PENGUIN BOOKS
TAJ

Timeri N. Murari has written novels, as well as screenplays and stage plays. His film, *The Square Circle*, made *Time* magazine's top ten best films. He adapted it for the stage and directed it at the Leicester Haymarket Theatre. His new novel, *The Arrangements of Love*, will be published by Penguin in 2004. He also writes a weekly column for *The Hindu*.

After many years away, Timeri N. Murari now lives in India. Visit the author at http://www.timerimurari.com.

Praise for the book

'Only a masterly historical novelist like Timeri Murari could skate so teasingly near the lip of a volcano. The structure of this novel is as fascinating as the building it describes.'—Bill Aitken, *Sunday Observer*

'A book of powerful simplicity . . .'—*Gloucestershire Echo*

'One can read into the symbolic undertones, and find this a complex and disturbing novel.'—*Asia Magazine*

Taj

A Story of Mughal India

TIMERI N. MURARI

PENGUIN BOOKS

PENGUIN BOOKS

Published by the Penguin Group

Penguin Books India Pvt. Ltd, 11 Community Centre, Panchsheel Park, New Delhi 110 017, India

Penguin Group (USA) Inc., 375 Hudson Street, New York, New York 10014, USA

Penguin Group (Canada), 90 Eglinton Avenue East, Suite 700, Toronto, Ontario, M4P 2Y3, Canada (a division of Pearson Penguin Canada Inc.)

Penguin Books Ltd, 80 Strand, London WC2R 0RL, England

Penguin Ireland, 25 St Stephen's Green, Dublin 2, Ireland (a division of Penguin Books Ltd)

Penguin Group (Australia), 250 Camberwell Road, Camberwell, Victoria 3124, Australia (a division of Pearson Australia Group Pty Ltd)

Penguin Group (NZ), 67 Apollo Drive, Rosedale, North Shore 0632, New Zealand (a division of Pearson New Zealand Ltd)

Penguin Group (South Africa) (Pty) Ltd, 24 Sturdee Avenue, Rosebank, Johannesburg 2196, South Africa

Penguin Books Ltd, Registered Offices: 80 Strand, London WC2R 0RL, England

First published by New English Library, UK 1985
First published in India by Oasis, Madras 1995
This edition first published by Penguin Books India 2004

Copyright © Timeri N. Murari 1985, 1995, 2004

All rights reserved

10 9 8 7 6

Typeset in Perpetua by Mantra Virtual Services, New Delhi
Printed at Pauls Press, New Delhi

For a lovely lady,
my wife Maureen,
with love

Only let this one teardrop, the Taj Mahal, glisten spotlessly bright on the cheek of time for ever and ever . . .

O King! You sought to charm time with the magic of beauty and weave a garland that would bind formless death with deathless form! Despite all this, the courier of your love, untarnished by time, unwearied, unmoved by the rise and fall of empires, unconcerned with the ebb and flow of death, carries the ageless message of your love from age to age. The mausoleum stands still and unmoving in its place. Here on the dusty earth, it keeps death tenderly covered in the shroud of memory.

—Rabindranath Tagore

Great Mughals Dynasty

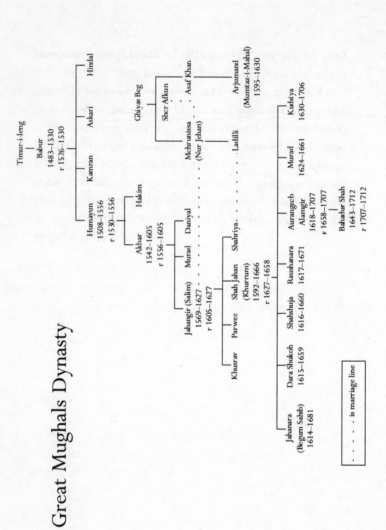

Timur-i-leng

Babur
1483–1530
r 1526–1530

Hindal   Askari   Kamran   Humayun
1508–1556
r 1530–1556

Ghiyas Beg

Sher Afkun ···· Mehrunissa
(Nur Jehan)

Asaf Khan

Arjumand
(Mumtaz-i-Mahal)
1595–1630

Hakim   Akbar
1542–1605
r 1556–1605

Murad   Daniyal

Jahangir (Salim)
1569–1627
r 1605–1627

Ladilli ········

Khusraw   Parwez   Shah Jahan
(Khurrum)
1592–1666
r 1627–1658

Shahriya ····

Jahanara
(Begum Sahib)
1614–1681

Dara Shukoh
1615–1659

Shahshuja
1616–1660

Raushanara
1617–1671

Aurangzeb
Alamgir
1618–1707
r 1658–1707

Murad
1624–1661

Kudsiya
1630–1706

Bahadur Shah
1643–1712
r 1707–1712

··· · · is marriage line

Author's Note

The past is prologue to the present. The tragic events that occurred over three hundred years ago still reverberate in modern India. The continuing conflict between Hindu and Muslim—and the creation of Pakistan—can be attributed to the actions of Aurangzeb, the son of Shah Jahan and Arjumand.

All the characters in this novel—except for Murthi, Sita and their children—lived three centuries ago, but I am sure that a man like Murthi lived and died building the Taj Mahal, along with twenty-two thousand others.

There was a man named Isa who walked in the shadow of the Great Mughal Shah Jahan. Other than his name, nothing else about him is recorded.

When it was built, the great tomb in Agra was called the Mumtaz Mahal, but over the centuries, with the erosion of time and memory, it has come to be known simply as the Taj Mahal. The jali (screen) which surrounds the sarcophagi of Arjumand and Shah Jahan is considered to be one of the finest works of sculpture in all India.

In my novel, the odd-numbered chapters cover the years 1607–30, and concern the lives of Shah Jahan and Arjumand: their love, their marriage, and Shah Jahan's eventual accession to the throne. The even-numbered chapters take the story on from 1632–66 and describe the later years of Shah Jahan's reign: the building of the Taj Mahal, Murthi's story, and Aurangzeb's rebellion against his father. Dates are also given according to the traditional Islamic system of dating from the Hegira.

TAKTYA TAKHTA?
(Throne or Coffin?)

—A Mughal proverb

prologue 1150/AD 1740

The world was thick with rain and it was not possible to tell night from day; they came and went unmarked as if blindness had struck men and beasts. Nothing could be heard except the river, roaring and thrashing like Siva's monstrous serpent. The earth broke under its might and gave up men, beasts, trees, homes almost gratefully, as if it could not bear their burden any more.

From under the great archway the ancient monkey stared out at the curtain of water that fell. He had never witnessed such rage in his life, and in his squeezed cynical face, there was a gleam of awe. His fur lay flat, streaks of dark rusty brown touched with grey, and where it had been torn away revealing black patches of skin; teeth marks, old and healed, puckered the flesh into a grimace. Huddled against the wall was his tribe of fifteen langours. He was not one of them. They were elegant, slim and silvery; he was squat and ugly, but he had killed their leader and now they worshipped him. He looked on them with contempt, and they accepted his authority submissively. On all fours, he stalked out. The rain broke on his back, as if angry at his defiance, but instead of retreating he moved down the steps into the neglected garden. His tribe, frightened of the storm, frightened too of being abandoned, screamed and then, miserably, followed him. The old monkey seemed unaware of the fury, examining the flooded fountains and the paving lying beneath the dense undergrowth; he tugged at a shattered piece and tossed it into the fountain. His companions were sullenly indifferent to their surroundings.

Under the wall, he sat back on his haunches and squinted up at the pure expanse of whiteness that he'd noticed through the darkness. It rose, cliff-like, in defiance of the all-veiling night. It seemed not merely to hold the blackness at bay, but to push it away so that there appeared an aura between the walls and the night. He did not mount the steps but circled around, wary from old habit. Reassured finally, he found a foothold in the marble and vaulted up onto the plinth.

There was an opening in the cliff, where the darkness had slipped in, and he followed it, stepping daintily over the shattered marble that littered the floor. The rain too had entered, leaving pools of water. He sniffed the damp and the desolation, caught too the sweet cloying of incense—he did not like that—and then the smell of man, sour, distasteful. He was curious and unafraid. He walked further, treading on crisp leaves and, seeing the carved screen convenient with holds, leapt nimbly to the top, avoiding the gaps ripped in the fabric of marble.

'Who goes!' a voice called.

The monkey stiffened, listening to the mad tapping of the cane. A man emerged from the lower chamber, emaciated, old, blind.

'Ah, it is you. I can smell you. Come, you do not need to fear me.'

His voice echoed. The rain could not penetrate the silence within the tomb. The monkey watched the man, knowing him to be blind and harmless, and his companions scuttled around, shaking water from their soaked fur.

'There is no food here. Only stone, and who can eat that? I have touched it all, and it is cold and smooth, like the surface of icy water. I do not know what this place is, or why it was built. Can you tell me, Hanuman?

The monkey scratched his chest and ignored the man.

'You do not know yourself. For you, like me, it is only shelter from the rain.'

the love story 1017/AD 1607

Arjumand

Was it thunder that woke me? I sat up, startled, listening. It was not yet the monsoon season, but the air was tense with that same sense of expectancy, and still, as if waiting to rage. I could hear nothing, except the first caw of the crows, the bulbul practising its enchanting scales, and the squirrels scolding shrilly. The sky was pale and clear with the smoke of night still lingering at the edges of the horizon. The mango and peepul and banyan trees outside the window appeared transparent in the delicate light.

It might have been my dream that woke me, although I could not recall it clearly. The thunder had struck at my heart which still beat hard and fast. Was it a warning? I felt no fear, no leaden weight to eternity such as the condemned man might on the dawn of his last day on earth. Instead, to my surprise, I seemed to feel a lightness, a delight. The excitement was not in the air, but in myself, in the sweet remnants of my dream.

I had glimpsed a silvery plain beneath a clarion sky, and in the shadow where earth and heavens met, it flushed with delicate red. In the far distance I saw an object, but could not distinguish what it was. A boulder? A man? It shimmered in the glare. What might my astrologer

3

foretell from this dream? Wealth? Happiness? Love? The common greeds of all who exist? Yet even without his guidance I knew the day ahead would be filled with meaning, somehow important. I was eager for it, impatient with waiting.

The *zenana* was still in darkness, but the commerce of the day had begun outside and I could hear the call of a street merchant, the creaking wheels of bullock carts, a child singing in a clear sweet voice. From far away the beat of the *dundhubi* proclaimed the appearance at the *jharoka-i-darshan* of the Great Mughal Jahangir. Each day, one hour before sunrise, he showed himself to the nobles and the people from the top of the Lal Quila. The sight of his person reassured his subjects that he still lived, that the kingdom was secure. He had to prove his existence anew each day. I could imagine him sitting on his silver throne, gazing east to the very edge of the earth where his empire ended. It was known that it took a camel train sixty days to cross from the eastern boundary to the western one, the land between Persia and Bengal, and a further sixty days to travel from the Himalayas in the north to the Deccan Plain in the south. The heart of this immensity was the emperor in Agra, but wherever he travelled in his empire, there was the centre.

The dundhubi was also the signal for our household to wake. The sounds were familiar; they had always been the same. All my life I had followed the movements from the noises: the slaves starting the kitchen fires, the rhythmic 'rush-rush' of the brooms, and the stirrings of the men in our household from the rooms below. Within, I heard the whispers of my mother and grandmother and aunt. Today I could hear a new note in their voices, an undertone of excitement as though they too had been woken by the thunder. I had thought myself to be the only one, and this largesse of anticipation scattered throughout the zenana disappointed me.

'Are you awake, Arjumand?' my mother called.

Usually the *haram* woke languidly, and it often took half the day for the women to complete their ablutions and dressing, but today there was a fluster of activity. Servants and slaves were running hither and thither, fetching and carrying and dropping as my aunt Mehrunissa gave one order, my mother another, my grandmother a third, and other wives and female relatives still more. Caskets of jewels, bolts of silk, boxes of ivory and silver and jade were being gathered together, for this was the night the Royal Meena Bazaar was to be held. Like a comet, it made only one appearance each year, in late spring, causing great excitement among the ladies of the Imperial court.

'Aren't you getting ready?' Mehrunissa asked me.

'Am I going as well?'

'Why not? You're old enough now. Someone might notice you and propose marriage.'

I was twelve years old in this year 1017, and nearly of marriageable age. I was my parents' only child and had led a cloistered, unexciting life. My education—reading, writing, painting, music, history, the Quran—was as much as was considered suitable for the narrow existence of a nobleman's wife. My arranged marriage would inevitably be a dry coupling of bodies and wealth. There could be no avoiding this future. I dreamed of romance of course; all girls do.

'Or propose something else,' one of my relatives suggested lewdly, causing great laughter.

'I have nothing to sell,' I said, ignoring the remark.

'You can sell anything—fruits, spices, carvings. It's not important. But of course,' Mehrunissa added slyly, 'if your stall has precious things on it, you will attract the great nobles, possibly even the Emperor.'

'What will you sell, Aunt?'

'Gold jewellery and the silks I designed.' She plunged her hands into one of her caskets, and lifted emerald and diamond bangles and necklaces, ruby rings and sapphires, then spilled them carelessly back. She frowned at the treasures.

'Do you think they're good enough?'

'What could be better?'

5

She shrugged, still doubtful, then glanced at me speculatively, secretively. Mehrunissa was an overwhelming woman, though very beautiful. She beguiled or bullied those who did not bend to her wishes, and even her husband, General Sher Afkun, whose bravery on the battlefield was unquestioned, fell silent in her presence. She wanted to dazzle and enchant. If she could have plucked the moon and the stars from the sky, she would have set them atop the great pile of precious metals and gems and cascades of silk.

'But they will not only come to buy, but to stare at us. They will stare and stare, but show no courage.'

'What other chance do they have to look on us? The ordinary market women can show their faces to the world and go where they like, but we have to spend all our lives caged in purdah.'

'It is better not to be seen, but to see everything,' Mehrunissa said sharply. 'It makes men wonder about us and dream.'

'And that is all they can do,' I said in exasperation. 'Who else will be at the bazaar, besides the Emperor?'

'Many of the great nobles.' She lowered her voice conspiratorially. 'Maybe even the prince Shah Jahan. Who knows what wonderful things will happen tonight?'

She sighed hopefully. All the women were transformed with excitement, but Mehrunissa seemed especially enchanted. This evening she could forget her marriage and her young daughter, and pretend to be a girl once more, dreaming of romance and composing poetry for an unknown lover who would, with a breath of magic, snatch her heart away. I wondered whether she already had one in mind.

'What things do you expect to happen?' I asked.

'I was just talking,' she said gaily. 'Where is Ladilli?'

'Still asleep.' Ladilli her daughter was, like me, an only child. She was my close companion, a shy, quiet girl, incapable of any boldness.

I did not have as much for my stall as Mehrunissa. I was young and unmarried, and apart from a heavy gold chain and some bangles, most

6

of my jewellery was silver. I heaped the anklets, ear-rings, bangles, necklaces and rings together, but they amounted to very little. They were worth hardly anything—a thousand rupees, perhaps less.

As I gazed at them the feeling of thunder struck me again, shook me. It was as if the dream were trying to return, to remind me that this day was to be different. I had seen the colour red, but could not tell whether it was a blood or silk—in dreams they run one into the other—and I heard a voice, a man's voice, soft with wonder, but could not tell what he had spoken. I had not seen his face in my dream; I only knew we were waiting for each other.

'You are very distant, Agachi,' Isa interrupted my thoughts. 'You don't look as excited as the other begums.'

Isa was a *chokra* whom my grandfather, Ghiyas Beg, had found and freed three years earlier. Though older than me by a few years, he was still small and scrawny. Isa told us that he had been stolen from a village south of Golconda by a magician while he was still only a boy, and they had travelled together for years. He had tried to escape his master, but had been caught and was being soundly beaten when my grandfather came upon him. He was allowed into the haram because he claimed to be a eunuch and this was attested to by Mehrunissa's own eunuch, Muneer. Sometimes I doubted this story of Isa's, but he served me more loyally than any woman would have done.

'I had a dream, Isa, and I was trying to remember it.'

'When you sleep, it will return,' he said.

'Possibly. Here, you can carry this.' I gave him my silver, wrapped in a silk cloth. 'Are the others ready?'

'Yes, Agachi.'

The bazaar was to be held in the gardens of the emperor's palace. This was hidden deep inside the Lal Quila which stood like a small mountain of red sandstone on the bank of the river Jumna. It had been built by the Padishah's father, Akbar the Great. It was Akbar who so generously gave employment to my grandfather when he first arrived

7

in Hindustan from Persia. They had met through the owner of a camel caravan who presented my grandfather Ghiyas Beg to the Great Mughal; if that had not happened we would have remained luckless and poor, like the thousands who crowded the streets of Agra.

My grandfather's advancement had been brilliant—but disappointingly brief. He had risen swiftly in the service of Akbar but, misjudging the emperor, he had been too bold in accepting bribes. It has the custom in Persia and Hindustan to accept gifts in return for favours, but Akbar believed his ministers should be above such practices, and dismissed my grandfather. Since Akbar's death two years ago, my grandfather had wanted to serve his son, Jahangir. It was possible that Jahangir had relented at last, for we were being shown great favour by being invited to the Royal Meena Bazaar. It is understandable that this event should have caused such great excitement in our household.

Our family procession from the house to the fort, a distance of four *kos*, was small: three palanquins. Muneer cleared the way through the crowds with a lathi which he wielded with cruel delight. I had protested to Mehrunissa, but she seemed to take equal pleasure in the whack of wood on flesh.

I chose to walk, with Isa following a pace behind me, preferring the dust, the heat and the wondrous sights of this vast city to the suffocating enclosure of a palanquin. There was no other city as large and as varied in the whole world. Here I saw men and women from Bengal, from Persia, Greece, Uzbeckistan, Cathay, feringhis from beyond the western seas, Afghanis, and people from every *suba* in Hindustan. Here the roadside bazaars sold the riches of the world: porcelain, gold, silver, ivory, silk, rubies, diamonds, spices, slaves, horses, elephants. Behind us trailed our own little procession of beggars. Isa gave each a *dam* or a *jetal*, depending on their wretchedness. Left to his own discretion, he would have driven them away with blows and curses. The poor are always harsh to each other.

We entered the Lal Quila by the Amar Singh *darwaza*. The Delhi darwaza and the Hathi Pol darwaza were reserved for the use of the Mughal army who occupied half of the fort. We passed the Imperial soldiers who wore scarlet uniforms, burnished armour, and were armed with swords and shields. We stepped from one world into another.

The fort itself is shaped like a great bow with the 'string' facing the river. Its walls are seventy feet high and ten feet thick, and the top is carved with serrations like the teeth of a saw. There are towers placed at regular distances along the wall, which runs for two kos, all manned by Imperial guards. We waited for a while in the Amar Singh courtyard with countless others before we were permitted to enter the narrow tunnel that led to the palace. The commander of the guards sat here on a raised platform and checked that we were indeed invited. The street now sloped steeply upwards, between two high walls. At the top of the slope the ground levelled out. Ahead of us was the pillared *diwan-i-am* with its wooden roof and beaten silver ceiling. The palace itself stood beyond the garden to our right on the eastern wall of the fort, overlooking the river. It was exquisitely constructed out of red sandstone, the walls and pillars covered in intricate carvings. In spite of its size, it seemed delicate and fragile.

However, the emperor himself seldom used it. He lived and slept in the *bargah* pitched in the garden. This is a huge and elaborate tent of many rooms, furnished with beautiful carpets from Persia and Kashmir, the walls covered with paintings and silk cloth decorated with precious stones. Timur-i-leng, the first Mongol conqueror, had decreed that none of his descendants should sleep under the roof of a building, and every emperor had obeyed this command. The remainder of the fort was occupied by the bazaar, the administrative offices and countless workshops.

There had been little change during the three years of our exile, yet I saw everything anew: the palace, the fountains, the courtiers in their brilliant plumage, the musicians, the jugglers, the elephants and horses, even the very air seemed to sing. It was not so much the occasion as the proximity to power. The empire had one heartbeat—Jahangir's—and we were all near it. The bustle and chaos and heat made one feel giddy: countless palanquins bearing the harams of princes and nobles pushed and jostled to unload their precious burdens at the steps of the palace. The emperor's haram occupied most of this building and it was not an easy place to enter, for, apart from his women, it also housed the incalculable treasure of the Great Mughal.

First we had to pass through a ring of Imperial guards, all armed with *jezails* or lances. They did not search the women, but the servant men in our company were inspected rigorously. The next ring, guarding the corridors within the palace itself, was composed of Uzbeck slave women. They were no less ferocious warriors than the Imperial guards, and equally well-armed. They were manly in their build, with strong broad shoulders, powerful arms and humourless manners. They searched each of us women, too familiarly at times, though some appeared to enjoy those energetic hands on their bodies. I did not. Within the haram itself stood the eunuchs. Their sole concern was to ensure that no man capable of lying with any of the women could enter the haram. But they have been known to be so influenced that they become careless in their task.

I had never seen so many excited women gathered together in one place as on this day. I couldn't count them all, but Isa, who seemed to know most things, told me there were more than eight thousand. It was possible: Akbar had had four hundred wives and five thousand concubines, and many of them still lived in the palace. Most of his marriages were merely political alliances, as were Jahangir's. These *mata* marriages ended after an agreed period of time and the women would return to their homes, heaped with gifts of gold from the Great Mughal. Those married by nikah stayed all their lives and were paid handsome salaries, granted great jagirs, and grew richer still through their efforts in trade and commerce. Women of many nations and tongues were gathered within: Rajput, Kashmiri, Persian, Bengali,

Tartar, Mongol, Tibetan, Russian, Circassian.

The palace was a vast honeycomb of rooms. They varied in size and in the luxury of their furnishings to accord with the importance of their occupants. The air was suffocating and sweet with perfumes that seemed to ooze from the walls, and I felt as if I were wading through soft and sulphurous flesh. Our progress was slow, partly due to the intense throng and partly because Mehrunissa knew many of the ladies, and stopped to greet each and every one effusively and lovingly; although later she would make some disparaging remark in a low whisper. Many of the ladies looked at us with surprise. But if Mehrunissa was guilty of insincerity, it was only equal to that which we met. At court affection is measured out carefully according to one's proximity to the emperor. I was far removed from him, therefore insignificant. But I could interpret each look: why had we been invited? Had my grandfather been forgiven? Soon I found myself unable to breathe, not so much for the lack of air—it came off the Jumna in cooling breezes—but because of the false friendliness.

I escaped to the balcony and looked down on to the palace garden. It was a peculiarity of the Mughals that they were filled with the desire for these oases of verdant beauty. The gardens gave them not merely a sense of permanence, but a reminder of the nomadic life of their distant ancestors; water, trees and flowers were then rare pleasures. Amidst a luscious green filled with every imaginable flower—roses, jasmine, frangipani, cannas, violets—and ringed with great shady trees, flowed a fountain. The water ran musically as thirty-six teams of bullocks drew water from the wells night and day. This sight alone was cooling and calming in the intense spring heat. The workmen had already begun to erect the stalls for the bazaar where I would sit, offering my small pile of silver. The earth lanes between would soon be hidden by carpets.

'There you are. I've been looking everywhere for you.' Mehrunissa dragged behind her a small, shy woman, as soft and frail as the silken clothes she wore.

11

'Your majesty, this is my niece, Arjumand.'

I bowed to Jodi Bai, Jahangir's empress. She stood waiting uneasily, even unhappily, as if expecting me to speak. I could not think what to say to this quiet, sad woman, and watched her as Mehrunissa chatted exuberantly about the bazaar. Jodi Bai was a Rajput and a Hindu, the mother of prince Shah Jahan. I had not expected my aunt to be so friendly with the empress, and this gaudy display of affection made me suspect her motives. Mehrunissa calculated such things with the precision of a mathematician.

'Oh, she's such a silly woman,' Mehrunissa whispered when Jodi Bai fled from us like a small bewildered animal taking cover in the long grass.

'Then why are you so friendly?'

'Because I can't be discourteous to the wife of Jahangir.' She looked back to the crowded rooms. 'Besides, I wanted to know what kind of person she was. What an empress! No wonder Jahangir drinks himself to death.'

'They say he drank before he married her. Both his brothers died from drinking.'

'And he won't last very long if he continues with her.'

'What are you going to do about it?'

'That is none of your business.'

She was gone suddenly, plunging into the throng of flesh and laughter and talk, like a bird swooping with the wind. I knew that beneath the beauty of my aunt flowed an ice-cold current of ambition. I could not foretell her ambitions; they were obscured by her secretive mind which was closed to everyone.

At the appointed time, three hours before midnight, we heard the distant women proclaiming: 'Zindabad Padishah, Zindabad Padishah.'

The noise welled gradually and as he came near, all the women rose to greet him.

Jahangir strolled on the specially laid velvet cloth, deep in conversation with my grandfather Ghiyas Beg. The Padishah wore a turban of scarlet silk from which sprang a long plume of nodding heron feathers. On either side of the feathers, set in claws of wrought gold, were a ruby and a diamond, each the size of a walnut. In the middle, holding the feathers in place, was a brooch set with a great, glittering emerald. Around his waist he wore a belt of gold, studded with diamonds and rubies. The sword of Humayun was buckled to his left side, and tucked into his sash on the right side was a curved dagger with a ruby inlaid hilt. A three-strand pearl necklace hung about his neck, and on each arm were gold bracelets studded with diamonds, a thick one above the elbow, and three around each wrist. His fingers too were weighted with rings holding precious stones, and on his feet were slippers stitched with gold thread and seed pearls. Behind him walked two men, one carrying a quiver of arrows and a great bow, the other a book. Behind the book bearer came an Abyssinian boy carrying pen and ink, for Jahangir had a passionate curiosity about the world, and would painstakingly record his every thought and impression.

My small stall was set at some distance from the entrance, in the shadow of a neem tree. Mehrunissa was near the brightest light by the fountain. I arranged and rearranged my jewellery, but no effort could turn it into a lavish display. The trinkets lay forlornly on the small blue carpet.

'Who will buy these, Isa?'

'Some most fortunate man, Agachi. I feel it.'

'He would be a fool. He would have a better chance anywhere else in the Bazaar.'

The nobles now no longer followed the emperor, but scattered to prowl the lanes between the stalls. I was not totally at ease without my veil in the presence of complete strangers, although secretly it was

13

what I had wished. It was not enough to do it merely for one night; the spirit soared like a bird sadly aware of the string attached to its leg.

My reverie was broken by my grandfather.

'You are well hidden, Arjumand.'

'This was the stall given to me. I am only a girl.'

He laughed. 'But what a beautiful one!'

I smiled. He always said that. I loved him. He was a kind, calm man, tall and slim, with eyes the colour of the evening sky, like mine.

'Will you buy something, please? Otherwise, no one will.'

'No, that is to be the luck of other men. It is early yet.' Then he whispered: 'But if they are all fools, I will return and buy everything. A good price for me, remember.'

'I saw you with the Emperor.'

'Yes. He was kind enough to note my humble presence.'

'What were you talking about? Will he take you into service?'

'I'll tell you later.' He pinched my cheek conspiratorially.

Then he was gone, and other men strolled by, boldly staring at me, whispering and laughing among, themselves, but lacking the courage to approach. The other ladies, like the women in the bazaars, flirted and called to them, but I could not act so boldly. Instead, I watched the tamasha: I saw Jahangir pause by Mehrunissa's stall, purchase something, whisper to her, and stroll on. She looked happy and delighted, but soon turned her attention back to the other nobles.

It was then that I sensed someone's eyes on me. They were insistent, wanting me to turn in their direction. I almost felt their caress. I was filled with weakness and when I turned I saw in the lane beyond, through the intervening stall, the prince, Shah Jahan.

Through the narrow opening of the stall between us, where the flickering candlelight created a barrier of dark shadow, I was held by his eyes. Jet black, longing, lonely, alight with a fire of their own, they held not the fierce flame of a prince, a ruler, a Mughal, but the glow of a boy afraid. I knew I was the cause of his fear and could not turn away

14

from him. He was the thunder that had roused me in the darkness. He was the red dream, not of blood, but the crimson turban of the crown prince. In my dream I had stretched out my hand to touch him, and he had clung to it knowing I was his only companion in the lonely and splendid existence of a prince. He moved out of my sight; it was my turn to fear, to lose suddenly a hope that I had not even known a moment before. I turned this way and that, searching the narrow lanes crowded with busy, laughing women and nobles. I wished them to disappear off the earth; I cursed them too. And then I saw him rudely pushing his way through them. He looked as if he ran, and then the hope, the placid calm, settled deep into me, and I was sinking into a soft, warm dream.

Shah Jahan

I, Prince Shah Jahan, no longer the boy named Khurrum, but Sovereign of the World and heir to the Emperor Jahangir, Padishah of Hindustan, though still only fifteen, strutting in the mantle as my father's favourite son, had been invited to attend the Royal Meena Bazaar. I had trembled with the excitement of the event, for my presence was a sign of the favour not only of my father but also of the court. They all adjudged me to be the heir to this vast empire, over my three brothers. To rule, to hold the sceptre of power, can be the only ambition of a young prince. On this night, I felt the bazaar would be a fortuitous event.

The Royal Meena Bazaar had been established by my great-grandfather, Emperor Humayun. It was a delightful idea for, by imperial decree, the women could appear unveiled in front of a chosen audience of men. The silken masks worn all year round were, for a single evening, discarded. The narrow world of the haram was to be turned inside out; for a few brief hours we would gaze on the naked faces of the noble ladies.

In spite of the heat and the stillness of the air, it seemed a current flowed through the palace as the evening approached. Stalls had been erected by the workmen in the garden and, doubtless, the women had chosen the wares they would offer for sale. I had heard they bargained and haggled like the women in the street chowk, and that the buyer purchased, if he were lucky, not only the wares, but the favours of the lady herself. I had heard nobles, a favoured few, boast about their conquests, sigh longingly of the pleasurable nights spent with a lady. I too was not inexperienced in these matters. I had lain with my slave girls and sometimes, for amusement, had gone with companions to the dancers in the bazaars and paid for their bodies. But I had learnt through experience that, because of my position, I could expect only fleshly pleasure from women. I did not listen to their whispers, for they whispered only to flatter me, to gain favours and wealth. The poets wrote and sang of love, of men and women wasting and dying from this strange sickness, but to me love was an illusion; the palace a desert of affection.

As I was bathed and dressed I smiled with anticipation and, seeing this, the slave girls teased me about the evening: I would meet a princess, oh yes. It had been forecast by the astrologer that the prince would be lucky. He would fall in love and live forever in happiness. I laughed at their teasing and did not believe them. And yet, I wondered: why was I excited? Was it the thought of seeing the faces of women I had glimpsed, heard speak, but never boldly looked upon?

The pleasurable game of matching voice to face, hands to face, eyes to face. What else could I look forward to: a night or two of pleasure, possibly a week, a month? I found this prospect tedious. I could choose any girl in this chamber to sate my lust. Yet, the air felt as if thunder waited. Was it a sense of dread?

Two companions joined me, the Nawab of Ajmer and a nobleman, Allami Sa'du-lla Khan. They were dressed as splendidly as I and, though older, appeared to be just as anxious and excited. They too had never attended a Royal Bazaar. They went to the balcony, looked out over

16

the garden; it was ablaze with lights, candles flickered in every niche, lanterns were hanging from the trees and stalls, and were caught and reflected in the waters of the fountain. They saw the shadows and heard the laughter.

'We must hurry, we must go.'

'Wait awhile,' I ordered. 'Drink some wine, pause and savour the pleasures to come.'

They obeyed, but only because I spoke. They did not recline, but hung over the balcony gazing greedily down, as if the fools had never seen women before. I wanted their company to pass the time, to talk of hunting and our sports.

'Sit!'

They sat, restive, straining like cheetahs. I felt no different, but a prince must always show control, otherwise he is powerless. But I lost their attention when we heard the dundhubi beating the approach of my father Jahangir. From the balcony, we saw him enter the garden, trailed by a serpent of courtiers.

For a moment, all fell silent, all paid homage, and then the chattering and the music continued.

'Wait a few minutes longer, until my father is occupied.'

When I judged that the frenzy had abated, and that the emperor would not be a distraction from my own entrance, we went down.

It was truly a bazaar; perfumed women squatted in their stalls in front of mounds of silk, cases of jewellery fashioned in gold and silver, toys, perfumes, ivory carvings, little marble statues. The air was sweet with their voices and laughter, and the soft sounds of music. My presence was immediately acknowledged and the women by the entrance laughed and clapped. Their eyes were bold and inviting, each calling to me to buy from her stall alone, some tugging at my sleeves like the chokras in a real bazaar. See my wares, sample this; it is cheap, especially for Shah Jahan. Look at this silk . . . here is a vase from Bengal. Their very lives could have depended on the sale, such was

17

their enthusiasm. I strolled through the lanes, noting the faces and bodies, some pretty, others not, old and young, thin and fat. They were all boisterous, bawdy, like birds set free from their cages, wheeling and chirping in the garden. Their chattering was incessant, a torment to me, and it was by chance, to avoid a persistent lady, that I turned away.

How can I explain the sudden helplessness, the suffocation of all my senses? She knelt in the lane beyond, quiet and alone, remote from the tamasha. True, it was her beauty, a perfect oval face, large eyes, a mouth like a budding rose and, in her shining black hair, a single strand of jasmine, that caught my eye, but it was her serenity that held me. She looked this way and that, seeing everything, and all with great amusement. A smile rose gently to her face, from within, quite unlike the shallow laughter of the other women. I saw what no other possessed: honesty. I felt that if I spoke, she would listen to me, and not hear the prince. My heart, my heart, it pained with beating, and when she turned and saw me through the opening, it stopped. I was truly afraid—and not even all the might I could command in this world could control the burst of fear—that she would turn away from me. I sensed immediately that any disinterest in her would not arise from flirtation, but from true indifference. Suddenly, I was no longer afraid. She remained still, looking at me, curious, amused and—what is it?—I felt as if we touched.

I cannot recall how I reached her side. I was there, and saw that her stall sold silver jewellery, a small and humble offering, and that she was assisted by a chokra. I could not contain myself; I was bursting with words and feelings.

'I felt as if we touched.' I spoke loudly, swiftly, unable to control the authority of my tongue which was more used to commanding than to revealing my heart. I tried again. 'But it was not possible at that distance. Yet I felt your arm gently on mine. To love swiftly is to chance life itself. It is a leap of trust like entering a battle without the protection

18

of armour, believing that somehow you cannot be killed. But even if you were killed, mere existence would not be worth it without you. You must tell me who you are. I must hear your voice and know you are truly real and not a dream that will disappear like water in this heat.'

'Arjumand Banu, your highness.'

Her voice was incense, soft, sweetly rising in the air. Unsettled by my intense stare, she lowered her eyes in modesty and began to bow in obeisance. It was enough to cause my heart to ache and I reached swiftly to stop her, touching her bare shoulder. I felt as if I had been struck.

'Your skin burns me, and causes my heart to beat like the drum of war.'

'Your highness only tells me what I already feel.'. It seemed then she slanted her head and brushed the back of my hand with her cheek. 'It is possibly the heat in the air.'

'No, no. That only strikes our surface, causing us some little discomfort. This enters deep into the flesh, simmering my heart, muddling my mind. I do not even know of what I speak.'

'The words are sweet, your highness,' she moved gently, and my hand fell away. I still felt the seductive softness of her cheek, like a brand pressed into my skin. 'Your tongue is too practised to stumble at the sight of a girl.'

'Here,' I snatched my dagger out. 'It if lies, cut it out. I cannot help its sweetness. It curls through the feelings in my heart and the only sound I can hear in my head is the blood repeating: "Arjumand . . . Arjumand." Did you not feel the same when we first looked on each other?'

'Yes, your highness. But it feels as if I have returned to sleep and entered the dream . . .'

'What dream?'

'I cannot tell it all. But when I awoke this morning, I felt as I did

19

when I first saw you here.' She searched my face carefully, seeing beyond skin and bone, gazing through my own eyes at what lay inside: 'You are real. This isn't still the dream.'

I knelt down in front of her, as she too knelt in her stall, and eagerly put out my hand for her touch.

'Feel the fever of my body again. You're awake, like me.'

Shyly she touched my hand, and once more we sensed in each the shock. It seemed the lightning that lit the skies in the monsoons leaped between us. I wished us to remain touching, but she withdrew, convinced now we were together and not separate in different dreams.

'I will sit here forever and look on you.'

She laughed, and the gentle sound made me feel as if I were tumbling through the notes of some strange and lovely music.

'We will grow old then, just staring at one another.'

'What better life could we have? I wish it were day, with the sun full on you. These shadows cheat me. They bend your nose, and yet it is perfect. They darken your eyes, and yet I know they are clear and beautiful. But even they cannot change the shape of your mouth or the curve of your cheek.'

'Do you only see so little of me? There are countless others in this palace who far surpass my beauty.'

'No. None can do that. What they reveal lies only on the surface. I see beyond your eyes and your face. I feel that I have known you all my life, and yet I know nothing. I cannot help but thank god that I saw you on this evening.'

'Yes,' and her voice fell to wonder. 'But I could have looked on you, day upon day, year upon year, and you would never have dreamt of my existence.'

'But I would have, I would have,' I said eagerly, wishing to persuade her. 'It isn't only the sight of each other that has drawn us together. Don't you feel it is beyond sight, beyond touch, beyond hearing? I felt your touch in my heart over distance, as you felt mine. Even through

20

the veil I would have known your love. It is so, isn't it?'

'It cannot be anything other, your highness.'

I wished she had not spoken those words. I felt a tremor, a vibration that started to shred the fabric of my feeling.'

'If I was not a prince . . .' I began.

'If you were less, I could not feel less.'

I looked into her eyes. They were wide, unflinching, allowing me to see behind the words she spoke. I felt the tremor cease, and could not disguise my joy. I laughed out loud, and heard her whisper: 'But how do I address you?'

'My love, my delight. You are my chosen one, my love.

'My love,' she spoke in a whisper, delighting my whole being, suffusing me with longing to hold her.

We knelt still, looking on each other, not wishing to miss a glance, a smile, a gesture. We could not tear our gaze away. Who knows how much time we passed in this manner. I could not have cared even if it had been a lifetime. I felt a touch on my shoulder, breaking the soft silence of our world, and looked up in annoyance. Allami Sa'du-lla Khan bowed apologetically, and seeing the swift flash of anger, merely gestured around. The crowd gathering around were barely silent, staring at us.

'Let them. I am Shah Jahan. Now withdraw.'

'Your highness, you should be seen elsewhere too. The women ask where is Shah Jahan, so we may bless him. You cannot ignore their wishes.'

'I will come soon. Withdraw.' He drew away, and I returned to my love. 'I will talk to my father about us.'

She bowed in acceptance. 'If it is his will . . .'

'It is mine,' I spoke firmly, and rose to my feet. She remained, kneeling, but her face lifted to continue looking on mine. I wished then to swiftly bend and touch my lips to hers, but I did not. She knew what I wished and smiled mischievously.

'There will be other times when we will not have to endure so many watching eyes.' From her stall, she picked up a piece of silver. 'Will not my love buy a memento? Having spent so much time, you cannot leave empty-handed, and I should at least have a rupee or two.'

'And what will you do with a rupee?'

'Give it to the poor. They have more need than we do.'

'The poor.' I could not hide my surprise.

'Hasn't my love noticed them? They live outside this palace.'

'When I am with you, I notice very little else. The world ceases its existence, and only we two live. If it is for the poor then, I will buy everything. How much?'

She frowned and studied her pile of silver jewellery, and then glancing up, gave me a smile full of fun.

'Ten thousand rupees.'

'I have a bargain.'

She began to laugh, peeking at me through the curtain of hair that fell over her face. I could not bear such happiness and wished like a thief to steal and ride away with her. Instead, I turned to my slave and placed the bag of money he carried on the floor of her tiny stall.

'I will see you again.'

'If it is your wish.'

Arjumand

And then he was gone. I had wanted him to stay, to sit forever, not even speak. His presence alone, the sense of him, would have been comfort, a balm for the pain, enough. I glimpsed his back, moving through the crowd, and then he was lost to my sight. He had disappeared, as if we had never existed but in my dream, and I was still waiting for it to turn into reality.

Isa scraped together the little pile of trinkets and looked around for a piece of cloth to put it in.

'Here.' I unwound my silk scarf, pale yellow with a border of fine gold thread, and carefully placed the jewellery in it. I tied the knot gently, and handed it to the slave.

'Count the money,' Isa said. 'What a profit for you, Agachi. Ten thousand rupees! Only a prince could be so generous.'

I felt a sudden unease. I craned my neck in search of Shah Jahan. What if, at another stall, another girl too received a similar favour? I knew it would not be so but I couldn't restrain my curiosity.

'Isa. Go and see if the prince is still in the garden. Hurry!'

From his glance, I saw he knew what I was thinking. The elation, the agony could not be disguised. I did not have the protection of the veil. He slipped away into the crowd; I held the bag of coins as a symbol of comfort. Gradually I became aware of the other women around me, the stall across the path, the ones on either side, those behind. I was encircled by their stares. It was impossible not to feel their jealousy. The bitter envy welled up in their eyes, and though they smiled when I caught their glances, I knew the coldness that was embedded in their hearts. They saw him only as the Prince Shah Jahan, and what they also saw was a reflection of themselves in a golden mirror. They could not look beneath, they could not look beyond; avarice consumed them. He was the bag of gold in my hands, the unlimited boundaries of an empire, he was Shah Jahan, Sovereign of the World. Their eyes made me feel dirtied; they wanted to believe that I had connived and calculated, spun the syrupy charms they practised, stupefied him with magic potions to capture his heart.

'He has gone, Agachi. He left alone.'

'Why did he leave?'

'Agachi, no one would confide the movements of Shah Jahan to a mere servant. All I know is that he has gone.' He hesitated. 'Everyone knows that he purchased your jewellery for ten thousand rupees. Some believe it was as much as a lakh. I told one idiot ten lakhs.' He laughed to himself. 'Do you wish to stay here?'

'What for? Let's go home.'
I could not sleep. The air was still hot, laden with incense and the evil whine of mosquitoes. I felt possessed.

Love is pain, an unrelieved longing. The world shrivels and dies, people disappear, and only *he* remains. It is like existing in two spheres: the body stays entombed in one, shaking, beating, hurting; the heart and mind adrift in the other. Those who love live a separate existence, one over which they have no control. This existence is light, yet burdened with fear; it soars, then plunges into darkness; it sings, and then dissolves into the bitter tears of parting. Hope, hope, hope, is the voice of the heartbeat.

I heard Ladilli come in as the light turned watery grey. She slipped into her bed and lay still. I pretended to sleep, but felt the presence of another person by my bedside, heard the soft clink of an anklet, a muffled rustle of silks. I peeped and saw Mehrunissa standing over me, staring intently. There wasn't enough light to read her expression, but I felt uneasy at her presence and the intensity of her study. She glanced towards Ladilli, and then she was gone.

the taj mahal 1042/AD 1632

It was a moonless night when Murthi first looked on Agra. He left his wife preparing the evening meal with their three-year-old son and the other travellers, and walked on alone in the immense darkness towards the glow of the distant city. It was a courageous act, and he was quite pleased that he should discover such bravery in himself. The night intimidated him. Above was the clear, vast dome of sky, which always instilled in him a sense of awe and utter humility. It reduced his worth to less than that of an ant stumbling through life oblivious to the roar of the universe. But closer were greater dangers: dacoits waiting to cut a traveller's throat for a coin; wild animals, old or wounded, grateful for easy prey. He looked back and saw the cooking fires, shrivelled and small. He thought of returning, waiting until morning, but still he trudged on, unable to control his impulse. He scrambled up a small rise, slipping in the loose mud and gravel, grasping a lantana bush for support, and reached the top of the hill. The land slipped down towards the Jumna. Beyond, imposing itself on the horizon, stretched Agra.

Murthi sighed in disbelief, and sat on his haunches, elbows resting on his knees, mesmerized. I will be lost here, he thought, I wish I had not come.

He felt a sickness of longing for his home, and the distant lights blurred as tears came to his eyes. He allowed them to run down his

25

hollow cheeks and into his grubby *jiba*. Expertly, he blew his nose to one side, and wiped his eyes and nose with the frayed *tuval* that hung from his shoulder. Home, like the night sky, was distant and now only a memory. It would be many years, he knew, before he saw his home again. He could not conceive of never going back—that thought frightened him. He knew he would return to his village, his family, his friends; he smiled when he imagined the stories he would tell them about his journey to the city of the Great Mughal.

He had not left his village of his own accord, but had been ordered to this harsh exile in the north. He was an Acharya, a carver of gods, as his family had been for generation upon generation. This gave him a sense of immortality, for it was continuity, not only of the flesh, but of the mind and spirit. Craftsmen like him had built the great shrines in Madurai, in Kancheepuram, in Thirukullakundrum, and he was honoured in his village for his carvings. Like his father and his forefathers, he could turn stone to silk, see the shapes of gods in granite and marble, and draw them out for the wonder of men.

But one day the thread of his life had snapped. He thought sullenly of the betrayal of the gods he had fashioned so lovingly.

His father had been summoned by their patron, the Raja of Guntikul, and informed in a jovial manner that he would have to travel to Agra. The Raja had heard that the Great Mughal, his distant cousin, a Muslim, was summoning artisans from every corner of the land to build a great monument to his dead empress, Mumtaz-i-Mahal. It was a Muslim custom to build tombs for their dead instead of simply burning them at the ghats. It would not be a place of worship. Out of generosity, the Raja was sending his finest craftsmen to help in the construction of this building.

Murthi's father had thanked the Raja for such honour, but pointed out that he was too old to make such an arduous journey. Possibly, one of his sons would be more suitable. The Raja had grandly accepted the substitution and had given some money for the journey, and the gift of

26

an ivory Krishna for the Great Mughal Shah Jahan.

It was only by squinting to pierce the glow that Murthi could distinguish the awesome silhouette of the fort. It was dark and brooding, with lights flickering in the turrets high above the city; a hill on the river's bank. He had passed many forts on his travels, but none as big as this.

The next day, in bright sunlight, it dwarfed the horizon. Its high red walls, the colour of the river water, frightened Murthi. His pregnant wife Sita huddled close to him for protection, and his son Gopi clung to his legs. His travelling companions, merchants, craftsmen like himself, all summoned to work on this monument, stared with the same awe and wonder.

'Even at night,' he said, 'it looks frightening. That is where the Great Mughal lives.'

'Is he a god?' Gopi asked.

'No. A man. But much, much bigger than our Raja. His land is huge, I am told.' He had no idea of the extent of the boundaries of the empire; he only knew that his journey of three months had been spent traversing only a small part of it.

'You can see him if you wish,' one of the merchants said. He had travelled often to the city and boasted of its wonders.

'To talk to?'

The merchant, a bania from Gujarat, laughed in delight at the man's stupidity.

'He would not notice someone like you. Before dawn each day he shows himself, from the jharoka-i-darshan.' He pointed to an opening in the battlements: 'There.'

'We will see him then,' Murthi said. 'He must be a wondrous sight.'

The river curled and uncurled towards the great fort and as they drew near, Murthi noticed a small building, the size of an ordinary

27

house, with a dome, and made of brick and plaster. The whitewash was streaked and blackened with the rains, and already there were patches of decay. It looked carelessly and quickly built. What drew his interest were the soldiers guarding it. There were about twenty of them, some lounging in the shade of the lime trees, the others on guard. They wore the Imperial scarlet, and the sun glittered on their lances and shields.

'What is it they guard?' Murthi asked. 'It looks a kutcha building.'

'That is the tomb of the Empress,' the merchant said.

'That? Then it is already built.' Murthi was angry. 'We need not have come all this way. Any fool could have built that. Why should I have been sent?'

'It is only her temporary resting place.'

'What was she like?'

'Beautiful, they say. But who knows?'

Murthi looked at the merchant and lost his awe. He knew the man to be empty and boastful now. All along his journey he had asked the same question: 'What was she like?' and he had always received the same answer. 'Who knows?' Nobody knew, and this disturbed him. He carved gods that were seen by all and worshipped by all; temples that soared joyfully up towards the sky, and to which men and women brought flowers, fruits and their prayers. How could he work on a building for a dead woman no one had ever seen? One day he would meet someone who could tell him what this woman was like.

the love story 1017/AD 1607

Isa

'You look tired, Agachi.'

'I didn't sleep well,' Arjumand said.

She sat in the shade of a rain tree, and though her face was in shadow, speckled with sunlight, I noted the darkness under her eyes. It formed shadowy crescents and the grey of her eyes was the colour of rain clouds. It had been some weeks now since that magical night of the bazaar and she'd only heard whispered rumours of Shah Jahan's love for her. Word went around the household that he was distraught and walked the palace corridors like a ghost searching for solace. Yet, she herself had had no word from him and waited and waited, fading before my eyes. A book of poetry lay open on her lap, but she never turned a page.

'When I sleep, I dream I am awake, and when awake I can only dream of him. I dream of his touch again, and how he looked at me and what he said, and the sound of his voice. It *was* real.'

'Yes, Agachi, I was there.'

I loitered. I had completed my duties of fetching and carrying, hurrying and scurrying for the household. It had been a smaller house when the family lived in the fort, but when Ghiyas Beg had been in

29

Akbar's service they had moved to this house. It had many, too many rooms, and was set within a huge garden. The garden was a copy of the one in the palace—every noble imitated the Great Mughal—but our fountain contained no water, only leaves, dust and dead flowers. It had been built by a noble, but he had somehow displeased Jahangir and lost his wealth and land overnight. Most of the land was directly owned by the emperor. Akbar had devised a system by which some of the income was received directly from the farmers into the treasury. The remainder was given in jagirs, small or vast, as rewards for service, and the income derived by the holder was taxed proportionately. The emperor could, on a whim, make princes of peasants and peasants of princes.

'Will he ever see me again, Isa?'

I noted the subtlety of the question. Doubtless she would see him often from behind the entrapping lattice of the haram.

'Of course.' It was the only comfort I could offer. I did not add, if it is your karma. I prefer that to their Muslim word of kismet. Luck. Karma implies the intricate patterns of the universe, the movement of forces beyond our perception. 'Would you like me to perform some magic for your entertainment, Agachi?'

'Those are cheap tricks, not magic.'

'The villagers believed it was. It all depends on belief, Agachi. How could God survive if we did not have belief?'

She looked up at me gravely, and then smiled. The smile was as if a single petal fluttered down to touch a still pool of water, the ripples gentle, barely discernible, but existing long after the petal had vanished.

'Yes, make some magic. Bring forth . . . Shah Jahan. Right here. In this garden, at my feet. Come, Isa. It is a simple request I make of the great magician.'

'Ah, Agachi, you are right. I only perform cheap tricks. If that badmash who stole me away from my own family had been any good, I would be able to conjure Shah Jahan out of thin air.'

30

She looked at me sadly. 'Can you not remember anything abut your family?'

Before I could reply, we heard a terrible scream from the house. It was a woman's voice, high and shrill, and even when it had stopped it seemed to linger in the air like a hawk unwilling to fall back to earth. We ran as fast as we could, jostled by the other servants and members of the household.

We expected blood and death; instead we found Mehrunissa stalking to and fro in a seething rage, but silent for the moment. Sitting on the divan, having failed to placate her fury, was her husband. We had no idea what had happened and we all waited and watched and waited. Ladilli had joined her father, seeking protection from the storm. 'Is that the thanks I get?' Mehrunissa shouted suddenly, to no one in particular, for none answered.

'It is an important position,' Sher Afkun protested. He was obviously repeating himself, for she ignored him.

'But where is it? Go on. Tell them where this important position is to be.' Her arm swept over us. 'Show them how generous the Emperor has been to us. And after all that I have done.' He remained silent and she spat: 'Bengal. Where is Bengal? It is one thousand kos away.'

'But I am to be the Diwan. It is a very important position. Bengal is a rich land. In what other way could the Emperor have shown his forgiveness to us?'

Mehrunissa did not falter. 'By giving you an appointment *here* as the Mir Saman . . . or something.' She turned from him, and believing herself unobserved by all others (I stood insignificant in the shadows) her face changed. Now she could have been alone, peering into her mirror at night while others slept. In that hour, we strip deceptions from our lives, revealing our secret thoughts and dreams like demons becoming real. What I saw frightened me and only half confirmed the whispers I'd heard. Jahangir lusted for her. He too had been struck down with longing on the night of the bazaar. It had indeed been a

31

momentous evening for this family. Jahangir was stamped in her face and eyes. Diwan, Mir Saman, these appointments were merely toys for the emperor to discard. Mehrunissa had turned her face to see in which direction the threads of power led, and having discovered it, like a simpleton suddenly seeing through the magician's trick, she knew how she could bend it to her will. It was a moment of naked fury, but before she turned around, her features had settled back into a dimpled smile.

She crossed, brushed her lips against Sher Afkun's forehead and pinched Ladilli's cheek, a painful gesture of affection which left a red stain on her daughter's face. 'I am sorry; I was angry. It is just that I was worried about my business.' She sighed dramatically, as if it were only a small matter that had so angered her. It was well known that she had a thriving business, designing and making clothes for the ladies of the haram. She even drew the patterns for the fabrics . . . flowers, fruits, geometric shapes, woven in gold and silver thread.

'What is done is done. I am very proud of you. Of course we will go.'

One day before their departure for Bengal, the household was honoured with a visit from Jahangir.

It is neither a simple nor an inexpensive matter to entertain the Great Mughal. Apart from the preparation of food and entertainment, there is the custom of presenting him with an abundance of gifts. The coin of the Great Mughal is gold and diamonds, horses and slaves. Nothing less can be offered; nothing less will be accepted. It places an enormous burden on those whom he chooses to visit, and I suspect he often does this out of malice or even merely for amusement. He can either refuse the gifts, perhaps taking a trinket as a courtesy, or he can take everything, depending on whether he has been pleased or displeased. In such a subtle manner have nobles been reduced to a state of penury.

32

On the evening of his visit, I guarded the gifts displayed on a precious Persian carpet. The women had stripped themselves of all their jewellery—bangles, necklaces, ear-rings, nose rings, anklets—and now they lay strewn on the carpet like sticks and stones, sinuous rivulets of gold, diamonds, rubies and pearls. The women of the haram looked strange shorn of their glittering plumage, like plucked peacocks.

There were also gold and silver plates and goblets, crystal cups, and a vase brought all the way from Cathay, more precious in its rarity than all the rest.

Ghiyas Beg was a man who understood Jahangir. His gift was simple but subtle. He had purchased it from a feringhi sailor, a drunken giant who frequented the bazaar. It was a long brass tube with small glass plates fixed at either end. I did not understand its use, until Arjumand crept into the room—like a little girl coming to tiptoe around a feast for the adults. She picked it up and examined it, peering first through one end, then through the other, pointing it at me as if it were a jezail. She began to laugh.

'What is it, Agachi?'

'It makes things large and small. One way you look tiny, but through the other I can hardly see you because you are so big. Here.'

She handed it to me, and went to the far end of the room. She struck a pose like a nautch girl, a hand on her hip, and then whirled around on her toes. I could not lower the glass until she approached and stared through the other end.

'You are foolish, Isa. Look through the other end too.'

'One end is enough, Agachi.' Reverently, I replaced the instrument on the carpet. 'It is a magic that even my master Lekraj could not have performed. But he was a bad magician anyway.'

'Would you like to punish him one day for how he treated you?'

'No. He has suffered enough.'

'You are a kind boy, Isa.' A shadow darkened her face for a moment. 'There is little room for that here.' I expected her to go on and explain her meaning. It was strange, for her life was filled with kindness, and she was the favourite of the family, even more so than Ladilli.

'My aunt sent me to fetch you.'

'I cannot leave my post.'

'Give me your dagger then. I will stand guard.'

It was an order, and she held out her hand. I hesitantly gave her the weapon, afraid that something would happen to her while I was gone.

'Will you tell me what she tells you?'

'Of course, Agachi.'

My reply made her smile, as if I'd paid her a compliment. When I looked back, she was still smiling, and had tucked my dagger into the waist of her skirt.

Mehrunissa sat in front of her mirror, applying kajal around her eyes while her slaves brushed her hair. She dismissed them when I entered, and went to her locked box, opened it and pulled out a small ivory case from the folds of clothing.

'Isa, you will guard this with your life.'

'Yes, Begum.' I reached out to take it, trying to be brave. It was obviously very valuable.

'You will tell no one that I have given this to you,' she held on to it, and glared at me. 'I will have you killed should anything happen to it. You understand, badmash?'

'Yes, Begum.' The fear was making me sweat, and my voice shook. 'I understand. What am I to do with it?'

'I haven't finished, fool. You will hand this, personally, to the Emperor.'

'Your highness, how can I approach the Padishah?'

'Because I cannot, fool.' Carefully she chose a rich piece of silk and wrapped the box in it. 'It is sealed. If I hear the seal has been broken, I will have the elephant crush you to death.'

34

I did not disbelieve her. It was a common manner of execution, an entertainment for the emperor and the people, and I was a slave for whom there would be no escape. Apart from fear, I felt hatred: why choose me? Could not her father, her husband, her brother present this precious gift to the Great Mughal? Then, through the mist of misery, I understood that they were not to have any knowledge of this gift. That made it even more dangerous, for I would have to be surreptitious.

Mehrunissa read my mind. 'You will give this to him openly, as a gift from you.'

'He may not accept a gift from a poor person such as I.'

'He will,' she said confidently, and returned to her mirror. I remained standing, clutching the ivory case, the carving pressing into my palm. 'I will be watching you, Isa. Remember.'

I saw her reflection, hard as the glass itself, shadowed by the candlelight. The image was impressed in my mind and heart, and until I had passed the gift to Jahangir I would be haunted and followed by those large, almond-shaped eyes.

Before leaving her chamber I hid the gift in the voluminous folds of my clothing and returned to my post. Arjumand saw the perspiration on my face.

'You look in pain. Are you not well, Isa?'

'It is nothing, Agachi.' I took back my dagger, warm from her hand, and avoided her gaze.

She placed the back of her hand on my forehead to see whether I had a fever. I was touched by her concern, but still could not meet her eyes. In contrast to Mehrunissa's threatening stare, they were gentle.

'I will not ask you what my aunt ordered you to do. It has made you unhappy.'

'Yes, Agachi. She is watching us.' I did not dare look, but Arjumand did, and shook her head. I grew bolder, reaching inside for the ivory case. Arjumand stopped my hand.

'No. I cannot keep a secret, and if you show it to me, I will tell

35

someone. Then you will be in trouble with Mehrunissa, and that won't be pleasant.'

'It won't be. Thank you, Agachi.'

Her trust in me only increased my misery. How can a servant serve many masters or mistresses and remain honest only to one? That was my wish, but it was not possible.

Once before, the day after the Royal Meena Bazaar, I had been summoned by Mehrunissa. She had sat cross-legged at a small ivory table, head bent, her hair like two dark shafts of rain on either side of her face, studying the *Ain-i-Akbari*. This lengthy treatise on government had been written by Akbar's minister, Abul Fazl. Matters of the empire fascinated her. Doubtless she was preparing herself for a position of importance. Finally, she looked up.

'Tell me everything.'

'Everything, Begum?'

'Last night, you fool. Every word that was spoken between them.'

'I did not hear. I . . .'

'You have the ears of an elephant, and I will have them torn from that stupid head if you don't immediately speak the truth.'

It was hard for me to be brave in front of Mehrunissa, impossible. I spoke. She listened carefully and then dismissed me. I wept at my betrayal of Arjumand, but did not have the courage to tell her of it.

We heard the approach of the Padishah: the dundhubi beating, the horns blowing, soldiers clearing the road. The Ahadi, his Imperial bodyguard, marched before him. He lay languidly in the silver palanquin, and slaves hurried in front scattering rose petals and unrolling Kashmiri carpets. The men of the household rushed out, and when he rose from the palanquin, they performed *kornish*, placing

36

their heads in their right palms, offering their homage to the emperor. Jahangir seemed in a jovial, even an eager mood, and embraced Ghiyas Beg with great affection. He did the same, with even greater warmth, to Mehrunissa's husband. To Arjumand's father he smiled and took his hand, and walked somewhat unsteadily into the house. His face was puffy, and when he spoke there seemed to be the whisper of another voice within him. It robbed him of his breath and he coughed again.

A pace behind walked his entourage of sword-bearer and book-bearer. In the *Jahangir-nama* there are no doubt many paintings of the beautiful Mehrunissa, but none such as the one I presented to the emperor at her command on the evening of his visit.

As was the custom he first examined all the gifts displayed for him, but chose just one object to signify his benevolence towards our family. It was the strange instrument offered by Ghiyas Beg, and when he placed it to his eye and found he was able to look up at the moon and see it as though it were only a few paces away, he laughed in delight.

'What is this called?'

'I do not know, Padishah,' Ghiyas Beg answered. 'I found it in the bazaar, and only wished it brought to your attention.'

'It is wonderful. I can examine all manner of things now—the stars, the animals, birds—I can even look upon the faces of my people and read their thoughts.'

Then they proceeded to an inner room where wine was offered to the emperor. In this matter he took pride in having curbed his appetite to twenty flasks of wine a day, even though he could not feel its pleasant effects without a few pellets of opium added to each cup. His great-grandfather Babur had recorded that it made him feel: 'whilst under its influence wonderful fields of flowers were enjoyed'. I served the wine and placed Mehrunissa's gift upon the tray.

'What is this?'

I bowed deeply. 'Padishah, a humble gift from me.'

Jahangir took the ivory box and broke the seal to open it. It was a painting of Mehrunissa. She lay on a divan revealing every part of her beauty for his eyes and he did not lift his head from the pleasure of gazing on that painted form. Her skin was fair as milk, her hair black, long, falling mysteriously over her bosom and down to her waist, and her face was heart-shaped.

'Who gave you this?' he asked me.

'No . . . no one, Padishah. It is a present . . .'

I was too frightened to speak further. Jahangir took it to the light to study it closely, and the flames obviously revealed even more delights. He sighed aloud; I knew he could not resist her. With her boldness she had captured his heart. Ghiyas Beg wished to examine the gift, but Jahangir only closed the box and held it.

'It is nothing, my friend. A puzzle. I must reward your servant for his cleverness.' He threw me an emerald ring, and I caught it deftly. 'Bid the women join us, Ghiyas. It will add to our pleasure to hear them sing.'

Ghiyas Beg could not disobey his command, and summoned the women from their place beyond the *jali* where they saw and heard everything. Jahangir gave them permission to remove their veils. It was his right to look on their faces. Occasionally he allowed special companions to look on the faces of his own women. To his disappointment, Mehrunissa was not among them. She remained in the zenana, waiting—she knew it would come—for his specific summons.

'Are they all here?'

'All except my daughter Mehrunissa, Padishah. Sher Afkun, you must fetch her.'

Her husband went reluctantly to fetch Mehrunissa. I noted his unease, but Jahangir was impatient. Finally, the curtain parted and Sher Afkun returned with Mehrunissa. She performed kornish, and remained bowed until the emperor gave permission for her to rise. I

38

felt, knowing Mehrunissa well, that she was laughing beneath her *beatilha*.

'You may remove it,' Jahangir ordered.

She did not immediately do so. Then quite slowly, she lifted the veil, and the emperor clapped with pleasure. It was on that same evening that Jahangir elevated Ghiyas Beg to the position of *Itiam-ud-daulah*, the Pillar of Government.

How swiftly this family's fortunes had changed.

the taj mahal 1042/AD 1632

'I carve gods,' Murthi said.

'There are none,' the clerk replied. He shuffled his papers and looked past Murthi. He barely saw the dark thin face, quite young but already dusted with grey stubble, or the hands, strong, scarred, calloused and clawed to clutch tools.

Behind Murthi, men and women waited patiently. There were thousands upon thousands; a fluid, humming river, filling gullies, drowning bushes, flooding trees. They squatted or lay patiently in the sparse shade. Children stared shyly around at the huge gathering; stallholders filled the air with their cries and the fragrance of their wares: samosas, bhajis, sweetmeats, dough, chai, oranges. The air was yellow dust, dry and searing, impossible to breathe. It had to be sucked carefully through the mouth.

'I am an Acharya,' Murthi insisted.

His words meant nothing to the clerk, and silence fell between the two men, cutting them off from the bustle. The flies buzzed; that, at least, was something Murthi knew. He would not move. He was tired and dispirited; still his journey had no end.

Their home was the maidan on the river bank, some distance from the fort. With countless others they slept, cooked and ate in the open, and at dawn, while others looked at the emperor, Murthi bathed in the

Jumna and prayed. Each day more workers arrived and slowly, unplanned and of its own volition, a small town grew. Passing traders stayed, building small platforms, acknowledging the permanence of these people. Huts, too, sprang from the dust, low, mean, raggedly thatched, but providing shelter from the sun and the night chill. Murthi's hut was only one small room, with a mound in the corner for cooking; Sita's utensils were three clay pots and a wooden ladle. Another corner was kept for worship: an oil lamp flickered at dawn and dusk in front of the image of Lakshmi. Their most precious possessions, Murthi's tools—chisels, a hammer, bellows—were hidden in a hole beneath the idol.

Agra had bewildered and excited him, and for days he had roamed with Sita and Gopi, shyly watching the continuous and dizzy movements of the crowds. They heard countless languages they did not understand, saw people from lands they never knew existed, and watched, for hour upon hour, the great camel caravans arriving and departing burdened with goods from Persia, Bengal, Samarkand, Kashmir, Rajputana. Nobles and princes passed them by, afloat on *howdahs*, trailing soldiers, palanquined women and servants in their wake.

Warily, they watched the great fort too, sighing in awe at its size and splendour, unable to imagine what it contained or whom it guarded. The fierce soldiers, dressed in scarlet and flashing armour, were a spectacle as they changed duty every hour to the beat of drums. One morning, an hour before dawn when the pale grey light just revealed the thin division between the heavens and the earth, they gathered with hundreds of others on the maidan between the river and the fort, to catch a glimpse of the Great Mughal Shah Jahan in the jharoka-i-darshan. A bell was rung, a golden chain was lowered.

'What is that?' Murthi asked.

'For justice. You attach your petition to the chain. I am told the Padishah studies it, and acts. Who knows?'

Murthi lifted Gopi up onto his shoulders and, peering up at the indistinct emperor, waited for some display of greatness. People *namasted*, hoping their whispers would carry up to the opening in the high wall. In return, they wanted to be blessed, to be protected by his power.

'Is he God?' Gopi asked, breathless with awe.

'No. A man. But for us,' Murthi spoke bleakly, 'it is the same thing.'

They waited; the emperor waited; unmoving as marble. The distance dividing them was the universe, and only one man could cross it, but he remained lifeless and still. Eventually, when the whole sun was afloat and free of darkness, the emperor rose and vanished. The chain was pulled up.

'Do people use it?' Murthi stared up at the opening.

'Sometimes.'

'Who is in charge?' Murthi asked impatiently.

The clerk, weary, spat to one side. He nodded at the fort and the marble pavilions that had begun to rise behind the high walls. 'He is,' he said, and laughed. 'Let us start again. You want employment . . .'

'I was sent here. I gave you the gift from the Raja for the Padishah.'

'He will receive it. I shall hand it over personally. Now, you are a stonecutter?'

'No. I am a craftsman. An Acharya. I carve gods.'

'There are no gods here. You must cut marble, or go. Others are waiting.'

Murthi did not leave. Behind the clerk were many brightly coloured *shamiyanas*, officials came and went, carrying sheafs of drawings and pens, speaking in concerned whispers. Sometimes they would come out to stare at the rock and scrub and the grove of lime trees behind the shamiyanas, refer to their drawings and gesticulate, then vanish again.

'I will talk to them,' Murthi gestured.

'If that is your wish. Go.'

Still Murthi did not move, but remained squatting, perplexed. He had pride. He could not squander generations of skill on hacking marble. He could not return, could not stay; he was adrift in misery and indecision. The clerk returned to studying his papers, pen poised, as though Murthi no longer existed.

'Will people pray in this building?'

'No,' the clerk finally answered. 'It is a tomb.'

'Ah, then you will want an image of the Rani.'

'No. The Quran forbids men to place their images on or in their buildings. And Allah himself has no size or shape.'

Murthi nodded as if he understood, but the clerk knew it made no sense to him.

'What was she like?'

'How should I know? Now leave, if you will not cut stone. There are others.'

A man emerged from a shamiyana. He was tall and slim, his beard neatly combed and attractively grey. He wore such fine and expensive muslin one could see through the folds of his kurta. His fingers were beringed and he wore gold bands on his arms.

Isa looked out on the crowd. Thousands of men and women, maybe as many as twenty thousand, Isa thought, waited patiently. The clerks who were hiring the workers sat at rows of small, low tables, recording the physical details of every man and woman: a scar, pockmarks, thick lips, warts, a cast in the eye. Each pay day, the description would have to tally before money changed hands. Akbar had instituted the custom for his soldiers so that strangers would not be paid. Isa watched one man who squatted restively in front of a clerk who was ignoring him. Nothing had been said for some time. The man looked up at him, stared, dropped his gaze. Isa returned to the shamiyana and sent for the clerk.

'Who is that man?'

'A fool. He carves idols, he says. I told him there would be none. He won't leave,' he shrugged.

'I asked, who is he? Find out where he comes from, then come back and tell me.'

The clerk returned to his position and picked up his pen. He did not understand Isa's interest, but he obeyed, and asked Murthi the questions. When he had recorded the answers, he return to Isa.

'He comes from Guntikul, that is south of . . .'

'I know it.'

'He is an Acharya. His name is Murthi. His father is Krishnan, his grandfather Lakshman. He was sent by the Raja. I offered him employment as a stonecutter, but he will not accept it.'

'Give him employment,' Isa said.

'But there's nothing for him to do here.'

'His skills will be used for other things. Make no mention of this. Watch and report directly to me how he lives.'

the five story 1017/AD 1607

Shah Jahan

'You are dreaming, your highness.'

'Cannot princes dream?'

'Not on the battlefield. I could have killed you thrice—here, here and here.' General Mahabat Khan's sword touched my throat, my heart, my belly. 'In war, the king *is* the heart. If he is killed, defeat is inevitable. When you become emperor, remember your grandfather Akbar's advice: "A monarch should ever be intent on conquest, otherwise his neighbours will rise in arms against him."'

'I am not yet emperor. There is still time to dream. I have had enough.'

A soldier took my sword and shield. The dust of our combat hung in the air, and the sand was pocked with our sweat. The general rolled along beside me as we walked to the *hamam*. His gait resembled that of Akbar, beside whom he had fought many battles. He was strong, thickset, scarred.

'You dream too much of that girl, Arjumand.'

'My dreams relieve desolate solitude. Generals no doubt lead dreamless lives.'

'So should princes and emperors.'

Ar-ju-mand. I dreamed helplessly and felt my body to be an abandoned palace, haunted by her spirit. She moved where no one had ever entered, and none other ever would. I had become her empire, her kingdom, her subject. The yoke was heavy, suffocating, embedded like metal in my heart. Only she could free me from pain, from this dreamlike existence in which I didn't know whether I was alive or in another world.

'What will I do?'

The general had been my personal tutor for most of my life, from the moment I had had the strength to lift a sword. He had taught me the princely arts of swordplay, horsemanship, wrestling, the tactics of the battlefield. I was, like all my ancestors, born brave. It could not be otherwise.

'Forget her,' he said harshly, shouting above the splash of the water. He enjoyed the luxuries of the court, the female slaves bathing him, massaging his body, giggling when he clumsily clutched a breast with one large hand. It enclosed the round ball of flesh perfectly, leaving a wet mark on her choli. 'I know it is the wrong advice to give to you, Shah Jahan, but I never was a good courtier. I am well versed in that court saying: "If the king saith at noonday, *it is night*, you are to say, *behold the moon and the stars*." But you have asked me and I have told you. Make of it what you will. Forget her.'

'I cannot.'

'You will, in time.'

'Months have passed since I saw her. But it seems only yesterday that we spoke and looked at each other. Even if I had a painting of her it would never be so clear. My sole pleasure is to relive the memory. I polish it as if it were the great diamond Humayun gave to Babur. It was said that it could feed the whole world for two days. She is of the same worth to me. Each time I dream I see her afresh, the silk of her hair, the ivory of her skin in the lamplight. What would it be like in daylight, I wonder? I am jealous, jealous of everyone whom God has placed

46

near her. Her slaves, her servants, her mother, father, aunt, her uncle. They are countless times more fortunate than I.'

'Become a sanyasi then, and wander the land in sackcloth and ashes with her image about your neck. Love is not for princes. You are not a soldier or a villager. You are Shah Jahan. You will marry whom you must. Not for love, for politics. Did Babur marry for love? Did Humayun? Did . . .?'

'He did. Humayun did.'

'And what disaster it brought on his head.'

Mahabat Khan ignored the convenient fact that my great-grandfather foolishly obeyed his father's instruction: 'Do naught against your brothers, though they may deserve' and brought disaster on his head. It was nothing to do with his love for Hamida. I would make no such mistake.

'Did Akbar? Jahangir?'

'I am told my father is obsessed by Mehrunissa.'

Mahabat Khan glanced at me, then towards the women waiting on us. Wisely, he refused to be drawn, warning me too. The emperor was still a long way from his tomb and he heard the softest whisper in the court. The wrong inflection on her name and our lives would be in danger.

Mehrunissa! She was a puzzle, an entangled coil which I had to unravel within the silent, private world of my own mind. Ah, if I could only speak to someone I could trust, someone who would not swiftly carry my words, reinterpreted to their own purpose, to the ears of my father. What did Mehrunissa wish for? I had been told that her ambitions were as limitless as the empire itself. She could not become empress, as my mother, Jodi Bai, was my father's first wife. But then, Mehrunissa was already married and could not be divorced; the watchful mullahs would not approve if my father married a divorced woman. I doubted she would be content to be merely a concubine lost in the haram, surrounded by other women and crushed with boredom. That would

47

leave her far from the throne. If my father is obsessed, I thought, he will somehow draw her nearer to him, and bend his ear to her whispers. She could be my ally then, echoing my own whispers: Arjumand, Arjumand.

'I have been seeking an audience with my father, but he delays me.'

'No doubt he hopes that your passion for this girl will fade and that you will regain your senses. Only then will he see you.'

'He must think I have forgotten her, for he has granted me an audience tomorrow. But the fire still burns within me. I shall demand . . .'

'Speak gently to your father. None can demand or command in this land except him. And be it on your own head.' He singled out a Kashmiri girl and pushed her across to me. 'Take one of these to douse the fire. It is only lust you feel.'

'No. It is love.' I waved the girl away.

'Well, remember my advice. Think carefully before you speak to the Padishah. Men often cut off their own heads with their tongues. All I can say is, remember you are the prince Shah Jahan.'

My palace lay further up the river from the fort. It was my own design, gradually perfected with the advice of my father's builders and artists. I spent lengthy periods of time with them, watching them construct models of the buildings my father had had erected in Agra and Delhi. It intrigued me that the hard, ungiving stone could be made as malleable as clay and used to create intricate designs. The Hindus, who were the greatest builders in the world, had discovered the ability of weight alone to hold up giant roofs and great walls. Their temples and palaces, like the one in Gwalior in which the beautiful archways are held by the balance of their own weight, are examples from which we have learnt. It is they who, on the orders of my grandfather, built the now abandoned palace of Fatehpur-Sikri. I have often wondered how, through their skills, stone can resemble wood, and how they perfected a system of construction to hold up a building for eternity.

My own palace was more simple. It resembled a waterfall. The building flowed down in steps to the water's edge, with the entrance at the highest level. Outside, on the roofs of each platform, I had laid out a garden and filled them with different kinds of flowering bushes.

Once my joy, now it was of no solace. It echoed the emptiness of my heart. At dusk, I gazed towards her house, just visible between the trees. I imagined her looking out towards me, and at other times watching as I rode through the city attending to State duties. If only I could catch a glimpse of her . . . but she was well hidden behind the cursed screens of purity.

'Prepare a woman and bring her to me.'

The night was cool, and the scent of flowers was as sweet as yellow wine. I would drown in flesh, forgetting that I had a heart and mind, and pretend I only possessed a body. The musicians, hidden behind a screen of bushes, played an evening raga. The melody was soft, melancholy, mourning the passing of another day. Forget. Forget. Forget. It was not so easy to blind the brain as if it were the eye, for there was no single point of memory, but a whole universe of recollection.

The woman they brought me was young and rounded with heavy, firm breasts. She wore only anklets and bangles, and her hair fell to her waist. Her skin was smooth and fair; touching it was like caressing gold. She smelled sweetly of perfume. Her companions removed my garments and turban and began to caress and touch me all over, using oils and the knowledge of their fingers to arouse me from the stupor of love and wine.

They whispered in my ears, promising me pleasures I had never known before, praising the length of my organ, its size, its strength; the woman herself trembled. I glistened with oils and was tantalized by their tongues, the feeling made me want to beg for an end to the exquisitely tender pain. Seeing my state of readiness, they turned their attention to the woman, rubbing her breasts and inserting gentle fingers inside her to draw out her sweetness. They bit and licked her nipples and soon she was so weakened she couldn't stand, but fell into their ready arms.

Their laughter was like music, for they enjoyed their labours as much as the woman. They parted her legs, lifted her and poised that warm, compliant body over me. Above her head the moon was a washed and wasted silver coin, trailing thin clouds, and the bright cold stars were specks of silver.

At that moment, I felt the women lower the girl carefully, opening her lips with their fingers, and there they held her suspended so that I could enjoy the pleasures of the moist gate. I was held by her flame; her heat ran up my thighs to my belly. They held her still, rubbing her breasts while she tossed and turned, wanting to descend the full length. Gradually, softly, slowly, whispering their wonder, whispering the pleasure I must experience, they lowered her until I was completely engulfed by her heat. Yet, they did not place her whole weight on me. She rose of her own accord, then slipped down slowly again.

'The bull has entered the deer,' I heard a whisper and felt the warmth of another woman lying beside me, caressing my body. 'Feel her . . . thrust inside her . . . she cannot escape you, lord . . . she is impaled on your lance . . . look on her ecstasy, lord . . . look, on your own strength.'

She rose and fell, rose and fell, and I felt myself rising too, being sucked upwards, and finally, unable to control my passion, I burst into her. Our cries soared with the music, silencing for a moment the busy night chatter of crickets. Then they burst into song again.

Oh, Arjumand!

The soldier guarding the entrance to the *diwan-i-khas* accepted my gold and ruby inlaid dagger. Not even I could approach my father bearing a weapon. The Padishah sat on the throne, surrounded by standing ministers, among them Ghiyas Beg, grandfather of my beloved. I bowed and my father greeted me perfunctorily. Since he did not grant permission for me to sit, I too remained standing.

The ministers took turns to speak, and my father listened carefully to their words. His attention, in the beginning of his reign, surprised them all, for they had listened to Akbar, who believed my father would never make a responsible ruler. Akbar had thought briefly of making my brother Khusrav the new emperor, but on his deathbed had changed his mind in favour of my father, who took to administration with zeal, speedily grasping the complexities of the empire and its business. Akbar had left us a stable state, a full treasury and laws that gave security and justice to our people. Against the protests of the mullahs, he abolished the *jizya*, a tax on the unbeliever, and as the majority of our subjects are Hindu it gave them comfort to be treated as equals to the Muslims. He reformed the tax laws for the farmers, changing payment from every lunar to every solar year and helping them financially in bad times. He banned child marriage and tried to outlaw *suttee*, the cruel Hindu custom of burning widows alive, but with little success. He had introduced countless laws, including the present system of governing the land through four ministers.

It was past noon when the routine of ruling ended and the ministers departed. The Padishah looked weary. His eyes were the colour of light cherries, not from exhaustion but from excessive indulgence.

'Khurrum!' He called me by my childhood name. 'Come closer.'

He embraced me. I smelled the familiar odour of sandalwood. The memory rose from distant childhood when he had played games with me if time and inclination permitted. He rose, yawned, and we strolled to his quarters, he squeezing me against him, wishing to press me into his flesh. Since my brother Khusrav's rebellion and the attempt to assassinate him, I had grown to great stature in his eyes. Apart from my name and title, I had also been given the huge jagir of Hissan-Feroz. Many years before Akbar had, briefly, granted my father the

51

same jagir. Yet I believed his affection for me also sprang from Akbar's lack of affection towards him. He wanted to redress the balance, not wishing me to grow up as empty and unloved as he.

'What is it you wish, Khurrum?'

Although he was aware of the reason why I had sought this audience, he revealed only Imperial politeness, as if warning me that this knowledge was not to be taken for granted. I would have to negotiate the matter within the delicate confines of protocol.

'Why should I wish for something?'

'You will learn that men seek an audience with the Padishah because they want what only I can give them.'

We entered his chamber; looking out over the Jumna. Its red sandstone walls were prettily carved, but did not match my idea of the splendid residence of a monarch. Slaves stepped forward to remove his turban, his golden belt and sash, and the golden dagger with a large diamond in its pommel. He took a cup of chilled wine.

'We are having problems with the Rajputs again. Mewar refuses to pay homage. He won't be satisfied until we destroy him. I thought Akbar's razing of Chitor would have taught him a lesson.' He lay back on the divan, brooding, and then, remembering my presence, smiled at me. 'Come, tell me, what is your worry? If I can, I will lift it.'

I knew I had to speak eloquently; I prayed that my tongue would be silvered with my longing. If I could not persuade him now, Arjumand and I were lost. My father drained his cup of wine and beckoned for more. His face was seamed by the profligacy of his youth. His eyes appeared blurred, hooded in that familiar manner whenever he listened intently. I could not judge his mood. Was it generous and kind? Was it harsh and cruel? His features were stern; the mask of an emperor.

'Padishah, Emperor of Hindustan, Seizer of the World, Defender of the Faith, Scourge of God, my father. You are looking well.'

'I am well,' he said agreeably, 'if it were not for my son behaving like some fawning courtier. You are my favourite, my most beloved

52

son; you need not behave with such formality in front of me.'

He pinched my cheek and caressed my face; his habitual gesture of affection. I bowed to his friendliness, not completely believing him. If I had not addressed him with such formality, he would have been displeased. I was, for the moment, in good favour, fortunate that he had permitted me to sit by him. His hand remained on my arm.

'Speak, speak,' he took more wine. Two more cups, and his attention would wander.

'I was at the Royal Meena Bazaar . . .'

'What a tamasha! I think I should have it arranged more often. Every month instead of only once a year. The ladies enjoyed it so much. What do you think?'

'If it pleases the ladies, then it should be held more often.'

'I shall have to give that some thought.' His attention was distracted by the slave massaging his neck.

'No, *there*, you fool . . . ah.'

'I know the time is nearing for my marriage to be arranged . . .'

His attention returned sharply, he was suddenly watchful.

'My happiness and the choice of my bride lie in your hands, and I will accept whomever you judge to be fit both for me and for the empire. At the bazaar, I saw a girl I found most beautiful. She sold silver jewellery. Maybe you saw her too. She comes from a very good family. Her grandfather is Ghiyas Beg, your Itiam-ud-daulah.' I paused for a moment, trying to judge the effect of my words. The Padishah said nothing, as if he knew what was to follow.

'Her aunt is Mehrunissa, daughter of Ghiyas Beg. She is the wife of . . .'

'I know her husband,' he said abruptly, his fingers impatiently tapped my arm. 'I have seen the girl. Arjumand. She is pretty.'

'She is beautiful,' I gently contradicted my father. 'My mind and my heart are filled with my feelings for her.' I drew breath but I couldn't control my tongue. 'I love her.'

53

'Already! A few moments with her and you say you love her.'

I heard an echo, soft and envious. When he was my age, he had lived desolately alone, in the shadow of Akbar, his life, his hopes, his dreams, all governed by my powerful grandfather. It was not possible to voice such a need for love. Akbar had none to give his sons. My father had married because Akbar wished for a strong alliance with the Rajput prince, the Rana of Malwar. If Jahangir had loved another woman, he had not voiced it for fear of Akbar. I hoped he would be guided in his decision by his memories, that he would grant to me the happiness he had been denied. From the gentle pressure of his fingers, their drumming ceased, I felt hope. I looked for signs in his face and eyes, his posture, in the folds of his silken *sarapa*, in the whirl of golden buttons and pearl and diamond ornamentation, even in the beam of dusty sunlight falling on a silver chest in the corner of the room.

And my father studied me. The look was curious, as if he were discovering a different person in his son. I imagined I read kindness and compassion there. He would understand my longing, my pain, for he too must be experiencing the same confusion of feelings for Mehrunissa. As a young man he had seen her once, when her father first entered the service of Akbar. It was probable that he had loved her then, but had not raised the matter with Akbar. I had learned of his infatuation for her from one of his favourite slave women, but he did not speak of such intimacies to me. He had stifled his love to obey his father; I was sure he would not now deny me mine. 'Akbar,' he began gently, reading my thoughts, 'often lectured me on the duties of a prince. It is our destiny to rule. God chose us alone for that purpose. We are not dacoits or brigands who have captured the empire. We are the descendants of Ghengis Khan and Timur-i-leng, and the empire we have carved from Hindustan sprang from our quality as rulers. A prince must consider only what will benefit his kingdom. If he thinks of himself first, and then his kingdom, it will be lost. You should read the *Arthasastra* of Kautiliya. That Hindu wrote wisely on the duties of a prince. Everything I do, I consider first how it benefits the empire, or how it affects the empire. When you mount the throne, you will learn to think in this way. Now, on the question of this girl, Arjumand, I consider it not as the father of a beloved son, but from the seat of the emperor looking at his crown prince. Our lives, my son, are not our own. They are the kingdom's. How will this marriage to Arjumand strengthen the empire? Consider it thus.'

I knew already that I was lost, and I could not think clearly for the heavy beating of my heart. In despair I spoke swiftly: 'It will make me happy.'

'Ah, badmash, you have not listened to me.' He cuffed me gently. 'Make you happy? I told you, our lives are not our own. A peasant can say, "I will do this," and do it. Who does it affect? Only himself, perhaps his immediate family. But if Shah Jahan says, "I will do this because it makes me happy," it affects the whole kingdom. What does Arjumand bring with her? Wealth? Power? A kingdom? A political alliance? Will marrying her make a friend of an enemy, as Akbar always advised? Will it extend the empire? If the answer is "yes" to every question, then you have my permission to marry her.'

The kindness remained in his eyes, but behind them I perceived the glare of power.

'You know already that the answers are "no".'

'Then the matter is decided.' He pressed me against him in affection, and I smelt the sour odour of wine on his breath.

'After your marriage for the kingdom, take her for your second wife, if you still feel the same love for her. You are young, you will forget this passion.'

'I want her as my first and only wife,' I began stubbornly. 'I will not . . .'

'Do *not* command within my hearing.' His brows drew together, and the glare became fierce, blotting out the kindness. 'You will do as I command. Enjoy the flesh of other women. There are so many. Choose whom you will for your lust and stop thinking of this girl. Now go, I'm tired.'

'I beg . . .'

'Go.'

I hesitated to obey a moment too long, and saw the anger begin to surface. I did not wish to enrage the emperor any further. I rose and bowed, but as I reached the threshold, he called after me.

'I have already chosen your wife.'

I did not stay to hear of his choice.

the taj mahal 1043/AD 1633

Murthi was bitterly disappointed. He peered at his wife through the weak light. The lamp was a small clay container filled with oil, the wick, several strands of twisted cotton thread, coiled in the oil, with a small piece jutting over the lip. He sighed, disturbing the flame; the shadows danced and stilled. Sita glistened, her drenched sari clung to her small, frail body as if she had been dipped in the river. By her side squatted his neighbour's wife, Lakshmi, holding the baby. Lika Sita, it slept. Murthi shuffled out and squatted by the entrance.

A boy was what he had wanted. Each day at dawn he had prayed for this child to be a male. Before Gopi there had been two sons; one had died at birth, the second when it was eight months old.

Ram, Ram, he whispered, why burden me with this girl-child? Of what use is she? Sons, I asked for. Sons who will learn my work, care for me when I grow old. One is not enough.

He looked for Gopi; he was playing *gilli* and *dandu* with the other boys. Murthi stood up and walked down the lane to the corner stall. A few men squatted around the entrance, sipping *araak* from clay cups. A city had grown up on the maidan, unplanned and chaotic. It crept outwards, swelling with each daily breath. Most of the dwellings, like his, were huts, though some were brick houses, built for officials. There were four great buildings housing the offices that administered their

57

lives and the progress of the monument. The city had been named Mumtazabad.

Murthi sipped a cup of the strong araak, and held himself aloof. The other men were labourers: coarse, bawdy, wanting only to get drunk, to forget their exhaustion. They were Panjabis: taller and burlier than he. He had discovered two families from his country, they spoke Telugu and, though not of his caste, at least they were a small link to home. One was a marble cutter, the other a bricklayer. Unlike Murthi, they had made the long journey north to seek employment. No Raja had ordered them into exile. There were some Tamils too, and Nairs, and they all, though barely familiar with each other's languages, at least felt some sense of identity.

They all worked, except Murthi. This puzzled and worried him. He was paid every day, lining up with countless others to receive his pittance, but each time he enquired, he was told: Wait. Other men who were not working received nothing. Why me? he often thought. He could not find an answer. He did not dare question the clerk in case his wage was stopped. Until two days before the baby was born, Sita too had worked. She would return the next day; they could not afford to live on his money alone.

Sita, with thousands of other women, had changed the course of the river. Why it had to be changed, none knew, but that was what they had been ordered to do. The river flowed in a channel quite distant from the site of the monument, curving nearer the fort. Slowly, painfully, while the men dug a new channel to bring the river closer to the site. Sita carried the fresh earth in a small wicker basket and dumped it into the water. The women were supervised; they would neither pause nor dally. Some men dug with iron picks, others shovelled the earth into the never-ending line of basins carried by the women. Day by day, month by month, the channel widened, gradually the river was dammed. Sita stopped thinking about it, only waiting for her wage at the day's end. And at nightfall other women took her place and worked by the light of a thousand lamps.

Thirty-seven men stood silently in the dusk, waiting for the emperor on the marble terrace of the fort. Isa stood apart; like them, he watched the activity across the river, the tiny figures scurrying through the shadows, bent beneath their different burdens.

A slave girl lit the lamps and placed candles in the recesses. The light flickered on the faces of the men. They had come from all parts of the world, summoned by the Great Mughal. Ismail Afandi, a plump jovial Turk, the Designer of Domes; Qazim Khan from Persia, the gold and silver smith; Amarat Khan, also Persian, a dour man with weak eyes, the Master Calligrapher; Chiranji Lal, a Hindu from Delhi, the lapidarist; Mir Abdul Karim, who had worked for the Emperor Jahangir and been given extravagant gifts of eight hundred slaves and four hundred horses. He, along with Markarrinat Khan, another Persian, were the administrators of the monument. All these men were masters of their crafts, the best—jewellers, painters, skilled builders—from Hindustan and as far away as Cathay, Samarkand, Shiraz. On the order of Shah Jahan, Isa had sent for them all, promising them great wealth in exchange for their skills.

The monument, carved in wood, painted, still incomplete, stood behind them on the marble floor. It was the silent ghost that haunted their lives. They did not look at it, but gazed across the river, and tried to imagine it transformed, towering over the earth, but none could. It was not real, but a dream. As the master craftsmen considered the monument they saw in it the familiar and the strange. It resembled the Guri Amir, the tomb of Timur-i-leng in Samarkand; but then again, it did not; Akbar's tomb in Sikander, but the lines were cleaner, sharper; the tomb of Ghiyas Beg, the Itiam-ud-daulah, but this was gigantic by comparison.

It had come to Shah Jahan in dreams, Isa explained, and they understood. As great artists, they too dreamed and saw the shapes and images which their hands then transformed into stone. It had emerged, afloat in the emperor's mind, part by part, a piece here, a piece there and, obsessed, he had had it translated into drawings, raging when his artists could not reproduce what he told them, lavishing on them praise and gifts when they captured his words and drew the image he remembered. It had taken two years for the dream to be coaxed from the shadows of his mind and made into the wooden model on the floor.

But still it was incomplete. They had made countless suggestions, but each had been rejected by the furious emperor. He cursed them and called them names, and they trembled, for violence contorted his face and mind, and death could lurk in the unreason of his anger. Isa looked at the model, unable to see any flaw. He had lived with it for so long, he could not think of it in any other shape or form. The tomb stood in the centre, rising above the marble plinth, the mosques on either side. It was serenely alone, uncluttered, and Isa loved its solitude.

In the workshops attached to the palace, hundreds of men bent over their drawings night and day, designing the most intricate patterns and shapes for the interior walls. The emperor drove them hard, rejecting most of the work, wanting it refined still further, made yet more beautiful until all the original ideas and designs had been lost a dozen times over. They were to imitate everything, yet nothing. It was as if in the purity of the wrought flowers Shah Jahan wished to purge the opulence of his power.

A tortuous battle was being fought within the emperor, and the struggle was reflected in the monument. He was trying to balance the suffocating and ornate magnificence of the Great Mughal with the simplicity of his obsessive love for his queen. He swayed between these opposing forces. Cupolas, minarets, domes of silver, ruby walls and diamond floors, sandstone buttresses and black marble platforms, golden stairs and emerald pillars and balconies of pearl. What could

60

such stupendous riches not create?

Such, the Great Mughal imagined, was paradise. Then the balance tipped, and suddenly he recalled the simple beauty of Arjumand, the spare, thin line of her eyebrow, the curve of her cheek, the straight nose, and the smile that did not tear at her face, but floated across the clear skin. And between each feature there was apparently—a trick of the imagination—an infinite, calm space. When he remembered all this, he would strip the riches that adorned the tomb, wanting to reflect only her beauty in its proportions. It was as if he wanted to build a statue or paint a portrait, transforming her nose, mouth and eyes into doors, windows and domes. White was the colour of mourning, so that when he gazed upon his creation, he and the whole land would be reminded that they mourned; that the pain in his heart was too great to be borne. Oh God, he cried silently, what did I do to her?

While he wept, Isa would remain still and expressionless, untouched by the tears.

Shah Jahan crossed the terrace slowly, his white robes blurring into the marble floor. He did not look at, or speak to, the assembled men, but walked slowly around his model. The men remained bent in kornish, although it had been decreed by Shah Jahan that no man should show him such humility. He felt their anxiety.

'Light,' he commanded.

'Yes, Padishah,' they chorused.

They ran to fetch torches, snatched candles from the recesses so that the terrace darkened, and only the model was aglare with lights except where the black shadow of Shah Jahan fell upon it.

In this light, he thought, the tomb looked too lonely, apart. There was, he had to admit, a simplicity that he enjoyed in the three buildings; the mosques were small and lowly as if to humble God for His cruelty. He frowned; he wished to break the solitude without unsettling the tranquillity. Something was missing.

He moved to the railing and the men fell away to gather again behind him. Night had fallen, but he could observe the labourers' shadows flitting between pools of light. He did not wonder about those tiny figures toiling endlessly to shift the course of the Jumna, working only because he commanded it. The water would reflect his monument, and he studied the placid, dark water, trying to imagine how the image would fall.

Mir Abdul Karim, tall and grave, approached and bowed low. 'Padishah, there is a problem.'

He waited for a signal to continue. Shah Jahan watched him. Abdul Karim perspired. He remembered the young prince, the stare chilling as a kite's. Now mantled with age and power, the stare was that of an old eagle, wise, but ruthless.

'The river,' Mir Abdul Karim faltered, clearing his throat before continuing. 'The changing of the channel is causing water to seep into the site of the monument, Padishah. The earth will not hold its weight. We should construct it further . . .'

'Drain it. Do not come to me with petty problems. You are the builders, not I.'

'Yes, Padishah. It will be done. But there is no iron-stone to fill in the foundation to prevent more water seeping in later.'

'Buy it,' he commanded petulantly. 'Why has the building not yet started?' He was met with silence.

Finally Isa spoke: 'Padishah, the model is not yet complete. The Quran forbids any change once building has begun. The builders await only your command.'

'I have to do everything,' Shah Jahan grumbled. 'You will prepare drawings for an addition to the tomb that will not spoil its simplicity.'

The men turned to look. Once more the lights blazed on the model. They stared . . . willed it to give them the answer, but it remained mute. And yet, it appeared to have life, to have begun its existence already.'

'Go. By tomorrow I want your answers. Isa!'

Isa remained. The men faded into the blackness of the garden below, murmuring amongst themselves. Shah Jahan turned from the railing.

'What was she like, Isa?' The Great Mughal sounded like a child wishing to be told a familiar story, like Akbar being read to by a slave.

From the hill to the east of the site, Murthi watched. He squatted patiently with Gopi and, playing in the dust beside him, Savitri. The baby had lived and grown, robust, healthy, good-natured. It irked him to have to look after her. That was a woman's work, but as he was unoccupied, Sita left the baby with him. When it needed feeding, he would take it to her, and she would hurriedly interrupt her labour to give the baby her breast.

Below, a crowd had formed. Astrologers had calculated the exact time for the ground to be broken for the start of the building, and the mullahs were gathered, gowned black as crows, to perform the ceremony. All work had ceased. Murthi waited. He heard the drums and the horns, and further up the river he saw the procession emerge from the Lal Quila. The emperor was carried in a palanquin, followed by soldiers, nobles and officials. It took some time to reach the site, and when the sun reached its highest point at noon, the prayers floated up through the still air. He saw the smoke of the incense, then the emperor kneeled and kissed the ground, then it was over. He was surprised by the swiftness and simplicity of the act. When a temple was to be built, the ceremony took days; countless offerings were made, the Vedas were chanted from dawn to dusk, fires burned orange with ghee and milk, alms were distributed to the poor. He was disappointed with this small tamasha.

Murthi spent his days feeling restless and bored. He would take out his tools, nine chisels of varying size, the smallest as delicate as a twig, looking as if it would snap in his strong hands. With a loud sigh, he would rewrap them in the gunny. He had taught Gopi the initial craft of caring for and sharpening these tools.

He had dug a shallow pit outside their hut, and then a narrow tunnel on one side which opened beneath the pit. He placed the long muzzle of his bellows into the tunnel mouth so that when he pumped the dust flew from the pit. He left the ground for a day to harden, then filled the pit with live coals. While Gopi worked the bellows, Murthi placed the tips of his chisels in the coals and, when they were glowing red, removed them with tongs, and beat them sharp with his hammer against a smooth ironstone. Finally, he dropped them in a vessel of water to harden. Then he allowed Gopi to practise, and they spent a great deal of time absorbed in their task.

One evening while Murthi sat outside his hut, he saw a group of men approaching. One or two he recognized; the others were strangers, all richly dressed. Their leader was Mohan Lal, a spice merchant. Usually he dressed shabbily, not wishing to reveal that he profited greatly from his trade, but this evening he wore clean, new clothes. Murthi rose hastily and namasted. Except for the ground, there was nowhere to sit. Some sat cross-legged, others squatted. Murthi ordered Sita to bring chai; the men protested, but only out of politeness, and waited for the tea to be served.

'I am Chiranji Lal,' a short, plump man spoke 'I have come from Delhi to work as a lapidarist on this monument. I have heard you are an Acharya.'

Murthi laughed with pleasure. 'Yes, yes. That is what I am, but this building has no need of my skills, so I have to work at something else. Are you an official?'

Suddenly, he felt uneasy. They had come to stop his wage. They knew he did no work.

'No,' Chiranji Lal said. 'What we have come for has nothing to do with the monument. There are many of us here who are Hindu, but

64

we have no temple in which to worship. We do not know whether we will be given permission to build one. We intend to approach the Padishah on this matter.'

Murthi waited. He felt their unease, and, looking from face to face, he saw their courage drain away as they thought of their petition. Over the centuries, the great Hindu temples had been destroyed and mosques had been built on their sites. Successive Muslim conquerors had crushed their belief, but they now felt change. Akbar had begun it with his *din-i-illah*, a free-spirited religion that embraced all gods. It was possible that permission for a small temple would be granted, but there was a risk.

'I cannot build a temple,' Murthi said. 'My family . . .'

'No. We do not want you to build a temple. You must carve us Durga to worship. Can you do that?'

Murthi was happy. He settled on his heels and nodded.

'I can do it. It will take time. I cannot begin work until I have received the vision.'

They all understood. It could take years for him to have the vision. The image of Durga—sister of Kali, eight-armed, riding a lion—was well known. She existed, but Murthi had to have his vision of her in order to carve her with imagination and subtlety, but without offending her.

'What stone shall I use?'

'Marble. It is all we have. We shall purchase a block from the merchant who is supplying the marble for the monument.'

They remained a little longer, discussing the details of payment. When they left, Murthi bounded in to tell Sita. His luck was changing.

A week later, it changed again. Murthi was summoned by the clerk who had hired him. He trembled, believing he had been discovered and would have to repay all his wages or be punished.

the love story 1018/AD 1608

seven

Arjumand

Hurt, hurt, hurt, hurt, hurt, hurt. The hooves of my horse, muffled by the dust, struck the earth with the dull rhythm of my heart. I was suffocating, not from the dust in the air, but from the pain in my heart. How swiftly the venom had reached my ears. The women, the eunuchs, the soldiers, slaves and servants, all knew of what had occurred as if they had been in the same room with Jahangir and Shah Jahan and had heard every word spoken between father and son.

How many times was it told—with false sorrow, gleeful sadness, feigned pity—and each bearer of the event embroidered the story just a little bit more. I remained alive, hoping bravely, only because I knew he loved me. He had spoken it boldly, to me and to his father. I dreamed about his words, whispered them softly to myself, imagining how he shaped them; imagining too, how, shorn of his princely power, the mantle of protection, he would reveal his vulnerability to me.

'You should ride in the palanquin, Agachi.'

'It is so airless in there.' I was riding a bay pony while Isa, armed with a silver-tipped lathi, strode beside me. he disapproved of my boldness, which was an affront to his dignity. Ladies of the court reclined in the shrouded palanquins, gossiping, playing cards, drinking, sometimes even discreetly entertaining men; only soldiers, slaves and maidservants rode.

'But what about the dust? It is worse out here. Inside, it will be cleaner . . .'

'Be quiet, Isa.' I spoke sharply. Even if I did feel discomfort, I refused to take his advice. The dust, reddish and fine, hung in a broiling cloud from horizon to horizon, north, south, east, west. It distorted the sun and the sky, and fell softly on the trees and bushes, dulling their bright green.

Jahangir moved, and the empire moved with him. We were two days out of Agra. On the third day, my party would leave the Imperial train and turn south towards Bengal. I was going to visit Mehrunissa and welcomed the escape from Agra and the cloying formalities of court. From where I was riding, I could see neither the beginning nor the end of the column. Somewhere, far ahead, Shah Jahan rode with his father. Between us flowed a river of men and beasts.

I beckoned Isa nearer and bent down to whisper: 'He must know that I ride far behind him. If he doesn't come to me soon, Isa, you will ride and give him this.' I took off a silver ring and Isa hid it in the folds of his clothes. 'Don't lose it.'

'I will guard it with my life.'

Horsemen were galloping back and forth, up and down the column, but none approached us.

At the head rode Jahangir and Shah Jahan. They were preceded by nine elephants, each bearing the Mughal standard of the crouching lion set against a rising sun; then four more carried green flags depicting the sun. Next came nine riderless white stallions bearing gold saddles, stirrups and bits, and behind them rode two horsemen. One carried a banner bearing Jahangir's title, 'Seizer of the World', the other rode with the dundhubi which he struck regularly to warn of the approach of the Great Mughal. Thirty men ran on foot before them, scattering scented water so that the emperor would have a sweet and dustless passage. On either side of him rode *hazaris* with their separate standards, each leading their thousand horsemen.

A little apart from Jahangir, and to his rear, rode four *wazirs* burdened with papers. These papers contained all the information necessary to inform the emperor about the land through which he was riding. If he should ask, they could tell him the name of the village and of its headman, its revenue, crops, fruits and flowers and, as Jahangir was an inquisitive monarch, they were constantly scurrying to and fro with the information he required for his *Jahangir-nama*. A little way from these men were two others. They carried a rope and, from the gates of the Lal Quila, they had begun to measure the distance Jahangir had travelled. The man in front made his mark; the man behind walked to it and placed his end of the rope to the mark while the first moved on again. Behind these two, came a third with his book, keeping count of the distance. If Jahangir should enquire, 'how far have we travelled?' the man could tell him. The fourth man carried an hour-glass and a bronze gong. On each hour he struck the gong.

A few paces behind Jahangir rode two horsemen with hawks on their wrists. Then came ten horsemen: four carried royal jezails enclosed in cloth-of-gold bags, the fifth bore Jahangir's spear, the sixth his sword, the seventh his shield, the eighth his dagger, the ninth his bow and the tenth his quiver of arrows. After the weapon-bearers came the Ahadi, soldiers under the direct command of the Padishah. These were followed by the three Imperial palanquins, each of silver and elaborately decorated with pearls. Behind them rode twenty-four horsemen, eight carrying trumpets, eight with pipes, and eight with drums. Then came the five Imperial elephants carrying gold and silver howdahs. The gentle swaying of the elephant invariably put the emperor to sleep. It felt like being rocked in a cradle.

Alongside these richly adorned elephants were three more. The beast in the middle bore three hands made of the finest silver, mounted at the top of a silver pole and covered with velvet. It signified that

68

Jahangir was an 'Observer of the Mohammedan Faith'. Another bore a similar sign proclaiming him to be the 'Augmenter and Conservator of the Faith'. The third one displayed a copper plate engraved with the words 'God is One with Mohammed'.

Four more elephants followed, their howdahs adorned with equally important symbols. One carried a pair of scales which meant the king dealt with justice, another bore a large flag which, when blown by the breeze, made the crocodile embroidered into the fine white cloth appear to be alive, writhing and snarling. It signified that Jahangir was 'Lord of the Rivers'; another beast carried a similar flag with the head of a fish, proclaiming him to be 'Lord of the Seas', while another carried aloft a golden spear, the 'Sign of the Conqueror'. These elephants were followed by twelve more carrying musicians.

All this grandeur of state came between me and my beloved. It seemed that he was at one end of the earth and I at the other. I could no longer bear the weight of his silence. It was well past noon, and I dismounted.

'Isa, take my horse and ride to Shah Jahan. Tell my . . .' I couldn't say the word, it stuck in my gullet out of fear, . . . 'my love that I am here. He must come to me. I must know what is to happen to me. Has his love for me ended? Must I wait? I will if he commands me to. I hate the woman who is to be his bride with a bitterness as great as my love.'

'Agachi, I cannot tell him these things.'

'Fetch him here then, and I will tell him. Mount.'

Isa looked down at his feet and then fearfully at the patient horse. Men and beasts flowed past us like a stream, the rush of a river around rocks.

'Agachi, I cannot ride. I will run.'

'It is too long a distance, and too long a time for me to wait. Mount now and hold fast to the reins. He will carry you swiftly to my beloved, and equally swiftly return you to me with his answer.'

Isa clumsily obeyed my command, although his face was creased

69

with unhappiness at the prospect of galloping on this horse. I waited only until he had settled and pointed the animal's head in the right direction, then struck its rump sharply. It broke into a gallop with Isa clinging to its neck. He would learn out of necessity. Another time I would have felt compassion and amusement at his plight, but now both had fled me.

A palanquin waited and I gladly took refuge in it to hide my tears from the many eyes that watched me. I rode with the haram, behind the entourage of the Empress Jodi Bai. She sat on an elephant in a *pitambar*, a canopied throne made of beaten gold and encrusted with precious stones. She was suffering from a strange, wasting illness and would have preferred to remain at court, but Jahangir insisted that she accompany him on this journey. Her beast was followed by one hundred and fifty Uzbeck warrior women armed with spears, and on all sides strode eunuchs carrying silver-tipped lathis with which they drove away any man foolish enough to approach. Then came countless elephants and palanquins bearing Jahangir's other women, each accompanied by her own retinue of slaves, servants and eunuchs.

Of course the business of state could not be forgotten or ignored while the emperor moved from Agra to Ajmer, or indeed wherever he chose to travel. Behind us came eighty camels, thirty elephants and twenty carts loaded with the royal records. A further fifty camels carried one hundred cases packed with Jahangir's sarapas, thirty elephants carried jewels which would be dispensed as gifts to those fortunate enough to have won his favour; two hundred camels followed loaded with silver rupees, one hundred with gold rupees, and one hundred and fifty camels carried nets to trap tigers or nilgais or cheetahs. There were also fifty camels carrying water for drinking and bathing, while large and colourfully painted carts carried the hamams, in which the emperor and we women could bathe in privacy. Behind all of us, guarding the rear, rode the Rajput Prince, Jai Singh, commanding eight thousand horsemen.

70

One kos in front of the column rode a man on a camel carrying a length of the finest white linen. If he came across a dead animal, or a human, he would cover the body with the cloth, weighing it down with heavy stones. This was done so as not to offend the eyes of the emperor. As often as not it aroused his curiosity, and he had his men lift the cloth so that he could see what lay hidden beneath.

The afternoon passed slowly. I looked out, watching the shadows of hills and trees stretch out across the land. I could see no sign of Isa. I wished now I had not been so impatient. He might have fallen and killed himself, and my message would then be lost forever. Selfishly I prayed that he lived; that he would reach my beloved. I prayed more fervently as dusk fell and the lights of the encampment began to burn on the plain ahead of us.

A whole day's march in front of our column, moved another large procession commanded by the Grand Master of the Royal Household. His beasts carried the *do-ashiyana manzil*, cooking utensils, food and every other necessity for the comfort of the emperor and his following. The Grand Master would choose a pleasant spot, near a river if possible, and there his small army of servants would erect a city of tents. In the very centre of this would be the emperor's quarters. His two-storeyed tent contained several rooms that matched in splendour the palace itself, including a diwan-i-khas and a diwan-i-am. Behind his quarters were those of the royal haram, and the whole residence was enclosed by a screen of scarlet cloth. The plan of this city had not changed from the days of Timur-i-leng. Everyone knew where he or she was to spend the night, to eat, bathe and stable the beasts. This prevented confusion when the column reached the site at nightfall. In fact, there were two such cities. While one was being used, another moved ahead in order to be ready for the emperor's arrival on the following night. As this was only a hunting trip, the Mughal army remained behind in Agra. It had been recorded that it took half a day for the emperor's retinue to pass a fixed point, and a whole day when his army moved with him.

71

I found my quarters in the tent of the haram. The women enjoyed these expeditions and were laughing and chattering as they prepared themselves for the evening's entertainment. I remained aloof, and when I had bathed and dressed I withdrew to lie down, refusing offers of food and companionship. I didn't need anything, my misery was food and companion enough.

Isa found me, my face to the wall, eyes tightly closed.

'Agachi, I couldn't find the prince. Each one I asked sent me to ask another. I am ashamed.'

'You tried. Leave me alone. Go.'

I couldn't turn to face him and only heard him creep away. A new emotion now welled up in me. Anger. How dare he neglect me? Even if he came to me now I would spurn him, dismiss him as I had Isa.

Much later I heard Isa return and whisper softly, 'Agachi, a messenger awaits you.'

'Who from?' I feigned ignorance, not wanting to hope.

'From the prince. Come.'

I wouldn't move, but remained huddled with my back to him.

'Fetch the message then. Tell him I will answer in a few days.' Isa did not move to go, so I sat up. 'I told you to go.'

'Agachi, I understand your anger, but he will not give it to me. Only you may receive it. Please come. You may regret it later if you do not.'

He was half hidden in shadow, but I could see the scrapes and bruises on his face and arms.

'I am sorry I made you ride.'

'It is one way to learn.'

I got up reluctantly. 'I will see this messenger and I hope he carries happier news.'

We went out into the cool night. The makeshift city sprawled as far as the eye could see, covering valleys and hills. Yellow lanterns and

72

open fires twinkled in the velvet black night. Tomorrow it would all disappear as swiftly as it had arrived.

The messenger was waiting in the deepest shadow to one side of the tent, well hidden from the patrolling soldiers and Uzbeck women. He looked a sorry creature, wrapped in a shabby blanket with the end of his turban masking his face.

'You have a message for me?' He nodded. 'Who from?'

'From myself, my love.' Shah Jahan whispered. 'Why must we always meet in darkness?'

'Perhaps his highness cannot bear to look upon me by day.'

'Why are you angry with me?'

'Tell me then how I should feel?' I spoke coldly, wishing only to escape his stare, forget that he existed and I existed. 'I have waited for months. A word, a whisper, any small token would have soothed the pain in my heart. All I have received from you, while I heard the words and lies of others, is silence.'

'I have endangered my life to come here in this guise. If I am caught, my fate will be worse than any beggar's.' He turned aside as a eunuch passed and I stepped with him deeper into the shadow. 'I could not escape my father's side, my beloved. He commanded me to ride by him all day, and at night I sat and listened to his poetry. Believe me, all I yearned for was to come to you.'

I felt myself relenting, but couldn't immediately still the anger that had flared in me.

'A messenger, then?'

'Who could carry the message better than myself?' He knelt down at my feet and bowed his head. 'Forgive me, forgive me.'

My heart melted. 'I cannot resist such humility. I forgive you, and can only blame love for my anger. It is a hunger which I cannot control. If love were food and drink, I would be a glutton and never cease consuming them.'

He took my hand and placed it against his forehead, then rose.

73

'It is I who am to blame for showing such princely control over my heart.'

Suddenly I felt a veil of shyness descend on me. I had never before been alone with my love, or any other man, and my thoughts and dreams now shrank from revealing themselves. But even if I were to say: 'I love you', what could he reply to comfort me?

'You have heard . . .?'

'I have.'

'I couldn't resist further without arousing his rage. I must remain the obedient son, and it is cruel that we must both carry the burden of my responsibilities.'

'Will he not change his mind?'

'It is not he, but I, Shah Jahan, who will not change. I could take you as my second wife . . .'

'If that is your wish,' I whispered. 'Even your concubine. My happiness is to be by your side.'

'No. That is not my wish. One day I shall be emperor, and it will be our son who will mount the throne.'

He learned forward and his mouth barely touched mine.

'How sweet you taste, like the petal of a rose.'

'It is only for you. Another would find my lips bitter.'

'And mine too, for another.'

We were suddenly startled by Isa's call: 'Agachi!'

The eunuch who had passed now stood peering towards us. His lathi was raised menacingly, and I felt my beloved groping to unsheath his dagger from beneath the blanket. I stopped his hand.

'Who is that?' the eunuch's high voice demanded.

'My servant. I am sending him on an errand. Go.'

'I will escort him out. Come, come with me.'

He pulled roughly at my prince and meekly Shah Jahan followed him out of the enclosure. I watched and watched until he was out of sight, hoping he would turn to look. But he was gone.

74

The taste of his mouth on mine remained all night and into the next day. It was cool and soothing, but no balm for my solitude. I would wait as he commanded, but promises made in passion can be swiftly forgotten by princes.

It was a relief to escape the confusion of so many men and beasts on the move. We travelled more swiftly, choosing our own pace and following our own route rather than having these dictated to us by protocol and the whims of Jahangir. Five hundred horsemen escorted me, as well as a dozen maidservants and Isa. But I stayed apart as much as I could. I did not want to make polite conversation or pretend to be happy, and I felt so alone. I was now sad, now angry, and even Isa was wary of my moods.

We camped each night in *serais*, the small fortified enclosures scattered throughout the empire for the use of travellers. Soldiers were not permitted within their walls and, as I preferred their protection to that of complete strangers, I slept in a *khargah*. It was cooler too. The malignant heat hovered just beyond the shadows of darkness, kept at bay by the cool night, only to stun us into stupor less than an hour after sunrise.

I lay in the khargah wooing sleep as I desired to be courted by my lover, but each night it eluded me. I would have preferred to sleep in the open and gaze up at the vast clear sky. It had the ability to distract, to make one wonder at the great universe that stretched far beyond one's own limited imagination. The sky gave a resonance to God and reduced us, even the Great Mughal, to puny creatures.

It would have given me comfort and hope. I could have skipped across the sky from star to star believing that their lustrous movements really did control the destinies of men, pushing them this way and that, changing the course of their lives. But what if nothing happened? If the stars did not control our lives, what did? My life was wretched,

75

hollow with uselessness. I wished I could abandon these trappings of power and wealth and wander the country like a sunyasi.

Who was she? Jahangir's last words to my beloved were: 'I have chosen your wife.' I had discreetly, painfully, enquired. No one knew, or they would not tell me. Did she really exist? Which princess was worthy of marriage to the crown prince? Was she Hindu? Muslim? I tried to imagine her as I stared up at the striped ceiling of the khargah, suffocating in the smell of incense. All around me my maids slept, and Isa lay stretched across the entrance. Beyond in the night, I was ringed by soldiers. But none could prevent the creep of my dark thoughts.

I heard several horsemen ride up to our camp and the challenge of the sentries, and then the soft murmur of voices approaching. Then Isa woke up and whispered to the men, before calling softly into the khargah: 'Agachi.'

I feigned sleep and waited for him to call again.

'Agachi, the Padishah has sent a messenger. He is to speak only to you.'

A maid brought me my robe, another lit the lamp. I went to the entrance and peeped through the lattice. A man stood in the shadows and Isa lifted the lamp so that I could see his face. The messenger was armed and had a scar that ran up his forehead and disappeared into his turban. He wore nondescript clothing under his armour.

'Who are you?' I asked, standing so that he could not see me and only heard my voice. He peered from side to side.

'The emperor's messenger, Begum. I ride in his Ahadi.'

'But you are not wearing the Imperial uniform.'

'His majesty did not wish my errand to be known,' he whispered uneasily.

I too felt uneasy at such secrecy. The soldier should have been wearing the Imperial scarlet, instead he looked like a dacoit.

'What have you brought? Give it to Isa. He will pass it to me.'

Isa slid two packages through the opening. One was flat, wrapped in silk; the other, in a velvet bag, was a small gold casket intricately designed with dancing figures. They were both sealed with the Muhr Uzak. 'They are for the Begum Mehrunissa, to be handed by you to her personally. They are gifts from the emperor.'

The cruelty of convenience! How it hurt me. I was worth nothing to Jahangir except as his courier. I could not marry his son because I was of no importance, but I could carry his love tokens south to Bengal, to Mehrunissa. Was he not aware of this irony? I could feel the fever of his passion for Mehrunissa in the objects I held; could be not understand my pain? He had commanded Shah Jahan to forget me. Could an emperor's command erase memory, vanquish love? But he had not commanded me to forget Shah Jahan. I could remain loving, while my beloved was to forget.

The soldier moved as if to leave.

'Wait. How is the empress?'

'She is . . . no better, Begum.'

Before I left the column word came to me that Jodi Bai had grown worse. She could neither eat nor drink; any food she ate was immediately vomited. It was a sickness which the hakim could not cure, in spite of all his herbal potions. Each day she grew weaker. The hakim had advised her against travelling any further with the emperor. The journey to Ajmer would only exhaust her further but, strangely, Jahangir had insisted that she remain with him. He claimed he would worry even more if he could not constantly attend at her side.

'And the prince Shah Jahan?' It took an effort to speak his name out aloud, to reveal my concern for him so openly.

'He is well, Begum.'

I waited breathlessly. He added nothing further, but stood there in dumb exhaustion. No message. No word. Shah Jahan continued to be the dutiful son.

'When will you be returning?'

'I will not return until much later. The emperor has commanded

77

me to ride with your party to Bengal.' He looked away, but not quickly enough. He held yet another secret.

'I have five hundred horsemen. How many have you brought?'

'Two hundred.'

'All Ahadi?'

He made no reply to this and his mouth became tight and drawn. He bowed, turned abruptly and faded into the darkness.

'Try and find out why they ride with us, Isa. But be careful.'

'I will be very careful, Agachi, though it is likely that I will fail. The Emperor's personal bodyguard won't chatter about his mission with a lowly servant.'

Isa failed, though not for want of trying. The Ahadi horsemen remained aloof from our party, riding a kos behind, keeping us within sight, but never forming a part of our train. All the soldiers wore the same nondescript uniforms, looking like rag-tag dacoits instead of Jahangir's hand-picked bodyguards.

They made the captain of my escort uneasy also. He was a young, handsome Rajput, a younger son of the Rana of Jaipur. The Jaipur princes had served in the Mughal army since the days of Babur and Humayun, and Fateh Singh was following his military ancestors. Occasionally he rode beside me to point out landmarks of interest and often would turn round to keep an eye on the Ahadi, always some way behind us.

The landscape undulated gently and changed imperceptibly. The vegetation grew more lush as we moved south, and we passed through jungle that was green and pleasant, full of colourful birds and animals. Here, the earth did not seem as hard and ungiving and each small village was surrounded by fields of wheat or chillies which burned a bright, dancing red next to the swaying yellow of the mustard crop.

For the most part the villagers hid from us, and only children peered out from behind doors or bushes, and watched with wide eyes. The villages were mud-walled, thatch-roofed, and protected by thorn fencing. I caught no glimpse of the women, except the bright, elusive flash of a sari. It was not only the landscape that changed, but the language, the customs, the mode of dress. Everything remained familiar—people, birds, animals—yet we travelled as if we held an unwinding thread that changed colour and texture as we moved along its length.

One morning, before we resumed our journey, Fateh Singh suggested that I might like to ride a distance of a few kos to Khajuraho to look at the temples.

'They are delightfully carved,' he said with a small, slight smile. 'You would enjoy them.'

I did not want all the soldiers to accompany us, the sight of them often frightened the villagers. I made the journey at dawn with Isa, a few maidservants, and a dozen soldiers led by Fateh Singh.

In the soft morning light the great temples hung in the sky like filigree, shaded a most delicate brown. There were four temples grouped together, and further on just beyond a dip in the land, I saw many others. There were perhaps thirty in all. They had broad bases and rose a hundred or so feet above the earth. A short ride past a giant statue of the Buddha and the fields of wheat that stretched out towards the dip, we came to the village. There could not have been more than a hundred souls living there and it was strange that such magnificent monuments had been built for so few people. A group of women were making their way to one of the temples; when they saw us, they hesitated, and then clinging together boldly kept walking, though they never took their eyes off the soldiers. They carried flowers and coconuts and plantains on brass plates, while from the temple came the soft chimes of a bell.

'The temples are seven hundred years old,' Fateh Singh said. He could not disguise his price in their antiquity. They looked newly carved. 'This was the Hindu Kingdom of Jijhoti. Note how tolerant that kingdom was.' He pointed right and left. 'There the Buddhist worshipped, there the Jain.'

On riding closer I noticed that there were many carvings, each set in a panel like steps leading to the sky. We dismounted and walked up to the temples, while the soldiers remained ever watchful.

The carvings were breathtakingly beautiful; men and women full of grace and loveliness, entwined in all manner of sensual poses. It seemed to me that somehow the stone had been turned into flesh by the touch of a chisel, and now this flesh was suffused with passion. The women were full-breasted, with long legs; the men handsome, their well-muscled bodies taut as if they were holding their breath while waiting for us to pass by. Such was the delicacy of the work that even the clothing appeared to be silken. One carving was of a woman caught in the act of undressing, with a cloth draped only over her lower limbs to reveal her full breasts; she had a scorpion frozen in stone on her calf. There were so many figures caught in different poses that they whirled and danced in front of my eyes, confusing stone with flesh itself.

Their luscious sensuality stirred my inexperienced passion. I imagined myself with Shah Jahan taking part in these wild dances of sexuality, frozen together in this subtle stone—our bodies forever joined in ecstasy. I felt the heat rise to my face, and was thankful that the beatilha hid my lascivious thoughts.

'It is strange that Hindus reveal such things in their places of worship.'

'Only because all things represent the grace and beauty of the divine,' Fateh Singh said. He pointed to some of the statues that were crudely shattered, and spoke with anger. 'See, even the Ghazi, the Scourge of God, stopped his own hand from destroying this beauty completely.'

It was true, for there could not have been another explanation as to why these temples had not been razed by past invaders. They had gazed upon these carvings, and had been moved by the passion and beauty of them. In other parts of the land many temples had been razed and on the sites mosques had been constructed. Islam lay on the face of Hindustan like the veil covering my face. In Agra, stifled by the court, I had only glimpsed this life, but once outside that circle of power it was revealed to me. for the first time I felt what it was to be a stranger in this land. It lay beneath our feet like a beast, tossing and turning, not fully awake and not yet really aware of our presence.

The women had finished their worship, and seeing that the soldiers stood some way off, came to look at me. They stood in silence, shy but openly curious. I spoke to them in Persian, then Fateh Singh addressed them in Rajasthani. They did not understand but giggled, and holding their saris to cover their faces, hurried off back to their village.

The priest stood watching us from the top of the temple steps. He was bare-chested and wore a white cloth around his waist, pulled up between his legs. On his chest was the sacred thread and his brow was marked with the three horizontal streaks of Siva. I climbed up the steps, but he barred my entrance. In the flickering light behind him I could discern the garlanded idol.

Isa joined our party half an hour later. He said that he had stayed behind to examine the carvings more closely, but I saw that his brow was still smeared with *vibuthi*. We never spoke of it again.

Thirty days later we arrived in Gaur. We lost sight of the Ahadi horsemen somewhere in the maze of streets and Fateh Singh presumed that they had gone to report to the Mir Bakshi. The first familiar face I saw was Muneer's. He embraced me and, while supervising the unpacking, he complained constantly about Gaur. I thought it was a most attractive place. It lay fourteen kos along the bank of the Ganga, and each successive ruler had left his imprint upon it. It was a holy city; the Kadam Rasul preserved the footprint of the Prophet. Gaur was also the granary of the empire and the inhabitants were wealthy.

My aunt Mehrunissa lived in one of the larger palaces, an airy, spacious building surrounded by a veranda and set in a large garden full of mango trees and many others fruits. It was a splendid dwelling certainly befitting my uncle's lucrative and important position as the Diwan of Bengal.

Mehrunissa came in as soon as I had bathed and dressed, and she looked radiant and pleased. I suspected that her happiness was due not to my presence, but to the gold casket that lay in my box. Around her neck she wore a gold key. Ladilli trailed her like a wraith and threw her arms around me. she had grown, but her manner had changed little; for me she would always remain a shy child, no matter what her age.

As soon as I had handed over Jahangir's gifts Mehrunissa ordered her eunuch Muneer to take them to her room. I thought that the papers would probably be a poem, for Jahangir considered himself an accomplished poet. I knew nothing of the contents of the gold box.

'Aren't you going to show me what's in it?' I asked Mehrunissa.

'No, I'm glad you can't open everything you get your hands on,' she said. Then, kissing me, she whispered: 'Don't mention these gifts to your uncle. He might misunderstand.'

She stood back, and then for the first time took note of my appearance. I knew that I had a wan pallor and had lost weight, but I did not need to tell her the cause. In spite of the great distance between us, Mehrunissa knew all that had happened.

'My poor thing,' she patted my cheek. 'You are very young. You will forget all about him.'

'I won't, I know that.'

'We will find you some amusements. He is not the only young man in the world.'

'I don't want another.'

She sighed in exasperation. 'Is it because he is the crown prince that you love him?'

'Of course not,' I said angrily.

She looked at me closely, trying to decipher the meaning of my reply.

'Shah Jahan is my beloved, not the crown prince. Even if he were a beggar, I would still love him.'

'What does your mother say?'

'The same as you, the same as the Emperor. "Forget him." As if those words alone could kill the feelings in my heart.' I took a deep breath and faced her. 'Help me, Aunt.'

'How?'

'Speak to the Emperor. Write to him. Tell him about . . .'

'But why should Jahangir listen to me? I am only a friend and have no power.' She hesitated as if she was about to add something else, but changed her mind, and instead smiled sweetly. 'I will try to help. That's all I can promise. Now I must distract you as best I can.'

Whatever the casket contained, it made Mehrunissa very happy. I pried and pestered her to reveal its contents, but she would merely shake her head, laugh, and then sweep me away to explore the city. Her delight was infectious and she was most loving and attentive to Sher Afkun, who wore an air of contented satisfaction. He was obviously enjoying his importance here in Bengal, and experiencing the delights of a position that was not overshadowed by the success of Mehrunissa's father. Mehrunissa's lavish display of affection, the excessive caressing of her husband's face and body, and the flattering endearments which so pleased him only made me feel uneasy. I could read her thoughts better than her husband, but it is said that men are easily beguiled by a kiss or a caress, and Mehrunissa was well versed in those arts.

'You must stay here forever,' my uncle said. 'You have made my Mehrunissa so happy. Until now she has been miserable—the heat, the sweat, the boredom—and though I have done my best to please her, I could not. Now you have come, and brought us great joy.'

'Yes, you must stay,' Mehrunissa said, laughing with him.

83

She knew that I was aware of the reason for her improved temper. 'Dear husband, will you arrange a *qamargah* for Arjumand's entertainment next week? It is so long since I've been out hunting. The last time was with Arjumand too, when we accompanied Akbar. Now that she knows how to fire a jezail, we will allow her to kill a tiger. They are bigger here than I have seen anywhere else. Arjumand, you will enjoy it.'

'Please do not trouble yourself,' I said. 'I no longer enjoy such sport.'

'Nonsense. You will arrange it, won't you?'

'Of course,' my uncle said.

The qamargah is a form of hunting that was first introduced by Timur-i-leng. Thousands of horsemen gather together to form a large crescent many miles wide, and slowly they move towards each other so that a ring is formed. Countless animals can be trapped within this enclosure: tigers, leopards, nilgais, langours, chitals. According to rank the hunters enter the enclosure one at a time to kill and animal by whatever method they choose: the jezail, the spear, the sword, bow and arrow. Akbar once entered on foot and was gored in the testicles by a nilgai, and spent many months recovering from the wound.

For this qamargah, my uncle had chosen the jungle east of Gaur. There were many tigers in the area, and he wished to show off Mehrunissa's hunting skills to the numerous officials and their families who would accompany us.

It was a festive party that made camp the night before. The tents were dotted around a pretty lake, and there was much food and drink. The men gathered in Sher Afkun's tent, the women in Mehrunissa's. Our enjoyment was no less uproarious than the men's, for Mehrunissa loved to arrange gatherings, and had hired singers and dancers for our entertainment. We drank wine and experimented with the *huqqa*, and listened for many hours to the performers singing about love and heartbreak and happiness. The hunt was to last for many days, and the

84

horsemen had already been sent on ahead to drive the animals to the chosen clearing. As Diwan, my uncle had the privilege of being the first to enter. Mehrunissa intended to accompany him and, as his special guest, I was to be accorded the same privilege. We would ride each on our own elephant.

In spite of the early start, our festivities went on until midnight. Even so, as we settled down to sleep we could still hear the boisterous merrymaking of the men across the clearing. Few would be capable of hunting the next day if they rose, as planned, at dawn. Some of the women murmured sleepily about those silly men, and I fell asleep to their laughter. In the distance, I could hear the sweet call of the chital.

At the hour when light throws no shadows, when it is neither night nor day, I was woken by the sound of shouting and the chilling clash of swords. In the darkness, we could not at first tell the direction of the fight, but then the sounds came across the clearing from my uncle's tent.

'What is it? What's happening?' The women were frightened and huddled together.

The shouting grew louder and mingled with the screams of dying men. Startled elephants trumpeted, men ran in all directions. A jezail was fired, a sword struck a shield. I tripped over a crouched woman as I made my way out of the tent. Suddenly I felt my arm gripped fiercely.

'Where are you going?' Mehrunissa whispered.

'To see what's happening.'

'Stay here.'

Her eyes were glistening in the half-light and her body was tense as she strained to listen to what was going on. I realized that she was not afraid, and worse still, she was not even surprised. She seemed to know exactly what was happening.

The uproar stopped as abruptly as it had begun. Silence hung eerily in the air, suspended like a hawk about to dive and kill. Mehrunissa slowly released her grip on me. After a moment we heard horses

85

galloping into the night. I shivered from the cold as I stepped outside. The stars were fading and a pink tinge like blood mixed in water was seeping across the dark sky. The grass felt damp underfoot. Across the clearing, a crowd of men had gathered around my uncle's tent. I pushed my way through to see my uncle lying with that calm and subtracted look of death on his face. A sword had been thrust deep into his side. His spirit now moved in another world, and we were left staring down at the abandoned husk. I knelt on the bloody grass and kissed him, noticing his faint and familiar odour, the musky tang of perspiration and perfume, but now joined by the sweet flow of blood. I cried then. I had a deep affection for him. He had been a kind and gentle man. His bravery as a soldier had given him a roughness, a bluster, that arose from the company of soldiers, yet still he retained an endearing shyness. Five other men were scattered in grotesque positions around him. An arm lay separately, the fingers clawed, as if it had been inching its way back to its body.

'Lift the lamp,' I commanded.

The light rose to bathe the faces of the other dead men. The nearest man had lost his turban, and had a scar that ran up his forehead into the thick matting of black hair—Jahangir's messenger. When I stood up again, the Mir Bakshi shrugged with only the slightest movement of his shoulder. His voice was bland, the red-rimmed black eyes quite devoid of any expression.

'Dacoits,' he murmured.

Mehrunissa wept long and loudly. I could not comfort her; a chill lay on my heart. Ladilli was the most deeply affected by her father's death, and she cried silently, continually. I kept her company as best I could, and she held tightly to my hand. Her father had been her closest friend, and now she seemed more lost than ever.

The Mir Bakshi sent his report to Jahangir: dacoits had killed Sher Afkun and he would move heaven and earth to find them. A messenger arrived from the emperor with condolences for Mehrunissa and

86

appointing her lady-in-waiting to one of Akbar's widows, Salima. Before departing from Gaur, Mehrunissa threw her great energy into planning a tomb for her husband. It was to be constructed by a lake on the outskirts of the city, looking east towards the jungle in which he had been murdered. It was to be a simple and inexpensive monument.

On our last evening in Gaur I sat with Ladilli, and noticed the gold casket I had delivered to Mehrunissa lying on the ivory table. Ladilli, still immersed in her sorrow, paid no attention to me. The key was in the lock, so I opened it and peered in. A diamond as large as my clenched fist lay nestled in a bed of emeralds. I knew it was the stone that Babur had returned to Humayun. Death would always be the companion of such a gift.

the taj mahal 1044/AD 1634

I am, Sita thought, like Sita, wife of Rama. She too followed her husband into exile. She could have remained at home in comfort, but she insisted on going with Rama into the jungle, because it was her karma as a wife. I wept when we left our home, wanting Murthi to make the journey alone: Rama's Sita was brave in her loneliness; I am not.

Sita yearned painfully for her family, mother, grandmother, father, sisters, cousins, and aunts. She missed the humble village nestled in the shimmering green rice fields, of which two small grounds belonged to her family. Countless days of her life had been spent planting, tending, reaping, drying in those fields. She missed going with the other women to the water tank some distance from the village, where they washed clothes, bathed, and gathered for gossip. She pined for the small temple, set on a rocky hill half a day's walk away.

There were no temples in Agra; she had only the little idol in her hut.

She thought of all this as she wound her way mechanically through the site, carrying her loads. She was small, supple and slim, her body muscle and bone, nothing more. She walked quickly, holding herself with her basket perfectly balanced on her head on a small ball of cloth to protect her skull. She had a fine, oval face with high cheekbones, brown quiet eyes and a generous mouth. She wore only one piece of jewellery, her marriage *thali*. The rest of her small collection, some gold bangles, nose rings and ear-rings, lay buried in the floor of their hut.

Sita stood patiently in line to receive another load of earth. It was wintertime in Agra and she had never known such cold. The previous winters had been mild, but this one killed; the old, the weak, the young, the unneeded, all died. It frightened her to wake in darkness with the moist, icy mist hanging still and menacing. She no longer wore a sari, but dressed in the Panjabi style of a kurta and pyjamas, layers that were now unclean because it was too cold to bathe regularly. In her village she had bathed every day, and now she felt her uncleanliness, which made her even more miserable.

The men worried at the earth. It was hard, dry and cruel; fighting the simple iron tools, rising as a brownish yellow dust falling in leaden chunks. All around her the other women chattered, but Sita understood nothing. The strange language increased her loneliness and made her clumsy. Now it was her turn again. She handed her basket to the man standing on the ground. He tossed it down the cavernous hole which plunged six hundred and eighty-eight feet to rock level, and received a full one handed up by a relay of men from the dark depths.

The foundations would take many years to lay. The design of the tomb was a series of piers straddling a series of wells which would eventually be connected by strong arches. The cores of these wells would be filled with rubble, and then the space between each with solid masonry. The piers would support the massive weight of the tomb, while the wells would prevent the river Jumna from seeping under it. The bricks were immersed in hot fat to make them waterproof for centuries to come. The mortar to bind them was also a special mixture: slaked lime and diamonds, raw sugar, lentils and lentil flour, crushed seashells and eggshells and gum from the trees.

Sita squatted down and grasped one side of the basket while the man took the other. Together, they lifted it up and placed it on her head. She adjusted the balance and slowly, gracefully, rose. It was an effort. Once upright, she made her way carefully through the confusion. The earth lay in undulating mounds, and Sita followed a narrow path, the width of a bare foot, to the bund. It was the start of a roadway, now only a foot high, but which would eventually rise and rise and rise, keeping pace with the level of the building. Elephants and bullocks would climb the gently curving slope of the bund, hauling loads of brick and stone. Sita dropped her load, and the squatting men beat the fresh earth hard with heavy blocks of wood.

She wound her way back by another route. In the shade of a dusty banyan tree a group of children were playing. The youngest were just babies, the eldest girls of four or five who looked after the others. Sita looked for Savitri and found her sitting contentedly in a pile of sand. She squatted and hugged her daughter, blew her nose, adjusted her clothes and then hurried back to join the line. She glanced back; Savitri was crying, reaching out, but there was nothing to be done about it.

In the distance she saw a group of splendid men approaching and heard the whispers of the other workers: the Padishah, the Padishah. She stood still and gaped with the others, as if a god had descended. The emperor crossed the earth like a storm, laying men and women low before him. Soldiers pushed and cleared a path through the workers for him. He did not appear to be aware of them. He mounted the bund, stood silhouetted against the blue sky, isolated from all around him, and stared at the churned earth. Then he looked up to the sky for a long silent moment, and, it appeared to Sita, saw something—something that towered over him which no one else could see. Then he returned to the fort.

Weary, Sita squatted by the dung fire. The smoke stung her eyes and she wiped them continually with the hem of her kurta. The clay pots simmered, one held rice, another dhal, a third brinjal, enough to feed them for one day. Each morning she wrapped the cold meal in leaves, making neat packets for herself, Murthi, Gopi and Savitri.

She was not well; it was a sickness she knew of old. She had not bled for many days and knew, unhappily, that she was pregnant again. She whispered a prayer: a son, Siva, Vishnu, Lakshmi, a son. If there had been a temple nearby, Sita would have bathed, dressed in a clean sari, woven jasmine into her hair and carried simple offerings to the gods. She would have given the priest a few coins to recite a special puja for her newly formed baby and prayed to the sound of the chanting that it would become a boy.

Hurry, hurry, hurry, hurry.

The words beat as if spoken aloud; his heart raced with them. Shah Jahan sat on the cushions staring at the model. His hand, an emperor's hand, soft, pale, enamelled with gold and diamonds, caressed the dome. The building weighed on him, hurting as if his bones too were made of white marble, settling into the flesh like an unhealing wound. Only when it was completed would the pain die, the wound close, the stone lift from his flesh. 'Something is wrong,' he whispered. 'Isa, fetch me Ismail Afandi.'

'It will be done, Padishah.'

Shah Jahan's hand continued its caressing movement, searching for the flaw. His ministers—the Diwan, the Mir Saman, the Mir Bakshi— stood silent and unmoving, none wishing to disturb the emperor's meditations.

Finally, the Diwan spoke: 'Padishah!'

'What is it?'

The Diwan rustled his papers. 'If you please, we should attend to some matters. The rains came late this year and the farmers have lost a lot of their crops. I must have permission to lessen their taxation, as Akbar decreed. But I find that is not possible. The Exchequer is expending a vast amount on the tomb for Her Majesty, Mumtaz-i-Mahal. What should be done, Padishah?'

'Later, later.'

'Padishah,' the Mir Bakshi spoke up. 'The Deccan princes are in open rebellion. We must send an army to subdue them. Who is to command the forces?'

'They are always a nuisance,' Shah Jahan replied. 'What do we ever achieve there? I tried, Akbar tried, my father tried. The matter can wait.'

'Yes, Padishah.'

'Now go. Approach me later.'

His ministers bowed and withdrew. Like the whole empire, they held their breath. The Great Mughal seemed to have placed his hand on the earth, smothering men and beasts and stilling all movement, permitting only the untold thousands of workers by the river to continue their frantic daily existence.

Ismail Afandi, the Designer of Domes, waited for Shah Jahan to note his insignificant presence. The emperor's hand rested on the dome. At his side a brazier filled with live coals radiated perfumed heat.

'It isn't perfect, Afandi.'

'Yes, Padishah.'

He remained still and subservient, his answer double-edged. The dome was perfect. Had he not built the dome for the great mosque in Shiraz, the dome for the Turki emperor's tomb? His skill had never been questioned, and this dome equalled the others. However, it was politic to agree with the emperor.

'It is flat . . .'

'Yes, Padishah.'

'. . . like the dome on Humayun's tomb. This one must not resemble anything else you have created. Do you understand?'

'A dome can be but one shape, Padishah.'

Shah Jahan's glance was a sword-cut, a slash. Afandi flinched. Sweat beaded his face. Why had he spoken? Foolish pride pricked at him that he should be instructed in his art by the emperor. Emperors ruled, he

92

built: a clean and decisive division of skills. He would not have undertaken the commission if this constant interference could have been foreseen.

'This dome will be different,' Shah Jahan said. 'It will be round, drawn up, as if it would float away.'

The emperor's hand hovered in the air as if he held an invisible ball. He knew what he meant, even if Afandi did not. His glance fell on the slave girls and he beckoned one; she knelt by him. He exposed her breast; it was small and firm with a dark nipple. He clutched it, but it did not satisfy him, so he beckoned another girl. Her breasts were larger, high, round and firm. The chill teased her nipples. He held one breast, squeezing and reshaping it.

'Like this, Afandi, like this, you see!'

'Yes, Padishah.'

He could not contain his shock. A woman's breast on a tomb? He was to forget all his experience to imitate flesh.

'Measure the proportions of the shape.'

Afandi drew out his callipers and gingerly encircled the breast. The girl remained passive, staring into the distance as Afandi wrote down the measurements.

'But at the base, I want it to come in——so——like her waist.'

'Yes, Padishah.'

All flesh is alike, Shah Jahan thought. It yields its pleasures sweetly, but it is only a vessel. What I held was no different from another woman's, yet vastly different from all others. Even in the dark, I could tell Arjumand from another. Now, though the memory fades, her shape, her scent, her softness burn into my senses. Yet, what I loved was not visible, it was contained within. The whispers that cannot be captured, the laughter that floats into eternity to be heard only by God, a glance with meaning only for me; these things filled me with such pleasure.

Oh God, to have had so short a time together; eternity would not have been enough.

the nine story 1020/AD 1610

Arjumand

'She is coming! She is coming!'

The women of the haram lined the balconies, clung to the latticed walls, pushed and jostled, squeezed into corners, peered over shoulders, climbed on stools and tables. Flapping greedily, like birds of prey, they peered down into the palace courtyard. I sat alone in the empty room staring out of the window at the Jumna. It moved placidly, the colour of burnt metal, touched by neither joy nor sorrow. Like the land and the sky, it had the resolute dignity of eternity. I sensed Isa's presence nearby. I felt his pity; it engulfed me. I couldn't turn, knowing that if I saw his face, I would weep.

'She comes . . .'

The excited cries from the other side of the palace filled me with dread and unbearable pain. Hope had been imprisoned these two years in the cruel silence of waiting. Now it knelt, bowing its head on the block, knowing the executioner's blade would not miss—*thuck!*—and it would roll helpless and lifeless, deaf to the tumult of the crowds. It was far better to experience this death, to open my fist and let my longing fall. But, through all this pain I still lived.

'Shall we see what Shah Jahan's bride looks like?'

Isa followed me to the balcony and the women noted my presence. There were many expressions of pity or compassion, some of triumph, some scarcely suppressing the glee that springs up when another is wounded. I pushed my way to the front.

The cavalcade halted below us and a girl was helped out of the palanquin by her slaves; she was embraced and welcomed by the older women waiting at the entrance. Stretching out behind her, winding out of the palace into the streets of the fort, was the caravan of gifts sent by her uncle, the Shahinshah of Persia, to the Great Mughal, Jahangir. Fifty arab stallions and mares, four hundred slaves, gold, silver, precious stones and, most important of all, the gift of the Shahinshah's friendship. It came in the form of a woman. She had been travelling for many months, escorted to the border at Kandahar by the Persian army and met there by the forces of the Mughal.

Kandahar was the pivot between the two empires, the heart of the arteries of trade, a rich and prosperous city. Possession of it fell to one or the other over the years, depending on the might of each army. At the moment it was held by Jahangir. Relations between the two empires were at best mercurial. Each viewed the other through the same prism of envy and wariness, each balanced the other's power on the fulcrum of Kandahar. Even in times of peace their friendship was uneasy. Many years ago, when Humayun lost Delhi to Shershah, he fled to the protection of the Shahinshah. The Persian emperor looked after him for several years, but only after Humayun had converted from the Sunni faith of the Mughals to the Shia faith. The emperor then provided him with an army and the aid of his youngest son, who died on the long march to retake Delhi.

The arrival of the Shah's niece in Agra was a sign that a new era of friendship was about to begin. Both emperors had elected for a gaudy display of peace, as this was in their best interests. Jahangir had commissioned his artists to paint a picture depicting the Mughal lion sprawling half into the Persian empire.

95

Princess Gulbadan was my age, slightly smaller in build, and moved with the awkward stiffness of acute shyness. It seemed to billow around her as she murmured and bowed to the many women who greeted her. Behind her stood a plump woman, her mother, and then came the many ladies-in-waiting.

Mehrunissa, though still lady-in-waiting to Salima, behaved as if she were the empress greeting her son's bride. No one could fathom Mehrunissa's motive for keeping Jahangir at bay. It was said that he was mad with love for her. I could not feel sorry for him as he had driven me into drowning despair. Only Mehrunissa herself now stood in the way of their marriage, for though the Empress Jodi Bai had recovered from her illness for a while, she had most mysteriously fallen ill once more, vomiting food and blood, and a week after the new sickness descended, she died. Jahangir, in his grief, had ordered a month's mourning in court, which everyone obeyed, but in the silence one heard the whispers: poison!

For love are such monstrosities undertaken. If one could die for wanting something, could one not also kill to attain it? Men have done this, women too. But I did not posses the power of the Great Mughal to achieve my end.

Mehrunissa smiled as she approached me with the princess. She knew how it would hurt me, but since I had of my own accord come to welcome the princess, she knew I was well prepared. I felt the eyes of the other women watching me, doubtless hoping that, distraught and raging, I would claw at the poor girl's face. Instead I smiled, and bowed when she stopped in front of me.

'My niece, the Begum Arjumand Banu.'

'I have heard of your beauty.'

'Your highness is kind. I cannot expect something of such little note to have travelled all the way to Ishfahan.'

For a moment our eyes met and I detected a faint, sad smile in hers, not for me, but for herself. Her eyes were brown, large, pretty

96

and wary; like those of the chital as it sniffs suspiciously at danger. Why she should have been afraid of me, I could not tell. She was to be married, not I. Could she have heard that Shah Jahan still loved me? The thought was poor comfort to me.

'It is not of such little note.' It seemed that she wished to say more, but Mehrunissa began to tug her away.

'I wish your highness happiness in your coming marriage.'

If she heard, she made no sign, and was soon lost in the crowd of women. She would have only a brief time to rest, for in three days she would marry Shah Jahan.

I wished that I could have escaped then, with duty over and bravery stretched, but I had to remain, smiling and nodding and talking. The Begum Arjumand Banu was another person, moving through the palace in an opium dream, walking in a nightmare, and I was hidden inside her, curled in a ball, eyes shut tight. All I wanted now was solitude, to sit in a corner of the garden across the Jumna in the lovely grove of lime trees where I wrote my poetry of words dipped in sadness.

'It will be cooler on the balcony, Agachi,' Isa whispered softly.

'I don't need fresh air. I need to be far away . . . to forget. I would like to go to the mountains. Would you come with me?'

'Of course, Agachi. I live to serve you. But will that be far enough?'

'No, it's just a wish. I will always think of him, long for him. There is no escape from that. Fetch me some wine, please.'

There was a brief respite from the celebrations when the princess was taken away to be bathed. When she reappeared the festivities would continue late into the night, distracting the ladies from the routine of haram life, allowing them to display their finest jewellery and wear new silks. Now they lay on the divans, whispering and giggling, and it seemed that every glance, every word, concerned me.

I took Isa's advice and moved towards the balcony overlooking the Jumna. As I passed down the hall, a furtive movement caught my eye.

In a cubicle, by no means screened from view by the curtain of fine muslin, three women lay together on a divan. Two were Kashmiri, with fair skins and long hair; they were gently stroking the Turki girl who lay between them. She had an oval face and a red pouting mouth, and her eyes were closed in ecstasy. Her hands returned each caress with the same soft stroking motions, moving up and down her lovers' bodies. Their languor suggested that endless time lay before them. They whispered, sighed, and kissed often, their tongues delicate and greedy as they probed each other's mouths.

My gaze was held by the pleasurable intimacy of these women. Other women passed by the cubicle, but paid no attention to the open lovemaking. For the first time I experienced an awareness of my own body, knew that there existed wonderful sensations yet to be explored and experienced.

The revealing clothing the women wore became an encumbrance, and they caressingly removed each other's garments. Their bodies shone with perspiration, partly from the heat without, but also from within. Each woman had dyed her nipples different colours and they had plucked the hair from between their legs so that all was revealed to their fingers, and to my eyes. The efforts of the Turki girl to return the caresses grew languid and feeble, while the stroking of the other two increased. They caressed each breast, kissed and bit at the nipples, while their fingers alternately entered her body and withdrew. The Turki girl shook and moaned in a pleasurable fever and the perspiration ran off her body as if she were emerging from the river. While one of the women continued kissing and thrusting, the other reached back to the pillow and removed from under it a long dark object, the thickness of a wrist. It was made of wood, and was as smooth as ivory.

The woman dipped her fingers in a bowl of oil and slowly, lovingly, spread it over the wood so it shone in the muted light. She was watching her companion kissing the girl's breasts, then her belly, and as if not wanting ever to reach the glistening tips between her legs, ran her tongue to the very spot and withdrew. Finally she knelt, and her long hair fell down over the open thighs of the Turki girl whose mouth was parted in a soundless scream that left her heaving and breathless.

The love they seemed to possess for each other transported them into a private world where nothing could disturb their concentration. One of the Kashmiri women used the wooden instrument to describe patterns around the girl's breasts and belly, the circling increasing around and around until she handed the instrument to her companion. She then shifted the Turki girl so that her head lay in her lap, and continued her caresses with her hands.

The other woman rose from her kneeling position, shook the hair from her face, and then gently inserted the instrument between the Turki girl's legs until it almost disappeared from sight. She withdrew it, and thrust it back, harder and harder each time, until the girl arched and the muscles in her belly rippled like a stream passing over rocks. Then all the frenzy subsided and she lay beached and lifeless.

I started, as if woken from a dream, and hurried to the privacy of the balcony. The cool breeze from the river chilled me, my clothes were soaked with sweat and my legs were shaking, my heart racing. I had discovered that in myself, in my own body, pleasure flowed from the same source as blood. This knowledge brought both delight and fear. The figures I had seen in Khajuraho, because of their remote beauty, held no excitement but the women, lusty, smelling of sweat and oil, and awakened the secrets of my body. I could not blame them; only a brave or foolish man would slip past the guards, so the women of the haram took their pleasure from each other.

How much greater than would be the ecstasy to be experienced with a man! And how sublime the pleasure I might have found with Shah Jahan.

Shah Jahan

I heard the tumult and knew that my bride had arrived. The Itiam-ud-

99

daulah had welcomed her on the outskirts of Agra and ridden with her procession. 'What is she like?' I asked Allami Sa'du-lla Khan.

He stood by the window, looking down. His posture was bored, restless; I knew he wished to escape this tomb.

'Who can tell, your highness? She looks small, delicate. She has pretty hands, I see. The rest is a mystery only you will discover.'

'It will be too late then.'

I fell silent. I was not a pleasant companion these days for I did not hunt or go out with my hawks. I refused to ride, would not fight, and I took no pleasure from my women any more. I drank, seeking oblivion in the wine.

'Go.'

Allami Sa'du-lla Khan looked at me doubtfully, unable to hide his eagerness to quit my company. I waved him away; he bowed and hurried from the room. I took his place by the window to stare intently across the haram. Arjumand could be there, within my gaze. I showed myself more openly, in the hope she too was looking across. But of what use was this? To look upon each other and not even have our fingers touch? I took out the poem I had composed for Arjumand. Unlike my father, I was no poet.

The lovely breezes of the dawn waft the fragrance of the rose.
Perfume rises from the earth where my loved one goes.
All worldly joy doth fade; all you who sleep, arise!
Her caravan departs; make haste, before the sweet scent dies.

Whom could I trust to deliver it safely? If only I could speak to her. The years of silence had left a swollen river of words in my gullet that choked me and prevented the passing of breath. I wished them to burst out in a great flood, but could only release this puny dribble of words.

'The Padishah will see you, your highness,' the wazir interrupted my thoughts. I hid the poem in the folds of my sash.

100

My father's appearance had changed. He had become quiet and brooding, his face was growing increasingly puffed and there was a sullen air about him. He could command all the world to do his bidding, but not his Mehrunissa. He plucked at his beard fretfully, it had lost its lustre. Even his sarapa and his jewels appeared to have dimmed. If I had not been in such a bleak mood myself, I would have smiled at such irony. We pined for love, and were both denied. Allah was indeed just, but there was cruelty in his justice.

'What do you want?' he said curtly, glancing up at me, perhaps wishing I had not come, resenting my reflection of his own condition. I reminded him of unfulfilled love, as my brother Khusrav reminded him of betrayal. He avoided us both as if he couldn't bear to face his own weaknesses.

But I was not as menacing as Khusrav. He had destroyed his chances with his mad greed. The madness had been planted in him by my grandfather Akbar who had unwisely chosen him as heir to the empire over my father. On his deathbed Akbar had changed his mind again, but he could not alter the destiny that Khusrav had chosen for himself.

I remembered how Khusrav, naturally, had not been pleased at my father's ascension to the throne. For a short time it had been placed within his grasp by Akbar, and once that obsession had taken hold it would not release him. Jahangir, aware of this temptation, kept Khusrav at court, until he escaped and led a rebellion. It was short-lived and two of the conspirators were executed by my father. Then the distrust between father and son was poisonous, and became worse when Khusrav planned to assassinate my father on a hunting trip.

The plot was to kill my father while he hunted in the qamargah. In the confusion of animals and men, the roar and thunder and screams of dying beasts, the deed could be performed invisibly. A dagger swiftly thrust, withdrawn and wiped; and then Khusrav's generous reward. But the *diwan-i-qasi-i-mamalik* heard the whisper even as Khusrav spoke to his conspirators. Even if the plan had not already reached

Jahangir's ears, I would have whispered to his agents because my own life would have been worthless should Khusrav succeed. Could the Great Mughal allow a brother such as I to live?

I cannot blame my father for what followed. I too would have acted swiftly and harshly, but because Khusrav was my brother, I was sad. He had been my closest childhood companion and, though we had not been born of the same mother, yet in the fawning world of princes we were friends. Together we learned the skills of warfare, riding and wrestling, and we read together; such a bond can become a burden. I also had one younger brother, Parwez, but we were not close. And there was an illegitimate boy, the Na-Shudari, Shahriya, whose mother was a Panjabi slave. He would be no rival for the throne. I was grateful for one thing: that Akbar had not poisoned my life. As with all emperors, his embrace corrupted.

My father did nothing until the morning of the hunt. Then he plucked Khusrav, like a ripened fruit, out of the grove of nobles. Many of them were silent supporters of Khusrav, and my father was aware of this, but wisely decided not to disaffect them with his accusations. Khusrav alone was to suffer for his treachery.

At an hour past dawn we were summoned to the diwan-i-am. It was a sombre gathering where no one so much as whispered. Khusrav and I stood directly below the throne within the gold railing. Behind us and within the silver railing stood the wazir and other high officials and with them stood the *gurz bardar* carrying the gold mace. One step lower, beyond the vermilion wood railing, stood the remaining nobles and the gurz bardar carrying the silver mace.

I stood as far away from Khusrav as possible. Of us all, he appeared to be the most carefree and at ease. He smiled and joked, but fell silent when the executioners, wearing their black caps, entered and lined up against the wall below the throne. Each carried his chosen instrument of execution. Above them we could hear the soft rustling of the women and catch glimpses of their shadowed faces peering at us through the openings.

My father entered, mounted the steps to the alcove and sat on the throne. Soldiers guarded the steps and none, even I, his Khurrum, could approach the emperor. Below him a clerk waited to record the proceedings.

At my father's signal the gurz bardar approached and touched Khusrav with the gold mace. Khusrav stepped forward with a show of courage, in his madness perhaps believing that Akbar's spirit protected him, and stared up at the emperor.

'Khusrav, Khusrav, what am I to do with you?' Jahangir spoke softly. 'It hurts me deeply to learn that you wished for my death. Did Akbar teach you to murder your own father? Surely not. It was not in his nature to commit such an evil deed. But what am I to do? Akbar crowned me Padishah. I sit on this throne by right. It is you who have no claim. Ask my nobles if this is not so.'

The nobles shifted uneasily. The emperor leant forward with a wounded, puzzled look. Khusrav made no reply.

'What do I carry in my hand?' the emperor continued in the same kind tone. 'Is this not the sword of Humayun? Akbar, with his own hand, presented it to me on his deathbed. He took his turban and placed it on my head. He decided then that I should be his heir. Why do you refuse to accept his decree?'

'Because . . .'

'Because!' Jahangir's roar unsettled the sparrows and they fluttered away. 'Because what? Is it some madness that drives you to kill your own father? What should I do to bring you to your senses?'

'Kill me!'

Khusrav's foolishness astounded us all. We could see the women's fingers, carmine and beringed, curling through the lattice as if trying to reach Khusrav and shut his mouth.

'*Taktya takhta*,' Jahangir mocked. 'Throne or coffin, we say, and now that you have lost the throne you wish for the coffin.' He shook his head in wonder. 'But how can I do this? You are my son. Humayun forgave his brothers because Babur ordered it. I cannot execute you. Your blood will not wash from my hands, it will only seep under the throne and weaken the ground on which it stands. Ah! You smile because you know I will not kill you. You read my mind wisely because I will not be the first to break the law of Timur—kill not your own kin. What then, Khusrav? Exile? Your face lights up at the thought. Can you believe that I will release you so that you can go and seek the protection of my wretched cousin, the Shahinshah, and return with the Persian army? No. I would be unable to sleep in peace. Yet, if you stay here, I will be uneasy of your jealous looks. Every day I would see your eyes gazing covetously at the Imperial sword and turban. Therefore, I have decided . . .' He gazed steadily at the clerk and spoke distinctly, so none should fail to understand. 'You will remain forever at court chained to a soldier. And to protect you from your own envy, you will be blinded.'

No one spoke. Khusrav's defiance crumbled and his legs gave way beneath him. The soldiers held him up and dragged him outside. Now the fingers of the women hung limply through the lattice, like damp leaves after a storm. They did not call, as was their right, to the emperor. Only their raised voices could now save Khusrav, but they too chose to remain silent. The clerk wrote down the sentence and it was passed to the emperor. He pressed the Muhr Uzak on it. Now no one in the land, not even the emperor himself, could save Khusrav.

Khusrav was thrown to the ground. The executioners fell on him, holding down his legs, his arms, and one straddled his chest while another held his head. The long thin spikes were heated in the brazier and when they were the colour of cherries, an executioner opened Khusrav's eyes. What did he see last? Not the trees, the birds, the blue sky, only the ugly faces of his tormentors. The hot spike was thrust first into one eye, then into the other. Each stab was accompanied by Khusrav's screams. He twisted and churned; his mouth was a gaping hole. Blood and tears ran down his face and into the dirt. The men rose and he lay weeping, covering the bleeding openings with his hands. The hakim knelt, cleaned the wounds and placed his herbs on the bloody slits before covering them with muslin.

I blame neither Khusrav nor my father for their actions. It was their kismet. Yet, I cannot forgive Jahangir's leniency. Khusrav lives, a ghost in chains, and so does his ambition. My father may believe that he has been exorcised of Khusrav's haunting, but I am not. His shadow will cross mine as I mount the steps to the throne.

When my father saw Khusrav wandering the palace at the end of the chain, feeling his way sightlessly through the splendid corridors, he would command the guard to take Khusrav away.

'Everybody wants something. What I want, none can give me.'

'That is not my fault, father.'

'What more does she want that I have not done?'

It seemed that the question ran continually through his mind. I could have answered aloud, but kept it to myself: the throne. He already lay in her palm and the longer she made him wait, the more secure was his love for her. She did not deny him hope, for she knew how he yearned to escape the loneliness of his power.

I cared nothing for his loneliness, only for my own. Could I trust Mehrunissa? Would she change his mind towards Arjumand, towards me? I was not unaware of the fragility of an emperor's affection for a son, but I could do little about that as yet.

'Doubtless her astrologer has advised her to wait for the right time.'

'Yes, yes,' he said eagerly. That's what I think too. Who is her astrologer?'

'I don't know. You have the power to discover any secret. Enquire, and pay him handsomely to change his prediction.'

'What if it's not his fault, but hers? See—I've written her a poem.'

He took a sheaf of papers from the table beside the divan. I saw that my effort for Arjumand was pitiful by comparison. For a moment, he considered reading it aloud to me, but changed his mind and instead stared at the words as if he were gazing on her face. The words had a soothing effect on his temper, for after he had replaced the poem on the table he smiled up at me.

'You must be eager to see your bride. Did you see the horses she brought? Beautiful. That scoundrel thinks he has got the better of us by just sending a niece instead of his daughter. Does he really believe that we are not good enough for his wretched empire?'

'That is the matter I wish to discuss with you.'

I spoke warily. There is nothing worse, not pestilence, nor famine, nor an enraged tiger, nor an elephant in musth, not even the natural elements in fury, than a wounded monarch. His snap, his snarl, could reach far beyond the walls of the palace and the fort, to devastate and destroy. His wound was not a fleshly one, inflicted by a *telwar* or a *jamdad*, but invisible, deep inside; he bled from the heart.

'What is there to discuss?' It was not his voice I heard, but the whisper behind it.

'Should we allow him to insult us like this? I am Shah Jahan, the crown prince of this empire, which is as large as the Persian's. He should have sent his daughter, not some insignificant niece. Of what importance is she to him? Akbar married the daughters of the Rajput Ranas, not nieces or cousins.'

'What you say is true, but it is too late. I have accepted her as your bride. To send her back would mean war.' He smiled kindly. 'I know your heart is with Arjumand. Make her your second wife. I give you permission.'

'I don't want her as a second wife. Why should I make her inferior to this other woman? Arjumand will bear my sons.'

'Are you stubborn as well as stupid? I command you to marry, and you argue with me! Madness has infected your brain. Love will pass. You are no ordinary man.'

'And are you?'

'What?'

'I said . . .'

'. . . and I heard. I have already fathered sons, for what they are worth—you are my favourite, and look at the trouble you are causing me—and what I do now does not affect the fate of the empire. I will take Mehrunissa as my wife, my companion in my old age. She will not interfere in my choice of an heir—I have chosen you.' His tone became querulous: 'Why won't you allow me this love? You are fortunate that you love and are loved. That is not the usual luck of princes. I gave love to my father, but I had none returned. I obeyed him in the matter of marriage too, unlike you. I love you, my son. There, I have said it. Akbar never let those words pass his lips. He spoke instead to that scoundrel, Khusrav, and look what it did to him—inflamed his brain. Now, late in my life, I love.' He sighed dramatically.

It was his kismet, his destiny, his luck, and it delighted him. He had found the garden of pleasure. He saw my discontent. 'I am told Princess Gulbadan is beautiful. One woman's body is like another's. Enjoy her.'

'How can you say that when you yearn for Mehrunissa?'

'Badmash, stop seeing your reflection in me. I am the emperor. What you do is for our whole good, not merely your own. Go.'

He turned away and removed the Imperial turban. A slave took it and reverently placed it on the silver table. My father's hair was flecked with grey; though he claimed great age, he was only forty. He had been worn down by alcohol and impatience after waiting for so long to mount the throne.

Through the jali the twilight, broken into intricate patterns, barely lit the diwan-i-khas. The red stone absorbed it, devoured it, leaving the room sombre, like the dungeons beneath the walls of the fort. I did not like this feeling of weight; it must surely affect the temperament of an emperor to be incarcerated in this bleak place. Though the candles and lamps were being lit, they threw black, flickering shadows across the walls. I would have changed this refuge for a lighter room, awash with the luminous pinks of dawn and twilight.

My father ignored my presence; he had returned to his poem and the wazir waited to lead me out. I bowed; it went unacknowledged.

Isa

Am I worthy of trust? It is a heavy burden to place upon the shoulders of a servant. By the nature of our position we are easily manipulated and intimidated by our masters. I turned this thought over in my mind as I trudged in the pitch darkness to Shah Jahan's palace. There was no moonlight and thin clouds obscured the stars, so that I could not see my own hand, let alone the path.

I had been woken by a cloaked figure. I smelled perfume—a woman—but her face was hidden.

'You are Isa?'

'Yes!'

'His Highness, Shah Jahan, has sent for you. Go.' And she was gone.

A thin mist rose like steam from the Jumna. I pulled my blanket close, covering even my face. The turban warmed my head, but my legs were cold. The palace was in darkness. I was thinking this summons had been a trick when suddenly the door opened, and another woman pulled me in. She was sure of her way; I was not. I followed her shadowy figure as well as I could, tripping over divans and cushions and carpets and tables. Impatient, she grasped my hand. We passed through a garden and went down some stairs near the rose bushes into another garden, then further on to a lower level still.

Shah Jahan waited there, wrapped in a blanket and sitting on a divan, staring out at the river. A golden ewer of wine stood on the grass by his side, he clutched the golden cup, drained it, and refilled it unsteadily. He swayed, peered, and waved me forward. The woman

108

faded away like the mist.

'You are Isa, her slave?'

'Yes, your Highness. Servant, not slave.' Would a prince understand the difference? Perhaps he had not heard; princes can have selective hearing.

'I am to be married tomorrow.'

'I know.'

'Quiet! I do not wish it. I do not want this . . . Persian! I am unhappy. That is a puzzle. A prince should not be unhappy. I have everything in life, except Arjumand. Do you hear me?' He leaned forward and the wine spilled. I made no reply, and he turned swiftly, the way a hawk does. I caught the glitter of his eyes.

'Fool. I said, do you hear me?'

'Yes, your Highness.'

'Listen. No other woman has ever had such an effect upon me. Arjumand! Have you felt like this, Isa?'

I could not reply truthfully.

'I said, have you ever felt like this?'

'No, your Highness.'

'You wonder why I speak to you of such things? Who else is there who can tell her how I feel without using my words to further their own ends? At court no one understands love, they know only convenience, policy. How is she?'

'Sad.'

'Ah, that word is enough. Sad, like me. Sadness that dims the sun and the moon. Sad. She weeps?'

'Yes, your Highness.'

'So do I. So do I.' He groped for the ewer again, but nothing flowed out.

'Wine, wine, bring me more wine.'

A slave came forward and replaced the ewer; the dew had gathered on its glistening flanks. I poured, because now he was incapable of doing it himself.

'You are so fortunate, Isa. A thousand times luckier than I am. Do you know why? You see her every day. You see her eyes come alight, the way she brushes her hair from her face; you see the movement of her fingers, the way she walks; you see her smile . . . that smile, slowly falling on her face, like moonlight on water.'

'Very seldom, your Highness.'

'Tell me how she passes the time?' He peered at me intently.

'Your Highness, she stares at nothing. She wakes, bathes, dresses, eats a little then sits all day with a book of poems in her lap which she rarely reads. Sometimes she rides far out of the city; sometimes we spend the afternoon caring for the poor. It takes her mind off . . .'

'No, no, Isa. Nothing must distract her from me. Tell her, please. I beg you. I will reward you greatly.'

'I don't need reward. But of what good is that to her?' I said bitterly.

He muttered to himself. 'Who will I ever find who can stop my breath as she does? This earth, even for a prince, is not filled with people. It is filled with only one. Arjumand.' He grabbed my sleeve and pulled me roughly towards him. 'If she marries another, I am lost. I can escape. I *will* escape. I cannot be abandoned by her.'

'It is you who have abandoned her.' I paused. 'Your Highness.'

'You are angry with me. Is she?'

'No.'

'She understands better. I have tried, but I could not persuade my father. He commanded and I obeyed. Was that weakness? I expect her to show strength by being patient. What right do I have to ask this of her, other than my love? You will tell her this in the same words I have told you.'

'And how long must she expect to wait, your highness?'

He made no reply.

'Forever?'

'No, not forever,' he whispered. 'That would break my heart too.

110

Not long.' He shook his head, trying to clear it of wine. 'Not long.' He fumbled with his sash and took out a crumpled packet, wrapped in silk. 'Here, give this to her; a poem, not much, for I am no poet. There is a letter here for her as well. Will she attend the wedding?'

'No, your Highness. That is too much to expect.'

He fell silent, now lost in reverie, pursuing elusive thoughts and feelings. The mist from the river had begun to creep over him, falling on his shoulders and gradually enshrouding him within its clammy coils. He was not aware of my departure.

The streets were still dark and deserted, and I moved quickly, not wanting to attract attention. As I walked I recited the prince's exact words over and over so that every one of them should reach Arjumand. Suddenly three shadows surrounded me. There came too swiftly. I was held, and struck from behind.

Shah Jahan

My marriage was not worthy of the name. I was woken from a drunken stupor by the dundhubi beating my father's appearance at the jharoka-i-darshan. Dawn, the light I loved for its sweet caress of the sky, came too soon. I was fetched by Allami Sa'du-lla Khan, servants, nobles and countless others to be bathed and dressed in the sarapa, ornamented with gold and diamonds. The vast ruby in my turban glittered like a third eye and the ceremonial jamdad, encrusted with diamonds and emeralds, was thrust into the gold belt encircling my waist. I felt bowed down by the weight.

A white stallion waited, glittering with gold saddle, bit, bridle, stirrups, and beside it stood a slave bearing a golden umbrella. The procession began, the tablas, the flutes, the *sankha* echoed in my aching head. Crowds of people lined the road: 'Zindabad Shah Jahan. Zindabad.' What need did I have of long life?

Horsemen pranced to the right and left, before and behind; there was no escape. We wound our way into the fort; my father waited at the palace. The osprey feather in his turban bowed and nodded in the breeze. He mounted and stood beside me, saw the exhaustion of wine and a sleepless night. 'It will not be painful,' he commented, much experienced in these matters, though newly-born to love.

We rode together. Ahead of us, slaves scattered rose petals in abundance, nautch girls danced and the drums grew louder and louder as we approached the palace haram. I glimpsed the women peering down; others waited to receive us. The mullahs too, the emblems of sanctity, of the formality of the ceremony, awaited. A gold pandal had been built within the palace. I was led to it and seated, and then the bride came to take her place before me. I had yet to see her face which was still covered by the beatilha. I could not pretend curiosity and I sensed that, in spite of the tamasha around us, she could feel my distance. She seemed to sigh as she settled down. Unlike that of the Hindus, our Muslim wedding ceremony is brief. A mullah read from the Quran, we murmured our promises to one another, then rose and accepted the blessings of my father, the emperor.

It was a day of music, of dancing, of joyous celebrations. Thousands of people were given a great feast, gold and silver coins were distributed to the poor. Nobles approached in a continuous stream bearing every imaginable gift: gold jamdads, boxes of diamonds, pearls, emeralds, slaves, horses, elephants and tigers were endlessly paraded in front of me.

My bride remained silent, her head bowed as if she mourned. I said nothing to her. Already a coldness had settled between man and wife, and I could not remove it. At twilight she was taken from my side by the laughing and blushing women to prepare her for the nuptial bed.

When she had been bathed and scented and instructed, and lay in the gauze of shadows, the women came to fetch me. I was led into the chamber, undressed and helped to lie beside her. Her body was young

112

and firm, her breasts high, rounded, with dark nipples. I felt her warmth, the perfume of her skin and hair.

I knew at daybreak the women would hurry in to examine the bedding.

the ten mahal 1045/AD 1635

Tap, tap, tap, tap, tap. It was a dry sound, musical with a thousand echoes. Under the shade of the trees and tattered makeshift awnings, protected from the terrible sun, the stonemasons cut and carved. The earth was grey with strewn chippings, the air white with a thin dust that settled on the hunched shoulders and gaunt faces of the men and boys. The hot coals of countless fires made the air hotter still, so that the dust writhed and twisted over the pits.

Murthi squatted by a slab of marble. He knew it had come a great distance from the quarries in Rajputana. Every day teams of bullocks and buffaloes dragged the vast blocks of stone. His was a coarse slab, measuring twice a man's height and the thickness of two hand-spans. His tools lay at his feet, as they had done for days now. Gopi tended the fire, keeping the coals hot in case of need. Murthi caressed the stone, tapped it with a finger—a daily custom—communicating with the heart of it. For hour upon hour he would watch it, squinting at the lines of the cut and the delicate patterns that were ingrained in the stone. Often he would burrow in his small gunny sack and take out the drawing he had been given. The measurements of the jali he was to carve were precise so that was not what worried him. He was unhappy with the design itself. It was geometric, unimaginative, made of refined vertical and horizontal lines. It displeased him; there was no beauty in

114

it. How could he carve straight lines? His hands obeyed more intricate laws of shape: curves, whorls, intertwinings, like the figures of gods in dance.

He thought back to the day when he had been summoned. Quaking, he had trudged to the clerk, expecting disaster now that the officials had discovered he did no work. They would demand that the money be returned; two rupees a day was not a lot, but too much for him to repay. Instead he was directed to a shamiyana, crowded with officials bent over drawings. He had remained standing, submissive, until one noticed him.

'I am Murthi, the Acharya.'

'Come, come.'

They were pleased to see him, and the man who had spoken made room for him at his side. The man was tall, quite thin, with a cast in one eye and hands like Murthi's: strong, knobbed. He was Baldeodas; he had come from Multan.

'We are alike,' Baldeodas said. 'Carvers. I am told that you carve gods.'

'Yes,' Murthi replied eagerly. 'But there are none here.'

'There is something else just as precious to be made. Do you understand drawings?'

'Of course,' Murthi said proudly. 'And I can read measurements.'

'All the better. Look. This is the jali that will be placed around the empress's tomb.'

Murthi studied the paper for a long time, absorbing the details. His strong, stubby fingers traced the lines, while his mind pictured the measurements.

'It will take time,' he finally said. 'A lot of time.'

'Of course. And the pattern?'

'It is very simple.'

115

'The Muslims,' Baldeodas whispered, 'like these things to be simple. Can you design a better one?'

'Yes,' Murthi said. 'Who should I show it to?'

'To me. But remember, no human figures. Their religion forbids such things. Flowers and leaves, that's what they like on their monuments.'

Murthi felt sad that they should be limited to such simplicity. What meaning did flowers have beyond pretty decoration? They could not echo the complex rhythm of the cosmic world. He remained still, no longer studying the drawing. Baldeodas sensed that Murthi was gathering his courage to make a request. The man had a stubborn patience in him; it was rock-like, drawn from the stone he shaped. 'What is it?'

Murthi looked down at his bare, dusty feet, the soles cracked and hard. They reminded him of his lowly station. Then, as he thought of what he was to create, he felt more courageous.

'If I am to do this immense work, is it not important enough for me to be paid better?'

'How much do you get?'

'Two rupees a day. It isn't enough for my family. My wife has to work too, so my children suffer.'

'I will discuss it with the *bakshi*. Only he can make decisions about money. What have you been doing until now?'

Murthi had been afraid it would come: 'This and that,' he said. Then he rose quickly, namasted and withdrew before Baldeodas asked another awkward question.

As if in a dream Murthi continued to contemplate the slab at his feet. Beside him Gopi squatted with equal patience. He would have preferred to play with his companions, but it was his duty to help his father and learn the skills that had been handed down through generations. He

116

understood that visions only came through prayer and meditation, and that it took time. Life was not meant to be easy. His father suddenly stood up and ordered him to sweep the earth clean around them. He obeyed. When a space the size of the marble slab had been cleared, Murthi drew a frame, and then, apparently at random, placed dots within the border. He used powdered chalk, as Sita did when she drew the decorations outside their hut each day after she had swept and washed. As another man might use a brush, Murthi swiftly drew his pattern with the chalk dust, squeezing out thin lines between thumb and forefinger. He worked for an hour, and after joining up the random dots he drew branches, flowers and leaves, like a creeper twisting and curling upwards. There was a central slim stem from which the plant twirled and whirled out to the frame. All the lines led back to the stem, but seemed quite separate. When the pattern was completed he stood back, deeply satisfied.

'I will fetch Baldeodas. Guard this.'

When Baldeodas saw what Murthi had drawn he was delighted. He walked round it, studying it from every angle, and then summoned the others to obtain their opinions. They were all pleased with the pattern for the jali, but before Murthi could start on the massive task the design would have to be submitted to the emperor. They could not bring the Great Mughal to this dusty site so an artist was fetched to draw the pattern on fine parchment.

When the commotion subsided, Baldeodas drew Murthi aside.

'The bakshi will pay you four rupees a day, when you start the work.'

That made Murthi happy. He would have liked more, but thought it best to be patient. He knew that Baldeodas drew twenty-two rupees a day, but then he was an important official.

'Saheb,' said Murthi. 'You know many things here. Did you ever see the Empress Mumtaz-i-Mahal?'

'No,' Baldeodas answered. 'None of us ever saw her.'

117

His answer disturbed Murthi. He had heard that she had been beautiful, but beyond that, had she 'ever really existed?

Isa and Mir Abdul Karim placed the design in front of Shah Jahan. He sat in the *ghusl-khana*, a cool, exquisitely designed room adjoining the haram, built from white marble and decorated with flowers inlaid with jewels. After bathing, the emperor would summon his advisers to this room while the slaves dried and oiled his hair. More slaves stood by ready to dress him and place the Imperial turban on his head. For a long time he studied the drawing of the jali that would be placed around the sarcophagus of his beloved Arjumand. Finally, he nodded his approval and returned the drawing to Abdul Karim.

'Who designed this?' he asked.

'Baldeodas, your majesty.'

'Good, very good.'

Karim did not withdraw immediately. The ministers waited, burdened with their papers, but Karim knew he had precedence.

'What is it now?'

'Padishah, the work is progressing well. The foundations are nearly completed. However, there is a problem that must be resolved. The contractor informs us that there is no wood for the scaffolding.'

'Nowhere?'

'None for such a high building. The monsoon has affected the forests. Cashew trees are scarce and the people are cutting them for firewood. The contractor has tried everywhere.'

They waited while Shah Jahan was dressed. The Mir Bakshi softly flicked at his papers in irritation. The matter of the Deccan was pressing on him. The *akhbar* he had received from his intelligence agents had reported that the little princes, aware of Shah Jahan's new obsession, were plotting rebellion. Worse, they were nibbling like mice at the southern edges of the empire. The Mughal army would have to deal with them, but he did not have the power to despatch such might. Then the Mir Saman had his continuing problems with the bad

118

monsoon. The crops were poor, trade was affected, income was down.

'Bricks,' Shah Jahan announced as the Imperial turban was placed on his head, and his ministers performed kornish to the symbol of power. 'Build the scaffolding from bricks. It is possible, is it not?'

'Yes, Padishah, but the cost?' The expenses left them breathless.

'Spend, spend. The treasury is full. I ordered that no expense was to be spared, and now you come to me with such a petty problem.'

Abdul Karim withdrew hastily. Bricks! The cost made him wince. It would be as expensive as using marble itself for the scaffold.

Isa would have left as well, but Shah Jahan gestured for him to remain, before addressing the Mir Bakshi. He turned his thoughts to the problem, wishing that Arjumand were by his side. How often she had advised him well on matters of state. Had he not given her the supreme symbol of power, the Muhr Uzak?

'I have thought deeply on the matter in the Deccan. We must subdue those wretched princes. I will appoint Aurangzeb to command the army. It will be good training for him. See to the details, and consult him. Now, what can I do about the monsoon? I am not God.'

'The granaries are full, Padishah.'

'Then it is not a serious problem yet. The next monsoon will be good. I know that.'

One by one he dealt with his ministers. When they had left, he went with Isa to stand on the terrace and survey the activity up the river. There a whole army was manoeuvering: men, women, elephants, bullocks and carts created a constant fluid movement through the dust and heat.

the love story 1021/AD 1611

Arjumand

My mother was compassionate at first. She comforted and cradled me, crooning sympathy, but she did not really understand my affliction. Love came softly, slowly, it did not strike like a thunderbolt. Love was kismet; if it came into one's life, one was fortunate. If not, a loveless life seeped away into the grave. Who complained? None. We were *saman*, to be bartered for wealth, position, political alliance. Love was not expected to be part of the bargain. It was only a fairy story, sung by poets. I was expected, like my mother, my mother's mother—and as I looked back further and further, I saw us pinioned by tradition— to marry the man chosen for me. Love, affection, companionship, these would creep in slowly. Years would pass and then, with some surprise, I would realize: I love this man. But who else was there for me to love? No one, of course.

Then my mother's concern soured to impatience, as I knew it would. I could not blame her. Years had passed and now I was old, in my sixteenth year, waning like the moon, my life long past its zenith.

'Who will marry you now?' was her constant refrain. 'You're too old. I'd already given birth to you by the time I was your age. I was a woman well settled, in a good position. I had . . .'

'Did you love my father?'

'What has that to do with it?' She spoke querulously, as if I had spoken of something unmentionable. 'You read too much poetry and fill your head with rubbish.' Then, in a softer tone, to placate me: 'You saw him once. Just once. How can you believe that you love him after only seeing him once?' The word sounded like the dundhubi beating the approach of doubt itself. I did not mention the second, fleeting encounter.

'Ten or a dozen times, believe me Arjumand, I would understand. Love grows slowly. It does not come by just looking upon a man once.'

'I cannot help that.' How could I explain to her, when even to myself the whisper was filled with disbelief?

'We've had enough of all this nonsense from you,' she scolded. 'Your grandfather has found a very eligible young man. I have seen him, so have your aunt and your grandmother. We all approve. You will marry him. He is a Persian, Jamal Beg. Your grandmother knew his father in Ishfahan. They are a good family and Jamal will rise high in the service of the Padishah.'

'I will not marry him.'

'Just like that! Oh God, what did I do to deserve such a daughter? Who put these stupid ideas into your head? Did I? I brought you up as carefully as I could. If I had spoken these same words to my mother, I would have been soundly thrashed. You will see him.'

'I will not.'

'Are you a fool?' she shouted. Her face turned pale, distorted by anger and anxiety. 'You are already three years beyond marriageable age. You are old, old! As a favour to your grandfather, Jamal has consented to marry you. Save yourself.'

'You mean I'm to save you. I am an embarrassment.'

'Yes, you are. All the women laugh at you. Don't you hear their whispers? They giggle when you enter the haram. "She waits for Shah Jahan and that badmash has married another and gone far away."' She sighed. It was a ritual. Her lovely grey eyes grew moist, like morning dew a tear dropped and slid down her face. Always, it touched my heart, almost made me waver. Yet I remained unmoved, stubbornly clinging to a memory.

'He has never lain with her.'

'Who told you such lies? They *are* lies, told just to make a fool of you. They give you this childish hope.'

'Everyone knows.'

'Not I.'

'Everyone, including you. The morning after they lay together, when the women inspected the bedding, there were no bloodstains.'

'It doesn't always happen. The long journey . . .'

'In which case, she was not what she was supposed to be.' I added cruelly. 'There was no blood. She told her ladies-in-waiting that Shah Jahan only spoke to her once on their marriage night. He looked on her body, then turned his back to her and said, "I cannot."'

'You were there, I suppose, listening and watching.'

'Others were. It is two years since that wedding night. Where are the children?'

'That takes time, for princes as for other men. Even Akbar, in spite of all his women, did not sire an heir until he went to that pir, Shaikh Salim Chisti. And even then the Empress had to live in an ashram before she could bear a child. It is the same with Shah Jahan. Anyway, what has all that got to do with you? He is married and you are not. What happens in his bed is no concern of yours.'

'It is his promise to *me*. He said he would come to me. I will wait.'

'Where is your proof that he asked you to wait?' She was triumphant now, crowing in victory. 'Come. Show it to me. When I can see that he was begged you to wait for him, then I will never—Allah be my witness—mention the subject of marriage to you again. I will be happy knowing that one day you will marry the crown prince.'

'I have none. You know that. Only his word.'

122

'His word! Isa's word. You believe the word of that chokra . . . that peasant saved from his just reward by your grandfather.'

'I believe Isa.'

'What,' she asked with cunning, 'if I were to prove he lied to you?'

'I wouldn't believe you.'

'You would believe that chokra and not your mother.' She shut her eyes, and the tears came as though my boldness had wounded her. I comforted her, but could not take back my words.

I believed Isa. They had found him at dawn, lying in a gully and left for dead. He had been tossed there like a pariah, curled in the rubbish. His face was drained of blood, the back of his head encrusted with it. I had no idea where he had gone. He was carried into the house, and I nursed him. When he was able to speak he told me of his meeting with Shah Jahan. He reached for the packet, but it was gone. Yet the ring, his precious gift from Jahangir, remained on his finger. How could I disbelieve him? I wanted to believe him. It was no different from our faith in God, even though no real proof exists. Belief sustains us. Isa had told me the truth; irrefutable, unshakeable. He wept because he had lost the letter. I did too. It would have comforted me during the long, heavy days that dragged by pulling me into old age. Who had committed the theft? Who knew? Surely not Jahangir? I suspected my own family who, out of concern for me, hoped to save me from the torment of waiting.

'You will see Jamal Beg this evening, and then we will decide what is to be done with you.' She left, grumbling to herself, bewildered by my obstinacy.

Shah Jahan

'Agra *dhur hasta*.' It lay a thousand kos south of where I ruled, in the name of my father, the vast jagir of Hissan-Firoz, which began forty kos north of Delhi, and ended here, in Lahore. Ranas, nawabs, amirs, farmers, peasants and traders, all paid me their tithe. My income was eight lakhs a year; I commanded ten thousand *zat*. I learned the craft of kingship. Yet, I felt empty, alone. If I had been struck I would have echoed like a dundhubi. The great distance between here and Agra lay heavily on my heart, a great plain separated me from Arjumand.

My princess grew sour, suspicious, evil. With the passage of each season, her temper grew dark, as dark as the monsoon sky which turns day to night. The beauty of Lahore, its wide tree-lined avenues, the cool pleasant climate, the spacious gardens, gracious buildings and palaces, the acting and dancing, the singers and musicians I gathered at my court, the charm of the inhabitants, the distant mountains and the valleys beyond the city, the privilege of her station; all these failed to please her. I could not blame her because in truth she had come such a vast distance only to lie unused in her bed. On our wedding night I had spoken those two words to her, and none since. She knew I was not incapable; other women drained the swollen lust of my body—I could not escape my needs. She also knew what came between us: Arjumand.

I had heard that she still waited. How could I not respect such courage? She humbled me with her loyalty, making my worth less than that of the poorest man in my jagir. Her life hung on the word of her slave: he had told her I loved her, and it was enough. Who watched us? My father, perhaps? If that were true, then what did his akhbar say about me, languishing here in Lahore? That I did not sleep with my wife, and pined instead for Arjumand? My sighs, echoing through the palace like the breeze whispering through eucalyptus trees, could be heard by my princess and she cursed Arjumand. Her life lay as ruined and desolate as Chitor after Akbar's conquest.

Marriage? I had given my word to Arjumand, yet here I was, trapped in the coils of state. Divorce? How swiftly I would run through that door, if it were open to me. A common man could repeat the words thrice and then walk free from a troublesome woman. But the prince had to remain silent, his tongue cleaved to the roof of his mouth by the

Padishah. Those words, 'I divorce thee', would echo across this empire and into the next; it would be the command for vast armies to march. I could set the Persian princess aside, banish her to a distant mountain palace, consign her to the oblivion of retired souls. The thought delighted me; it failed to delight her. Bitterness had taken root, and she would not be moved. She would play the role of the senior wife, barren and unloved, for what else could she do? The princess knew my thoughts. She understood; her food was tested—once, twice, thrice. Her eunuchs permitted no one to enter her quarters and, when she travelled about the city, her Persian soldiers marched with her, swords drawn. She walked in the shadow of two men: the King of Kings and the Seizer of the World. They were mountains and beside them, I was a speck of sand.

So I waited.

And Arjumand waited.

Arjumand

I heard that he sent me poems and letters wrapped in silk, but like the stolen packet they never reached me. Neither did they lie tattered, trampled and dusty on the Panjab plain, but found their way into the cool perfumed hands of Mehrunissa, as did mine to him. They travelled no further than the boundary of the city before their swift return. By chance Isa discovered them. He had not pried in her boxes; he had seen her eunuch, Muneer, take my packet from the hands of one of the diwan-i-qasi-i-mamalik.

Only recently my aunt had finally succumbed to the overtures of Jahangir. He had already become her puppet. She chose the time well for her capitulation. I had asked her over a year ago, why did she wait if she loved him? I could not understand; if I had been her I would have moved swiftly. We have so little time on this earth. She replied: 'Jahangir is Emperor. He can have all his desires, whenever he so wishes. If he points his arm to the east or west or north or south, the whole Mughal power will march until he commands it to halt. There must be a few things in life even an emperor cannot acquire easily. I will be one of those things. In his eyes it will give me greater worth than the throne itself. If I had swooned immediately at his interest—and how many of his discarded women did so?—he would have lost all desire. Already he calls me in his poems, Nur Mahal. I am the light of his palace, the candle in his heart.'

Our household was bustling with the preparations for the marriage. Dressmakers, jewellers, cooks, mullahs, singers and dancers, garland-weavers and decorators streamed in and out. The emperor was delirious; poems now flooded from his pen. Messengers galloped the short distance to place them reverently in her hands. The verses amused her. I suspected she did truly love, though it was not the emperor she loved, but the golden throne.

Mehnurissa had become completely absorbed in the design of her costume. Her churidar was made of the finest red Varanasi silk and woven with her own design of gold-threaded whorls; her *gharara* was also of silk, so transparent as to be almost invisible, with delicate threads of gold running down its length; her blouse, boldly designed to reveal most of her bosom, was patterned with delicate squares of gold thread. She would wear an elaborate red *touca* richly beaded with diamonds and pearls, and her beatilha was so fine that it would not shadow one facet of her beauty. Jahangir had sent her many gifts: a necklace of pearls, each the size of a grape; another that fell to her waist, heavy and intricately made of gold and set with emeralds. She would wear earrings too, and each emerald was the size of a pebble. Her bracelets were clamps of gold and more emeralds, and her gold anklets tinkled as she walked. There were rings for all her fingers and a stud for her nose. They all delighted her and she would caress the stones, constantly admiring herself in the mirror.

In a rare quiet moment I asked her: 'Why did you intercept our letters?'

'The Emperor commanded it.'

'I don't believe you.'

'Arjumand, you are of my family, my own beloved niece. Why should I want to step between you and Shah Jahan? A union between you and the crown prince would be to our advantage. Soon, I will be Empress of Hindustan, and I don't want a stranger to be married to Shah Jahan, better my niece.'

She sounded sincere, and her smile was sweet, but her assurance left me full of doubt.

'Why would Jahangir want to prevent us writing to each other?'

'Matters of state.' She spread her hands in a gesture of helplessness, but she was too intelligent to be unaware of what she meant. Mehrunissa did not merely parrot the statements of others. 'The princess is already very unhappy. She told her uncle, the Shahinshah, about it in a letter . . .'

'How do you know that?'

'The Emperor told me. Of course he had them intercepted. He has no wish to displease the Shahinshah . . . yet. He is very sympathetic to you and Shah Jahan. He understands the nature of love, but at the moment he does not wish to encourage your relationship too openly.'

'But Muneer gets the letters for you.'

'I am to hold them in safe-keeping. I promise you that I have not read them, nor will I ever read them.'

'Give his letters to me, then.'

'No. If the Emperor commands me to, I will. He has not done so.'

In such pale sympathy lay the serpent of deceit. She could hide behind the throne. Surely it was to her advantage to have me rather than the Persian princess close to her? If so, she should encourage us; yet she held our letters. Her behaviour confused me, frightened me a little. Mehrunissa stretched up and gently smoothed the furrows on my brow. I saw a spark of amusement on her face, as if she were toying with me.

'You will get lines on your face, Arjumand. We cannot have that.' Then she enquired in her softest voice, 'What did you think of Jamal?'

I shrugged. I could not condemn a man just because he was not the one I love. Jamal had been presentable, stocky, neatly dressed, given to ornate gestures. He laughed too often as if he wished to please the Itiam-ud-daulah, which I knew he did. It would be to his advantage to take me off my family's hands. Who else would do such a favour and marry a sixteen-year-old woman? If he had been suspicious or reluctant about the proposed match, he did not reveal it. Surely a man would want to know why his future bride was still unmarried. Possibly, he knew. The ghost of Shah Jahan would haunt the marriage, but such was his ambition that he was prepared to tolerate it. He played to my invisible presence, drinking only lightly, always attentive to my grandfather and father, aware that I was watching from behind the walls of chastity. I did it to placate my mother, who sat beside me pointing out his handsome face and polite behaviour, as if he were a trinket to be acquired in the bazaar. Gradually she fell silent as she sensed my stubborn disinterest. She wept for her own heartbreak and I tried to comfort her.

'Will the Emperor ever give his permission for us to marry?' I asked my aunt.

'I promise I will speak to him,' Mehrunissa said solemnly. 'I promise I will try to persuade him, but it will take time.'

'How much time? Four years I have waited, he has waited. How much longer? I cannot bear it. At times I feel as if I am dying.'

'Be patient.'

'For how long? I am not like you, Aunt. I cannot understand your love. How could it bear the waste of these years?'

'I have explained all that to you already. Here.' She gave me her handkerchief and I wiped away my tears. The kajal turned it dark and streaky. I crumpled it. 'Does he still wait?'

'Yes.'

'How do you know?'

'I know. You would too, if you had read his letters and poems.'

I could not believe she hadn't; her curiosity was too powerful.

'He will not have changed. Please speak to the Padishah.' All could do was beg. The pain of it humbled me. Even a street beggar could not know such desperation as I. If I had to approach the emperor, I would do so. I would rise before dawn and be the first to stand outside the walls of the fort below the jharoka-i-darshan, and when the wazir lowered the chain of justice, I would ring the bell, attach my petition and watch it rise into the sky. Justice, justice—the chorus of the poor.

'Haven't I already promised you that I will speak to Jahangir?' She wiped the smears from my cheek. 'He will be persuaded. Now go. I am busy.'

At last he came.

He rode at his father's side into our garden, his brothers behind him. And after them came great flanks of nobles, glittering and shimmering in the bright sunshine like rare and gorgeous birds. Velvet and rose petals protected the hooves of their prancing horses, women whirled and danced in front of them, the musicians reached an ecstasy of noise. The *punkahs* of peacock feathers cooled his brow in the heat.

Jahangir wished to display humility towards the Light of the Palace, to observe tradition. The groom would ride to the bride's home for the marriage. This was a replica, I was told, of Shah Jahan's wedding. The steamy air reeked of perfume, of gold, of gifts. A thousand nobles attended the ceremony, each bearing gifts which were paraded and recorded, then carried off to the treasury, the stables, the haram, the zoos.

I did not notice very much. I only watched Shah Jahan. His eyes constantly swept the enclosure, knowing that I was waiting behind the lattice, and then I knew that he had not changed. He stared intently, unblinkingly, towards me, the handsome face barely suppressing its longing. He wanted me to go to him, but of course I could not leave the ceremony. There was to be a great feast in the palace garden that evening. It would be our chance; a brief and only one.

Shah Jahan

'Bring her to me, Isa. Quickly. There, to the darkest corner, where we cannot be seen.'

In darkness! Should love use such stealth? But where else could we meet? The garden was ablaze; candles and lanterns lined the walls, flanked the pathways, hung from the trees. The lights shimmered in the fountains. A few nobles and ladies were strolling in the garden, watching me, bowing as they passed. I wished they would ignore me, forget I was Shah Jahan. The air was filled with music and the melodious voice of Hussein, the court singer, who sang of love and conquest. If only I could make this crowd vanish; then we could be alone in this enchanted place. We could listen to the lovely songs together, but now I only heard their heedless cruelty and felt defeated by the melancholy of our frustrated love.

I withdrew into the shadows. She walked slowly behind Isa, dawdling as if she were taking an evening stroll. But I noticed the coiled impatience in her walk, her eyes searching the shadows, her face poised on that precipice of fear that perhaps I would not be here. She had changed. Memory, you cheated me. You kept her a girl of thirteen years old. How cruel. Why had you not made her taller—transformed the young girl's body into that of a woman. You did not narrow her waist, curve her hips and swell her breasts. You made no effort to tell me how she walked—with a graceful sway, her back and shoulders held straight. How differently she moved from the others—she seemed to float above the earth. But essentially she remained unchanged. Her churidar, gharara, touca and blouse were of the same pale yellow and silver colours that I remember from that first night.

But why curse you, memory? If you had shown me her new beauty, how much more fiercely would I have raged at our separation, how much more bitterly sadness would have cankered my brain?

Arjumand

'Where is he?'

'Just there.'

I saw nothing, only the darkness beyond the light to the edges of the earth. If I stepped over now, where would I fall? I felt chilled, the soft hairs on my arm alert. I had, until this moment, been cosseted in hope, afloat on dreams which had been my sustenance; all my life could have been spent in their company. I was frightened. Like water on sand, they might evaporate once I stepped into the shadows, leaving my heart dry and dusty. Possibly when he saw me he would no longer love me. He would be bemused, would wonder why had be loved this woman for so long? What did she have that had first attracted and held him? He would search my face, my eyes, and see in me another person, not his lover, not Arjumand, but an old woman, haggard, strained, desperate. He would bow politely and then be gone. And for me there would only be an eternity of darkness. I stopped. I wanted to turn, wanted to run. Fear engulfed me.

'Come, Agachi.'

'I . . . I . . . need air.'

'He is waiting.' Isa came near. His face turned from the light, and for a moment I saw sadness in his eyes. 'Eagerly.'

I stepped from the light into the darkness, but really I went from darkness to light. I glimpsed the dull gleam of his gold belt, and, like a third eye, a star, the glitter of the diamond in his turban. 'Arjumand.' His whisper and his outstretched hand, strong and steady, guided me to him. I cursed the darkness because I could not see his face. Before I could speak, he kissed my hand, then inside my palm, my fingers. His

131

beard was soft and silky. Then I took his hand to my lips and held the palm against my cheek. Comfort flooded over me, such peace. His touch healed me.

'I was afraid . . .'

'Of what?'

'That you would look at me, and your love would wither away.'

He chuckled in delight. 'And I have been standing here being poked and prodded by these branches, shivering with fear that you would not come, that you would send a message through Isa sending me away.'

'And would you have gone?'

'No. I would have remained here forever, frozen in pain, welcoming death. These wretched shadows—I cannot see you. Come over here. There is a beam from that lantern.'

I obeyed. He looked at me in silence and with tender greed, as if he feared he might never see my face again.

'You have only grown more beautiful, but there is sadness in your eyes.' He leaned across and kissed them. 'Why? I am here now.'

'For how long, my love? You look at me as if you will never see me again.'

'No. I only look on you so intently because my eyes are not large enough to see all your loveliness. I want to look and look. There will never be an end to the looking, even when we are together in the sunlight. There, the sadness has gone. You are happy. How your eyes change! They make me weak when I look into them.'

'Now it is my turn. You are even more handsome than I remembered. Your face has changed. It has grown stronger, and I had not noticed these marks.' I caressed the small, barely visible pits in his skin. They gave him vulnerability.

'I was a child when I fell ill with the sickness.'

'A child?' I could not help but laugh. 'It's hard to imagine. I wish I had been there to see you. I can't see your eyes, they are in the shadows.

132

What do you feel?'

'Happiness.'

'I can see that now. I love you.'

'I have waited so long to hear you say those words. Say them again.'

'I love you.'

'And I love you.'

His lips were dry and sweet, soft as a petal, his skin cool and scented. His body was young and muscled. How could just his gentle touch free such furies inside me? It was the same frenzy I had felt in my blood when I watched the three women in the haram.

'How long must we wait?'

'Not long, my love, not long. Soon my father will give his permission. He will have to.'

'I have spoken to Mehrunissa. She promised me that she would try and persuade him to change his mind. Perhaps he will listen to her.'

Though he did not move, I sensed him withdraw, as if he'd slipped away.

'What is it? You frighten me. Why does one always tremble with fear when one loves so much?'

'In case it escapes; in case it is an illusion. Don't ever fear. I will love you always.'

'Then what is the matter?'

'If she can move him in this matter of ours, in what else might she be able to bend my father's will?'

How swiftly ecstasy dies! We still remained in our secret light, but we were imprisoned by it. He was no common man, unfettered like a farmer or a hunter. He was the crown prince Shah Jahan.

'She will not be able to change his mind about you,' I said fiercely. 'He loves you too much. Look how he writes constantly of his beloved son in the *Jahangir-nama*. Your are his heir. He has written it. Even Mehrunissa cannot change that.'

'Who knows? And if I have you, what do I care?' He spoke lightly,

133

but could not disguise the concern. The throne was a thundercloud and we stood in its shadow.

'She told me it would be to her advantage for us to marry because I am her niece.'

'Yes, yes.' He sounded relieved. 'She would never harm you. How lucky I am to have found you, my love. Without love the world is a lonely place. It is like wandering endlessly in the desert. I know, because I can see my own dusty footprints.'

'How will you escape, my dearest? You said . . .'

'Yes. I have planned it. Be patient. Soon, you will hear that Shah Jahan has been given permission by the Emperor to divorce the Persian princess.'

'I will wait, as I have waited, and I will willingly grow old in the waiting. I could not love anyone else. I would prefer to die than live without you.'

Isa's sharp whisper startled us. 'The Emperor's wazir comes, Agachi.'

We peered into the lighted garden. There was no hesitation in the wazir's approach. We had long been noticed, and had been given an allotted amount of time; now it was ended. Shah Jahan kissed me swiftly, fiercely. From the deep pocket of his sarapa he pulled out a packet, thrust it into my hand and whispered: 'Let this be always with you— to remind you of my love.' He stepped back into the garden, and walked across to meet the wazir.

My breath had gone; it had slipped away with him. Even my heart could not beat, for he held it, carrying it with him as he faded into the crowd. In the light I looked at what he had given me: it was a rose. The petals were made of rubies, the leaves and stem emeralds; here and there, artfully placed, a diamond shone like a tear of dew. I kissed it.

Isa told me that one hundred different dishes were served at the wedding feast. The food was served on gold platters borne by slave girls. The plates we ate from were also of gold, and each guest was presented with a gold goblet for the chilled nimbu pani. The dishes placed in front of Jahangir were all sealed, and the seals were broken in front of him. Then slave girls sampled each dish before serving him. There were fifty roast lambs which had been steeped in spiced yoghurt, hundreds of tanduri chickens, bowls of murgh masala, mutton saag, chicken chaat, seekh kebabs, shammi kebabs, pasinda, doh peesah, roghan josh, shahi korma, naan, chapati, paratas, burfi, badam pistas, gulab jamuns, and every imaginable fruit that Hindustan could produce: mangoes, grapes, papayas, wood apples, pomegranates, watermelons, oranges, plantains, guavas, pears, lychees, custard apples and nungus.

I ate nothing. I did not even smell the food. I could not help staring at my beloved as he sat beside his father. My eyes did not leave his face.

The emperor, drunk with love for Mehrunissa, his heart sodden with obsession as if she were the most priceless object ever to be lodged in his vast treasury, had spent weeks composing a long and eloquent poem to her. He read it out to all of us at the feast. It lasted an hour, and Mehrunissa was compared to the most splendid things in the universe—the sun, moon, stars, diamonds, rubies, pomegranates, pearls, ivory. How bitterly envious I felt that he could declare his love openly.

'She is my Nur Jehan,' he intoned solemnly when he came to the end of his epic, and drank deeply from the golden cup to the Light of the World who, having shed her coyness, now watched his performance with a critical eye. She leaned towards him and whispered; he set down the cup and clasped her, kissing every part of her face. Whatever she said made Jahangir smile and then arise, helped by the slave girls. Then, with Mehrunissa, he retired to the bedchamber already prepared by the women.

After my beloved left, I returned to the garden. It was deserted now, except for two solitary figures. One was seated while the other stood nearby.

135

One was Prince Khusrav. Unable to move freely, he sat where he had been placed by his guard, staring sightlessly into his own bleakness. I sat down beside him.

'Who is that?' He turned, squinting as if I were sitting a great distance away. For a moment I thought he knew me, but then his face went blank.

'Begum Arjumand, your highness.'

'Ah! The love of my favoured brother.' He reached out and touched my breasts boldly, taking delight in my start. 'I am allowed some liberties. You are a woman of beauty, I am told. That is what I miss most, looking on beauty: girls and women, flowers and trees, the moon changing from a cut in the sky to a great silver ball, the light at dawn before the sun has risen above the horizon.' He dabbed at the involuntary tears that streamed continually from his damaged eyes.

'Why have you joined me?'

'I was alone.'

'You are a clever woman too, not merely beautiful. If you had said "because you were alone", I would have driven you away. Look around. Is anyone watching us?'

'Some of the women.'

'I will tell you what they are saying to each other. "Why is that Arjumand wasting her time sitting with Khusrav; what can he do for her? She is being foolish, because the Padishah will not be pleased." Has my father satisfied his lust for that Persian whore?'

'That is a cruel word. She is my aunt.'

'Look into my eyes, if you wish to see cruelty.' He turned away swiftly. 'Yet, I am often told he was generous. He could have taken my life.'

'Would you have spared him, had you taken the throne?'

He smiled wolfishly. 'Possibly.' His denial sounded hollow. 'I was a happy boy, until one day my grandfather Akbar placed the dream in my head. He condemned me with that dream. Now I hate him more than

136

my own father. Allahu Akbar,' he whispered mockingly. 'God is dead and his disciple suffers. His loving embrace was my downfall. It would have been better if he had spurned me. I would now be the governor of some province, content to accept the generosity of the Padishah. But,' he smiled coldly, 'like a stallion eager to lead the race, I ran too swiftly and stumbled.' He brooded in silence for a while and, feeling he wished to be alone, I rose. 'Where are you going?'

'Home. It is late.'

'Come. I will show you what Akbar once showed me when I was just a young boy. It was his curse, and it changed my life.' He rose, and tugged at his golden chain which was looped around his waist and held by the soldier. 'I am not sure which of us is the dog. He is only a guard, and must respond to my princely tugs. But I cannot slip the chain, and in that, he is my master.'

They walked into the palace, and I followed them through many brightly-lit corridors until we were deep inside the building. Here, the corridors were heavily guarded. Khusrav whispered to the commander who looked at me closely, and then permitted us to pass. We descended the stairs and the air grew cold. We passed more soldiers, and finally reached the last door. At each post, we had written down our names in the records which were kept by the guards. We had to remove all our jewellery and weapons; Khusrav, his dagger and belt, his gold armlets and his rings; I, my necklaces, ear-rings, and even my anklets, though only the gold rose was of value.

'What you are going to see,' Khusrav said, as the heavy door swung slowly open, 'is the heart of the empire. Whoever holds this room, owns Hindustan.' He turned to his soldier. 'Unleash me. I cannot escape from this place.' The soldier unlocked the gold chain and remained outside while we entered. The soldier gave me an oil lamp and closed the door behind us. It was cool, silent, still, as if nothing had ever lived within these walls.

I lifted the lamp high, and could not control my trembling. A million fires leapt in response to the yellow flame, as if they had waited through eternity for its light. The whole room blazed, and beyond I saw many other rooms from which winked smaller fires.

'What do you feel?' Khusrav whispered.

'Fear.'

'Yes. It is fear one feels first, for here are countless reasons for fear. An emperor's soul could be purchased with this, so what chance do we have? This sight strips us of all our senses and our minds become bloated with greed. There is a ledger somewhere. Hand it to me.' I picked up the great file. It was bound with leather and very heavy. 'Let the blind man choose.' He opened it at random. 'Read. Fill my ears while you feast your eyes.'

I read from his pointing finger. 'Seven hundred and fifty pounds of pearls, two hundred and seventy-five pounds of emeralds, three hundred pounds of diamonds . . .' I looked up. They lay in tubs, row upon row, like grapes in a common bazaar stall. Semi-precious stones too: agates, opals and beryls, moonstones and chrysoprase. He turned the pages again and jabbed his finger down. I continued. 'Two hundred gold daggers encrusted with diamonds, one thousand decorated gold saddles, two golden thrones studded with jewels, three inlaid silver thrones . . .' Once again he flicked through the pages. 'Fifty thousand pounds of gold plate, eight gold chairs, one hundred silver chairs, one hundred and fifty gold images of elephants studded with jewels . . .' I faltered.

'I know. It is difficult to read such words and breathe. We are suffocated by our longing.' He took a cautious step forward, stopped at a tub of rubies, sullen as blood, and plunged his hand deep into the stones. 'That is what I did when I was ten years old and Akbar brought me here. I remember the corruption that stole into my heart then, for he showed me everything, and promised that it would all be mine one day. Such heartless cruelty.'

Taking my arm, he led me into the other rooms. The sight of such riches, though it did not fill me with greed, made me dizzy. There was too much to behold, and my eyes widened at the sight of such immense wealth. There were silver candlesticks, gold cups, silver plates and mirrors, tubs of topaz, coral, amethysts, boxes of necklaces and rings. Chinese porcelain, hundreds and thousands of silver plates and cups, tubs of uncut diamonds. They were all dusty, lifeless. If this was indeed the heart of the empire, then it was a cold one. It did not beat, pulsing its blood throughout the land to its people, but lay still and useless.

'I would like to go now.'

He turned his sightless eyes on me. 'This is what purchased that Persian whore.'

'And did not Akbar likewise purchase you?'

'Yes,' he admitted softly. 'Seeing this cannot but change our hearts.' We reached the door and he turned around as if to take a final look. Possibly, he was remembering the young boy doing the same thing. 'You have not touched or taken anything?'

'Of course not,' I said shortly.

'Don't be angry. This place brings out every one of our weaknesses, and it is easy to believe that one tiny stone will not be missed. But it is counted daily, tallied and re-tallied. If anything is missing we would all lose our lives. The soldiers will have to search you. And me.'

I submitted to the guard's lecherous hands, knowing it would not be possible to leave otherwise. The soldier attached the chain to Khusrav again.

'Once more I am brought to heel,' he mocked. 'My little army.'

That staggering amount of riches, the glimpse into the golden heart of the Great Mughal, left me uneasy. It did not induce sweet dreams, but nightmares. It forced one to assess one's own worth, which was as nothing in comparison. I had no envy for such wealth; it could only be a golden prison from which one could never escape, a stifling encrustation around the heart. How could love and loyalty and trust survive in that cold room? They would drown in the bottomless well or riches.

We returned to the garden. In spite of the warmth and stillness, the air tasted fresh. It was good to see trees, flowers and people again.

'Well, do you love Shah Jahan more because of what I have shown you?'

Khusrav peered at me in a deliberate and twisted way that he had adopted, as if the light were not clear and he could see only at an angle.

'No. Even if he were not a prince, I would love him.'

He fell into thoughtful silence, sifting my words. 'Blindness has some advantages,' he said at last. 'Faces lie; voices do not. I believe you. Who stands by us?'

'No one.'

'Because I cannot see, I listen carefully. Listen to me, Arjumand,' he groped for my wrist and caught it tightly, squeezing the flesh. 'You believe that your aunt whispers your name: "Arjumand, Arjumand," into the ear of my beloved father as they lie together. No. I will tell you the name she whispers for Shah Jahan: "Ladilli, Ladilli, Ladilli".'

the taj mahal 1047/AD 1637

Murthi sat, his eyes closed, his breath shallow. He prayed, as he always did. The clatter of the day faded, serenity descended, smoothing the harsh lines on his stubbled face. He knew the vision would come: it never failed. True, it had taken longer than usual, but the distractions were many. He was no longer in his village, living in his own home, happily engaged in the sculpture of deities. Four years had passed since Chiranji Lal and the others had approached him to carve a Durga for their temple. Deferentially, once or twice, they reminded him about it, but they were patient. The temple was being built, brick by brick, slowly, furtively. In a deep and dark grove beyond the limits of the city, it rose up. The ground had been consecrated, pujas performed by a priest, blessing sought of the gods and doubtless received. The emperor Shah Jahan had unwittingly provided the bricks and marble. They were purchased for, and then diverted from, the great tomb that rose on the banks of the Jumna. The contractor, a Hindu from Delhi, perspired profusely as he secretly put through each temple transaction. It was not criminal, just dangerous. The great Muslim emperors had practised tolerance, and Shah Jahan did likewise. But twice, goaded by the mullahs, he had destroyed Hindu temples at Varanasi and Orcha. The fury had died down, but for how long, the gods only knew. A temple built right under his nose would again inflame his anger. Rambuj, however, was not worried that he daily courted death. He skimped on materials for the great tomb. Instead of an exorbitantly expensive marble block, he would provide a panel, and pay *dastur* to the masons. Here and there they would build with brick and face with marble, garnering a rupee here, another there. If discovered, the corrupt would of course be executed.

The vision came: Durga rose, seated on a maned lion, smiling. She was the malignant form of Devi, wife of Siva, and her eight arms held the thunderbolts of destruction. He had carved her before, once. He could not copy for he was an Acharya, and though the form of the god did not change, each stone had to show some subtle difference of pose or expression.

In a corner of the hut, wrapped in gunny, lay a block of marble. Murthi unwrapped it reverently. It was square and rough; each side measuring from Murthi's knuckle to elbow. After great deliberation he chose the smoothest side and brushed off the loose grit.

'Water.'

Sita passed him a brass lota. Murthi poured, and scrubbed the surface clean with coconut husk and sand. It was a perfect piece, chosen with care. It had come from Makrana in Rajputana, where men quarried night and day, cutting deep holes and stuffing them with gunpowder, exploding entire hillsides. From there it was hauled by elephants and bullock carts to Agra. The relay never ceased.

When the face of the marble had dried, Murthi chose a fine brush, a small pot of black dye, and after long hesitation—where should he start?—and another prayer for guidance, began the meticulous drawing of Durga. It would take many days to complete it to his satisfaction; weeks would pass before he would choose a chisel and cut the first chip.

He remembered how it had taken him months to transfer the drawing of the jali to the uneven surface of the slab. One mistake, one irregular line or curve, would distort the stone and mislead his skilled hands. His original design had been elaborated: the creeper stood in a frame, and within the frame he had cut delicate flowers and leaves a fraction below the surface of the stone. These would be filled with coloured pastes that would eventually become as hard as the marble. His one small section of the jali alone—more men worked on the other panels—would take him his lifetime to carve. One day the whole structure would be placed around the empress's tomb. He knew he might not live to complete the work, but Gopi would, and every day he learned a little more of his father's skill. Murthi sought perfection, prayed for it. It was his dharma to travel such a vast distance to carve this jali. If the gods had not intended it, he would have remained in his village.

Baldeodas watched his craftsmen at work. He did not deny himself the credit for designing the jali. That was expected; he was the chief sculptor. The design had to be executed in exact detail on each panel of the jali: not a single leaf, or twig, or flower could be different. His men knew that. He moved from one slab to another, intense and critical. He had permitted Murthi to draw the pattern first. His was the model and the others reproduced it in the age-old tradition of skilled artisans. They did not deviate, but controlled their hands, controlled their passion, so that no one would ever be able to say which man carved each panel of the jali. It took time. Baldeodas knew the Quranic saying: 'Slow is of God; hurry is of the devil'. He prayed to his gods. If there were any imperfection, any flaw, he would kneel to Shah Jahan's executioner. He sweated in the presence of death. The ghats smoked on the Jumna, the ashes of the dead turning the air grey and malodorous.

Baldeodas liked Murthi best; the little man was quiet, stubborn, proud. His work would be perfect, if only because he could not tolerate imperfection. He was less sure of the others. They were imitators and might lose interest, lose concentration and allow the chisel to slip, destroying the symmetry.

'You must begin,' Baldeodas told Murthi.

Murthi squatted on top of the marble slab. His tools lay in order on the earth, *kum-kum* marks on the chisel heads. They were blessed. Murthi chose his first chisel, tested the point, clasped it between his palms and bowed his head in prayer. It was brief: 'Maha Vishnu, guide my hands on such a long journey'. Gopi handed him the mallet and Murthi delicately placed the chisel on the stone at the top left hand corner within the border, and tapped out the first chip of marble.

Shah Jahan laughed. The sound was humourless, reflecting only dry satisfaction. He was told that the foundations had been completed and now work could begin on the tomb itself. It would rise to a height of two hundred and forty-three feet from floor to finial, and the height would exceed its breadth by fifty-six feet. The building was designed as a square, each side measuring one hundred and eighty-seven feet, but the thirty-six foot wide chamfers at each corner, would give it the appearance of being octagonal. It had taken five years to rise to the earth's surface from the great depth they had plumbed. There was still the high plinth to complete after they had finished the tomb. Again, it would create an illusion—that the tomb floated. Everything was, after all, an illusion. He wished he could know that it would be completed in his lifetime. It must be; he could not die while it stood unfinished. No one else loved her as much as he had. No one.

'Ismail Afandi waits, Padishah,' Isa announced.

The emperor beckoned; the Designer of Domes performed kornish. Behind him a model was carried in by an apprentice and set carefully in front of the emperor. It was of the dome, standing two feet high.

'Shabash,' Shah Jahan said. 'It is perfect, Afandi. You understood my instructions.'

'Yes, Padishah.'

Shah Jahan rose from the divan and circled the dome. He seemed

144

pleased but then his face darkened. 'It is beautiful, but how will it hold its own weight? In wood it looks easy, but in marble? Surely it will collapse and fall?'

'Padishah,' Afandi was delighted to display his cleverness. 'See.' He lifted the dome to reveal another beneath. 'To achieve the height you wish, we must build two domes. The inner will support the outer, taking the weight. From base to finial this will measure one hundred and forty-five feet. Never before has anything been built so high.'

The emperor clapped Afandi on the back and Afandi simpered with pleasure. He had not been completely truthful about the design, but that did not matter. He would have continued his boasting, but the emperor smiled thinly and it chilled him. Shah Jahan scrutinized him deliberately, his eyes reduced to slits.

'You have been clever, Afandi. It is true; nothing so high has been built. But I have examined the tomb of Sikander Lodi in Delhi and the domed temple in Purjarpali. The double dome on Lodi's tomb was inspired by the temple dome. It was the Hindus who first devised the double dome. My great grandfather's tomb is of the same construction, I believe.'

'That is true, Padishah,' Afandi whispered. 'I have examined those buildings. It was the only possible way to achieve the height.'

'Good. We learn from others.'

1048/AD 1638

'Hurry,' he whispered.

He was sitting in the diwan-i-khas, watching his workers toiling. He felt restless, impatient. His gaze drifted over to the small, ordinary brick tomb that held Arjumand. The plain little dome was squat and ugly. He was stabbed by pain when he thought of her there, within reach but so far away now, just as she had been in the beginning. Fate continued to play its cruel tricks.

For a fleeting moment he wished that she could see the Taj Mahal rising up. By day it was going to be more beautiful than the sun; by night its loveliness would distract men from looking at the moon. He felt his bleak solitude once more. Thinking back, he could not recall the exact words he had spoken to her in the palace garden on the night of his father's wedding. He remembered telling her that the world was like a desert without her, his life made of dusty footprints. Now she was dead, and he would never escape that desert. He had not bothered to search for a new companion, of course; no one could replace her. Shah Jahan smiled grimly at the irony of it: he was the ruler of an empire and he was unhappy, alone.

He shifted on the divan to watch the late afternoon sun turn the latticed walls to gold before sliding off into dark patterns on the floor. At twilight the light changed in this room. It became red, strangely magical. Long ago, he had argued terribly with his father in here. Jahangir had been drunk and distracted with love for Mehrunissa, and Shah Jahan's pleas had gone unheard. In his rage he had vowed to transform the dull red walls of this room. Well, he had done so, but it was a petty victory. What was being constructed by the river would be his real achievement. His name would reverberate for century upon century. They would say: Shah Jahan, Sovereign of the World, the Great Mughal, built this. Or would they say: here lies his Empress, Arjumand.

Arjumand! He wept, surprised to find that tears still flowed so easily.

'I destroyed her, I destroyed her.'

The words were wrenched from him, against his will, as if he wished not to know what had hurt him for so long. But tears could not ease his pain.

He had spoken out loud, and Isa heard him, but gave no sign of it.

'Padishah, the Mir Bakshi craves an audience.'

The financial adviser entered, bowed, saw the stain of tears and looked away, with disguised impatience. The emperor's mind remained distracted, the time was not propitious, but the Mir Bakshi could not wait. From dawn to dusk, doubtless even in sleep, the emperor was obsessed with that tomb. What time had he for the affairs of his empire? It lay neglected while the clouds of ruin gathered. His ministers struggled on without his guidance.

'Padishah,' the Mir Bakshi spoke forcefully, without preamble. 'The Deccan. The rats are nibbling. We must act swiftly. Akbar said a monarch should be ever intent on conquest. We have done nothing, and now they rise against us.'

'You always speak of Akbar, Jahangir, Babur,' Shah Jahan grumbled. 'Is the matter so urgent?'

'Yes. We must march south soon.'

'I cannot leave Agra,' the emperor snapped. His tone silenced protest.

'Who will command his army, then, if not the Emperor?' the Mir Bakshi enquired softly. 'The presence of the Emperor will subdue those rats. They will lose courage when they see him at the head of his might.'

'I cannot leave,' Shah Jahan replied. 'Aurangzeb will go.'

'It should be your eldest son who leads the army, Padishah. Dara. The Deccan rabble will think Aurangzeb too young, too inexperienced. They will not respect him, nor the Great Mughal.'

'I have told you that I cannot leave,' Shah Jahan said petulantly, losing patience. 'Aurangzeb will go and Dara will remain here. He is my beloved son. I cannot let him go to war. Arjumand loved him dearly, too. She would not forgive me if he should come to harm. He will be Emperor after me.' He paused for a moment. 'Prepare the army to march within the month. Aurangzeb will command.'

The Mir Bakshi withdrew, unhappy, but relieved that a decision had finally been reached. Aurangzeb, that strange silent boy, revealed nothing of his thoughts and appeared to be only a shadow skulking about the palace. Dara was loved by all; he would make the better commander. But the emperor had decreed that Aurangzeb should lead the Mughal army. The Mir Bakshi shrugged: it would give the boy some experience.

Sita stood in line in the crowd, waiting for her day's pay. She was listless, weary, her mind drifted and she shivered. Winter was long past but still she felt chilled. The evening was hazy with dust, turning the orange glow of the sun to a brown glare. Her sweat cooled, her clothes stuck to her body; she would bathe before she prepared the evening meal. She stood patiently, too listless to push and shove for her money. It would come.

At times Sita felt she had never left her little village, that she still lived there, if only in her thoughts. Nothing had changed; the huts, the tank, the distant temple. Her mother and her father were the same. At twilight, when the coconut palms threw long, thin shadows and the bony cattle slowly returned from pasture, she would help her mother prepare the evening meal in the kitchen. They would talk softly of the day, of marriages, deaths, births, flirtations, crops, age-old feuds and Sita's own future. There were years still to wait, but a tentative choice had been made secretly by Sita and her mother. From her birth, her mother had watched the young men of the village until at last a choice was made. The boy was of their own caste, handsome, playful, aware of Sita. They shyly observed each other in passing, never speaking, content to be guided by destiny. Both families were pleased. Then, suddenly, he was gone, nobody knew where. One day he had taken the cattle out to graze, and they returned alone, without him. The whole village turned out to search for him, but no trace was ever found. A wild animal took him, they said. Sita felt as though she had been hurled from a cliff. She mourned deeply and humbly accepted the second choice: his younger brother, Murthi.

The crowd had dispersed, the clerk looked up at her. His pile of coins had dwindled and his book was smudged with entries.

'You are . . .?' he asked brusquely.

'Sita, wife of Murthi.'

He looked down his ledger, found her name, stopped, and peered up. She was pretty enough, but she had a glazed distant look. Her skin was muddy, the washed brown of the Jumna as it trickled through Agra. The river was weak and sluggish like the pulse of a dying man. The woman standing before him reminded him of that.

'You have not worked for some time.'

'I wasn't well,' Sita said softly. 'I had a baby. A boy. It died. I was sick for many days.'

'Ah,' the clerk was sympathetic.

He looked down at his ledger and tapped his betel-stained teeth. There was an entry against her name which puzzled him. Who would take such an interest in this one soul? She was just another villager. They swarmed over the earth and left it unrecorded, like this woman's dead baby consumed by the fires. But he could not disobey the directive on the ledger. He counted, twice, a pile of coins and delicately moved them towards her. She looked at them with bewilderment, almost with fright.

'I have only worked one day, Saheb. This is my first.'

'They are yours,' he began, then thought again and placed his hand over the pile. 'You are the wife of Murthi, the Acharya?'

'Yes.'

'Take them, then. They're for the days you never worked. Don't tell anyone at all about this.'

'You are very generous, Saheb. But I am afraid you will get into trouble.'

'I can take care of myself,' he said blandly, quite boastful, although a moment earlier he had briefly entertained the thought of withholding the money. She would never know who had ordered him to pay, but the thought of discovery frightened him. Let her believe, then, that the generosity was his.

Feverishly, she tied the coins into the knot of her saree and tucked it back into her waistband. She tried to rise, but the excitement had made her dizzy and she toppled over.

the love story 1022/AD 1612

Isa

Like the earth, our faces reflect the furies or kindnesses of nature, but our souls are hidden. In repose, Arjumand's face reflected enduring solitude, a wistful sadness that rose like morning mist from her soul. Her misery gave her a luminous beauty, a heartbreaking resonance. But on occasion I also saw a sudden spark, like a jezail at night, flash in her eyes: the flicker of hope. She had resigned herself to loss, though since their meeting in the palace garden, hope rose strong once more. Fate twisted and tossed her.

Then, like a dreamer waking, she would brighten, revived by the comfort of that brief memory of Shah Jahan, and continue with her life. She moved from hour to hour, from day to day, plunging herself into every activity: riding, painting, composing poetry, visiting the hospital she had built for the poor with the money Shah Jahan had paid for her jewellery—as if by pretending not to care she could trick fate into relenting, and win for herself the destiny she pined for.

Once a week the beggars lined the street, squatting on the bund between the drain and the wall of the house. They were leprous, maimed, deformed, contorted, whining, each holding out a bowl. Through chance, I had narrowly escaped a similar fate many years

151

before, and now I had no wish to have anything to do with them. Yet I walked slowly behind Arjumand, and each time she leaned over, I pulled her gharara away from them with my staff, not wishing, even accidentally, to touch them.

'Stop doing that, Isa.'

'Agachi, they are unclean. You will catch their diseases.'

'It is only my clothes.' Crossly she pulled her hem out of my reach and went on as before. Carrying food in heavy clay pots, other servants staggered beside us. Arjumand dipped the ladle in each of the pots and poured the contents into the bowls, at the same time placing a chapati in the beggar's hand. 'You blame them for their own misfortunes, don't you, Isa?'

'Yes, Agachi. Most are badmashes. They make a better living than even the spice merchants.'

'If you were one of them, wouldn't you want to be fed?'

'Yes, Agachi, but . . .'

She ignored my protests, as she usually did. When Arjumand settled her mind on a matter, no one, not even her mother or grandfather, could dissuade her. She could have despatched me alone, or even Muneer, to this work of charity, but insisted on doing it herself. In the stale, still heat the beggars stank, and I held my breath, not wishing to inhale their affliction. It corrupted the air. Arjumand seemed not to mind, but busily ladled food, and moved steadily down the endless line. Flies buzzed, settled, buzzed. The beatilha protected Arjumand's face from their irritation.

'Where do you sleep?' Arjumand asked a young woman. She was a fine looking girl, but she had lost an arm and her frayed garments barely covered her nakedness.

'Anywhere.'

'It is warm, Agachi,' I spoke coldly. 'The stars are shelter enough. Countless times, I too have slept . . .'

'But you no longer do,' she turned and raised the ladle. 'I am asking

152

them, not you, Isa. And please don't sulk. Only I have that privilege.'

'But you seldom use it, Agachi.'

She laughed. It made the beggars smile coarsely, as if she had told the fools a joke. If I were not there to protect her, who knows what might have happened. I could not truly comprehend her concern for these wretches, though she did once explain it to me.

'My grandfather was poor, too.' She was sitting on a stone bench under a peepul tree and drew patterns with her slippered foot in the dust. 'I've known no other life but comfort. I feel sad when I see people living in the streets, hungry and poor. Something should be done to help them.'

'That is in the power of the Padishah.'

'Kings and nobles do not see such things,' she said drily.

'Then why should you. Agachi? They will not enter this beautiful garden.'

'I think of the stories my grandfather told me. After he was waylaid and robbed on his journey here, he did not eat for days. It was a frightening story, but without suffering, a story has little meaning. Is the pain of love so different from the pain of hunger? They both set a craving in the body that must be satisfied. Like these people I have been humbled. Their bellies cry for food, my heart for love. Have you ever been hungry for either, Isa?'

She tilted her head, squinting against the beams of sunlight piercing the leaves, and studied me carefully. Like her aunt, she had the disturbing ability to give the impression of being able to read one's thoughts.

'I have hungered often. The body refuses to die. Besides, I stole when I could no longer bear my hunger.'

'The first Emperor, Babur, did the same thing as you. And for love?'

'Twice, Agachi.'

'And you gave up. Shame on you, Isa. You should fight.'

'My fate decreed defeat. The first I lost, the second is unattainable.

153

With time love can fade, but it never dies. It has remained with me, like the hunger of the poor people. Agachi, I could have done this work for you, if you had commanded me. Your family, quite rightly, stays at home.'

'I wanted to do it myself, not command you to do it. The Quran says we should give alms and do good for the poor.'

'But these are not all Muslims.'

'Very few are,' she said sharply. 'We look after our own people. The Quran does not say we should only feed the believer.' She turned to look at me and I saw the shine of humour in her eyes. 'Is that not right, Isa?'

'It is, Agachi.'

'Are you truly a Muslim?'

'Oh yes, Agachi.'

That made her laugh, as if she knew a secret which would never be revealed. I was grateful for her loyalty to me. She was the only one who would ask such a question, for she was as bold as her aunt at times. But I couldn't imagine her aunt, now the empress Nur Jehan, labouring among the stinking poor under a beating sun.

It was midday and, apart from our small company and the beggars, little stirred. A few pi-dogs, etched in skin and fur, sat patiently to scavenge morsels. Two horsemen rode towards us through the haze. The horses' hooves, muffled by the dirt, kicked up pools of dust that gently fell back on the road. The riders wore clothes unfamiliar to me: tight pyjamas, jibas tucked in, and their legs encased in leather from toe to knee. They had faces as dark as mine, but I knew it was not their natural colour. Their skin was probably much lighter, for there was a red tinge of burning to their darkness. Their manner was haughty, as if they rode not on horses but in the clouds, and as they approached they stared down at us with bold eyes. Arjumand, sensing my distraction, looked up from her task.

'What are they?'

154

'Feringhi.' They slowed to a trot and I noted the heavy swords they wore.

'I have heard of them,' Arjumand said. 'They constantly worry my grandfather for trading concessions. He does not like them at all. He says they are devious and crooked, and often break their word. They complain constantly, wanting the world to sway to them, he says. When the Padishah asked that they should not persist in stamping the image of the woman they worship on the passes of Muslims wishing to pilgrimage to Mecca on their ships, they refused to listen. Let us ignore them.'

'Yes, Agachi.'

She returned to her work. There were only three beggars left to feed, but I could not easily obey her command. The feringhi swayed unsteadily in their saddles and from their manner I knew they had been consuming arrack. Their grey eyes were rimmed with redness, and their faces were puffy. They talked to each other in a strange language which sounded as if the words escaped from their mouths sideways, sliding down with their spit. They laughed as they spoke, and one nudged his mount towards me. They looked, not at me, but at the curved shape of Arjumand. I sensed mischief. The sun shone through her light garments, and her slim, firm body was distinctly outlined. I stood between her and their eyes but then, with no warning, the stocky man in front spurred his animal and pushed me down. As I fell, I grasped my dagger . . .

Arjumand

I heard Isa's warning and turned.

He had fallen almost beneath the horse. I rushed to help him, but the fat feringhi moved his horse between us. I smelt its sweat and then, worse, the man's—bitter and unclean, stale with dust. It was unbearable. Heat imposes its own laws, one must bathe every day. He was not of this land, and practised his own custom, which was to bathe only once a year. The only weapon I held was the ladle and I struck the horse with it. The ladle broke in my hand: 'Get away!' My command only amused the men. They laughed coarsely. The second man was bigger, just as unattractive, and his beard was yellow and dirty. I tried to retreat, but the beggars blocked my path, their hunger greater than their fear. The servants stared open-mouthed, and poor Isa struggled to rise, but the horsemen kept butting him down again.

'Leave us alone.'

'We won't go until we see your pretty face,' the fat man spoke our language crudely. Without warning, he leaned down and snatched at my beatilha, ripping the cloth and exposing my face to their greedy eyes. I felt as if I had been struck; the pain could have been no worse. I had had no experience to teach me how to deal with these men. My life, sheltered and protected, left me helpless now. I was shaking with shock, that these men should have behaved so rudely, and with the shame of being stared at by such filthy creatures. No strange man had ever seen my face, and now I stood open to the stares of the beggars and these evil feringhis. They laughed and jeered, but in my confusion I did not hear them. My shame swiftly turned to rage. I felt as if I had been violated and defiled.

'Get out.'

'She is a beauty.'

And then for the first time in my gentle life, I felt a new and unpleasant emotion: hatred. It burned swiftly, a flame enveloping my senses. I wanted to kill them now, but the only weapon to hand was Isa's lathi. I picked it up, and struck one horseman on the thigh. He yelped, and the horse shied away. I struck it, struck him, struck the other. The fat one gripped the end of the lathi and snatched it from my grasp, as if in his anger he would strike me.

'Do you know who I am? My aunt is the Empress Nur Jehan.'

156

The name wrought magic. The man who held the lathi dropped it as though it scorched his hand. Their laughter ceased, silenced by their fear. Wordlessly, they turned their horses and spurred them down the road, not looking back. I watched until they were lost to sight, wanting to remember every detail.

Isa lay in the road, weeping. Tears cut channels down his dusty face. I went to him to help him. He was reluctant to stand up, and kept his head bowed.

'I failed you, Agachi.'

'You were brave. There was little you could do against two such men. Wipe your face.'

'I will kill them.'

'No. And don't tell my family. I do not want them to know what happened.'

'But Agachi, if you tell your aunt, she will inform the Padishah. The Emperor will have them executed immediately.'

'No, Isa. I told you. My family will never allow me out again if they hear of this. I will not forget what those men did—ever. One day, they will be delivered to me.'

Later in my room I wept uncontrollably. My tears sprang from anger, from humiliation, and I could not understand why they had taken so long. I shook too, as if I had a fever. I wished to see no one, feigning illness. My mother came and touched my brow; it was too warm and she left me alone in my darkened room. I grieved and ached with pain, a strange pain unlike any other. It felt like a wound inflicted deep inside, festering. I had no wish to hate anyone. No thought of it had ever occurred to me until today. How dare they humiliate me? Was I a devadasi? A nautch girl to be cheaply used? Were all the feringhi alike? From what my grandfather said of them, I suspected that they were.

God defend me from the unbeliever.

Men, not God, are the last resort for justice. I believed Khusrav's warning whisper: Ladilli, Ladilli. The name fell on me like a stone. From enchantment, I tumbled to despair. It *was* possible. Mehrunissa could not easily mould me to her wishes, but she could control Ladilli, and through her, Shah Jahan. My brain become feverish and my blood pulsed so fiercely I could not sleep. My love had given me his promise, but his fate, like mine, was beyond his control.

My father was an adviser on matters of finance to the emperor. I appealed to him and to my grandfather. Surely the emperor would hear their voices above the whispers of Mehrunissa. But they were both remote from my daily existence, concerned with matters of greater importance than the heartbreak of a mere girl, or the stubbornness of a daughter whose presence continued to plague her mother, for other men had been brought, other men refused.

It was a matter of conspiracy, not discussion. I hovered for days, waiting for them to be alone, trying not to attract my mother's attention. Doubtless, she realized what I was about, for, one evening, she pointedly left them alone with their wine and huqqa. They reclined against the cushions, talking softly of matters of state. Mehrunissa's position strengthened theirs; the emperor now heard three voices speak the same harmony of thought.

'Come, Arjumand. Sit by me.' My father patted the divan. My grandfather smiled kindly. They both looked on me with some concern. The similarity of expression made them look very much alike, except for my father's youth and his greater height. But it was only the stoop in my grandfather's shoulders that made him appear the shorter of the two. Despite the whiteness in his beard, he certainly matched my father for spirit and energy.

'You know why I have come to you?' I asked my father in a low voice.

'Yes. Your mother told us. You know you have been a great worry to her. If something worries her, then she worries me.' They chuckled in the usual manner of men complaining of their women. 'What can we do?'

'Speak to the emperor for me. Shah Jahan wishes to marry me.'

'We are aware of that. The whole world is aware of his love for you, including the emperor. You are both stubborn children.'

'If all know this, why does he not act? I wish I were a child still, then I wouldn't understand the meaning of time. It races for me now.' I paused, then hurried on nervously. 'I've been told Mehrunissa wishes Shah Jahan to take Ladilli as his second wife.'

They sat up. 'Who told you?'

'Khusrav.'

'His ears are sharp,' my grandfather said. 'Too sharp.' He looked at my father. I could not read his thoughts, but when he looked at me I saw compassion in his eyes. 'That will not happen. We shall talk to the Emperor tomorrow. It would not be wise to force Shah Jahan into another marriage that he doesn't want. It will only cause a rift.'

'What about Ladilli?'

'I'm sure your aunt will find her a suitable husband.'

I left them; when I observed them from behind the lattice, they were deep in discussion. I felt triumphant. They would thwart Mehrunissa, if only to prevent a conflict between father and son. My cause had become political, but I did not care now.

Mehrunissa regarded her defeat as only a minor setback. I had been summoned to the palace haram by Muneer, now tawdry with riches. He wore gold rings with large diamonds, rubies and emeralds on every finger and gold bands on his arms. He had grown fatter, a reflection of his importance. As my aunt's chief eunuch, he held a position of immense power. Great men paid bribes to be heard by her; his least whisper cost a lakh, I was told.

Mehrunissa occupied a suite of rooms overlooking the Jumna, the choicest in the palace. The gentle breeze through the jali ruffled the piles of papers by her side on the rich woven carpet. Her silver desk, a gift from the Rana of Gwalior, was carved with scenes from the Mahabharata, and on it lay the Muhr Uzak. I had never seen the Imperial Seal before. It was the height of a stretched span and made of solid gold. The top of the handle held a large diamond, and its sides were inscribed with Persian writing. It was designed to fit comfortably into the fist of the emperor and it was too large for her hand. It took strength to lift the heavy Imperial Seal. I pressed it into the wax and there was the impression of the Mughal lion above the single name: Jahangir. In this cold lump of metal was concentrated all the power of the empire, and now it lay always on Mehrunissa's desk.

She took it from me impatiently. 'It isn't a toy.' Carefully she replaced it in the velvet-lined golden box. The surface was smooth and worn with use, the gold almost fading.

'You are happy?'

'Very. When can we marry? It must be soon.'

'Always so impatient.'

'Impatient? Five years we have languished in waiting since we first saw each other.'

'Lower your voice. I was being playful.' She patted my head as if I were a child to be placated. She flicked through her papers, peering at this one and that, found one and carefully extracted it. She did not hand it to me, but gave me the gist of what had been discussed: 'Our problems never directly concerned you. Jahangir wished for an alliance with Persia; that is very important to our wellbeing. We don't wish for war in that direction. Having married Shah Jahan to the Persian princess, we couldn't then order her home. Shah Jahan has informed me . . .' I noted the sudden change in her imperious expression, '. . . that the princess is sterile. She cannot bear any children. Of course, she has protested that it is the fault of Shah Jahan, that he has never slept with her, but how can we believe that? I decided it would be best to dissolve the marriage. Not divorce, mind you. The Shahinshah would not approve of that. She will be sent back to Persia. Naturally, I have been generous. She will take with her five camel-loads of gold coin, eight camel-loads of silver coin, all the jewellery that was presented to her as gifts from the Emperor—in all two camel-loads. For the Shahinshah himself, we have sent an equal number of gifts including elephants, horses, and five hundred slaves.' She peered at me through her falling hair and smiled. 'Are you satisfied with what I have done?'

'Yes, Aunt.' I sat still, but filled with almost unbearable excitement. 'Now that we have rid ourselves of the Persian, when can we marry?'

'Ah, you are eager. Remember, Arjumand, marriage isn't all that one expects or hopes for. If the man is a donkey, one has to carry the same burden.' She didn't say any more, though doubtless she spoke of Jahangir who, having tired of ruling, was now occupied with his poetry and painting and the *Jahangir-nama*, and of course, continued to take pleasure in wine. 'We will consult the astrologer. He will decide the date of your wedding.'

It was to be held at dawn, almost a year to the day after Mehrunissa's wedding. I wanted it to take place immediately, but the stars decreed this was the first auspicious day.

Mehrunissa, her generosity now bountiful, designed my wedding costume: a churidar of yellow silk, heavy with gold thread and an intricate gold border, a blouse of the same pattern made of a fine material that revealed more of my breasts than I had done before.

'It is what men most like to see,' Mehrunissa said when I protested. 'Even Prince Shah Jahan.'

My touca was perched delicately on my head. The material was flimsy and fine and was held in place by a heavy gold brooch like a spider's web, with a large and flawless diamond in the centre. The touca was also bound with a string of fine pearls. From the Imperial treasury my aunt gave me a ruby necklace; the gold and the red stone lay in layers on my chest, and for my ears there were tiny gold lamps with ruby flames. My arms, from elbow to wrist, were covered with gold bangles and my anklets were wrought with countless tiny bells. She even painted my face, streaking gold powder below each eye.

I knew she wished to make amends to me for her devious machinations over the years, and gladly I allowed her that relief.

I could not sleep. At sunrise Shah Jahan would ride into our garden on a white stallion. I moved through a mist and dreaded that at any moment I would wake up to find that my life was never to change. To reassure myself, I would look around—not at the bustle of the household—but outside. In the darkness I could see the dim outline of the pandal erected in the garden. Soon the workmen would decorate it with flowers, roses and jasmine—and jewels. It stood like a monument to five long years of waiting, and the moment the ceremony was completed, the pandal would be dismantled. I wished it could remain as a permanent symbol of my happiness. Here Arjumand married the man she loved.

I stared hard and long, but the light never changed; perhaps the great forces that move the sun, the moon and the stars had chosen this fateful day to cease their movement. The stillness was terrifying. Seeing me alone and silent, Ladilli crept in. We had not spoken for some days, and that had bewildered her. I knew she was not to blame, but what else could I have felt, except fear and distrust? She sat beside me and gently took my hand.

'I'm so happy for you, Arjumand,' she whispered. 'You deserve nothing but happiness now. You've been so brave and strong all this time. I don't know how you lived through it. I know I couldn't have.'

'You will, when you love.' I squeezed her hand, but I couldn't immediately embrace her.

'Will I? I doubt it.' She had an irksome placidity. There was a stillness in her, soft, yet vulnerable. 'I will marry whomever my mother tells me. How could I do otherwise? She will shout and scream and cajole. You know how she chooses her weapons wisely. With my father dead,

162

I have no ally. I will do as I'm told.' She sighed. It was a small, wise sound, quite unafraid for the future because she accepted it unquestioningly. It was I who fought, who experienced the pains of love and disappointment. Life would never scar Ladilli. 'We will be friends again, won't we?'

'Yes.' I replied quietly. 'It was my fault. I was angry.'

'Who could blame you? I was not told until I noticed you were angry with me. When I asked my mother, she said it was only an idea that I should marry Shah Jahan.' She shrugged, unsurprised. 'I don't think she really meant it.'

'If it were possible she would have arranged it.' I stopped, knowing how easily Ladilli could be upset. 'You will come and visit me?'

'Yes, often. Who else do I have? It will be easy now that my mother is Empress. She is very preoccupied with her work, and I've never seen her so satisfied before. It's not the marriage that makes her so happy.' She stopped and giggled. 'I still cannot believe that the Padishah, the Great Mughal, is my father. Of course, he isn't the same as . . .' She caught her breath and checked the tears. She still thought often of her father. 'No, it's not the marriage. That alone could never satisfy her. What she wanted most is to be occupied, to be useful, to be powerful. Now she's happily immersed in matters of state. She plunges into them like a diving crane. She only wishes to match wits with men, and win. Women bore her with their talk of children and clothes and tamashas.'

'Is she pleased with me?'

'Oh yes,' she bubbled, and then became subdued. 'I think so, but of course she doesn't confide in me. You're happy and that should make her happy, too. One day you will be the Empress Arjumand.'

'Yes,' I agreed adding silently, Ins'h'allah. And how would Mehrunissa behave when that day came?

Shah Jahan rode behind Jahangir. Their sarapas, one scarlet, the other deep red, intricately embroidered with thick gold thread, splashed with emeralds, pearls and amethysts, spread out splendidly on the rumps of their horses. Jahangir scattered gold and silver coins to the crowds as he passed. The early sunlight glittered on the diamonds in their turbans, on the chains around their necks and on the gold scabbards of their swords. Shah Jahan controlled his happiness in solemnity.

They dismounted; the music ceased. The silence felt as if the whole world were holding its breath. They took their places opposite me. The men sat on one side, the women the other, and in between were the mullahs. We faced each other. I saw him, but he could not see me; the heavy veil hid my face. He was only a blur through the netting, but I could not take my eyes from him. The mullahs read a passage from the Quran, and then pronounced us married by nikah. The book, bound in leather and decorated with gold, was passed to Shah Jahan. He wrote his name and then it came to me. I saw his curling letters, and carefully wrote my name beneath. My mother helped me to my feet, and led me back to the house. It was only an hour past dawn; streaks of the long night still remained in the pale sky. I looked back to see Shah Jahan formally embracing Mehrunissa, my grandmother and other relatives.

Then I went to sleep, still clothed in my marriage costume, dreamlessly and contentedly. When I was woken at dusk I felt as though I had shed all the sorrow, all the pain. My body felt utterly restored, vigorous and light.

Mehrunissa had arranged a great wedding feast in the palace and the toasting and singing continued late into the night. After a while I was taken away by my aunt and mother and the older women of the household to be prepared for the marriage bed. Slaves bathed me with slow, soft deliberate hands, caressing my breasts, my thighs and buttocks, and slipping gentle fingers, only the tips, inside. I had little need for arousal. My senses burned fiercely. I was dried with tenderness and then perfumed: my hair, face, and breasts were annointed with precious unguents. They combed my hair until it gleamed like a raven's wing in bright sunlight, and added kajal to my eyes and red paste to my lips and nipples which were hard and erect.

'Don't be afraid,' my mother whispered as she led me to the bed. The platform was gold, and it stood on the carved legs of a lion.

'I'm not. Other women lie with strangers on their wedding nights. I will lie with Shah Jahan.'

She sighed. 'It doesn't make any difference. This will be the first time for you and love does not make it any easier. The women will help you to achieve pleasure.'

I lay down, afloat on the divan. My body was covered, my hair spread like a peacock's plumage on the pillow. Beside the bed, on either side, two women waited silently. Another two softly fanned the air with punkahs. The warm, perfumed air stirred, the incense swept over me. From somewhere outside I heard the soft melody of a night raga being played on the sitar. It balanced a mood of joy and sadness, and echoed my sense of tranquillity and promise for the night. As I waited my thoughts drifted to the women I had watched enjoying the pleasures of each other. Soon I would know the pleasure of love.

My prince knelt, silent, tender, and kissed my face, my forehead, my nose, my eyes, my mouth.

'At last,' he smiled. 'My exalted one.'

'And you are mine.'

My eyes devoured him; my hands touched his beard, perfumed and glistening, lost themselves in the curling hairs on his chest. I smiled. I had never seen him bareheaded before. I knew a lingering feeling of disbelief, as if he might vanish.

'You're happy?'

'Very. And you?' It seemed our words could only be short, breathless, hurried.

'Yes. I love you. We will never ever be apart again. Where I go, you

165

too will come. And where you go, I will be by your side.'

'Is that your promise?'

'Yes.'

'I will never permit you to break your word to me, as long as I live.'

'That will be forever.'

The women took his robe. He lay beside me and the hardness burned like an ember against my thigh. We lay gazing on each other as the women began to caress our bodies gently. It seemed that we were being embraced by a god with countless arms. I looked down, noticing with excitement the contrast of our bodies, his so firm, dark, muscular: mine pale, soft, and rounded. It seemed that this was the very first time I had seen myself, that for years I had had no knowledge of my body's physical shape and secrets. Two women played on my body with delicate fingers as if it were a sitar, arousing each part slowly and knowingly, brushing my breasts, my nipples, the curve of my belly, and sliding fingers gently between my legs, then down my thighs until I felt that even my toes were instruments for pleasure.

Shah Jahan sipped his wine and the women stroked his body too with no less care. They teased his nipples, traced circles around his belly and caressed his organ slowly. In their hands it grew larger still, straightening, glistening with the oils they rubbed into it, until it appeared to strain away from him. One of the women took my hand and placed it on him, and I felt the stone hardness there, never imagining such strength could exist between a man's legs.

Their hands and tongues plied my body with tantalizing delicacy, stroking and sucking my nipples erect and hard so that they ached as if they would burst and their fingers glistened with unguents and my own moisture. Shah Jahan's touch was harsh and greedy. He squeezed, a nipple first, carefully rolling it between his fingers, then increasing the pressure and with a sense of distance studied the painful pleasure that swept my face.

'You will discover wondrous experiences this night, my chosen one.' My love spoke softly. 'Pain and pleasure are inseparable in the act of love. In the pleasure, like a serpent, lies the pain. It is God's balance within our bodies and in our hearts.'

He bent first to kiss, then to bite, and as I arched, wallowing in the fever of pleasure and pain, I felt the thrust of the women's fingers deep into me to counteract the sharpness of his teeth on my nipples. I felt another caress me with oils, parting the lips of my body.

'She is ready, my lord,' a woman whispered.

He knelt between my legs, staring down, devouring all he could see in this ghostly light. The women drew my legs up. I lay vulnerable now, completely exposed to his eyes. A woman took my hand, stretched it out, again made me grasp his hard organ.

'It has an eye but cannot see. Guide it within.'

My prince was experienced. He understood my innocence. Gently, he lowered himself, patiently allowing me to guide him into the warm, soft refuge between my legs. It seemed fire entered with him, my body and senses dissolved. He went deeper. I felt every minute touch within me as he sank deeper and deeper. The pain was sudden and sharp. I cried out. A sting that was swiftly gone, extinguished and soothed by the pleasure again. I could not believe I could admit such length, such breadth into my small body. A wave swept within me, beginning from my thighs, softly curling and licking and heating my whole body. We were slippery with oils and perspiration. A woman patted our faces dry.

He began to move slowly, rising and lowering, never placing his weight fully on me, the only sense of his touch an exquisite pleasure within me. He had begun so gently, but as he began to increase his pace, a frenzy slowly took over his face. His breath grew harsh. As if my spirit were escaping slowly, I was being drawn deep into his body. It grew sweeter, painful, rushed. Hurry, hurry, hurry. He hurried now, taking me with all his strength and then, as the waves of pleasure

167

threatened to engulf us, we both cried out. He was still, shuddering. I could not move, could not breathe. He fell on me, and I felt the fury of the dying waves of feeling. But gradually they lessened until I felt calm and serene. The sitar still played, from another world.

At daybreak, when we rose from sleeping in each others' arms, the women came to inspect the sheets and were satisfied.

1023/AD 1613

'You cannot come with me.'

'I will. You made me a promise, my beloved; I cannot let you break your word to me.' We were lying together on the lawn of his palace, in the clear moonlight that threw black, sharp shadows. I rested in his arms, as I had done every night since our marriage. The peace I felt soothed me. I could not pray for more, dream for more, only that it last forever. We made love often—did others so frequently, so greedily, as if they could not remember the last hour? We were never parted for long; an hour, two, and I felt myself bereft until he returned. 'Why do you try to break your promise to me now?'

'Look at you,' he drew back and gazed proudly at the slight swell of my belly. I too stared down. How serene I felt. My heart, my body were so filled with our love, and there it lay for us to see. He caressed the swelling, stroking it continually. 'It will be a long, hard campaign. I cannot risk taking you there.'

'There is no choice. I don't care if it is hard and difficult. I don't care if the comfort is lacking. I want so much to travel with you.'

'The child . . .'

'He will come too. My dear one we must never part. You promised, and now I hold you to it. A prince cannot withdraw a promise to his wife. We will go together to this battle. I cannot live alone again. Never. It would be like the five long desert years.'

'It won't be the same. You're with child, you're my wife. You have your family, a position in the land.'

'The child cannot talk to me or love me as you do. It will only remind me that you are gone. I don't want to run back to my family, and what difference does my position in the land make to the empty ache in my heart? "Princess" is of no comfort. It just sounds cold and aloof; it keeps people at a distance, in distrust.'

'You are foolish,' he laughed, partly from pride, partly from worry. I tried to smooth the creases from the corners of his eyes. 'I beg you, my beloved, to stay behind. It is going to be dangerous and difficult, and the battle will be fierce. The Mewar Rajputs have fought us since the very first time my ancestors came down from the mountains and conquered this land. Even Akbar couldn't defeat them. He destroyed Chitor, but he couldn't destroy them. I fear they may be unconquerable.'

The moonlight fell on his face. It was dark and silvery, his eyes hooded and brooding. His beard looked strangely pale, ageing him suddenly. I could not bear his doubts. I took his face and kissed it, then gazed into his eyes.

'You must never say that. You are Shah Jahan, Sovereign of the World. I know you will be the one to defeat the Mewar Rajputs. I feel it.' Though he smiled gently, the doubt remained in his eyes. I have not seen such uncertainty in him before. 'Why do you think Mehrunissa chose you to lead the army?'

'I am crown prince. My father no longer wishes to go into battle.'

'No. Jahangir only does what she tells him to do. He plays at being emperor in the diwan-i-khas, but it is she who holds the Muhr Uzak. I saw it once on her desk.'

'I have heard it is now kept in the haram, but I thought it was only a rumour.'

'It is there. I know my aunt well. She only gave the appearance of accepting defeat over our marriage; it was but one battle in her life. The fight continues, and we are not even aware of the forces raging around us, my beloved. She chose you to lead the Mughal forces, over

169

general Mahabat Khan, to test you. She thinks you will lose the war. She knows you will lose. If the great Akbar couldn't defeat the Mewar Rajputs, how can Shah Jahan, a young man with little experience of warfare?'

'I will not lose,' he said fiercely, spurred by the challenge of possible defeat. His mood could change as rapidly as his father's.

'You cannot. For our sake.' I touched my belly. 'For his sake. If you are defeated, Mehrunissa's power will only increases. Even if you win, she will not lose much. She will be able to crow loudly over her choice of leader, but then she will watch you even more carefully.'

We lay quietly and I awaited his decision. I felt afloat, suspended in the thin light. My appeal had been not to his heart, but to his mind. As crown prince of this vast empire, he could survive with the loneliness of his heart, but not the loneliness of ambition. One was a sadness; the other a danger. He needed, not lovers, but a friend. Akbar had had the general Bairam Khan to guide him. Only I truly cared for Shah Jahan. If he did not wish to succeed, I was content. If he did, then I was the only person in all the world in whom he could securely place his trust.

Shah Jahan

The State of Mewar lay some six hundred kos to the west of Agra, beyond Jaipur. The land of the Rajputs was harsh and unforgiving, desert and scrub grass and lantana, of no use to anyone. Everywhere we felt ourselves watched from the stern granite forts that sprang from the rocks and the hard earth. Who could tell what they defended? Their little kingdoms might be no more than a field or encompass some hills and desert. The Rajputs were the only Hindu military force who continually opposed the Great Mughals. Many had been conquered and, through our pracice of conciliation and marriage, turned into friends and allies, but a few were still recalcitrant.

The Ranas of Mewar had fought us for one hundred years. Nearly fifty years ago, Akbar had besieged the Rana's iron fortress, built high on a rock. The sides were sheer as ice and it had taken him a year, even using a *sabat*, to take the fort. The Rana himself had abandoned it before the siege began, withdrawing deeper into his inhospitable kingdom. Akbar knew of this, but still the remaining Rajputs had fought long and fiercely, with a madness he could not understand. He had sustained heavy losses in the siege, and enraged, for the first and last time in his rule, had ordered the massacre of all the defenders of the fort. The Rajput women, of course, committed *jauhar* before the stronghold was captured. Their funeral pyres were the signal of defeat.

Certain Rajputs marched with us, Jaipur to the left and Malwar to the right. Minor princes leading their few horsemen followed behind, hidden by the dust. When they did not fight with us, or against us, they continually fought each other. Their own petty feuds drained their blood and their unity, but it suited us to encourage these feuds and thus distract them from ever uniting against the Mughals.

I looked back. I led one hundred and fifty thousand men and beasts into battle. Seventy-five thousand were mounted on horses and elephants—Rajputs, Jats, Mughals, Dogras. The balance were *siphais* and *banduq-chis*. Forty cannons were hauled by elephants over this difficult land. Apart from my own warriors, thousands followed to feed and care for the army. Fifty thousand carts of grain accompanied the force, and uncountable live cattle and goats and chickens. If food became scarce, we would purchase provisions from villagers, but we would not rob. We were no longer conqueror but rulers, and could not disaffect the peasants. The din of movement was ceaseless; the creak of elephant girths, the jingle of bridles and bits, the rumble of carts, squeaking wheels, the crack of whips, the dundhubi beating, horns blowing, the sharp call of commanders to their men.

In front of me lumbered five elephants bearing the Mughal standards. As always I rode Bairam. I had named my elephant after Akbar's general. He was a wise, brave beast who feared nothing, and his tusks were tipped with iron. To one side, a syce led my horse. Shaitan. Behind me Arjumand rode in a rath. There was enough room for four people to sleep but only her maid, Satiumnissa Khananam, rode with her. Beside her conveyance, constantly within call, rode the hakim, Wazir Khan. He looked uncomfortable and tired, unused to hardship, and doubtless would have preferred attending Arjumand in the luxury of the palace, but she would not be dissuaded. I was proud of her loyalty and bravery; another woman would have stayed behind, waving from the balcony before returning thankfully to the cool comfort of the palace and the companionship of the ladies. In her company I could not but be courageous and fortunate. Isa arranged the small comforts of her household, riding ahead each day to ensure that the night's accommodation was cool and clean and comfortable, bathing water and food prepared. He would ride back then, an exhausting task in this heat, to ensure her well-being. He was as concerned for her as I was.

We were twenty days out of Agra—the army moving at the pace of Bairam, who could never be hurried on a march—when I received a report that the Rana of Mewar, on hearing of our approach, had withdrawn into his fortress town of Udaipur. I had expected as much. He could not match me with men, only with strategy.

That night I conferred with the commanders of the hazari. They were resigned to a long, patient siege, and that was the only advice I would receive from them. I sat alone when they left, wrapped in a quilt, brooding. It was a chilly night. Isa crept in softly. His face was pinched and drawn. It frightened me.

'What is it, Isa?'

'Her Highness . . . she has begun to bleed.'

fourteen

the taj mahal 1049/AD 1639

Famine gripped the empire. The monsoons had failed, and even the snow-fed rivers were now only streams. The earth was dusty and hard, and the fields cracked and deserted. The ghats burned night and day to the mournful, eerie music of the conch, ushering more victims onto the pyres. Men ate what they could—dogs, roots, bark, for the bazaars held no food—and when there was nothing to eat, they lay down and died. The highways of the empire were littered with the dead: men, women, children, cattle, goats, horses; those who were not taken to the pyres were consumed by jackals, dogs and vultures. Trees, grass and flowers withered and died and the landscape took on a uniform colour, a dull brown, the hue of death. The sky too became the same colour.

The tomb stood abandoned, only a few feet high, its marble dull with dust. Behind it the river was a trickle, a thin pulse of stale water. The bed lay exposed to the harsh sunlight like the dry belly of a reptile.

Sita lay on the floor of her hut, sheltered from the glare, but not from the heat. From that there was no escape. It hung within the four low walls, stifling, still, waiting. She was thinner now, and could see her bones in the muted light. The children lay beside her sniffling and crying, but she was unable to comfort them. They did not want love, only food.

173

Murthi squatted outside, his knees stuck up in front of him like broken sticks poking out of the hard ground. He blinked, watching the approaching cloud of dust, wondering what moved in the plain beyond his vision. The others near him also looked at the darkening skyline.

'He has come back,' Murthi whispered hoarsely. His voice was weak but he did not have the will to raise it and call Sita.

'Yes,' his neighbour spoke bitterly. 'What good will that do us? He doesn't see that his people are dying of hunger; he only cares for that tomb.'

'Ah, I heard that in Lahore the people approached him and he opened the granary there. We should approach him here when he shows himself at the jharoka-i-darshan tomorrow.'

'Do you wish to die?'

'What difference does it make how one dies? I am starving now. If I am punished for asking to be fed, it is better. Will you come with me?'

His neighbour, the Panjabi, scratched his thin face cautiously as if to make sure that his flesh still hung there. He looked back into his home. One child had already died, another barely lived, and his wife lay inert.

'We must get others. A huge crowd gathered in Lahore, I heard.'

'There will be others.'

'You must lead us then. You can present the petition to the Padishah.'

Murthi agreed. He could afford to be brave; he was protected. But by whom? He still had no idea, but in the great fort across the river a hand shaded him. He had enquired, but nobody replied to his questions: 'Who cares for me? Who cares for us?' The minions of the emperor merely shrugged and turned their backs. When Sita had fallen in front of the clerk she had been carried, almost lifeless, to her home. Without Murthi's summons a *hakim* came. The man wore silks and jewellery which reflected his great standing. He was the emperor's personal physician and he attended Sita, prescribing medicines and having them

174

delivered. Murthi, overcoming his awe, had tried to enquire: 'Who sent you?' The hakim didn't reply. He murmured that he was passing and had noted the plight of the woman. Murthi knew he lied, but namasted in gratitude.

He came back again some days later to see if Sita had recovered. Her colour and strength had returned. Then food came, sent from the palace kitchens: fish, eggs, milk, vegetables, all in abundance. Murthi didn't enquire again as to the identity of his benefactor. Instead, he asked the hakim, pointing to the rising tomb:

'Bahadur, did you know the empress?'

'Yes,' the hakim said softly, and he looked for a long time at the tomb.

'What was she like?'

'A brave woman,' the hakim said. 'Too brave, if that can be considered a failing.'

Clearly the hakim did not wish to discuss the empress further, but his words delighted Murthi. At last, a man who had known her had spoken with awe. Bravery was something he associated only with mythic figures—Bhima, Arjuna—not with ordinary mortals.

The horizon sliced the orange-red rim of the sun as Shah Jahan stepped out of the bargah. Isa waited, wazirs and soldiers and courtiers waited. He strode across the marble floor and the dundhubi beat his approach to the jharoka-i-darshan. Except for Isa, his followers stood behind at some distance, waiting respectfully beyond the gold barrier. Shah Jahan seated himself on the cushions, looked out towards the pale horizon, then to the unfinished tomb and lastly down at the people. The crowds sprawled out across the maidan to the river, and across to the other bank. Their faces were upturned, dark dots in white clothing. The gold chain of justice was lowered without his command. It rested a moment, then the bell was rung.

'Why are they not working?'

'They are starving,' Isa said abruptly.

Shah Jahan noted his tone, but said nothing. In the lemon light of dawn, he studied Isa's profile. How many years had they known each other? He could hardly remember the beginning, the Royal Meena Bazaar and the chokra squatting beside Arjumand. It was difficult to see the boy in this man. Their lives had been bound together for so long that he had never really seen Isa. He knew little about him. Isa served him with intimacy, but never stepped over the bounds into familiarity. He never spoke of Arjumand; her name seemed to have been forgotten. He used to call her Agachi. That never changed within his hearing. Shah Jahan mouthed the word: Agachi, Lady. But he could not capture the same intonation, the same . . . affection. Had Isa loved her? Possibly. He wanted to talk to him about her, discover something new. Each person reveals part of themselves to one, part to another, never the total sum of themselves to a single person. But Isa remained aloof, distant, formal. They were, finally, in spite of their common bond, not friends.

The wazir plucked the petition from the chain of justice and glanced towards the emperor. Did he wish to study it, or should it be sent straight to those officials who deal with such matters? The emperor, sunk in thought, did not see him. Isa stepped forward and furiously snatched the paper. The wazir simmered at the affront. He would have protested but decided instead to hold his tongue. Isa unfolded the papers. He snapped his fingers and a soldier stepped forward with a lantern. The yellow light fell on the petition, on the emperor's face, which looked worn and tired, as if he were gradually fading from the world.

His Most Exalted Majesty, Dweller in Paradise, the
Second Lord of the Constellation, the Great Mughal,
King of Kings, the Shadow of Allah, the Scourge of God,

176

Sovereign of the World . . .

Impatiently Isa flipped the page. The wazir shook with anticipation, waiting for the bite and snarl. Such insolence, such disrespect would be punished. But the emperor smiled thinly, seeming to mock himself, and allowed Isa to read through the petition. The wazir could not understand the relationship between the two men. Another man in his position would have grown rich and fat, but Isa held no title, no great jagirs, no wealth, nothing. The emperor could crush him like a grape, but the hand was always stayed. They seldom directly addressed each other. Sometimes there seemed to be an underlying antagonism between them, more on the part of Isa, than on the emperor's, but they were never apart from each other. Isa moved in Shah Jahan's shadow. Or did the great Shah Jahan walk in Isa's? It puzzled the wazir.

. . . the King Shah Jahan. We, your people, humbly
petition you. For two years there have been no rains.
The rivers have dried, the crops have withered, there is
no food. We cannot live. Our children have not eaten
for many days, and they die of hunger. We have stripped
the trees of bark and eaten the roots and, like our
children, we grow weak and die. We appeal to your justice,
your bountiful generosity: feed us.

Shah Jahan peered down. The people stared back silently. The sun had risen, revealed itself to the earth, and its light crept over the upturned faces, illuminating them one by one.

'Who leads them?' the emperor enquired.

Isa glanced down. 'The first name is Murthi. Many others follow.'

'Who is he?' There was whispered menace in the emperor's tone.

'He carves the jali,' Isa said.

'How do you know this?'

177

'I know.'

The emperor waited. Isa said no more. Shah Jahan did not pursue the matter but made a silent note of it. It interested him. It interested the wazir even more.

'What would she have done?' The emperor's whisper reached only Isa's ears.

'She would have fed them.'

'Then feed them. Open the granaries. Open the treasury, buy food wherever it can be found. Those who hoard—execute them.'

Shah Jahan rose from the throne, held up his hand in a vague gesture of blessing to the people. As one they bowed. The silence broke and he heard their murmurs as he moved back to his quarters. Isa remained for a moment, watching the huge throng slowly disperse. They could not have known the emperor's decision, but soon it would be posted on the doors of the fort. He peered down, unable to distinguish individual faces. He had been acutely aware only of the emperor's curiosity.

1050/AD 1640

The tomb rose, block by block, creeping up to meet the sky. Parallel to every wall rose the brick scaffolding. Two teams of masons laboured arduously in a race with each other. At the same furious pace, keeping level with the height of the tomb, the bund rose. It lay like a muddy snake nearly twenty kos long, curling through Mumtazabad. It was the width of one cart, but here and there it had been widened so that a second could pass without toppling over. Elephants and bullocks dragged the slabs of marble and cartloads of bricks up the incline in an endless procession. At the top, teams of men would slip a rope around each new block of marble, attaching the end to the pulley that always remained a few feet above the level of the building. The mahout would urge his elephant forward, lifting the block into position, then slowly

178

lowering it to rest on the one below Each slab fitted squarely, immovably, seeming to sigh as it accepted the place allotted to it by destiny.

Carefully, Murthi brushed away the marble dust with his calloused, chipped hands. Three years had passed since he had begun, and a square foot of the jali had been revealed. It seemed as if the stone was no more than a shroud veiling the design, which had only to be prised away from the intricate pattern within.

Murthi flexed his hands, stiff from holding the chisel. Each day he began at dawn and finished at dusk, with a brief respite for his midday meal and another for a cup of chai brought round by the seller. Gopi squatted by the fire. Every time his father discarded a chisel, he laid it in the coals until it turned coppery grey, then he dropped it on the ground to cool. Gopi had inherited the same patience and stubborn concentration as his father. He watched him wrest the pattern from the stone, chip by delicate chip. Learning came from watching; it came from practice. He never doubted that he would have the skill to follow his father. How else could it be? His ancestors had practised the craft; it was in his blood, and he never dreamed of doing anything else. His life was dedicated to the discipline of stone. When there was time, he would chip away at a small discarded block of marble. He had drawn a little tiger on the flattest side and had patiently begun to carve the beast. If he finished it to his satisfaction, he would sell it in the market for a rupee.

Murthi sucked a last mouthful of smoke from the beedi and threw it away. He picked up his chisel, and began softly to tap, monotonously tap. Only the keenest ear could pick up the subtle variations in the sound. Louder, softer, gentler, harder. It came gracefully, almost unconsciously. Rarely when the work went well, Murthi allowed his mind to wander. He remembered his father, his village; thought deeply ill of the Raja who had dispatched him to this distant city. He hoped he had died by now. Then his thoughts turned to his elder brother, how he had disappeared so mysteriously, as if plucked from the face of the earth. He recalled his cheerful manner, his bold, adventurous ways. He had never wanted to follow their ancestral profession, but no doubt if he had lived to grow older, he would have. What else was there to do? Murthi had been very fond of his brother. They had been friends, not yet of an age for antagonism, slights and jealousies to harden. He still missed him, but over the years the memories had gradually faded.

Murthi noticed the jewelled slippers from the corner of his eye. The stones looked like pearls, and the threading was gold. He looked up sharply. A tall, elegantly dressed man stood there. Murthi couldn't quite read his expression; it resembled one of triumph.

'You are Murthi, the man who signed the petition?'

'Yes, Bahadur,' Murthi replied cautiously, for the man might be an official.

Murthi had expected trouble after putting his name to the petition. To their great surprise, it had worked. The granaries had been opened, food distributed to all to tide them over. The emperor also threw open the treasury and gave away half a million rupees as alms. That had been a year ago, and slowly his dread had faded and been forgotten. Now it returned in a rush; instinct warned him to fear this man.

'Come with me.'

'Why? Where?'

'You dare to question me?' the man asked harshly. 'I am the Emperor's wazir. Come.'

At twilight, the marble walls in the diwan-i-khas turned to pale gold. Even the precious stones set in the inlaid flowers took on a different light. Topazes became diamonds, jade became emerald. Nothing retains its nature from beginning to end, Shah Jahan observed, things changed unexpectedly, harshly, unpredictably.

He reclined on the divan, listening to the music, hardly seeing the women, soft, perfumed, dancing for his pleasure; others knelt at his side, filling his cup, stroking his forehead, fanning him. On the other side sat his son, Dara. Shah Jahan looked at him with open affection and rested an arm across the young man's shoulders. They spent many evenings together; the younger man a comfort to the older. Dara had an open face, alert, intelligent, and his eyes were Arjumand's.

'What do you want me to do?'

'Nothing, father. Let them live in peace. It is their manner of worship and there was no temple here in which they could pray. They have built this one discreetly. It harms no one.'

'They should have petitioned me.'

'You would have refused because of the mullahs. They would have demanded that you raze it to the ground.'

'They still do. They insist.' Shah Jahan sighed in irritation. The mullahs were a continual thorn in his side; he had no peace from God's men.

'How is it that men who claim to love God have such a narrow vision of him?' Dara asked. 'I have never understood that. The Brahmin priests are no different. They too are strident in their beliefs, and it is impossible to discuss these matters with them, or with the Jesuits. We should follow the example of Akbar: toleration. Akbar believed it was the cornerstone of the empire. If we destroy their temples, the Hindus will rebel. They are our subjects and they must feel they can live and worship in peace in the empire.'

Shah Jahan pinched his son's cheek. 'You are like Akbar. You too will be as great as he.'

'It will be enough to be a humble disciple of his. He wrote that justice must be equal for all men, for Muslim, Hindu, Buddhist, Jain, Sikh, Christian.'

'Yes, yes. I don't disagree. But even the Sovereign of the World feels the hot breath of the mullahs on his neck.'

Shah Jahan knew that all power was limited, including his own. It ended just beyond vision where even an emperor's hand hesitated, drew back. He could check his mullahs' religious zeal, but only briefly. When they became too demanding, he would slacken the rein briefly to divert them, to support their belief in him as the Scourge of God. It was not in his nature to persecute. He glanced at Dara. When his time came, would he be able to control them? Or would he antagonize them with his avowed tolerance towards all religions? Akbar was strong, breaking only those he could not placate. Was Dara another Akbar? In his affection, Shah Jahan believed he was. He had also inherited Arjumand's courage. 'I will allow it to stand.'

Dara laughed in pleasure at his father's judgement. He knew it was right. The Muslim Mughals ruled, but this was the land of the Hindus and they had to be given freedom to worship.

The wazir entered, bowed, and announced: 'His Royal Highness Prince Aurangzeb wishes an audience, your majesty.'

On his father's command, Aurangzeb entered. He stood for a moment at the entrance and let his glance sweep the room. The sun had darkened him, war had hardened him. He looked leaner, straighter, more commanding. His eyes rested longest on his brother, and though the black orbs were unfathomable, his lips twisted a little, revealing fleeting contempt, then a kind of wistful envy. Aurangzeb bowed, and remained standing. He was not given permission to sit, and knew the audience with his father would be brief. It always was, as if his father had little to say to him, except to give his commands.

'*Shabash!*' his father clapped, 'you are as I was. You frightened those Deccani rats into submission. But will they remain thus cowed?'

'Yes, they will.'

'Why are you so confident? We have all tried, but the moment we turn our backs they pick up their swords again.'

'Because I am Aurangzeb.' It was a surprising, but not boastful remark. He stared back at his father and seemed to grow still taller. 'They know I will not be kind or lenient. They know I will give them no quarter.'

Shah Jahan studied his third son. This one resembled an eagle, the eyes fierce and glittering, ever watchful, the nose hooked like a beak, and his whole stance one of leashed defiance. He sensed enmity, which would have to be contained. Finally, coming to a decision, he nodded.

'They need to be watched constantly, then?'

'Yes. And ruled strongly, otherwise they will go back to their old tricks.'

'Good.' Shah Jahan was satisfied. 'Then I appoint you Subadar of the Deccan.'

Aurangzeb blinked in surprise. He glanced at his brother, who said nothing, but appeared to smile. Aurangzeb did not move. The appointment, a hereditary office for the crown prince, would keep him distant from Agra, distant from the court, distant from power. But distances could be measured both ways.

'As the Emperor wishes.'

'Good,' Shah Jahan rose and embraced Aurangzeb. The gesture held no affection, only formality, the token of relationship.

'Come, look at it. Tell me what you think.' He waved to the open sky beyond the marble arch; the tomb stood in the dying light.

'I have seen it,' Aurangzeb said shortly. He thought it wasteful, extravagant, but remained silent.

'For myself, I plan another tomb. There!' Shah Jahan pointed to the bank opposite the Taj Mahal. 'It will be the same in every detail, except that it will be built of black marble. A bridge of silver will join the two.'

'I will see that it is built,' Dara said.

Aurangzeb remained silent. He bowed to his father's back, then deliberately stared long and hard at his brother. The veil lifted, hatred lay beneath.

the fifteen the love story 1023/AD 1613

Shah Jahan

They waited above us, peering down; we waited below, peering up. A whole month had passed since we had laid siege to the town. We encircled the high walls of Udaipur that rose out of the steeply sloping earth. The walls were sheer on all sides; a single curving road led up to the heavy wooden gates. I could not discern faces on the battlements; doubtless they mocked me. Now and then a jezail fired, a man fell. The cannon returned fire, but the weakened shots bounced off the walls; the defenders jeered. My men sat or lay in what shade they could find, content to remain alive and safe.

'Do as Akbar did,' my commanders advised, 'Build a sabat.'

'I'm not Akbar, I am Shah Jahan. A sabat will take a year, and will cost me as many lives as it cost Akbar.'

A sabat is a long, sinuous tunnel that rises like a cobra from the ground and up to the battlements of a fort. Built of wood and brick and sealed with mud, wide enough to take ten horsemen riding abreast, it is protected from above by a roof of wood and hides. In the walls are embrasures through which jezails can keep up a constant fire on the defenders. It is a living, moving fort. The men who build it work in the open and, naturally, die. Akbar lost twenty men a day for a full year as

184

they built his sabat. The heavy losses enraged him.

'Mine it, then.'

'It is too strong, and the ground too steep.'

They returned to their shamiyanas, downcast, disappointed. I heard their whispers: *Shah Jahan cannot command*. I heard too Mehrunissa's whisper echoing from Agra, creeping over the land, a tentacle slowly coiling around me: *Shah Jahan will fail*.

I rode round and round the walled city—how many times? Each day I hoped to note a vulnerability, some weakness that I could probe and break. The walls remained unchanged; the sloping ground denied an enemy any fighting space. The Rajputs had sufficient water and food for a year, and enough fierce warriors to defend the city for longer than that. A direct assault up the steep path would mean the loss of countless lives or, even worse, defeat. I heard faint music, and caught glimpses of the bright red and yellow and blue costumes of the Rajputana women as they looked down on my progress. The colours vibrated in the sunlight, their brightness blinding, a contrast to the dull brown of the land. 'Akbar, guide me; give me direct battle and I will be victorious. This rock I cannot conquer.'

Arjumand

My beloved returned each twilight disconsolate, I loved him, he barely noticed. I comforted him, he scarcely cared. He paced, restless, brooding, his eyes dark as night, as dangerous too. None could approach the prince, except I.

The household lay three kos from the fort. My tent was pitched by the side of a lake. Around us lay the ruins of an abandoned palace, the wails tumbled and broken like crones' teeth. At night, as I lay in his arms, we heard the wild pigs, the nilgais and tigers come to drink, wary, alert. Later, up in the dark surrounding hills spotted with jungle, we could hear the sweet warning cry of the chitals, followed by the

185

chatter of the langours and the short, harsh bark of the sambars. The tiger hunted. We heard his distant muted roar—even the earth trembled to it—and then the silence, the return of whispering activity in the jungle after danger had passed. The tiger had killed. At dawn, in the mists curling up from the water, we saw the sambars standing in the lake feeding on plants, and herds of nilgais taking water before the heat of the day gripped. The first gentle rays of sunlight gave the lake a feeling of holiness.

These sights and sounds, the orderly movements of nature, healed me. They gave me comfort and renewed my strength. I had bled for many days, weeping bitterly, for I knew the blood was not mine, but that of the innocent child. The hakim's face was grave; he could not staunch the wasting life. I sweated, I burned, my skin turned to chalk, my body was a weight too great to carry. The army halted, silent and patient, and I felt my beloved hold my hand, kiss my face, whisper words of comfort and love.

Death had written a line on my face; it could never be erased. I felt old with grief. Turning my face to the wall of the rath I listened numbly to the squeak of the cartwheels and the thunder of the moving force. Had I grown too old to bear a child? Five squandered, barren, empty years—I raged at such waste, raged at my imperfection, my failure to carry a child.

'It is gone,' Shah Jahan whispered. 'We will make another soon.' He wiped the silent tears as they fell, kissed and tasted them. 'If . . .'

No, don't say it. You are not to blame. I held you to your promise. Even next time, it will be no different. I will come with you. We must never be apart.'

'I should have known you would be stubborn.'

How else would we have married?'

He laughed and held me. Before, I had needed his comfort and strength; now he needed mine, but he was withdrawn, as I had been.

'I hear Mehrunissa's whispers,' he said, 'and begin to believe them.'

186

'They cannot survive in there forever.'

'I cannot live here forever. Even my own men mock me. I see their glances as I ride by, I hear their murmuring. They know I am beaten.'

'You are not. You are not.' It had become a ritual before we slept, whispered so none could hear. It was small comfort. Our wills alone could not breach that high fort. 'What do they eat? What do they drink?'

'I have been told they have enough for one year. An eternity.'

'It is only a year, not forever. One day they will have to come out.'

'Only when we have gone. Already Mehrunissa grows impatient, I'm told. "Just one little fort, and Shah Jahan cannot capture it. Should I send Jahangir? Should I send Mahabat Khan?" If they come, I'm defeated.'

'What will happen,' I whispered, 'when you have gone, and the Rajputs come out to the fields . . .?'

He understood.

His eyes grew bright and wide, their darkness vanished. He woke Isa and ordered the musicians to play, the singers to sing, to bring wine. We drank and laughed, the past no longer had the power to hurt us. We had cast it from us. None understood our gaiety; they smiled indulgently, believing we only laughed to overcome our sorrows. When the dancers and singers tired, we dismissed them and returned to the bedchamber. When we loved, our passion was no less than the first time.

Shah Jahan

I scourged the earth.

Like Timur-i-leng, I destroyed. For one month I devastated the land, laid waste the crops, cattle, pigs, hens, sheep, goats, camels and, when they resisted me, the people. My men rode: east, west, north, south, tearing at the heart of the land, crushing its soul. Wells were poisoned, lakes filled with the carcasses of animals. At dusk the singed earth caused clouds of dust and smoke to veil the evening sun, and from the ramparts of the town, the Rana could look on the death of his kingdom. Fires raged, villages vanished from the face of the earth, peasants stood desolate, afraid, watching my horsemen trample their crops, their saman, their dreams, their lives. Jungles burst into flame and the animals fled.

I knew the Rana saw it all. The fort was silent, grew afraid, those brave walls seemed to shrink, to cringe each time another blaze flared, taking a home, a family, children, a livelihood. Even warriors tilled the earth, drank water, ate food, loved their wives and children. They could not be sustained by bravery alone, they could not eat courage. Now I knew the Rana's weakness. If nothing remained of his people, his land, there would be nothing to rule. He would become a hollow prince, living in a hollow town on top of a hollow hill.

For thirty days I showed my strength to the Rana. Each dawn, riding Bairam, I took my place at the start of the road that led up to the gates of the town; each dusk I left. Half of my forces had remained in siege. A whole army was not needed to lay waste the earth. He could not escape, could not despatch his horsemen to defend his land. A walled town is always defensible, but it cannot attack, and eventually becomes a prison. I waited. I read the Quran, the memoirs of Babur, poetry. I ordered the musicians to play; they entertained me and perhaps the doomed people in the fortress took pleasure in their music too.

One morning, the gates opened; an emissary came forth, escorted by a dozen foot soldiers. They were unarmed. The countless ranks of my army fell silent, so silent that I could hear the approaching footsteps on the dry earth. The Rana's pradhan was a Brahmin. He bowed and stared up at me. His gaze barely veiled his arrogance, and his forehead blazed with his caste mark. The fool expected me to greet him first. I said nothing.

'The Sisodia sends his greeting to the Prince Shah Jahan. He has watched you destroy his kingdom, and it has saddened him. He cannot understand the harshness of the Prince Shah Jahan, or his policy of warring on peaceful people. Akbar would not. . .'

'You address Shah Jahan, not Akbar. While you ramble on my men continue their work. What does the Sisodia want? Surrender? Or the death of his kingdom?' I returned to my *Babur-nama*. If Babur had had my cunning, he could have recaptured Farghani. But then, he would not have turned south to Hindustan, remaining instead to rule that little kingdom all his days.

'Surrender,' the pradhan spoke swiftly, harshly. The word choked him. 'Command your men to stop.'

I felt victory in my hand. 'First, the Sisodia himself will approach me. He may ride. He may have an escort of ... one hundred armed horsemen.' Like Babur and Akbar, I understood the wisdom of conciliation and the necessity for leniency. In the *Arthasastra*, Kautilya, the political sage, advised the prince not to accumulate enemies unnecessarily. The pradhan remained expressionless, but his eyes softened, his narrow chest expanded, like a cock puffed to crow. His master's pride would not be broken; he would ride out from his fort like a Sisodia.

Bairam turned and plodded through the ranks of my men. They parted respectfully and bowed, paying homage to my wisdom. I forced myself to conceal my own pride and excitement, and I only paused to despatch a brief message: 'Inform my father, the Emperor: Mewar is defeated.'

'Allahu Akbar!'

I could not contain my exultant scream. I threw out my arms and embraced the sun and the sky, the earth and the winds, the jungles and the rivers. Sovereign of the World! The name was fitting; I could have borne no other. My elephant was a chariot that rode through the heavens, and all the men paid homage. Shah Jahan! Shah Jahan! Shah Jahan! The dry wind whispered it, the kites screamed it from the skies, Bairam's feet crushed the earth to its sweet rhythm. I felt unearthly, god-like, not even the universe could contain my joyous spirit. My elation had begun when that gate opened slowly, creaking in the expectant silence; it released a cool spring within me, welling, bubbling, rushing until it burst out of my lips. I could think of nothing in my life to equal this; all else paled. It was as if I had not lived until now. No, I was wrong. My first sight of Arjumand—that had been something greater, but different. That had been the intoxication of love; this was victory!

Arjumand

Shah Jahan removed his slippers and slowly, with dignity, lowered himself onto the cushion. He looked so young, so proud, my heart hurt with loving him. Reluctantly, I took my eyes from him and peered through the lattice at the crowd in the diwan-i-am. The nobles were pressed against the vermilion railings; they flowed into the grounds beyond, standing on tiptoe to catch a glimpse of my prince. Khusrav, Parwez and Shahriyar, his brothers, stood behind him, their faces alike closed, sombre, unreadable; what jealousies had been aroused? 'I knew he would succeed,' Mehrunissa whispered in my ear. 'He will become a great prince.' She hugged me, as if it were I who had achieved this victory. 'I will always help him. Tell him he can depend on me.' I felt the calculating caress in her eyes.

Victory brought power, and I was to be courted for what that could achieve for her.

Behind the silver railing stood a slight, bewildered youth, the son of the Rana of Mewar. 'What a wild young boy!' Mehrunissa laughed, mocking him. His turban barely contained his mass of hair, but perched on his head, wound Rajputani fashion like a coiled unwieldy rope. His dress was not fashionable and though he looked arrogant, it was obvious that he was afraid and in awe of the gathering. Karan Singh was a gentle, though untutored boy. It had been pleasant to enjoy the company of

190

such innocence, such curiosity. At court such qualities are swiftly crushed. He had questioned Shah Jahan about all manner of things during our journey from Mewar to Ajmer. It was in Ajmer—while we awaited Jahangir—that our first child, conceived in such joy beside the lake nine months earlier, was born. We had prayed for a son. God gave us a daughter, Jahanara. She was a beautiful baby and we loved her. Jahangir, delighted with victory—he considered it his—had brought the court here, one hundred kos from Mewar, to celebrate. Ajmer was a small crowded town, quite ancient, filled with low flat-roofed buildings and surrounded by the Taragarh hills. There were two venerable mosques: Arhai-din-ka-Jhonpra and the Dargah. My beloved gave thanks for the victory and for our daughter in the Dargah. Akbar had built a small fort in the town but Jahangir preferred to pitch the Imperial tent on the shores of Lake Sagar. All day a strong cool breeze blew across the lake from the hills.

The emperor entered and mounted the throne. He smiled down at my beloved, clapped in delight and pleasure, and the nobles hastily echoed him Every face shone with happiness, as if cast from the same mould.

'I am pleased with my victory over Mewar,' Jahangir announced. 'Where my father Akbar failed, I have succeeded. I only wish he were here with me to celebrate my victory He would have been proud of me, as he never was during his lifetime. My noble spirit always desires, as far as possible, not to destroy these old families. I only wish to live in peace and harmony with them. For this reason only, I have asked nothing of the Rana of Mewar . . .' He looked down on Karan Singh. Karan bowed awkwardly. It was not correctly done, but Jahangir forgave him. '. . . except to send his son, Patrani of Mewar, to stay here as my guest for a time. The Rana will keep his kingdom, and all I ask of him is his loyalty and his love . . .'

'Don't snort,' Mehrunissa pinched me. 'Allow him to be Emperor. We all know those were the terms Shah Jahan set. It pleased Jahangir, and that should please you.'

'He should at least mention my husband's name.'

'. . . I am proud of my son, Shah Jahan, for having followed my instructions well. I have raised his rank to ten thousand zat and five thousand sowar . . . .'

'Doesn't that please you? You are rich now.'

'. . . and I give him permission from this day to pitch me red *gulabar*.'

'I told you he would not forget your prince.'

Red, but not of blood—that was the dream that had haunted me for all these years. I had thought the stain of blood on the divan had shown the meaning of my dream, but I was wrong. I laughed and clapped. My beloved was now confirmed in the rank of crown prince. First the hereditary jagir of Hissan-Feroz, now the hereditary gulabar. Jahangir plied Karan Singh with costly gifts and the ceremony continued.

1025/AD 1615

When was my son Dara conceived? A woman can tell these things, not through calculation but by instinct, by love. The very moment the child was formed was on the night of this great event. It could have been no other time. Dara was conceived in joy, in happiness, in laughter and loving. I remember the embrace, the kisses, the heightened pleasure of our intimacy. Our bodies were passionate, our blood sparkled with lust. What we felt that night, we wove into our child. He drew his spirit from that moment.

I do not know how it should be, but we create the natures of our children long before they are born into the world. They feed not only on the body, but on the mind and the heart and the air we breathe. Dara caused me no pain, or possibly I did not notice it in my happiness. He came swiftly with the sunlight at dawn. He did not cry, but lay in my arms looking around him with great curiosity. His eyes were Shah Jahan's.

I could not give him up to the women who waited eagerly to nurse the baby prince. It was an honour for those whose breasts held milk to have the prince's lips on their teats. They would be rewarded with riches and honour, and their station in the haram rose. But I placed his searching mouth to my own breast, aching to have him suckle me. I ordered the heavy-bosomed wet-nurses to withdraw. I felt I had to be careful. Their milk might change our beloved baby, fashion his spirit after their own natures.

The first to come and visit me was Shah Jahan, his face drawn, weary with the night of vigil. He had suffered the same pain as I, or perhaps even a greater one. He kissed me first, thankful that I lived, and lay beside me contented and exhausted. Then, delicately, wondering, he examined our son.

'He is as beautiful as you,'

'Sons cannot be beautiful, they must be handsome.'

'This one is.'

He placed his finger in the small fist, and the baby grasped it. It seemed they were of the same spirit, in love on the first sighting, the way we had felt towards each other. Both smiled in admiration of each other, and when the prince bent to kiss his son, Dara chuckled with laughter.

'Your beard tickled him. I only pray he grows strong and straight like you.'

'He is my heir,' Shah Jahan whispered, and then softly into the delicate ear of the child. 'One day you will become the Great Mughal.'

Mehrunissa looked down curiously at Dara, her head tilted, squinting as if she looked through a beatilha. She would have pinched his cheek, her usual token of affection, causing him to cry out, but I stopped her hand.

'What do you look at?'

'I was admiring him,' Mehrunissa smiled. 'I think he looks like Shah Jahan. Jahangir is very pleased. He has sent a gift.' Slaves staggered under the weight of an enormous gold cradle. It hung from a bar held up by two stands on either side. It was the height of a tall man, and there was enough room for a small boy. The sides were engraved with strolling elephants. Mehrunissa kissed me, hesitated a little too long, then brushed her lips against Dara's fragile forehead. Our gestures betray us more than our words. I watched as Mehrunissa slowly, deep in thought, walked away from my bedside.

Isa

I loved Dara as if he were my own son. When my duties permitted I would search for him. If he was with Arjumand or the prince, I would not disturb him, but if he was with the maids I would steal him from them and we would go out onto the lawn to play. His skin and hair were soft and he took great pleasure in my caresses, held my fingers as if I were his father He was not yet of an age to be able to distinguish one from another. Soon he would. He looked like Arjumand, except for his dark eyes; those belonged to his father.

It was a placid, pleasant household. We lived in harmony, and it was a relief to escape the intrigue of the Imperial palace. I believe Arjumand would have been quite content to live here forever, forgotten by all her family. She loved her husband deeply and spent as much time as possible in his company. They enjoyed a rare intimacy, since most husbands and wives prefer to remain strangers, except in their coupling.

Mehrunissa, however, would not allow such tranquillity. Shah Jahan's victory had only increased her power. She glowed in its reflection and, when the Deccan once more began to grow restive, she whispered the prince's name to Jahangir.

1026/AD 1616

'You must remain behind, Agachi. I will care for the Crown Prince on the journey.'

194

'No. You are not his wife. We promised each other.'

But she sighed as we watched the confusion of packing for the hardships of the Deccan. It was early winter, a good time for the campaign, further south the heat of high summer burned the skin.

'But remember what happened on the journey to Mewar. Your condition doesn't permit travel.'

Her belly was swelling once more; she moved stiffly, tiredly. The new baby had started too soon. She should have rested for a year or two. The hakim confided this to me, after examining her. He was concerned; his concern infected me. The road to the south was rougher, harsher, and the battles possibly fiercer.

'You are beginning to sound like an old woman. Maybe you would prefer to remain behind in comfort?'

'Where you go, I will serve you, Agachi. But please consider; should Dara too make such a journey? He is too young.'

'He will become used to it,' she sighed, as if she foresaw endless, endless travel.

The baby was born near the lower rim of the empire, another son — Shahshuja. Arjumand, exhausted after the birth, gave him to a nurse to suckle.

The landscape, the people, the climate, all were inhospitable. The hills were a dull purple, sharp as teeth, rising above a mass of jungle containing isolated villages and petty princes.

Burhanpur was a small fortified town in a valley by the Tapti river, and there was a constant bustle of boats plying between here and Surat. The river lapped the palace walls, and from the parapets we could glimpse through the haze the brooding great rock fortress, Asirgarh, which is the highest in Hindustan, a whole day's climb from the plain to its gate. It had taken Akbar two years to capture it, and only by his cunning had he finally succeeded.

The palace was a small, simple building of brick. There were no quarries for sandstone or marble here. The haze of heat was relentless, causing every rock and shrub to waver. Humayun, Akbar, Jahangir, and now Shah Jahan, all had come to live in this palace, to battle against these petty princes who so persistently caused problems. Why could they not peacefully accept the rule of the Great Mughals, instead of dragging them down here again and again?

Shahshuja's birth had been long and painful. Arjumand's screams and whimpers burned my heart. Afterwards she was tired and listless, and lay in her room looking out on the unchanging hills, the sluggish river and blazing sky. Occasionally she would enjoy the undulating shadow of a drifting cloud, its movement briefly darkening the hills. We were a thousand kos from Agra, and we all felt as if we were inhabiting a strange, burning world in which we were the only living things.

Her body did not immediately return to its beauteous shape, but remained swollen, heavy, as if it still contained the child. I suspect that disturbed her—women care about such things—but she did not speak of this to Shah Jahan. When he returned from conferring with his commanders, she would behave cheerfully, laugh and talk and play with Dara and Jahanara, giving the impression that she had been in the same happy mood since dawn. But Arjumand was to have no respite. Having waited so many years for her beloved prince, his children now tumbled out of her body. Only nine months later, she gave birth to Raushanara. The girl child was suckled by a village woman whose baby had died, and Arjumand was grateful for the respite. But her affection for Dara never changed. She would cuddle and cosset him, shower him with her kisses. Shah Jahan too seemed to take an equal and continued delight. The others he merely examined, held, and briefly kissed. The favourite had been chosen; he had cut his place in their hearts, and none could take his place now. How deliberately parents make a choice between their own children!

'Isa, you will go with my beloved into battle. You must defend him against his enemies.'

'I will accompany him, Agachi, but I am not a warrior. I will do my best.'

'If he should die, I will too. My heart will break. I hate these people for causing such danger to Shah Jahan. And yet he enjoys himself, as if it were a game in which no one really dies. He is like a child delighting in a new toy.'

'The Mughal army is not *a* toy, Agachi, You should be proud that he commands such might. He will be victorious once more.'

'I know, but my fear remains, A chance arrow, a lance, a musket ball, and I too shall cease to live.'

So I accompanied Shah Jahan into battle, but not with any pleasure. I sat crouched uncomfortably behind him in his howdah. Bairam smelled war; he was draped in chain armour and as we marched he trumpeted grandly. The other elephants responded and their roars echoed in the hills. The ground shuddered with moving horsemen, flowing like quicksilver down into gullies, over hills and into ravines. The battleground had been chosen, a plateau near Elhchpur. Against us were ranged the armies of the Nizam Shahi kings.

I looked around as we approached their forces, scarcely heartened by the sight of the thousands Shah Jahan commanded. Around us rode his own Ahadi, and behind followed Mahabat Khan, the watchful shadow of Jahangir. The old general went to war coolly; he lay in his howdah, legs crossed, with his hands behind his head. I presumed his posture was intended to calm and encourage all who saw him. To our right rode the prince's new-found friend, Karan Singh. The Mewar prince preferred horseback. Under his dark turban he wore a metal helmet and his body was covered with finely wrought chain armour. On the left rode the prince's old companion, Allami Sa'du-lla Khan. Shah Jahan wore only the lightest *char-aina*, which consisted of two well-padded square metal plates to protect his chest and back, and two smaller pieces to protect his sides, all held together with gold clasps. His helmet was decorated with nodding plumes and was damascened with gold, and chain-mail flowed down his back. His jezails were carried by bearers who walked beside Bairam. They too were well protected. Only I was unprepared for battle, wearing jiba and pyjamas, miserably vulnerable. I prayed constantly.

Shah Jahan raised his right arm high in view of all to his right flank, and twisted his wrist once. For a long minute, nothing moved. Then ten thousand horsemen wheeled away from the main army and began to troop south. He performed the same action with his left hand, and another ten thousand wheeled to the north. These were the tips of the buffalo horns, set in motion to attack the flanks of our enemies. In front of us moved the cannon and the banduq-chis. We reached the edge of the plateau and far ahead the enemy army began to move towards us.

Shah Jahan lifted both arms high, and we halted. The tested method of warfare was to permit the enemy to enter an embrace, to deceive him into believing he would succeed by attacking. The barricades for the banduq-chis were placed in position, and the siphais prepared their weapons. Far away to the south and north, twenty thousand of our horsemen would be circling towards the enemy.

Shah Jahan turned to glance at me. His face was calm, but those dark eyes were alight, a fire burned inside his head. He resembled a great beast, coiled and bristling, preparing to spring.

'You're frightened, Isa?'

'I cannot lie, your Highness. Yes. I'm not used to war.'

'I cannot ease your fears. Every army has the same objective: victory. And one part of that objective is to kill the commander. If I were not

198

seen by my men—even for a minute—they would presume me dead, and retreat, I am their heart. If I die, they die in spirit. The enemy will try his best to reach me. I think you chose the wrong elephant.'

'You should have refused Agachi's request, your Highness. You should have demanded I remain by her side.'

'Who can deny Arjumand anything. Can you?'

'No, your Highness.'

His attention returned to the approaching enemy, mine to prayer. Cowardice is a miserable thing. I wallowed in self-pity, in extravagant promises to the divine; if they would but protect my life, I would perform every imaginable sacrifice to their greatness. In this moment, I was stripped of all pretence; my soul bared for inspection. I could not remember the words of the Quran nor recall the meaning of that faith.

In the dark sanctuary of my soul, I prayed to Siva. I begged forgiveness for my deception, my abandonment of my gods in a feigned conversion. Surely Siva would understand that in this Muslim world, I, a poor Hindu, could only advance my own small ambition—to survive by declaring, with my lips only, to be of their faith. If f should live, I would perform puja; I would have *homam* performed to his divine presence; I would give all my savings to his temple; I would feed the poor; I would make pilgrimage to Varanasi, Badrinath, wherever he demanded. In humility I would shave my head.

My prayers were interrupted by a swelling murmur from the men. The Muslim warriors began to shout, softly at first, then louder: '*Ba-kush, Ba-kush*', the Hindus: '*Mar, Mar*'. In my fervour I shouted also: 'Mar, Mar.' Shah Jahan, startled, turned. 'You too wish to kill, do you, Isa? We will give you a sword.' His own weapon was suddenly placed in my hand. In the confusion, he failed to hear—or possibly he had, and thought it of no importance—that I had given the Hindu cry.

The enemy moved towards us, a mass of dust, horses, men, elephants. They seemed only to want to roll over us inexorably and crush us. They had no strategy, save the clash of force against force. Shah Jahan laughed when he saw how close they huddled, unable to deal with the twenty thousand horsemen closing in on their flanks. They had some small arms but no cannon. When they were within range, Shah Jahan lifted his right arm and waved forward. Our cannons immediately opened fire. Furrows of flesh and metal were cut in the ranks of the enemy. Once more the cannon fired, more furrows. The screams of men and beasts were muted, unable to lift themselves above the continual thunder of jezails and cannon. Shah Jahan stretched both arms wide apart and slowly brought them together until his palms touched. In the hazy distance, blue with smoke, brown with dust, I saw the horsemen attacking the flanks. The sun glittered on swords and blood, steel hit steel, elephants trumpeted, horses screamed. Men hacked men as if they were trees to be lopped, limbs and heads fell, bellies opened and gushed blood. The earth absorbed it, turning dull and dark. The air rang with the chants of battle, with the call to kill: 'Ba-kush, Ba-kush; Mar, Mar.' Bairam stood immovable: none of the enemy could reach us.

At midday, the battle ceased. The enemy fled, abandoning weapons, their dead, the wounded animals and the crying men. Five thousand of them died, one thousand eight hundred and fifty of our men. The Mughal army went through the battlefield, plunging swords into the dying, removing gold rings and valuables from the dead. I looked up; vultures circled overhead. How did they know? Did the sound of battle reach those scaly ears? Did the gods whisper the news in the winds? They came from all directions, beating at the air as if applauding the slaughter. Shabash, shabash.

1028/AD 1618

Arjumand

A gold chair was placed beside the throne of the emperor, but Shah

Jahan remained where he was, seated on cushions in front of the throne. To one side was a huge golden plate filled with precious stones, diamonds, rubies, emeralds, pearls. Beside it was another filled with gold coin. His brothers stood behind him, and behind them were ranked the nobles of the court.

'You're quiet,' Mehrunissa said.

'I am feeling very proud.' I rested my forehead against the cold lattice. I hoped there need be no more victories. It was a relief to leave the Deccan and return to the cool air of Agra, refreshing, after the stifling heat of the south. I prayed the empire would lie still for many years and that we could live together in the serenity of our love. 'But I am a bit tired. It is all the excitement. Each time we return, my prince rises in the estimation of his father, but I hope there will be some peace now, so that we can live normal lives.'

'Shah Jahan is a great leader. Everything depends on his father and the troubles of the empire.'

'Send Mahabat Khan next time, please, Aunt. I would like to stay here for a while.'

Who asked you to march with him? If Jahangir went to the Deccan, I'd quite happily send him off and stay here.'

'We promised each other never to be apart.'

She shrugged. Then be it on your own head. You're mad to want to go with him everywhere.'

'He wishes it too.'

'Next time, stay in Agra.' She peered at me through the shadow. 'You look tired.' Her hand touched the curve of my belly. 'Again. Do you two never stop? You must rest, Arjumand. Refuse him.'

'How can I?' I couldn't help my tears marring this great occasion. 'I couldn't bear to see him sad.'

'Let him be sad,' Mehrunissa said harshly. 'What does he think you are, a cow? In five years you have had five babies.'

'Four,' I said absentmindedly. This is the fifth. The first was not born.'

That is more than enough. Send him to another woman to slake his lust. My God, the man must be a bull to make such demands of you.' Her voice lowered. 'I don't permit Jahangir to lie with me more than once a month. If his lust cannot be controlled, I tell him to sleep with one of the slaves. Let me present you with some female slaves.'

No. I will satisfy my husband as long as he desires only me. He has not taken another wife, nor has he wished to lie with any other woman.'

But each time you conceive another baby. Look at your body; look at mine.'

Her waist was slim, her skin shone with health, her long black hair fell in thick ropes to her waist. I couldn't deny her youth; mine appeared to be fading, like a rose petal pressed between the pages of a book, thin, worn, fragile. 'I don't look old.'

'You will if you continue to make babies. Don't you see the peasant women? Fat, ugly and heavy, surrounded by brats? You will begin to look like that.' She gave me a sly look: 'Obviously you must enjoy it yourself. But too much enjoyment is also bad.'

I couldn't deny the enjoyment. At times, it was more than physical. I could not be aroused to the same fervour of passion as he, nor feel the lust I had felt as a young girl. My body felt remote, as if I lived in another world and couldn't feel the touch of his lips and hands, nor the insistent movements of his body. Yet, looking up at him absorbed in his pleasure, I too felt an enjoyment. If my body's ecstasy was a pretence, that in my heart was not. On the night of his victory, I could not command my body to spring attentive to his touch. It lay passive, hurting still from Raushanara's birth. The soreness had remained longer than before, my passage felt inflamed with his thrusting. Battle aroused him; my love calmed him. I loved him; I could not deny him.

'Use your hand,' Mehrunissa said.

'I tried. He doesn't enjoy it.'

'What kind of a man is he? They don't care how their juice is drawn from them, as long as it is. Boys, other men, goats, cows . . .

'He only wants to lie with me.'

She raised an eyebrow to heaven, then fell into pensive silence, her chin resting on her fist, staring at Shah Jahan. I should not discuss our love with her. With Mehrunissa it became a state matter. Who knew how she would distort even such a private thing to her own ends?

The dundhubi beat the approach of Jahangir. Behind him came my father, carrying a heavy leather-bound book, Jahangir walked slowly, leaning against my grandfather. He seemed to have aged, while Mehrunissa only grew younger. He stopped once to gasp in air, as if he couldn't draw enough into his body.

'He doesn't look well.'

'He's in excellent health,' she said sharply. There's nothing wrong with the Emperor, so don't start spreading rumours, otherwise you will get into trouble.' Her anger failed to hide the uncertainty in her voice. The Emperor will live for many, many years.'

'Of course he will,' I countered sincerely, and for the moment she was comforted.

Instead of mounting the throne, Jahangir went to Shah Jahan and kissed him fondly. They embraced each other with great affection, then turned, arms around each other, to face the nobles.

'I am proud of my son, Shah Jahan. Once more he has proved himself to be a great warrior. He has defeated those Deccani rats. They lost one battle and, like the cowards they become when the Great Mughal approaches, they have given up the war they threatened. Peace, they cry to Shah Jahan. They accepted all my terms, and the treasury now overflows with their tributes.'

The emperor spoke for an hour, pausing only now and then to breathe very deeply, as if he were drowning, and to allow the nobles to express their enthusiasm: Zindabad Shah Jahan, Zindabad. He would have read out his poem in praise of Shah Jahan, but it was mislaid and could not be found.

When the oration was over, Shah Jahan sat down again on the

cushions. Attendants carried one of the gold plates to the emperor, and he dipped his cupped hands into a mound of precious stones, then poured them over Shah Jahan's head like water. The rainbow of stones cascaded down on my beloved; like dew they clung to his turban, his sleeves, gathered in shining pools on his lap and around him.

Again Jahangir poured the diamonds and rubies, and again and again until the plate was emptied. Then other attendants held forward the plate filled with gold coins. They fell like drops of sunlight. Shah Jahan kept his head bowed, as the coins clattered and rolled over him. It was the darshan of a father's love and trust. If there had been a more precious element in the empire, Jahangir would have used it to bless his son.

Still the lavish show of affection was not yet over. Jahangir took the volume from my father and held it above his head, as if it were the highest symbol of his limitless authority.

The most precious gift a father can give his son is the sum of his thoughts. Through them he imparts not only his love, but his experience, his observations, his knowledge. This is the first copy of the *Jahangir-nama*. Shah Jahan will find things in this volume that he may disagree with, but that is his choice. But he will not discover any untruth about my affection for him. In all respects he is the first of my sons, and I pray to Allah that this, my most precious gift, will be the cause of good fortune for him. Other copies have been despatched to the cities of the empire so that all may know of a father's love for his son.'

Shah Jahan humbly received the book. He kissed the covering, and his father's hand. Jahangir helped him to stand and led him to the gold chair by the throne. He seated Shah Jahan in it, then took his place on the throne. No prince had ever before been allowed to be seated in the presence of his father at court. His rank was also raised to thirty thousand zat and twenty thousand sowar.

I was the first to read the book. It was a thing of rare beauty. Paintings adorned every other page, most of them executed by

Jahangir's favourite artist, the Hindu, Bishandas. I did not read it merely for the praises of my beloved—admittedly I lingered over those more than other passages, my fingers caressing his name—but to try to understand Jahangir. He wrote of many things: of Laila and Majnun, his cranes who had been captured when a month old, and raised by his own hand. They had travelled with him to all parts of the empire so that he could observe their habits, how they pecked each other to signal change when they hatched their eggs, how the mother fed grasshoppers and locusts to her young. He told how, observing a star fall from the skies, he rode out to its grave, had it dug up and discovered that it was made of metal. He had had one sword, the Alamgir, fashioned from the star. In order to discover the true nature of courage, Jahangir had ordered that a lion's intestines be closely examined to discover the source of its bravery, but he could find no physical explanation. Nothing in his vast empire was unimportant to him, be it miracles or daily administration, natural wonders or a method of breeding pigs. I learned much about my father-in-law from the *Jahangir-nama*, including the admission that he had ordered the murder of his father's favourite courtier, Abdul Fazl, and that he had thrown the man's head into the latrine. His book was honest, he even confessed that he drank too much: twenty flasks of wine laced with fourteen berries of opium every day. He also recorded the tragedy of his unrequited love for his father, Akbar. Love can wound, for its lack or for its abundance!

It was noon, but the sky was dark as dusk when Aurangzeb was born. The earth was wet with rain, and the trees and grass and plants were vivid green like a parrot's plumage. The nights were noisy with the endless chant of frogs. The monsoons pounded the earth, bent and broke trees like twigs, shaped a new course for the river that roared and thundered past the palace red with silt as if blood mixed with the waters. Water dripped from leaf to leaf, from roof to gutter, collected in ankle-deep pools in the courtyards. And each time it paused to take breath, the air smelled clean.

It was in such a cauldron, in a season when the night was turned to day with cold blue flashes of lightning and thunder shaking the walls of the palace, that Aurangzeb first cried. He cried not from fear—his dark eyes looked on all fearlessly, he listened without cowering to the din of nature—but somehow in anger. He raged, his clenched fist beat the air as if to hurl the thunderbolts back up to the sky. He was a thin baby and I did not expect him to live, except that I saw the fierceness of his spirit, a determination to survive. He hovered then between the sky and the earth, battling against the elements within and without. With such a presence of death in him, how could I love him? I turned away and allowed others to nurse him. If he should die, I wouldn't suffer.

But he lived. Jahangir's personal astrologer, Jatik Ray, corpulent with success, cast his horoscope. In the flickering candlelight the shadows leapt and danced in brooding celebration, and he made his calculations. The paper was damp with moisture, the ink ran like black tears from the written numbers. We waited. My new son, lying in the arms of Satium-nissa, apparently took an interest as well; there was curiosity in his tiny, wizened face. I felt a foreboding I could not understand. It was the thunder, I suspected, changing the mood of us all, quiescent, lurking, waiting to rage when the lightning ceased. 'Greatness,' Jatik Ray whispered finally. 'His are the stars of a great king. He will rule over an empire even larger than this. Surya rules his life, he will shake the world.' Jatik Ray stopped, as if he could not read further portents in the life of my son.

'Tell us,' Shah Jahan commanded.

'It will be a sad life; I cannot foretell more, except, Jatik Ray assured us hastily, 'that it will be a great one.

He could say no more, but closed his books, stealing another surreptitious look at the child before he left.

'He tells us the same things for every one of our children,' Shah Jahan laughed. 'Even Jahanara. I believe only his predictions for Dara, because I know what he will become when I die. It is I who control their destinies, not the stars or the numbers cast by that fool.'

With the great wealth the Padishah had showered on my beloved, the gold and precious stones, the rank of commander of thirty thousand zat and ten lakh sowar, I could afford to build hospitals and schools for the poor. The hospitals were for the women for they had need of the greatest care: their worth was less than that of the cows that roamed the streets of Agra, scavenging fruits and vegetables and rubbish. What chance had they, when I myself could not prevent the continual filling of my womb with the seed of Shah Jahan. Like me they could only protest in mute silence and carry the burdens in their bellies like stones of servitude. My own hakim, Wazir Khan, attended them in their misery, and I visited them daily in the company of Isa. But even I could not change the custom of educating only the male children. The schools were not only for Muslim boys, but Hindu and Sikh, and every other religion in the land. The female children I could not rescue from the prison of their homes and the drudgery of domestic work.

My activities had attracted the attention of Mehrunissa. I heard the whisper that came from her, it was a warning: she already behaves as if she were empress. The people's needs are the concern of the Padishah, not her.

Mehrunissa, Mehrunissa, Mehrunissa. The dundhubi beat her name solemnly across the empire. The heart of its power was in her hand: she stretched a finger, taxes were raised or lowered; another finger, an official fell or rose; a third, and commerce ceased or flowed anew; a fourth, and laws were enacted and repealed. Jahangir still played at being emperor, holding daily audience with his ministers in the ghusl-khana, revealing himself in the jharoka-i-darshan at dawn and again

207

late in the afternoon. At that hour, when the shadow of the fort fell across the maidan, he would come to watch the elephants fight, or the executions. The methods of punishment were chosen to suit the crimes; the crushing of a man's head by an elephant (it was said Akbar had a beast which would make its own judgement as to whether a man should die or live), disembowelment or the executioner's sword, or … there were many, all performed on the maidan.

But Mehrunissa ruled. The murmurings of the nobles were soft, insidious; they were meant not to reach the ears of Jahangir, only of those who were receptive, those who desired an end to her authority. But the emperor and empress were so close to each other that it was impossible to divide them.

These were not my concerns. I only listened for whispers against my beloved, and there were none. He remained in favour with Jahangir, spending much time in his father's company. His cause was strongly supported by my own father and grandfather, and if Mehrunissa thought differently, she never spoke out loud to either of them.

My indifference was also personal, deeply personal, and there was, besides, something else to occupy my thoughts. The seed of Shah Jahan had lodged once more in my belly. I could no longer remember when these conceptions occurred. I had been so innocently joyous at Dara's birth, but during the others, I cared not even which season it was. I told no one but, claiming a mild illness, had Isa fetch Wazir Khan. When he came I ordered the women to stand on the far side of the room out of our hearing, but within sight, for I could not be attended alone by a man. I lay on the divan, shielded from his eyes by a heavy curtain. He knelt beside me, and thrust his hand through the opening. I held it, and heard his startled exclamation. I should have guided it for his examination. Some women use illness only as an excuse to feel a man's caress.

'I know the symptoms. You don't have to examine me.'

'Again? It is too soon, your Highness. I told you that at least a year should pass; your body must rest. Your spirit is very, strong, but alas, your body cannot match that strength.'

Tell my husband. I cannot refuse him.' I squeezed his hand. 'I want you to give me a potion.' I heard again the treachery of my own words, the drumming of blood in my face. I wanted to murder the seed of my beloved prince, my own heartbeat.

'Your Highness, it is not wise to administer it so late. One hundred days have passed.'

'I will make the judgement of what is good or bad, you fool.' I meant no rudeness, but was unable to contain my fearful impatience, the dread of that enormous weight crushing my bones, my blood, my belly.

'Your body will grow used to it, and each time will throw out the child. This is your sixth conception.'

'And it will be the last. Bring your potion to me personally or accept the consequences of my anger. No, no, I'm sorry. I spoke from despair. I will give you gold.'

'I have served you long, your Highness. I will do as you command, not for gold, only because it is what you wish. But next time, even should you order my execution, I will refuse. One day you might not recover from the sickness it brings on in your belly. Refuse your husband.'

'Yes, it would be better to refuse, but for how long can I plead exhaustion?'

'A year or two.'

I could not help laughing.

'Would you remain without a woman for so long?'

'I have four wives, your highness, so none is abused by my need. Shah Jahan should . . .'

'That is enough.'

He fell silent immediately; gently he removed his hand and left. There came an urgent, uneven clatter of feet on the marble floor.

'Agachi,' Isa called. 'I have heard that the emperor is ill. Some say he is dying . . . .'

the sixteen

the taj mahal 1050/AD 1640

The tomb was a skeleton, its spindly bleached bones silhouetted against the clear night sky and the sturdy brick scaffolding. It was lifeless, cold. Shah Jahan had imagined light and space; instead it was oppressive, a dead thing. It weighed him down. He had failed. He beat his head; the attendants feared his rage. Afandi sweated and coughed out the dust that hung in the central chamber. The floor underfoot was covered with rubble, the air dank with mortar, raw stone, the sweat of thousands. Above him, the dome was like a smashed skull, revealing the heavens. When completed it would weigh twelve hundred tons. He prayed. He saw the lips of Muhammed Hanif, Sattar Khan, Chiranji Lal, Baldeodas, Abdul Haqq move silently. The others had furtively receded into the darker shadow.

'It is as yet incomplete, Padishah,' Isa interrupted.

Shah Jahan spun around, his sarapa throwing shadows over the walls, as if a great bird's wing were beating there. He noted who spoke, who interrupted, and the glare died. The sarapa settled on him and lay still, a hawk's plumage smoothed.

'Soon it must be. Soon. Do you hear me, Hanif?' Shah Jahan peered into the shadow. Hanif, the chief stonemason, reluctantly detached himself from the protection of the others.

'It will be done, Padishah. Very soon,' he spoke softly, placatingly.

211

The walls and the balconies were completed, but there were still great gaps where the jalis would go, where the windows would be fitted; they were not Hanif's responsibility. Others should accept blame. Already the smaller domes were nearly finished. The hall in which the men stood already soared eighty feet above them and their voices echoed in the vast space.

The emperor looked round. Workmen crowded the corners, peered down on him from balconies, stared up from below, unmoving, silent as if each dark body had been chiselled into the white stone for eternity. His presence had frozen them, crouched, kneeling, standing, carving, carrying. Only when he had departed did they move and breathe and whisper: the Padishah, the Padishah.

Sita screamed. Murthi, waiting outside, started up and then settled back on his haunches. The women were with her. He sucked a beedi and with each pull of smoke, breathed; Ram, Ram. It must be a boy. One son is not enough. She screamed again. Gopi and Savitri clutched at him in terror. He held them. It is only a baby, he calmed them— dismissing her suffering. It was his dharma to make children; his woman's to bear them. He was proud of himself; his loins held power. With luck, news of this birth would reach the ears of his protector. Perhaps a gift would be sent, a silver cup or even a gold one for a son. He was no closer to the solution of that puzzle; it made his head ache. All these years, the shadow had hovered protectively, invisible only because it hid behind the walls of the fort. He shuddered at the memory of his suffering at the hands of the wazir.

The wazir had taken him to a corner of the site away from the others, furtively.

'Who are you?'

212

'Murthi. I carve the jali.'

'I didn't ask what you do, fool. Do you know Isa?'

'No. Who is Isa?'

'I ask the questions, fool. Isa, the emperor's servant, his slave, the lackey who walks in his shadow.'

'Bahadur,' Murthi spoke boldly, 'how would I know a man of such standing? I am just a carver. I work for Baldeodas.'

'You signed that petition.'

Murthi thought about denying it, but he could not. His swift bravery drained away. He had done it for his wife, his children, other men's children. A man could not die without performing one act of courage. He had done his, now he had to accept the consequences.

'Yes. Have I angered the Emperor?'

'Of course.'

'But he did give us food.'

'That doesn't lessen his anger. He sent me to find you. I can curb his rage, if you will tell me what you know of Isa.'

'Nothing, Bahadur. I know nothing of this Isa. I have told you that.'

'Then I cannot help you. You will have to suffer. Come.'

The wazir gripped Murthi's arm and marched him away from the site, along the river and into the fort. Murthi stared around him in terror. No one paid any attention, they did not notice him as they performed their various tasks. He was taken to the far side of the fort, to dark and forbidding buildings, and handed over to a soldier. He did not hear what the wazir whispered, but the soldier grabbed him roughly, removed keys from a wall, and took him into total darkness where countless men and women lay, some crying, others silent, hopeless. He was thrust into a cell, the door slammed. Murthi found himself in the company of thieves, murderers, adulterers. He wept, unable to comprehend his crime. He carved gods; how could they permit this injustice? For two days he crouched there, silent, sullen, always afraid. On the third the door opened and a jailer called.

'Murthi!'

Murthi shuffled through the stink of his fellow prisoners, his feet clinging to the filthy earth floor. He sensed the end.

'You are Murthi? Hurry, I don't have all day.'

The jailer led him into bright, dazzling sunlight. A soldier waited. He was not grabbed roughly, but touched lightly.

'Follow me.'

He followed the soldier numbly, and suddenly found himself outside the gates of the fort.

'*Chulo-ji, chulo*,' the soldier shooed him away and turned his back.

Murthi stumbled away, bemused by what had happened. Then, starting from his stupor, he bolted. He ran towards the river, terrified of being caught again in the nightmare. He saw that a crowd had gathered on the maidan below the jharoka-i-darshan, where Shah Jahan sat on his golden throne, looking down. It was afternoon and Murthi crept along with the crowd to observe the tamasha. An elephant stood swaying in the centre of the maidan, in front of a stained wooden block; flies buzzed around it. A group of men wearing tight-fitting caps walked out from the fort. Between them they held a fainting man. Murthi stared, barely recognizing the ashen face, slack with terror; it was the arrogant wazir. The man was hurled to the ground. The executioners placed his head on the block, others held his arms and legs. He screamed as the shadow of the elephant fell on him. The great beast lifted its right leg on command, held it a moment as if to find its balance, then delicately, slowly, brought its foot down on the wazir's head. The executioners leapt away nimbly as the skull burst. Murthi turned and pushed through the crowd, shaking with fright. It could have been him, not the wazir, who was held under the elephant. Who had reversed their fortunes? Could it have been the mysterious Isa? Whoever he was, Murthi was determined to find out about the man.

'Hazoor, you have a son,' the women called to him.

Murthi beamed, clapped, and hurried inside. Sita lay stunned and tired, wet with sweat; her face had the calm placid look of one who has gone through immense agony. Murthi examined the child. A boy. A boy. Now his old age was assured of comfort.

1054/AD 1644

Isa watched Shah Jahan settle on the platform. It was the emperor's birthday. Twice a year, according to the solar and lunar calendar, the emperor's weight was matched in gold. This was a Hindu tradition, *tuladana*, adopted by Humayun over one hundred years earlier. Each successive Mughal had followed the custom. This was Shah Jahan's lunar birth date, and the ceremony was held in the privacy of the haram, whereas the solar ceremony was performed in public. The ladies jostled around the scales. The stand was made of gold and stood as tall as a man. From the gold crossbar hung the platform on one end, and on the other a great bowl to receive the coins. Slaves placed bags of gold coin in the bowl, piling them carefully, until the emperor was slowly lifted from the ground. The ladies shouted and clapped, Shah Jahan smiled and the tally was taken. He weighed one hundred and sixty-two pounds. The gold coins were removed to be distributed to the poor.

Shah Jahan's pleasure was brief. It was as if the light were extinguished in his eyes. He left the ladies to enjoy the celebration feast and listen to the singers, and hurried down the haram corridors. Isa followed. They entered a corner room. Moonlight pierced the jali, silvering the marble. The hakim kneeling by the divan immediately rose from attending the still figure. Shah Jahan waved him back.

'How is she?'

'Your majesty, she scarcely breathes, and there is little I can do. I have placed cool cloths on her body.'

Shah Jahan knelt by Jahanara. He could not bear to look on his beloved daughter, the image of Arjumand. She had been desecrated. Her face and body were brutally scarred, the skin black; he could still smell the odour of burning. Twenty days ago her clothes had caught fire from a dropped candle, and two of her maids had died trying to smother the flames that enveloped her body.

'Jahanara, Jahanara,' he whispered. She could not reply. He scarcely saw her body rise or fall to breathe. Her hair was stubbled, her skull charred.

'Great wealth awaits you, if you save her life.'

'We can but pray to Allah,' the hakim replied, praying he could save her—for the Padishah's gifts would make him rich beyond greed.

Dara was there too, his eyes sunken with the exhaustion of the long vigil by his sister's side, and he rocked in prayer. Isa stood, remembering Arjumand's screams fading into the harsh Deccan hills. For what had she borne all that pain? For this, her disfigured image lying on the divan in terrible agony? Jahanara whimpered, echoing her mother all those years ago, and Isa remembered the sunny child, loved almost as much as Dara. He stifled his affection with each wave of pain that washed through the princess's ruined body. It could not be helped, the body was not of iron, or stone, and broke easily under the onslaught of pain.

He heard a commotion outside and looked out into the corridor. Striding swiftly towards him, his shadow rising and fading along the walls, came Aurangzeb. His clothes and face were dusty, sweat cut ravines down his face; he reeked of effort and exhaustion. He had ridden swiftly from the Deccan, a journey which would have broken a lesser man. Aurangzeb moved erect, coiled, as if pain were not within his understanding.

'Isa, she lives?'

'Barely, your Highness.'

Aurangzeb plucked the dagger from his belt, and handed it to Isa.
The prince bowed to Shah Jahan, ignored Dara and knelt down beside
Jahanara. His black eyes glistened. In his young, turbulent life, she had
been his closest companion. He held the beads in his clasped hands
and prayed. He neither wept nor wailed; his prayer was silent, fierce.
He did not observe the emperor stare at him with astonishment, as
though he saw a ghost. Astonishment gave way to suspicion, the
emperor's eyes narrowed with mistrust. Dara leaned over and
whispered in his father's ear. Aurangzeb's sudden appearance had made
him uneasy too.

'Who told you to come?' Shah Jahan asked.

Aurangzeb made no reply. His prayer continued. Respecting this,
Shah Jahan waited.

'Who asked you to come?'

'No one. She is my sister, and I was afraid for her life. I could not
wait uselessly out there.'

'You rode alone?'

'The Emperor's son cannot ride alone.'

'How many?'

'Five thousand horsemen.'

Shah Jahan cocked a mocking eyebrow.

'So many? Is Aurangzeb afraid he will be attacked? Or does he plan
an attack?'

'Neither.' Aurangzeb looked at his father. His eyes were neither
defiant nor fawning. His stare was flat, as if they were equals. 'My rank
is fifty thousand zat, I came with but a handful. Whom can they harm?'

'No one.' Shah Jahan said coldly. 'You will return immediately to
your post. How dare you leave it without my permission? You and
your men will leave this very hour. How long did the journey take
you?'

'Ten days and nights.'

'So long?' Shah Jahan mocked.

217

The Quran commands us to pray five times each day, and I obeyed it.'

'You will return in nine and pray six times. And remain there until I, your emperor, give you permission to wander all over the country. Go.'

Aurangzeb's lips tightened. It was impossible to tell whether he meant to smile or snarl. He bowed to his father, stared for a long time at Jahanara, his face softening, then turned and left the chamber. Isa followed, holding out the prince's dagger.

'I will arrange for you to bathe and eat, your Highness.'

'You heard my father,' Aurangzeb said. 'I cannot stay.' He hesitated, glancing back to the room, as if he wished to question Isa, then stopped himself. But Isa sensed the question. The baffled expression was so familiar: What have I done? Why does he not love me?

But Aurangzeb only gripped Isa's arm, then strode back down the corridor, his shadow darkening and fading behind him.

1056/AD 1646

Reverently, Murthi carried Durga to the temple, wrapped in a gunny sack. She was not heavy, but Murthi stopped to rest often. He did not wish to fall and shatter the marble, perhaps break one of her arms. She had used up so many years of his life. It was piety, rather than the labour and time he had spent on her which prompted his great care— if you harmed Durga, she harmed you; but goodness was repaid with goodness.

The temple was nearly finished. It was tiny. The gopuram touched the lower branch of a banyan tree and the *garbhagriha* was barely the height of a man. Sunlight turned the marble walls a mottled lemon-yellow. The low outer wall of brick, built to satisfy tradition rather than for protection, had yet to be completed. Chiranji Lal and a small delegation waited. A priest had journeyed all the way from Varanasi to consecrate the idol. Great mounds of rice, ghee, milk, honey, curd, incense, coconuts, plantains and flowers lay waiting. The puja, which varied in length according to its importance, would take not hours, but days. The Brahmin was a slim young man, smug with learning but lacking in experience. He was bare-chested, with the sacred thread crossing his shoulder down to his waist. A knot of hair sprang from his shaven skull like a spring of water from rock. Musicians with flutes and tablas sat on a faded carpet to me side. The priest took the idol, unwrapped it, and carefully positioned it on the platform. Durga's arms sprang from her body like branches. Murthi had painted her crown gold, and the border of her sari blue and silver. Her breasts were voluptuous. She sat on the lion as if it were a throne. Her expression bore the most subtle hint of a smile. You had to look carefully to see exactly how it was done, just a faint tilt in the lips. The goddess stood half in shadow, half in sunlight, accidentally reflecting the spiritual division of her world. Murthi heard the awed intake of breath and felt immeasurable pride in his achievement. This was his dharma; to carve gods. Murthi the Acharya.

'I cannot stay here,' he was regretful, though he had often witnessed this ceremony. The *sastras* would have to be recited in their entirety, the idol dipped in the river, bathed in milk, honey and ghee, fires lit to consume the rice and ghee. Only then could it be installed in the garbhagriha. Between it and the pedestal would be a thin copper plate: the deity's true power arose from the symbols etched in the plate The men understood; he was employed to carve the jali. He took darshan from the priest and returned to his work.

The jali lay on the dusty earth, half completed. It looked half clothed too, a little like the priest, the lower portion draped with crude marble. The graceful stem sprang from the ugly mass, so delicate and fragile that it was not possible to believe they were of the same stone. One soared; the other lay inert.

'How is your mother?' he asked Gopi as he began work, tap, tap, tap.

'She weeps and lies with her eyes shut tight.' The boy's face was lined with worry.

'She is tired from work, but she will soon recover. She is not as strong as she used to be.'

He worked all day in concentrated silence until the light began to fade. He had barely revealed one leaf. It sprang from the mass, only the tip showing, bent to an unfelt breeze.

They walked slowly, Murthi stiffly after his labours. He smelled the smoke of cooking fires, caught odours of food in the currents of air. Mumtazabad was clean and orderly. It might have been in existence for centuries. It had a settled, familiar feel to him, as if he were in his own village. The streets, the people, even the pi-dogs were all familiar now. He felt at peace. The idol was completed; only the jali remained. A few more years, then they could return, not rich, but comfortable. He looked back, catching a glimpse of the incomplete dome rising up through the trees. The sun had turned it a luminous pink. The rest of the tomb was shrouded by the brick scaffolding. When he returned home he would tell his old friends of this wonder. Doubtless, they would not believe him. Men needed to see it before they could understand. A sketch in dirt was only dirt, the imagination could not transform it into marble, could not make it soar into the sky. He wished the great tomb were complete. He would like to see where they placed his jali, how it would catch and break the light, how the shadows would fall on the marble floor. It did not matter that his name would never be known, that was unimportant. Who knew the names of the rishis or the men who built the great temples of Varanasi or who carved gods on the sides of hills and in caves? Life was duty.

Women crowded the entrance to his home, crouched and whispering, peering in.

His heart thumped.

'What has happened?'

'Sita is dying.'

220

He pushed through. Sita lay, barely breathing. Her face was still, pale; he knew the signs of a life slipping away, unchallenged.

'Go,' Murthi ordered Gopi. 'Run to the fort. Tell the soldiers to inform Isa that my wife Sita is dying. We need the hakim. Run.'

the seventeen love story 1031/AD 1621

Arjumand

I grieved when my grandfather died. A part of me ceased to exist; he took it with him. We begin life whole, the sum of many people: fathers, mothers, grandfathers, brothers, cousins, sisters. And then, as they die, one by one, each death lessens that whole. We shrink, we shrivel, whittled down until all that remains from the subtraction is our self.

He died in his sleep. We were summoned, and I looked on his calm, peaceful face. It was difficult to imagine the youth who had journeyed from Persia to seek his fortune in the service of the Great Mughal Akbar. The youth was hidden inside the old body, hidden by the folds of silks, hidden by the grief of the Great Mughal Jahangir, the Empress Nur Jehan, the Prince Shah Jahan, the Princess Arjumand, Princess Ladilli. Princes, nobles, ranas, nawabs, amirs, all came to pay their respects to the starving boy hidden in the great man. Jahangir had ordered a month of mourning for the death of his Itiam-ud-daulah, his Pillar of Government, his wise counsellor, his companion.

I kissed him, familiar odour of his scent was fading, already the sour stink of death hissed out from within. My beloved kissed him and wept too. They had grown close, the old man and the young, as if each sought the other's protection. Mehrunissa wept loudest. He had not

222

only been father, but her friend and adviser, her mentor. He had guided her destiny as God had guided his. She seemed more than bereaved; for days she appeared to be in a dream. She neither ate nor drank, but sat staring out at the waters of the Jumna. For years she had leant on her father and could now barely support herself. But her subdued state did not last long. Though death always waited its turn, Mehrunissa consumed life. Jahangir granted her permission to construct a tomb for the Itiam-ud-daulah. It was to be built in the city, on the banks of the Jumna. She hurled her great energy into choosing the builders and the design. She knew what she wanted.

Jahangir thought it ironic that he had skilfully evaded death, that instead it had fallen on Ghiyas Beg. His own illness lingered on, left its marks on his face. He found it difficult to breathe in the dry heat, and constantly wished to move further north. His love was Kashmir. He was eager to sit in the gardens he had designed and watch his fish, each wearing a gold ring, swim among the fountains. But his reason for going there was not only his health; he looked wistfully north to the great mountains beyond their barriers of rock and snow, towards the land of his ancestors. I had heard it whispered he wished to conquer that land. He dreamed of ruling Samarkand.

I had been unhappy, too, in the year before my grandfather's death. There were reasons for this: I was to bear yet another child. Once more my belly swelled, once more the despair descended on my spirit. The last time, the hakim's potion had succeeded, and I had been ill and weak for days, the divan constantly stained with blood. But the release from the stone in my womb had been a comfort in my drugged mind then.

Afterwards, I decided to resist my beloved more firmly. When we lay together he could sense the stiffening of my body as he caressed my breasts—how sad they looked, they were veined like marble, and they

223

felt weary with their weight.

'Again?' he whispered harshly. How swiftly time carries slights, as if they had occurred a moment ago. 'I feel I am lying with a corpse.'

'Why do you say such cruel things to me?'

'Because you no longer love me.' He spoke spitefully, triumphant as a boy wishing the accusation to be denied.

'I do love you. My love has not changed from the first moment I saw you.'

'Then why do you deny me?' He lay back, no longer addressing me but the ceiling, wanting me to beg his forgiveness. Oh, the weary hurt of loving. 'If you still loved me you would be eager for me to lie with you.'

'I'm tired. I have recently lost a child, and my body still aches.'

'I wonder how you lost my child,' he said, deceptively innocent beneath the cruelty of his demands for inexhaustible love. 'Twice now. How many more times will that happen?'

'Such things happen to a woman. Who can predict them?' I whispered fearfully. I could not tell whether he had guessed, or whether he knew. I prayed he had not heard a false note in my denial.

'I know,' he held me tenderly, his anger suddenly dissolved. 'Men cannot understand the pain of women. I am always greedy for you. I cannot hold my love in check. Each time I see you, I only wish to kiss your face and eyes, embrace your body, lie between your legs.' His lips brushed mine. They were soft like petals, gentle, forgiving, as if it were I who had sinned.

'When you are better, we will love each other, I can wait.'

'It will be some time. The hakim said I should rest before I have another child.'

'Forever?' The harshness came and went, like breath escaping in the cold, and I could not control his fear, his anger.

'Of course not. I do not mind if you lie with one of the slave girls until I am ready for you.'

'So that is all you think I'm worth—to lie with a slave girl. You're too good for me now.'

'Please, you twist my words to suit your own meaning.'

'What other meaning can they have?'

He sat up, his back rigid with fury. I touched, he winced as if my fingers were coals. But if my touch could hurt him, his words burned me. I could only placate him by submitting to his love, but I could not do it. The power of his seed frightened me; it was unimaginable. Neither his father, nor grandfather, nor great-grandfather could so swiftly fill a woman's womb, and keep it filled as if it were a gourd. Our few pleasurable hours alone together were lost now, wrecked by his anger, spoiled by my stubbornness. Why was love so difficult, demanding, exhausting?

'None other than what I meant.'

He half turned, startled at my raised voice. I defied his stare, refusing to lower my gaze coyly.

'Your father and grandfather lay with their slave women. If you cannot control your lust, spend your juices in them. Look at me. I am a woman, and I love you, but you treat me like a brood-mare in your stables. Children, children, children—how can I care for you if I spend my life broken under the weight of your child pressing on me like a stone?'

'Maybe I should take a second wife.'

'And a third and a fourth and a fifth. Akbar took four hundred. What stops you? Let them exhaust themselves.'

He bowed his head and was silent. Finally, I turned away from him and shut my eyes, I did not wish to remember our words, the anger in his face, the sound of my strident voice.

'I could not,' he said softly.

Before I could embrace him and beg his forgiveness, he was gone. For thirty-five days no word was spoken between us. We had promised never to live apart and here we were, in such close proximity to each other, yet all the empire could well have lain between us. This pain was worse. If we were apart, I would know he still loved me. Here, he kept himself aloof and occupied, not even glancing towards the zenana as he came and went. I watched, not only with my own eyes, but with others: Isa, Allami Sa'du-lla Khan, Satium-nissa, Wazir Khan, all watched. Did he weep? Did he whisper my name? Did he too feel as if he were a living corpse? No, they replied, their voices hushed in deference to my sorrow, he laughs and plays. So I did likewise. I invited all the nobles' wives to dine at the palace. Dancers and singers entertained us each evening. I laughed too loudly, talked too much, applauded until my palms ached. I hardly knew how to live in such emptiness, in such hollow gaiety.

'Isa. You will construct a small stall in the garden where he sits. Do it swiftly, quietly. It must be ready tonight.'

How could a prince bow his head in humility to a woman? He was made of gold and marble, but I was only made of flesh and nothing could be as terrible as the pain of living without Shah Jahan's love. I would submit willingly to the most demeaning humility. The pain could be no worse. But what if he should reject my offering? I could not bear to think of that.

I put on my yellow churidar and blouse and touca. My silver jewellery was no longer a mere handful, now it filled boxes. I chose only what I remembered. Isa made the stall, covered it with carpet. I took my place and spread my wares. The night was so quiet; the moon hung in the water like a silver sword.

'Will he come?' Isa asked.

'I don't know. Pray that he will. Bring wine. Order the musicians to remain silent until he enters the garden.'

'Do you wish me to stay?'

'Yes … no … stand there.'

He took his place in the shadows. I sat, arranging and rearranging my trinkets as nervously as I had done that first night so many years before. The past always returns. What if Shah Jahan did not come? He had ridden north, south. He was hunting. He stayed in his father's palace. He was with a nautch girl. He drank with companions. He would enter, laugh at me, and go to his own bed. My head ached with all the possibilities. Nothing gave me hope; I did not deserve such happiness twice in my life.

I did not see him come. He stopped at the edge of the moon's shadow. He must have stood there for some time, then he strode swiftly across the lawn to my stall.

'Ah, my little bazaar girl, how much is your jewellery?'

'Ten thousand rupees.'

'I have none. Will ten thousand kisses be accepted?'

'From Shah Jahan, one will be more than enough.'

I received the ten thousand that night. I also received his seventh child.

One morning Ladilli came to see me. She seemed to be afloat in the early breeze, wafted about as though unable to control her own destiny. Her gentle transparency, a fine mist which one could penetrate but not disperse even by flailing one's arms, made me lose patience. It was always difficult to judge her temper, even anger was cloaked under placidity.

'What is it, Ladilli? If you're just going to sit and sigh, do it from the other side of the room. I can feel the weight of your breath,'

'I am to be married.'

'You should be happy then,' Her face showed no expression. She was old for marriage, even older than I had been when I married Shah Jahan. But she accepted her fate unquestioningly. 'Are you?'

She shrugged. 'My mother told me this morning. I am to marry Shahriya.'

227

'Ah!' I could think of little else to say.

I had never liked Shah Jahan's younger brother; he unsettled me. In court he was known as Na-Shudari, the 'good-for-nothing'. His face appeared to be made of moist clay, the flesh constantly adrip. His features never wore the pleasant looks of other men's. His mother was a slave, and Jahangir had heaped her with gifts and then sent her into retirement in Meerut. He was a cruel choice for Ladilli.

'Refuse.'

'Arjumand, you know I cannot do that. My mother will shout at me for days. I can't bear it. I find it easier to say "yes" at once.' She clutched my hand. 'You speak to her. You're strong, and my mother will listen to you.'

'What can I say to her? Is there someone else who pleases you?'

'Yes!' Light flooded her face. I could not help but feel a great sadness for that brief glint of happiness. It would be extinguished forever. 'His name is Ifran Hassan. He's a noble.'

'I've never heard of him.'

'He's not a particularly important man. He has a jagir near Baroda.'

'Have you spoken?'

'Of course not. But I know he likes me; he sent me this.' She wore a small silver locket around her neck. It was round and could be opened; nothing lay inside. 'I had a gold one made exactly like this, and sent it to him.'

'I will speak to your mother,' and I gently disentangled my hand, knowing that in so doing I was disentangling my life from hers. Mehrunissa would never be moved. 'It will be difficult. Your Ifran Hassan is a very minor noble. Shahriya is a prince.'

Immediately I regretted my harshness Her shoulders sloped as if she had overheard a whisper, condemning her life to be forever unfulfilled. I could only offer false hope. In a few days Mehrunissa would confirm her choice more forcefully.

'You're right. She won't even listen. A prince! That fool.'

It was the only spurt of anger I had ever seen in her. It startled her too; she flushed, rose and hurried out.

Shah Jahan

I was displeased by Mehrunissa's choice of my bastard brother as her son-in-law. He had been spawned by a slave, and lived almost forgotten. I saw him once or twice with his companions reeling drunk through the palace courtyards. His life had been obscure, of no significance, and now Mehrunissa's hand had reached into that dark oblivion and pulled him into the light. I had been her first choice for Ladilli; her second was judged just as carefully. I did not care who Ladilli married, but I could see the path of Mehrunissa's reasoning. She would be in control of Ladilli and, through her, Shahriya. Emperor Shahriya perhaps, the buffoon emperor, an idiot king.

'Even my aunt wouldn't dare,' Arjumand said. 'You are the first of Jahangir's sons.'

'But for how long?' I turned for advice to her father, Asaf Khan. His long face was secretive, schooled in the discipline of politics. I loved his daughter, I owned his loyalty. 'You see the Emperor daily. Am I the first of his sons?'

'Yes.' Abrupt, sparing of words. I found no consolation there. 'Mehrunissa gathers enemies.'

'Who doesn't? But she holds Jahangir, and I hold nothing. Now she holds Shahriya, and I hold nothing. My father is a sick man. Which of us will he choose?'

'The one she chooses.' Arjumand whispered, She knows I'm not like Ladilli, I will oppose her,'

Our time of peace was ending. Mehrunissa had begun to push me towards the edge of the precipice. On one side, I glimpsed a chasm, a bottomless abyss from which none returned, not even princes. On the other side, an impassable mountain.

'What shall I do?'

'Nothing,' Asaf Khan said quietly. 'What can you do? You must wait. If you move suddenly, Jahangir will take fright. He is preoccupied at the moment with his health. He yearns for Kashmir.'

'Is he now aware of what my aunt does?'

'Yes. She is wise enough to keep him informed. He approves of Ladilli's marriage to Shahriya. He thinks it an excellent match. He laughed and told me: "Just think of what you have won, old friend. Your sister is an Empress, her daughter a princess!"'

'And . . . .'

'That is all he said.'

'Did he say nothing of Arjumand?'

'No. Possibly he thought it unnecessary. Do not read meaning into his silences.'

'What else can I do? He ignores Arjumand, and in so doing he slights me.'

'He is distracted. We have problems enough reading Mehrunissa's words. Let us wait and see. I will support you in the ghusl-khana.'

I did not have long to wait.

They told me the magnificence of Ladilli's marriage surpassed even my own. Mehrunissa gave gold plates and cups to the guests, precious stones to the women, and scattered gold and silver coins to the people, and the feasting lasted three full days.

I did not attend, claiming illness, Arjumand could not; the child she bore died an hour after being born.

A little while after the wedding, Mehrunissa made her move. I was ordered to march south.

The Deccan simmered. The perpetual heat in that part of Hindustan seemed to keep it boiling with rebellion. Who could govern from such

230

a distance? Even if I did march south and defeated those rats a second time, what greater reward could my father give me? Could he bathe me a second time in gold and diamonds? He would only murmur: Shabash. And if I should fail, Mehrunissa would triumph. How could a prince who could not crush the Deccan rule Hindustan? My past victories would be forgotten. She would not mention those when I returned defeated.

It was also a great distance from Agra. I would not be able to hear the whispers at court until countless days later when Asaf Khan sent me news.

In haste I sought an audience with my father. The court was in the throes of preparing to move north to Lahore. Kashmir beckoned, drawing the emperor, the centre of power, further away from the Deccan even than Agra. Jahangir reclined in the ghusl-khana; a white cloth chilled with ice had been placed on his forehead. His eyes remained closed though the wazir announced my presence. He was breathing through his mouth like a lion, expiring in the shade, panting for his last hold on life.

'The air,' my father whispered, 'it is reluctant to enter this old body. It shuns me. In Kashmir . . . ah, Kashmir . . . there it smells so sweet, rushing in, unafraid of me.'

'Do you wish me to return to the Deccan?'

'You received my orders. Why come and ask me all over again?'

One eye opened like a prison door creaking. A light glittered within. 'I don't know why you constantly bother me.'

'This is my first audience for some time.'

'It feels like the hundredth. Is that all you want? I wish to return to my dreams of lying by the fountains in my garden and listening to their calming music.'

'If I am to march down to the Deccan . . . .'

'You babble. Just now I told you that you were to take command and to remain there until we have subdued those rats. If . . . if . . . what is

231

this "if"? The emperor's word isn't an "if". This is not a bazaar in which you bargain and say "if . . . ."' The eye reddened and burned like a brazier of coals. He shouted: 'I am commanding you to march.'

'I beg forgiveness, your majesty. You take offence at a slip of my tongue. I did not mean to question your command.'

'I should think not.' The eye began to lose its fierceness, to close. 'I will take offence at what I wish.'

'Am I forgiven, your majesty? I could not leave thinking I had angered you.'

'Yes, yes. Come.'

He beckoned. I knelt, and he embraced me in an absentminded manner. If he were to go north and I south, I would not want acrimony to linger in his mind. It would become the fuel for Mehrunissa's whispers. Yes, yes, she would say. He thinks he is already emperor. That is why he questions and quibbles.

'I beg your permission, Father, to take my brother Khusrav with me. He has been chained up in the palace for many years and the journey to the Deccan would mean a change in his dull life.'

He seemed hesitant, as if considering whether to open he eye once more. It remained closed, only a thin razor of light glimmered. 'And he will be out of your sight, not a constant reminder of his betrayal.'

'Why not? He is a nuisance, weeping all the time. The sight of him makes me melancholic. Added to my illness I find it intolerable. Take him, take him.'

We left for the south a few days after my father went north. He had announced his intention of only visiting Lahore, but he could change his mind; Kashmir beckoned still. We embraced before he left. He seemed stronger, but who could tell if we would ever see each other again? He waved Khusrav away.

'*Manzil mubarak.*'

'Manzil mubarak.'

I saw Arjumand's father. Asaf Khan promised to send a messenger out to the Deccan every seven days, reporting on the state of the emperor's health and Mehrunissa's thoughts. The two were bound together. If he failed, she would move swiftly to choose a successor; if he strengthened, she would delay. She had appointed my brother Parwez to the position of Subadar of Lahore, and had taken Ladilli and Shahriya with her. As Arjumand and I and the children travelled further south, I felt that we were floating down a river that was carrying us beyond the edge of the horizon.

Khusrav stayed chained to his soldier. They had grown accustomed to each other, and he did not wish to be parted from his only friend. I trusted neither of them and commanded Allami Sa'du-lla Khan to place a constant guard on Khusrav. I believed his eyes had healed somewhat and that, even if he did not see as clearly as I, he saw. After our first meal together, I commanded him to keep his own company.

'But I am told I ride with you only because of your affection for me, brother,' he said.

'I thought it would break the monotony of your imprisonment.'

'Imprisonment! In a golden prison! How could that be dull? I listen to the rumours and the gossip, and in my perpetual darkness calculate the meaning of each hiss and whisper. "Why?" I always begin my reasoning with that word. "Why?" Why did Mehrunissa marry her daughter to that drivelling idiot, Shahriya? But we all know the answer to that. It is easy. "Why?" Why does Shah Jahan take his blind brother south with him?'

'I have told you once. Now, eat. Have some more wine.' Isa filled his cup. Khusrav peered at the liquid in the gold vessel, but did not touch it, 'I cannot remain long in your company. I have to discuss the campaign with my commanders.'

'Ah, yes, of course. I have an important brother. Commands, orders—he raises an arm and ten thousand horsemen ride.' He sighed, and the tears flowed. They came and went at will. 'If only I had been as wise as Shah Jahan. I rushed in blindly ... I amuse you, don't I? Then, I was blind in the mind, now, I'm blind in the eye. Two blindnesses. What ill luck! If only the first had occurred before the second, I would still have both sights.'

'You do see.'

'A little. You begrudge me that? A dim, shadowy Shah Jahan sits in front of me. He shows his impatience; possibly, he is even showing his unease. I affect my beloved father in the same way. I sit and stare at him and he runs away. If I had been as wise as Shah Jahan, I would now be riding at the head of these thousands who will die at his bidding. But are they enough? Shah Jahan would command many times that amount twenty, thirty times—but he can't. Not yet.'

'I am the first of his sons.'

'But are you the first of Mehrunissa's? That is the question.'

He whispered then. 'You should ask what Khusrav would do.'

'What would Khusrav do?'

'Kill her. Swiftly. Before she makes her move. Despatch horsemen now.' He gripped my arm tightly. 'Without her whisperings, you will remain Jahangir's first son until the day of his death. And that will come soon, God willing.'

'She is too well guarded. Now it is my turn to ask—"why?"'

'Because her death would hurt him. He would weep, as I have wept. He would stagger through his palace, blinded with anguish. He would stumble and fall into an abyss of loneliness. Forever.' Khusrav chuckled in delight and clapped his hands. He dreamed night and day of Jahangir's death. I could not blame him. But I did not believe him.

'When you ask "why?" and receive an answer, you then have to ask another "why?" Why does Khusrav want Mehrunissa's life?'

To save his own.' He peered at me. 'Taktya takhta. I want neither throne nor coffin, my brother.'

The heat became intense, the grass shrivelled and died; the rocks and earth grew malevolent, the sky was a burnished shield. I dreamed too of Kashmir, not for my father, but for relief from Khusrav's implacable hatred. Arjumand lay in her ruth. The heat was scarcely kept at bay by the punkahs. She never complained, but always smiled her love for me. Her smile had not changed; it illuminated her beauty, though it seemed to rise more slowly now. But when it came, I couldn't contain my pleasure or my love. She was also heavy with our seventh child. We no longer discussed whether she should remain in comfort in Agra. I would never bend her will, and by now I did not want to. Her presence was a constant comfort to me.

I kept Dara always at my side. He rode a white pony, and his curiosity about this land was unending; I taught him, for he had begun his training. The other children remained with their servants, behind Arjumand's party. My other two sons, Shahshuja and Murad, were quiet, obedient boys; only Aurangzeb revealed an independent and stubborn spirit. He did not stand as high as my hip, yet approached me boldly and requested permission to ride by my side. I refused it. He was too small and would need constant attendance. There was a curious and disturbing woodenness in his countenance when he was in Dara's company.

Dara understood the nature of power. It flowed where I flowed, stopped when I stopped. It eddied around me, visible from horizon to horizon. I knew the fount was my father, but as the distance between us increased, so did my power. Other men ruled the land we passed through—ranas, amirs, diwans, mir bakshis—but while I was present in their suba, my authority surpassed theirs. The journey was slow; a prince cannot pass unnoticed. Each day at dawn, noon and dusk I held court, granting audiences to all who approached to pay homage and present gifts. And each time I halted, a feast awaited which could not be refused. So I listened to endless, repeated professions of loyalty and affection. The words never changed, only the orators.

Two days before we reached Burhanpur, we came upon some soldiers by the wayside; a hundred men commanded by the Mir Bakshi.

They were accompanied by the chief Sadr of the suba. They waited by a pillar of human skulls, which rose to the height of two men and was of a comparable diameter. It was built of mud and brick, and was encrusted with heads. They had neither eyes nor flesh, only the bones remained. The building of such pillars was a custom first practised by Timur-i-leng. This one had been built by Akbar, a monument to his vengeance. We no longer followed this tradition.

On the ground near the horsemen three men lay bound.

I gave permission for the Mir Bakshi and the Sadr to approach. They came reluctantly; my presence was not welcome. The Sadr performed a perfunctory kornish. The Mir Bakshi was more respectful. I ignored both, and rode over to the prostrate men. They were alive, bound with ropes, bare-headed. Blood caked the side of one, matted the beard of another. The third looked unharmed, but more tightly bound. They lay contorted, impassive faces pressed into the dirt. They expected no justice from me.

'This is a trivial matter, your Highness,' the Mir Bakshi said. His authority was temporarily subdued while I stood near. 'It should not concern the prince.'

'What have they done?'

'Nothing, Lord,' one of the bound men shouted out.

At a signal from the Mir Bakshi, a soldier struck the man with the haft of his spear.

'You will strike only when I command it. In my presence nothing is done without my authority.'

The Sadr rode forward. He came too close; I gestured him to move away. He made no effort to fawn, but glowered.

'These men were going to kill the thakur in that village.' He waved beyond the hills. 'We prevented a murder. Show the Prince the weapons.'

Three rusty swords fell to the ground, then a dagger.

'Why did they want to kill the thakur?'

'Who knows why these peasants do anything?' he said dismissively.

'I asked you a question. Answer swiftly. I will not tolerate the pious insolence of a mullah.'

'It was some grudge,' he whispered, realizing that it was only his holy profession that protected him from sudden death.

'Tell me,' I addressed the bound man. His eyes reminded me of those of a trapped tiger, full of helpless rage that he should be cheated of life so meanly.

'Your Highness, this thakur is an evil man. He makes our lives a misery . . . .'

'That is no reason to plan murder.'

'No, your Highness.' His eyes were icy. 'I had a pretty wife whom the thakur coveted. He took her against her will, kept her prisoner, used her, and when he tired of her he gave her to his men. She died from their cruelty.'

'Why did you not seek justice?'

'Justice?' He looked bitter. 'The thakur is Muslim. He is a friend of the Sadr and the Mir Bakshi. I am Hindu. When I went to them, they told me that it was not their concern. What could I do? I wept, I cried, I begged. They laughed at me. When she died, I sought my own justice. This man is my brother, this my cousin. We did go after the thakur, but we were caught. You may execute us.'

When hope is dead, men grow bold. His stare did not waver, he had not whined. I respected him.

'What is your name?'

'Arjun Lal. My brother is Prem Chand, my cousin Ram Lal.'

I turned to the Sadr: 'Is this the truth?'

'He did not come to us about his wife. It is only now he makes up this story.'

'Of course I know he is lying. What else does one expect from a Hindu?' I turned my horse's head, as if to ride away. 'What was her name?'

237

'Lalitha.' His glare was powerless, malevolent, full of loathing resentment at having been tricked.

'Release them. Execute the thakur.'

Burhanpur had not changed. The harsh sky, the hawks, the coarse plants, all were the same. The palace still stared sullenly across to the familiar purple hills, as if it resented having been rooted all these years to that one unchanging vision.

Arjumand gave birth to a female child. It died within the week. She remained listless and tired, Isa told me, though when I returned from my skirmishes with the Deccani rats, she showed only her happiness at my approach. She spoke little of her loss, but laughed and sang, and listened delightedly to my account of our success.

'Each time you win,' she told me, 'think of Mehrunissa. Her power lessens as yours grows.'

'What power have I here, so distant from my father?'

'This.' She swept the hills with her hand. 'You are the Mughal here. You have men, you have land; your father cannot take them from you; only you can present them to him. This is your conquest.'

She spoke the truth. Here, I was indeed the Great Mughal. All surrendered their forts, their territories to me. I accepted on behalf of the Emperor, but in my own name. Consoled by this, we led a peaceful life; we had each other, we had our children. Only the heat and flies were unwelcome fellow travellers. News reached us that my father's health had improved, and the messengers from Asaf Khan kept us abreast of court affairs. And Mehrunissa stayed her hand.

What lasts? Nothing. All life is impermanence.

It was a still, breezeless night. Arjumand slept. In repose, she became again the girl I first saw. The lines of age and weariness fell from her lovely face, turning it into a child's. I would gaze on her, in the shadows, night after night, until sleep claimed me.

I was woken by Isa at dawn. I crept from the bed and followed him into the corridor. A messenger from Asaf Khan waited: the emperor was ill, near to death.

I stood on the balcony, watching the sun strike the hills. They remained a stubborn purple, taking pride in their defiance.

'Send Allami Sa'du-lla Khan to me. Tell him to bring two soldiers, men we can trust.'

Khusrav's room was dark, the light had yet to enter. He lay sprawled asleep, his soldier in a corner on the floor. In sleep his features too changed. He appeared not blind, but whole, the childhood companion of my youth. He felt my presence, awoke and sat up. He peered into my eyes, and knew what they held.

He whispered: 'Taktya takhta?'

the eighteen
the taj mahal 1056/AD 1646

The tomb was ready. It rose from the surrounding dust and dirt and debris of building, from earth rough with ruts, holes, bunds, shattered marble, broken bricks, timber. It still looked skeletal against the blue sky, a pillar of ice casting its shadow over the procession that approached from the small, makeshift building on the bank of the Jumna.

The mullahs led the column, reading from the Quran. Then came Shah Jahan, his head bent in prayer, his fingers swiftly counting the pearl prayer beads. A few paces after him walked his four sons: Dara, Shahshuja, Aurangzeb, Murad. The coffin followed: a simple block of cold marble, unadorned, bending the backs of the men who sweated under its weight. A ramp sloped from the ground to the tomb's entrance, nineteen feet higher. The procession climbed slowly, the air filled with their murmurs, and the smoke of incense lingered after they vanished inside, then, like the vast crowd that had gathered to watch the ceremony, it slowly dispersed.

Only Isa stayed behind, watching from the marble balcony down the river. The tomb seemed to him earth-bound, disproportionate: it looked too thin, too tall, somehow emaciated. Of course it was not complete. The vast plinth had yet to be built, twice the length and breadth of the tomb, a huge marble lake on which the tomb would appear to float. And then would come the minarets and the two mosques, and finally the garden. Isa knew its staggering cost: one thousand and thirty-six sacks of gold had been used to cast the railing that surrounded the sarcophagus and the great lamp that hung from the dome. An equal amount of silver had been used for the doors. Every imaginable variety of precious and semi-precious stone, in incalculable numbers, had been set into the flowers and plants that adorned the interior. Diamonds, rubies, emeralds, pearls, topaz, jade, sapphires, turquoises, mother-of-pearl, bloodstone, wonderstone, cornelian, crystal, malachite, agate, lapis lazuli, coral, glass stone, conch-shell, onyx, garnet, beryl, chrysoprase, chalcedony and jasper. They had been chosen and set with mathematical precision by master jewellers not only to reflect the changing light, but to cast the most favourable astrological configuration on the coffin. The great quantity of marble had been a gift from the Rajput princes. Twenty thousand workers had laboured night and day for years, and would continue to do so, yet Isa knew the Mughal treasury beneath his feet had hardly been tapped, as if just a handful of water had been scooped from the Jumna.

He paused at the entrance to the diwan-i-khas. In the shadows stood the peacock throne. It had been built by Shah Jahan, but despite its splendour and the honeyed light that caressed its feet, it looked desolate, abandoned. It was a gold platform set upon four lion's legs of gold. The platform was some three feet wide and five feet long, covered with cushions. Above it hung a canopy, also of gold, supported by twelve pillars each the thickness of a man's arm, encrusted with emeralds. On top of the canopy were two golden peacocks that appeared more splendid than the live birds. Their jewelled feathers reflected every colour with an equal brilliance. Between them stood a tree bearing fruits of emeralds, rubies, diamonds and pearls. It had taken the court jeweller, Bebadat Khan, seven years to fashion the throne.

Isa sat down on it, attempting to feel the power of the Great Mughal, but only found it uncomfortable. As he sat, a strange emotion entered him, rising from the throne itself—a chill, terrible feeling of loneliness.

Murthi ignored the procession. He battled with stone, fierce, relentless, untiring. Tap, tap, tap; with each chip he cut at his own heart. It would be finished soon, soon, soon. He worked harder, faster, never slacking. With each tap, he heard the minutes, the hours, the days pass. He ran a race with time; now they were neck and neck. Another year of life, another year closer to death. His clenched hands ached, the knuckles knobbed, in winter, during the rains, they hurt, and he had to force them to grasp around the chisel. Gopi worked on the other end of the jali, scrubbing the marble with coarse sand. At the very top it had begun to take on the smooth sheen of glass. Murthi was proud of his elder son. He worked with his father's stubborn patience. Up and down. Up and down. Up and down. The younger boy tended the fire, played at it, throwing twigs and chips to make the sparks dance.

Murthi was lonely for Sita. At first it surprised him; then the pain welled, choking him. It was as if she still reached out to draw love like blood from his heart. He remembered her youth, her laughter in the village, her shyness on their wedding day, all wasted now. He had squandered them with his deliberate coldness. She was supposed to bear children, and had disappointed him. She had grown weary, not only in body but in spirit. Oh, he never meant it. It could not be helped that he had known from the start that she had no affection for him. She had been chosen for another, and had only accepted him when his brother disappeared, as if he were a discarded length of material she'd picked up from the roadside. And all he'd done was punish her and, by doing that, punish himself too.

The hakim had come, but it was too late. He touched her pulse; it was still. With her life, her age had fled, only youth and memory remained. It was as if all had been hidden beneath the surface and now showed through. Murthi had knelt down and touched his lips to her forehead. There were grey streaks in her hair; he had never noticed, he saw only her beauty, the curves in her cheeks, the silken texture of her skin.

The women had bathed and dressed her. They combed her hair, placed kum-kum on her brow, a garland around her neck. They remained behind, watching the procession, listening to the conch, hushing the crying baby, as the little group of mourners passed through the streets of Mumtazabad to the ghat.

Isa watched the bier pass. It was a simple affair made of thatch with bamboo poles. She was light enough for only four men. He caught a glimpse of her face, just the nose and the eyes he remembered; the rest was hidden by the garland of rose petals. He did not accompany the procession to the ghat. Standing apart, he watched the priest murmur the sastras, sprinkle the ghee and rice, light the pyre. It took time. At first the flame shimmered, wavering in the sunlight, then slowly darkened and rose.

Death subtracted, Isa remembered.

The palace was closed. It was empty; the soldiers, slaves, courtiers, wazirs, musicians, singers, and servants had been driven out. All was silent. Dust eddied, crisp leaves scraped across the floor, pigeons crooned softly.

Shah Jahan sat not on a throne or a divan or carpet. He knelt on the cold floor. He did not move, he made no sound. He neither ate nor drank. He remained thus for eight days and eight nights. His soul was a black and melancholy place, harbouring no thoughts. His heart knew no feeling. He did not weep, he did not beat his temples, he did not cry aloud. Isa watched, keeping a sleepless vigil.

Every hour the emperor writhed and struggled to contain the demonic force that tore at him. With each passing of the storm, he would subside, drained, weary, but never rising.

At first, Isa thought it was a trick of the light. Sunlight and shadow passed in turn across the walls of the ghusl-khana, and each time they passed over the emperor's face they drew something from him, as if water were washing his image from a slate. When the emperor first knelt down there were seven white hairs in his black beard. With each passing hour, day and night, the beard whitened. Isa watched the years hasten, laying their toll on his flesh, staining white every single hair. Lines appeared, first one, then another, like the earth cracking before his eyes. By the dawn of the eighth day, Shah Jahan's face was that of an old man, his beard fully white. He lifted his face towards the sun.

'AR-JU-MAND!' The roar was that of a mortally wounded tiger. 'ARJUMAND! ARJUMAND!' Hour upon hour he called her name until he could only whisper. 'Arjumand.'

Isa listened to the echo in the palace, as if a thousand voices called her name, AR-JU-MAND. From the corners, from the graceful archways, from the pavilion, it rode on the soft cool breeze, lingering on and on, and finally faded.

Shah Jahan gestured. He could not rise. Isa lifted him. When the emperor stood, Isa was startled. Before they had been the same height. Now, he could look down on the emperor. He examined Shah Jahan closely. He looked shrunken, visibly dwindled in his clothes.

Death subtracted.

Murthi too looked diminished. He trudged away slowly from the dying flames, supported by his son. Ash floated and fell on his clean white jiba and dhoti. He did not notice the grey on his clothes.

'She's gone,' he told Isa, bewilderment in his voice.

'I know.'

244

'I thought she loved only you. I didn't treat her well for that.'

'Did you ask her?'

'Never. You were a ghost. We didn't speak of you. It seemed at times the way she looked at me … I imagined her longing that I would turn into you.'

'Yes, you imagined. She had forgotten me. If you too had forgotten, forgiven, she would have been happy. It is too late. But you have him and the others.'

Isa reached out to his nephew. Gopi shied away, then overcame his awkwardness and allowed Isa to pat his head. He was tall for that, and the gesture came years too late. Isa drew a gold coin out of the air and held it out.

'How did you do that?'

'When I was a boy, I was stolen from the village and sold to a magician. I can still remember some of his tricks. Here, take it.'

Gopi received it with awe. On one side was stamped the Imperial crest, the other bore the likeness of the Great Mughal.

'Is there anything you want?'

'Nothing!' Murthi said harshly, and walked past Isa, not looking back.

Murthi had not meant to show such anger, but saw that his brother took no offence. His bitterness increased. For fourteen years he'd laboured. What waste! His brother could have lifted him into a position of power, given him riches, but he had not helped. Isa was prosperous, fed, jewelled, clothed in silks. His hands were soft, unscarred, while Murthi's were cracked and chipped, Murthi himself aged beyond his years and aching in body and soul.

After the wazir's execution, Murthi had been determined to find out who Isa was. It was Isa about whom the wazir had questioned him. Each evening, Murthi enquired in and around the fort: *Who is Isa?* Some knew, none knew. A slave, a friend, a minister, a magician, an astrologer; he held no title, no jagir, no zat. Nothing was explained. So he waited to see this Isa. He caught glimpses of him, as the Great Mughal came and went, but he was too distant. Soldiers always stood in the way. At last, chance brought the Great Mughal to the worksite. Shah Jahan had come to examine the jali. Baldeodas fawned and scraped, explained and pointed. The sculptors stood in reverent silence. Shabash, Shah Jahan said to each in turn. He lavished praise only on Baldeodas.

'Who is Isa?' Murthi whispered to a soldier.

'That's him, there!'

Murthi stared, gaped. Through the flesh and silk, he saw the ghost of his brother, Ishwar. Surely the years had deceived his sight, tricked his memory. As the Imperial party began to move away, Murthi gathered his courage.

'Ishwar,' he called.

The man paused, then turned. He detached himself from the emperor's side and approached Murthi. Isa did not notice Shah Jahan turn too to see who called.

'You are my brother Ishwar!'

'Yes.'

They did not embrace. It had been too long. Isa waited patiently, expecting Murthi to say more.

'You had the wazir executed?'

'Yes.' Isa's smile chilled Murthi. 'The fool believed by imprisoning you he could imprison me. He threatened to tell the emperor I had used my influence to help you and protect you. He was jealous of the emperor's trust in me, and sought to trap me. I took him to the emperor and ordered him to repeat everything. When he had finished the emperor asked me what I wished done to the wazir. I said: execute him. He was executed. You saw.'

'Who are you?' Murthi could barely understand the power of Isa. A man had been executed by his word. 'You hold no rank, no office.'

'I serve the emperor.'

'Did you ever see the empress? What was she like? I must know. Tell me . . . .'

'It would take too long. She was brave. She loved too much.' He spoke a word softly to himself in a different tongue—Agachi. 'Shah Jahan will never harm me. The wazir did not understand who I am.'

'Who are you?'

'I am the memory of the Empress Mumtaz-i-Mahal.'

In contrast to Dara's splendour, Aurangzeb looked austere. He wore cotton and no ornaments, not even a ring.

They were sitting in the haram in the company of Shah Jahan. The women were unveiled except for Jahanara. She sat shrouded, not from modesty, but to hide the terrible scars. On her recovery she had pleaded with Shah Jahan to forgive Aurangzeb, and the emperor had relented. He returned the jagirs and titles to his third son; he even appointed him Subadar of the Deccan and increased his zats.

Shah Jahan observed his sons. They differed in every way, not merely in their clothes, Aurangzeb silent and watchful, Dara exuberant, open, full of wit. During the feast Dara spoke out on all matters, discussing and debating with other guests. How like Akbar he was—tolerant, concerned for his people, bitterly opposed to the oppressive influence of the mullahs.

'Do you too believe in din-i-illah, like Akbar?' Aurangzeb enquired politely. It was the first time he had spoken all evening.

'Akbar believed himself god. I do not. Din-i-illah was the religion he prescribed for his followers, a blend of Islamic, Hindu, Christian, Buddhist. Men cannot worship in such a confused manner. I only believe they should be free to follow their faith, and if I can promote a reconciliation of their beliefs, I shall be well satisfied.'

'We should call you a Padishah-ji,' Aurangzeb commented. He bowed, mocking.

'And should I address my brother as Hazrat-ji? You are well known for your piety.'

Aurangzeb glanced swiftly at his father. The emperor had caught the exchange, and broke off his own conversation to await Aurangzeb's reply.

'Yes. I have only humble ambitions. I bow to the commands of my father. If he is pleased, I am too. I cannot subscribe to your way of thinking. I am a devout Muslim. When I have served my father to his complete satisfaction, all I wish for is to retreat to a quiet place where I can worship.'

'I must remember that,' Dara said.

'I will remind you.'

'Look! Look!' They were interrupted by the women calling from the window. They pointed.

The moon had slid from the clouds and the sky was silvery grey. At a distance, the Taj Mahal lay on the water. They looked on it, breathless. The pure white marble blazed in ethereal beauty. It was as if a beautiful woman gazed into a mirror which faithfully returned every perfection. There seemed to be in that reflection an inner light that turned the surrounding water as dark as night. They did not lift their eyes to the building itself—the dome like a gigantic pearl afloat in the night sky— they looked only upon its image. It filled the heart and eye to abundance, to silence, to prayer. When they finally lifted their gaze, the tomb looked melancholy in the cold light, seemed to radiate, through the mantle of splendour, an eternal sadness.

Aurangzeb withdrew while the emperor gazed. A glance had been sufficient. He left the palace and rode alone into the city, winding through still and sleeping streets until he came to a door by the mosque. He knocked and entered a small low building. The room was simply furnished with a carpet, divan, cushions. Aurangzeb bowed deeply to the reclining man. The man hastily rose, surprised, and bowed even lower.

'Be seated. It is I who will remain standing in your presence. A man of God is worthy of more reverence than an emperor's son.'

Shaikh Waris Sarhindi did not accept the prince's invitation, he stood too. He was an orthodox Sunni, a mullah like his father Shaikh Ahmad Sarhindi. Akbar had defied the father; Jahangir had imprisoned him. Now Shah Jahan paid the son scant respect as he campaigned for his father's cause: the supremacy of Islam and death to the unbeliever.

'I have been in the company of my brother Dara. I find it too rich, like the food.' Aurangzeb belched. 'Whom will you support?'

'Your Highness, of course. We all will. You will restore the faith, you will be the true Scourge of God.'

'I promise.'

the nineteen love story 1031/AD 1621

Arjumand

Through my sleep, I felt my beloved leave. I woke and heard whispers. The early dawn, such a faint light, was luxuriously cool, but cruelly brief. The edge of sunlight would soon hurl a torrent of heat that would not end even at dusk.

I rose and looked out. My prince stood on the balcony lost in thought, then turned abruptly and hurried down the corridor. He moved to the west wing, towards Khusrav's quarters. I saw the shadows of others follow him. Isa came to me.

'What is it, Isa?'

'The Emperor is very ill,' he said and shrugged. 'Again.'

'What did my husband want?'

'Allami Sa'du-lla Khan,' he added softly, 'And soldiers.'

I ran through the corridors. Allami Sa'du-lla Khan waited with two soldiers outside Khusrav's room.

'Where is the prince Shah Jahan?'

'Inside, your Highness. Shall I call him?' 'No.'

It was still dark. I could barely see the two shadows joined in conspiracy. I heard Khusrav's fierce whisper. It was harshly loud and filled the room with his mocking, 'Taktya takhta?'

And then, after silence, my husband's implacable reply: 'Takhta.'

'No.' I whispered.

My beloved stared at me, but did not move. His voice was hard, like the hills, and his words had the same immovable quality.

'Go. This is my business.'

The soldier uncurled from sleep, and drew his weapons. He looked first at Khusrav, then at me. He hesitated, uncertain of his move.

'Strike. Strike quickly,' Khusrav whispered. 'He is unarmed. Kill him, you fool.' Khusrav crouched on all fours. The soldier continued to hesitate. His head swung towards the door, and he peered as if trying to see through the walls. He was a young man, his face still creased with sleep, his beard black and straggly. 'I will make you governor of Bengal when I am Padishah. Strike!'

My beloved crouched waiting. He could have called out, but remained silent. The soldier was aware now of men outside. Slowly, he lowered his sword. Khusrav hissed in despair, in rage.

'It is not your destiny, your Highness,' the soldier said. 'I am your army, but I am only one man. There are too many battles to fight before you will become Padishah. You have already lost so many. God meant it not for you.' Carefully, he placed his sword and dagger down on the carpet and approached Khusrav. He knelt, took his hand, pressed it against his forehead. It was a gesture of love, a sad farewell. Khusrav bent forward and embraced the soldier.

'Oh God, my dreams,' Khusrav whispered. He released his friend, and took a heap of jewellery from the small table: rings, gold chains, arm bands. 'Here. Keep these in my memory.'

'I've no need of such riches, your Highness.'

'Take them. Let someone benefit from the fool Khusrav.'

He thrust them at the soldier; a ring fell and rolled, neither looked at it. The soldier rose awkwardly, his hands filled with gold and diamonds. They might have been stones from the river bed. He stared at Khusrav for a while, trying to remember his face; the room was

251

light now. Then he looked towards Shah Jahan.

'I cannot kill a prince,' but before my beloved could acknowledge the confession, the soldier added coldly, 'I leave such killings to princes.'

In surprise we watched him leave. He walked with the dignity of a victorious man. Khusrav chuckled. 'A wise man. He leaves the killing to princes. Without us, without our ambitions, soldiers revert to men. Doubtless he will return to his village and tell his children stories about the madness of his prince.' A thought occurred to Khusrav and he touched Shah Jahan's shoulder gently: 'Don't harm him. Let him go. At least one of us spoke with honesty tonight. Tonight? Today. I speak as if time matters and I should be accurate.'

'Leave us,' Shah Jahan repeated to me.

'Why?' said Khusrav. 'Don't you want the beautiful Arjumand to be a witness to my death?' He turned towards me, squinting. 'She is of the same blood as that whore Mehrunissa. She sent you.'

'I came without her command. I am not my father.'

Shah Jahan took my arm to lead me to the door. I pulled away from him.

'You must not kill him. Please, I beg you, my beloved, my husband. You must not kill him.'

'Must not? It has to be done. He still has some followers; his shadow falls on the throne. Let it fall in a coffin.'

'Send him into exile. Keep him chained. Lock him in prison. Do not kill him.'

Shah Jahan looked at me with dark anger. I knew he would not be moved. I had never seen such determination in his face before; it frightened me.

'What affection do you have for my brother?'

'None. I only speak because of my love for you. His death will be our curse, a curse on our sons, and on the sons of our sons. Look at him. His blindness already haunts us. His death will drag us down. If you kill him you will be the first to break the Timurid law. Your ancestor

Timur-i-leng first proclaimed it three hundred years ago: "Do naught unto your brothers, even though they may deserve." It has been obeyed by every prince since then. Babur told Humayun, Humayun Akbar, Akbar Jahangir. They have obeyed that law, whatever the provocation. It is the law that protected Khusrav from your father's anger. Khusrav's blood is your own, you must not spill it. It will stain our lives for generations.'

Shah Jahan began to laugh. He roared and then embraced and kissed me.

'I didn't know I'd married a superstitious woman as well as a beautiful one. All that will happen is that the throne will be secured for me.'

'I don't want it at such a price.' I pushed him away. I couldn't control the dread that rose in me. Like smoke, it choked me. 'I dreamt, on the day we met, of red. It was the colour that stayed in my mind when I woke. I did not know then what it meant. When I met you, I thought it was the crimson of the crown prince. I was wrong. It was blood. It will wash us away, my beloved. Spare him.'

'Listen to her,' Khusrav croaked. 'I'm not afraid of dying. Each day I have woken expecting the assassin. But even my father obeyed Timur-i-leng's law. He couldn't kill me. You must not either. I swear I will renounce the throne, not for my own sake, but for yours.'

'Everyone offers me his life not for his sake, but for mine. What generosity.' Shah Jahan turned to me and with great gentleness took me by the arm and led me away from Khusrav. 'I have listened to you, as is our tradition, but I cannot allow him to live.'

'And what,' Khusrav called after him, 'will happen to Parwez and Shahriya? Are they to die too? But they're not here, alone and helpless; they are in Lahore, surrounded by the army.'

'No. Please, my beloved. You can't.'

'I must. Go.'

I wept all day for my husband, my children, myself. I had never

253

known such fear as that which now enveloped me. It shook me and squeezed tears of despair from my eyes. The red of my dream was blood; it always had been. I had interpreted it, to my own inclination, as the turban of my beloved. I had not lowered my gaze and seen the bloody hands. My tears could not wash them clean, but dropped and dropped and, as they touched his flesh, they too turned into blood. Even the tresses of my hair with which I wiped them turned red.

I tried to stop my ears, but the sound still seeped through my fingers. Even if I had suddenly become deaf I knew I would have heard the whispers. The soldiers had gone in. Khusrav turned to Mecca, to the sun, knelt in silent prayer, then rose to stand at his window so that he could look out on the world. He did not wish to look on the faces of his executioners as he had done on those who blinded him. He accepted without a struggle the cloth with the coin knotted in the centre that they wound around his neck. They took his body and placed it in a simple coffin. I was not told where they buried him. How many of the murdered does the earth conceal?

It had been done in haste, too much haste. Once more a message came from my father: Jahangir lived. It was followed by another from Jahangir himself:

> I have received your report that Khusrav died of the colic forty days ago. I pray he has gone to the mercy of God. I have received alarming intelligence that the scoundrel Shah Abbas, Shahinshah of that accursed kingdom, Persia, marches on Kandahar. We must meet him with the greatest force I can command. You will march north with *all* your forces immediately.

Khusrav's spirit rose up out of its hiding place; I felt it weave an ominous spell round us. In the months after his death, I constantly felt his mocking presence. It watched me to sleep, then awaited my awakening;

it hung with the low dark clouds over the hills, throwing a gloom on the land. All at the palace felt it and we moved softly, quietly, not wishing to startle Khusrav's ghost. I prayed, not five times, a dozen times every day. I read the Quran; it could not move the despair that clung to me. And now came Jahangir's orders: march.

My beloved did not reply immediately to his father's summons. He paced the balcony, stopping to stare at the hard, ungiving hills. I knew what he saw. Not just the land, but *his* land. He had fought; men had died; these rocks and gulleys and forts were his empire. If he left it would fall, and without it he would be reduced to the subjugation of his father. And Mehrunissa.

'I can see her hand in this,' he told me.

'But the Shahinshah does march on Kandahar.'

'I know, but why does my father want my forces?'

'You are the most experienced of his sons.'

'But he says "the greatest force I can command". Not "you" can command. Why doesn't he remain on his sick bed? I could beat the Persian scoundrel on my own. If we march, I will lose all this.'

'And if we don't . . .?'

My question went unanswered, but not ignored. I watched him weigh our future. If he refused to obey, it would enrage Jahangir, They were in deadlock, and for days he paced the balcony. How Khusrav must laugh. It seemed as if his spirit had flown directly to Lahore and whispered into Mehrunissa's ear. Because she knew. A message came from my father that Jahangir had transferred all Shah Jahan's jagirs to Shahriya, including Hissan Feroz, the traditional lands of the crown prince. She had pushed her idiot good-for-nothing son-in-law one step closer to the throne, pushed herself one step further towards ruling after Jahangir's death.

'I am already lost,' Shah Jahan said. 'She has moved too quickly. I cannot strike out when my father dies. She will proclaim Shahriya emperor. He has become the first of my father's sons.'

'Decide then whether you will march on Kandahar. It would be best to tell him you must wait until the rains are over. That would give us more time.'

'What use is delay unless I can use it to my advantage? I cannot allow my father to push me aside so easily. How could his love just evaporate like that?'

'My aunt sucked it out of him.'

'I must please him, but also show my strength. I will march north after the rains, and he must allow me to command all the forces. And he must give me the jagir of Panjab. That will protect my back against Mehrunissa and my brothers.'

It did not please Jahangir. He raged at my beloved. He called him *bi-daulat*, even writing the name in his *Jahangir-nama* so that all should know my beloved was 'the wretch'. He commanded him to remain in Burhanpur forever, but to send the army immediately.

'Without my forces I'm nothing at all.'

'By withholding them, you will enrage your father once more.'

Since Khusrav's death,, thunder roamed the skies outside, rolled within my heart making me tremble for my beloved. I could not mention Khusrav's name for fear of reminding Shah Jahan of the curse that had descended so swiftly on our lives. We felt abandoned on a rudderless raft racing blindly into eternity. We loved each other. That was our only comfort. Our love was all the magic we could command; it held fear at bay. We bestowed it on each other through our touch, our lips, our bodies, enfolded in it we felt ourselves invisible to the surrounding world.

'It is too late,' he whispered, 'I know it. Mehrunissa has spread her poison. It cannot be stopped.'

'Send Allami Sa'du-lla Khan immediately to Lahore. Beg your father's forgiveness. He will grant it, and then we can march to Kandahar.'

He smiled: '"We?" How many times must I tell you, you must not

256

come to war. You could be harmed.'

'I will never let you go alone. Send Allami Sa'du-lla Khan.' An hour later Allami Sa'du-lla Khan rode.

The weeks passed, and we waited. The rains flooded the valleys making the palace moist and warm, filling the rooms with the odour of rot. My spirits were further lowered by a new pregnancy, with the early sickness and the weakening. Then Allami Sa'du-lla Khan returned. The cloud in his face was dark as the ones above our heads.

'Jahangir would not see me. I waited for days. I was not even permitted to attend the diwan-i-am. Mehrunissa advised him to turn me away, and she has ordered everyone at court never to mention your name in your father's presence. You have ceased to exist in your father's eyes. That Na-Shudari Shahriya now struts about the palace with the red turban, threatening to kill you if you should ever show your face there.' Allami Sa'du-lla Khan laughed without humour. 'He waves his sword about, frightening everyone, describing how he will cut you to pieces in personal combat. Mehrunissa applauds each show of his arrogance.'

'And Ladilli? How is she?'

'She hasn't changed, I hear. I received a message from her, sending you her affection. It was not written, in *case* her mother discovered it on me. She has two children now. I only hope they will not grow up to look as hideous as Shahriya does.'

'What's wrong with him?'

'He has a disease. He has lost all his hair, and his eyes stream. His skin too seems to come off, like fur dropping off a street cat.'

'Poor Ladilli.'

'Enough,' Shah Jahan said. 'I cannot sit here and allow myself to be abused by Mehrunissa and my father, letting that fool Shahriya boast of becoming emperor. If they are in Lahore, I can reach Agra before my father can. Is the treasury still there?'

257

'Yes. But soon it is to be moved to Lahore to pay the Emperor's army.'

Shah Jahan

I marched north swiftly. I had wanted Arjumand and the children to remain behind, for there would be little rest for any of us. She stubbornly refused, though each day she grew heavier with child. I suffered to see her discomfort. More cushions were placed under her to soften the jolting of the rath, but each evening she collapsed in exhaustion.

It seemed that, even as I had spoken my decision, news of it had reached my father's ears. I was no longer even bi-daulat; worse, far worse, I was the usurper. I had no wish to ascend the throne before my time, I only wished to preserve my destiny, not overtake it. I thought that if I captured the treasury I would be able to reason with my father. Certainly it would not be possible to reason with Mehrunissa. She knew that once I gained control I would leave no room for her anywhere near myself, my family or the throne.

They brought me the news that Kandahar had fallen to Shah Abbas, The rich heart of the empire's trade was no longer under our control. I vowed that when I ruled, I would recapture it. The fall of Kandahar enraged my father further. It had been ruled by us since the time of Akbar, and Jahangir felt that he had failed his father. I was, of course, to blame; he would march south to do battle with me. I was told he wrote in the *Jahangir-nama*: *What shall I say of my own sufferings'? In pain and weakness, I must still ride and be active, and in this state must proceed against such an undutiful son.*

His words hurt me. I had been provoked by his indifference, by his inability to close his ears to Mehrunissa, to keep his word, his love, for me. Yet no ill of him had passed my lips. Still he raged.

1032/AD 1622

It was on the twenty-fifth day of the march that I knew I would not succeed. Agra was still far distant, and the whole strength of the Mughal army now lay between me and Agra. My father had decided not to command. He could not fight his son, could not be responsible for my death. He obeyed the Timurid law. But I had broken it, and I heard the echo of Arjumand's words. She had never spoken them again, but I knew they filled her mind and heart as they now filled mine. The army was to be commanded by my old tutor, General Mahabat Khan.

He was an experienced and wise commander. He gave me no choice of battlefield but through his swiftness, forced his on me. Balockpur was a small village on the edge of a plain surrounded by low hills, bald and barren and offering little cover. I would have chosen the hills themselves. My force was smaller, more manoeuvrable, and by using swift horsemen I would have been able to attack swiftly and then retreat. But he was aware of my tactical advantage in such circumstances. The open plain forced me to confront the might of the Mughal face to face.

On the eve of battle, I rode out alone, unable to sit in the silence of the gulabar: the heat in there consumed my flesh in sweat. Arjumand lay on the divan. The hakim informed me the baby would be born that night. A good omen or bad? If it lived, good; if it died, bad. If it were a boy child, good; if a girl, bad. We grasp at signs, believing they will shape destiny by their chance presence. If my dripping sweat struck the ant, I would be the victor, if it missed, the vanquished.

It was not a clear night. The half moon was shaded by wisps of low cloud and the stars looked faded and distant, as if they had withdrawn their influence over my destiny. If only they would come closer, move the earth by their force, bend fate to my bidding. That was an idle wish. Did they really care? Could they even see these armies waiting for dawn's light? I studied the face of the sky as closely as I had studied the terrain. Where did my star lie? There, beyond the most distant of stars.

259

Its light reached me, winking good fortune on my cause. But then, ominously, for there was no wind, not even the slightest sigh of a breeze, a cloud slipped between it and me. Possibly, it had not been my star, but Mahabat Khan's.

Of the low surrounding hills, the one nearest appeared the highest, a knob of earth, boulders and lantana bushes. I picked my way to the top, and stared back at the village engulfed by the army. I could discern the movements of my men, horses, elephants, the whispered voices, murmured prayers, the cooking fires whose countless sparks scattered over the black earth. The army flowed into the distance and the sight of the encampment gave me reassurance. These men had fought for me for many years; we would be victorious once more.

I looked north towards the Mughal army, held my breath. I saw them faintly in the distance; so vast the very sky might have been a part of their forces. The fires dotted the whole horizon for as far as my eye could see, and then rose up and up into the sky, winking and fluttering malignantly, beckoning me to my fall. How would he attack? With the buffalo? He had the strength to send thousands of horsemen to encircle my force. Would he wait patiently for mine, and embrace me as we rode into attack? How would old Mahabat Khan think?

Gravel rattled below me. Isa made his way through boulders and bush, and came to stand at my side. He bowed, then turned to stare at the Mughal forces, appraising our chances. His face revealed nothing.

'It is a female child, your highness, but it did not survive.'

It was a bad omen, I knew. I bowed my head in prayer for the baby.

'Arjumand?'

'She is well, but tired. The hakim said she must sleep. You have a visitor. Mahabat Khan asks for an audience.'

The old man was in a jovial mood. He had drunk two cups of wine and stood leaning against a tamarind tree. Beside him were his soldiers, a dozen in all, wary, watchful.

'Your Highness, I would have waited inside, but the surroundings were not appropriate for a meeting with a prince. I do not usually drink warm wine—how spoilt I am now—but you had none chilled.'

'The boat cannot come down here daily. I apologize. You have a message from my father?'

'None. Oh, he's in good health, complaining constantly about his rascal son.'

'I thought I was "bi-daulat."'

'That too. It depends on his moods. They swing to extremes, much worse than before.' He spat. 'He only listens to that . . . woman. I do not bow to an emperor now, but to an empress. Every hour I receive her messages. Attack, attack: destroy Shah Jahan. I must be victorious. Do I need more men? Do I need more cannon? I can command what I want.' He took a step towards me. I heard Allami Sa'du-lla Khan's warning grunt and the rasp of his drawn sword. Mahabat Khan raised his arms. 'I have no sword. I wish only to speak to your Highness in private.'

We walked away from the others, but not too far. I remained wary of my old companion. He was successful because he had a sly and useful mentality; it sprang traps when least expected.

'I am a soldier,' he laughed. 'Not an assassin. I leave that business to others. You cannot win tomorrow. I don't wish to humiliate my old pupil, for we were friends once. If you surrender, Mehrunissa assures me she will treat you with great respect.'

'Mehrunissa! And my father? I do not care about her promises. What did he command?'

'That we are not to take your life.' I glimpsed his eyes, sharp as starlight in the black night. 'You are of the Timurid line.' I felt the sadness of his sigh. 'You should not have killed Khusrav. That was bad.'

'I will take care of my own destiny.'

He stood quietly, awaiting my decision. I was grateful for his courtesy. He could have sent a messenger rather than come himself. 'I cannot surrender.'

'I expected as much. It would disappoint me greatly if Shah Jahan capitulated before a battle.' He chuckled. 'Even when he knows he cannot win.'

'Allah will guide us.'

'Allah guides us all, some into pits, others to the tops of mountains. Who knows His will?'

We walked back to his men through the village. It was at peace. Cattle lay chewing hay, serenely indifferent to our presence, to the impending battle. Goat kids suckled milk from their mothers, children peered out to see the prince and the general of the Mughal army stroll as if they were at court.

'You will stay to eat with us?'

'No, I must return to my men. There is a lot to do tonight. I must try to remember all that I taught you. I hope you haven't grown too clever for an old man.'

'A cunning old man.' I chuckled.

'And you are a cunning young one. You've had years of experience since I first taught you. Experience is no more than instinct; it will guide you better than a thousand words of instruction.'

'I will listen to it then.'

Arjumand

I was asleep when he returned, sunk deep in the opium of exhaustion. It lay on me, cocooning me in pleasant darkness. No light, no sound, no touch could penetrate, but something told me, darting deep into the black warmth, that he came. Servants, maids, Isa, the hakim, none could have disturbed me, but his presence did, as if he had entered my sleep, and gently carried me back into the light. He knelt beside me in silence, looking down with dark, soft eyes. He touched my cheek, then bent and kissed me, stroking my hair. It was his favourite gesture of affection, to keep caressing softly, calmingly.

262

'It was a daughter, I am told. I feel sad that it did not live.' We held and comforted each other for a long while. It was the will of Allah that it did not live.

'We have enough children. I didn't mean to wake you. I came only to look at you. You must sleep again.'

'Soon. There is always time for that, my love.' His brows creased and I smoothed them. 'We will win tomorrow.'

'Mahabat Khan came to see me. He wished me to surrender. He is obeying your aunt's orders.'

'She is worried then. If you win, you will have won everything. What place would there be for her?'

'If I lose, I lose everything.'

'Not everything. You dismiss me so quickly?'

'You would remain with a defeated prince?' He smiled down on me.

This defeated prince, will he be different? Will his love change? Will his eyes change? Will his touch change? Will his heart change?'

'No.'

Then I will stay with him. The world holds no interest for me without Shah Jahan.'

I awoke again to the noise of men preparing for battle, the orders and commands, the squeak of tightening girths, the harsh rasp of swords being sharpened, the movement of cannon, the hoofbeats of nervous horses. I longed to hear instead the chatter of the crows and the parrots, the bulbul practising its sweet calls preparing a dawn raga, the scold of squirrels, the scrape of brooms sweeping the courtyard, the call of fruit-sellers outside my window. I felt uneasy, hating these discordant sounds, hearing only their menace.

'Isa.' He came, even though I barely whispered. He always heard me. 'Where is my beloved? Call him.'

263

'He has gone, Agachi. He came to see you, but your sleep was heavy.'

'Why didn't you go with him, badmash? I gave you an order to be by his side always.'

'He sent me back. He wanted me to stay here and make preparations.'

'For what?'

'Escape, if need be. Agachi, you must rest.'

'I wish people would stop ordering me to do things. Rest, rest, rest—it only weakens me more. Prepare my rath. I want to see the battle.'

'It would not be . . . .'

Our encampment was small without the army, only myself, the children, the servants and a few soldiers who remained with me for protection. My sons were eager to reach a vantage point from which to look; they had no idea of the importance of the conflict. They believed their father, like all fathers, to be invincible, and they wanted to see the flight of the Mughal army.

Boulders lay in the path of the cart and most of the low hills were impassable. At last we found a suitable position about a kos from the plain. Dara and Shahshuja crouched in front of me. Aurangzeb stood at a distance; quiet, intense, but with a disturbing and watchful stance, expecting neither victory nor defeat. I lay, propped on cushions, peering through the heavy curtain towards the approaching dust storm. At such a distance it was not possible to distinguish much, except for the flow of men and beasts, but still I looked towards the centre of our forces, knowing that hidden somewhere in the dust Shah Jahan rode at a stately pace on Bairam.

Our army was so puny! My heart sank. The Mughal forces stretched out far beyond the edge of the plain. They shook the earth, sweeping over the ground like a huge wave. As they neared each other, I heard the faint cries of the soldiers, reaching us no louder than whispers. Two groups of horsemen wheeled away; they would have to ride a great distance to flank the Mughal army, its wings spread wide, like a great bird's shadow. Cannon fired; the battle had begun. On both sides men and beasts fell, re-grouped, advanced, fell, re-grouped, advanced. The horsemen moving east and west did not ride far—a kos, possibly less—before changing direction and charging the Mughal army. They meant to cut the great wings, and one of them appeared to crumble under the impact of the charge, to waver and fall back. The other remained in close formation. Dust drifted towards us, a yellow-brown mist that obscured the heart of the battle itself. The men behind pushed forward, waving swords, hitting shields, shouting. They made a steady and heartening advance, but finally even they were lost to sight.

All day I watched and waited. All was noise and blood. Neither side retreated, but remained firmly rooted in their positions. Like a tide, one part would retreat, then surge again, retreat and surge. Our line wavered, but held. I knew that if it broke and scattered, it would mean Shah Jahan had fallen.

Dusk came early, not pleasant with a cooling breeze, but hot and dusty, muting the sun's glare to an opaque yellow that hung over the earth. We did not remain to watch further. The men would break off to rest, recover their dead, die from their wounds or bind those which were not severe. By the time we reached the village, the first of the men began to trickle back. They were caked in dust and sweat, weary beyond their will and strength. Some carried their companions, moaning with pain, some fell and lay in a dead sleep, others plodded on and on. Some would surely die; what chance had they to live with those bloody rents in their bodies?

Night had fallen, the fires were lit and the food cooked before my beloved came to me. His eyes were red; his face looked no different from the others—dusty, exhausted, his beard the same dull colour as

265

the earth. I fetched wine and he drank greedily. I wiped his face with a tuval, which turned brown with dirt, but the cold touch also removed some of the weariness.

He spoke first to Isa: 'You have prepared everything?'

'Yes, your Highness.'

He touched my face then, apologetically, a gesture for forgiveness.

'We must ride quickly. There isn't much time. By dawn, they'll know I have been defeated.'

the taj mahal 1067/ AD 1657

Gopi squatted by the marble panel and delicately chipped a sliver free. He brushed the stone with a hard, calloused hand, and continued to wrest the flower—a marigold—delicately from the marble. He resembled his father in posture, in patience, in skill. Beside him, Ramesh heated and sharpened the chisels. They worked in the shade of a gulmohar tree outside the wall surrounding the Taj Mahal.

Ten years had passed since the completion of the tomb. The work, however, went on. A great plinth had been built, which gave an illusion of weightlessness to the tomb. At the four corners stood the delicate minarets, tall and slim as palm trees. Their presence satisfied the emperor. They gave balance and harmony to the plinth, which would otherwise appear to be a desert of marble. On either side of the monument were the mosques. They were small and humble, as if bowed in obeisance to the splendour of the tomb.

But it had not been designed and built to stand in dust. With equal care and concern the emperor had commissioned the *bagh*. It was to lie at the foot of the great tomb. The bagh was divided into four quarters; the raised stone pathways running north to south, and east to west, meeting at two lotus fountains carved from marble, and between the paths were wide canals. The still sheets of clear water would reflect the shimmering tomb, but in order not to distract the eye, fountains

267

would be placed only in the north by south canals. To make it worthy of the tomb, Shah Jahan spared no cost in creating the garden. Underground pipes, vast storage tanks and a series of manual draws fed a continuous stream of water to the trees and plants—mango, orange, lemon, pomegranate, apple, guava, pineapple, roses, tulips, lilies, irises, marigolds. The main supply of water was carried by earthenware pipes buried beneath the paved walkways. To ensure that each fountain received exactly the same quantity of water so that their jets rose to the same height, the water was not fed directly into the copper pipes that supplied them. Instead, below each fountain was a copper pot. The water ran the length of the canal, filling each pot, and only then did it flow through the pipes and spring up into the air. The water for the fountains and the garden was lifted from the Jumna by teams of bullocks, poured into the draws and fed into the tanks. From there it flowed down. The pressure of the water decreased as it flowed towards the southern end of the garden. This was a deliberate calculation. Close to the tomb, Shah Jahan wished there to be only flowers, but further away, to shelter the supplicant, there would be trees.

Not once did Gopi look at the Taj Mahal. His head remained bent, and when he raised it somehow he would manage to avoid the sight of the towering monument. It still filled him with bitterness.

His father had been unable to complete the jali. He had grown old and frail, his hands incapable of holding the chisel. They had stiffened and frozen into claws, so Gopi continued to work on the few inches that remained. Compared to the vast tapestry of his father's work, it was a paltry amount, but still it could not be hurried. Everything had to be exact. It had taken him a year to reveal the last part, and then, as if it were clay, he carved into the marble border a motif of flowers—perfect marigolds and lilies with stems and leaves. They were filled with a blend of *safeda* and *hirmich* and colour pigments. These were the same as the materials used for the frescoes he had seen in caves, painted centuries before by forgotten artists. The filling set as hard as marble, and was glazed so that it shone like the stone. Gopi smiled at the memory of his father's immense pride in their accomplishment. He had praised Gopi as if he had done all the work. It seemed to Gopi that after his mother's death his father had softened, become dreamy, only communing with another world. The four of them had made a pilgrimage to the small temple to give thanks. A few other people had attended, furtive, wary, for despite its insignificance and sheltered position, it seemed a vulnerable place. Durga was anointed with saffron and kum-kum, draped in silk, garlanded with a gold and diamond chain. They offered fruit and flowers, and the offerings were blessed and returned. When they left, Murthi had acquired a peaceful look.

'We will go home to our village,' he announced. 'Your mother missed it very much. If only she could come with as. But first we must see our jali. I want to see where it will be placed, see how the light falls on it.'

Workmen wrapped the jali in gunny and placed it reverently on a cart. They watched the cart until it was lost to sight in the bustle of workmen and beasts. Gopi saw his father grow small as if the cart carried part of him away. The jali represented seventeen years of his life, and all his skill.

'When they have placed it,' Murthi said, 'we will go.'

They prepared themselves for the long journey home. It would be exhausting and difficult, but Murthi was determined. When they had discarded what they did not want and bundled together what they would keep—Sita's jewellery would be the dowry for her daughter, Murthi's tools, a small leather bag of rupees—they went to the Taj Mahal.

They approached the soldiers guarding the Taj Mahal, but before they could pass they were stopped.

'Where are you going?'

'Inside. To look.'

The soldiers looked at Murthi, at his sons and daughter. There was no doubt: their faces, their clothes, their manner, all told what these people were.

'You cannot go in.'

Murthi was shocked. 'But why?'

'You are Hindu. It isn't permitted. Now go away.'

'So I am Hindu. What is wrong with that?' Murthi said. 'I worked for seventeen years on this tomb. I was never asked if I was Hindu. I carved the jali, it now stands around the tomb of the empress. I only wish to see it, nothing more. Then I will leave in peace.'

'You cannot enter. You can look at it from here.'

'I only wish to see my jali. The light. . .'

I have told you. It is impossible for you to enter. Hindus are not permitted in here.'

Murthi remained rooted. He was stubborn, but then, so were the soldiers. They blocked his path, not menacingly, but exasperated that the fool wouldn't understand. Gopi gently tugged at his father's arm, but his hand was pushed away. Murthi stood staring at the building, trying to glare through the vast marble walls.

It was only at dusk, as the light faded and the tomb seemed adrift in a hazy pink glow, that he allowed himself to be led away. His face was seamed and he had grown frail. He had to lean on his sons; his daughter led them. The journey to Guntur was forgotten. Murthi lay down in the hut and could not leave. His spirit was bound to a piece of marble; he had given it life, and only by looking on it could he feel he would be free of it now.

Gopi approached his uncle, Isa. He thought, as he sat in Isa's splendid chamber at the palace, how dissimilar the brothers were. It was possible that only the splendour of state disguised Isa. His face was fuller, his body stronger, and there was confidence in his bearing.

'My father is dying.'

'I will bring the hakim.'

'No. The hakim cannot cure him. You can. He wishes to look on his jali, but they will not let him enter. Please could you ask the emperor for permission to allow your brother to visit?'

Isa looked down the river to the Taj Mahal. It shone harshly in the midday sun, the marble glared back at the sky and it stood isolated and alone. It needed a companion of beauty, but there was none in this world. Isa had thought long about the tomb; it had life, it breathed. He imagined the rise and fall of the stone as it sighed. He realized it was lonely. It was a perfect thing in an imperfect world, and that was an awesome burden. Perhaps Shah Jahan's own tomb, a reflection in black, would one day be its companion. But why black—a malevolent colour? Perhaps the emperor wished to remind the world of his guilt. His tomb would stand for the same eternity as the Taj Mahal, but it would be a shroud, not a silken veil. By day it would look ugly, squat and misshapen in the sunlight; at night, it would cease to exist, while the Taj Mahal grew and glowed, played with the light as it did with the water. Even the river would not reflect black. It would be his punishment to groan and suffer under blackness, to dwell forever and ever in the dark. The emperor wished the world to know that he had destroyed the only person he had ever loved.

Could their lives have unfolded differently? Isa could not say. To have loved less would have meant not to love. Love was not to be measured out in portions like food or water, regulated so that it did not overflow. Was it possible to have loved more and, by loving more, snuff out life itself?

'Your brother is dying of a broken heart.' Gopi broke the silence.

'For that I have no cure. What can I do?'

'You have the power to execute men. You can save your brother.'

271

'Power? What do you understand of power? You think that, because he is the Great Mughal, his power is unlimited? It is limited, because he is only a man. He can take life, but not give it, he can change the course of rivers, but he cannot create a drop of water. He can make you a noble, but cannot give you nobility. He can pretend he is a god, but he isn't. If he were, he could breathe life into the dead, and the tomb would never have been built. Nor does he have the power to change the laws of the gods or those who impose them. We are Hindu, we cannot enter.'

'Even you?' Gopi mocked, disbelieving.

Isa did not reply.

Murthi weakened, pining. Death whittled his flesh, chipped at his face; it used him as he had used marble; shaped a corpse from bones, flesh, blood and heart.

Isa walked with his nephews to the ghats. He watched Gopi light the pyre, repeating the words of the priest. His brother had shrunk; he was lost in the mass of flowers. The flames rose, biting into wood and cloth and flesh. He stayed until only ash remained and his nephews squatted by the charred site, staring and waiting for their father to rise in the wisps of smoke.

'Will you return to the village now?' Isa asked Gopi.

'Why? I cannot remember much of our village. I only agreed to go because my father wished it. I must find work here to support my brother and sister.'

There is still much work to be done there,' Isa pointed to the Taj Mahal.

Gopi wanted to refuse, to curse the monument, but said nothing. It had fed his father and family; now it would feed him.

'I will work, as long as there is work.'

272

The emperor's appetite for women had never abated. Slaves, devadasis, nautch girls, princesses, begums; the most beautiful, the most voluptuous, all lay with him day and night. He could not be sated. A demon lived between his legs; he had taken a potion to increase his powers and it had blocked the passage. He could not pass urine and writhed in agony. He clutched at Isa, like a child afraid of demons, until the hakim administered a strong potion of opium.

While he slept, Isa went to the battlements of the Lal Quila and looked out over Delhi. He heard the whispers already racing through the city: the emperor is dying, the emperor is dying. Doors closed, shops were barred, chai and paan wallahs melted back into the night. Once he had received the summons, Dara rode swiftly, and his horse's hooves echoed through the still city and far beyond into the empire. It reached the ears of Shahshuja, Subadar of Bengal, Murad, Subadar of Gujarat and Aurangzeb, Subadar of the Deccan. Isa sensed them stir in their distant palaces.

In the darkness, down on the maidan, he saw figures gathering below the jharoka-i-darshan. One, two, ten, a hundred. Inside the palace, the nobles slipped in silently, gathering in the diwan-i-am to stare up at the empty *awrang* beneath its canopy of gold.

All looked east. The blackness began to fade, the sky turned a delicate gold; it was dawn, but the emperor did not appear. The nobles and people waited, even as the sun rose high and beat down on their backs.

Isa knew their thoughts: The emperor is dead. And he heard the people below weep, for he had been as a just and wise father to them. They wept too for the unknown.

Shah Jahan woke to pain, teeth bared, and whispered to Isa: 'Agra . . . Agra . . . I must look on her.'

'He cannot be moved,' the hakim said.

273

'Cure him,' Dara and Jahanara begged, but the hakim cowered at his own ignorance.

Dara summoned a wazir: 'Issue a proclamation. The Emperor Shah Jahan is at present unwell. He will recover soon. Send it to all corners of the empire.'

The wazir obeyed the command. He posted a message on the gates of the Lal Quila and sent messengers racing across Hindustan. But other messengers rode swiftly to Dara's brothers: The Emperor is dying and the Prince Dara has taken command of the empire.'

For two further days and nights the emperor lay in a drugged sleep. When he finally awoke, the pain had fled from his body, but his face was etched with exhaustion.

'Agra. I must go to her. Isa,' he ordered, 'tell the Mir Manzil to prepare my journey.' He looked then to Dara and saw the anxious look in his eyes. 'What is it, Dara?'

'My brothers have declared their intent. They believe you are dead. Shahshuja now calls himself Sikander the Second, and Murad has struck coins.'

'And Aurangzeb?' Shah Jahan could not disguise his dread.

'Nothing,' Dara said. 'He has spoken not a word, but he moves now towards us with his army.'

'His army? His . . .'Shah Jahan shouted. 'My bi-daulat sons. Their greed outreaches their affection. Take me to the awrang. I must show myself.'

The nobles were summoned and the Ahadi formed their ranks around the diwan-i-am. Shah Jahan, supported by Dara and Isa, mounted the steps of the alcove and settled slowly on the peacock throne. The nobles noted the toll of his illness: the shake of his hands and the weakness of his neck. He had lost strength. They noted too the authority of Dara.

'I am well,' the emperor spoke, but his voice barely reached their ears. 'My beloved son and the only loyal one, the Prince Dara will rule

274

until I am strong enough to take up my duties once more.'

Isa saw a veil, dark and dreadful, descend on those upturned faces. He could read their thoughts: Is Dara strong enough? Isa knew from what he saw that the emperor had made a mistake. Out of love, he had placed the empire on the shifting sands of divided loyalties.

'I order my sons to return to their posts on pain of punishment. I am still Padishah of Hindustan.'

It took ten days to reach Agra and immediately they arrived the emperor entered the great tomb and the silver doors closed behind him. He knelt at the sarcophagus and kissed the icy marble.

'My beloved, my beloved . . .' His whisper echoed up into the dome. 'What should I do now? Our sons march against me. They will not obey the commands of their father, the Emperor. My words are but dust in the wind. I fall ill and they turn against me. Our beloved Dara is my sole support; our love has nourished loyalty in his breast. I have sent him into battle against his brother Shahshuja and I cannot breathe for fear, I never feared for myself in war,, but now for another I tremble like a coward. Watch over him . . . guide him . . . give him your strength, my beloved Arjumand.'

Shah Jahan kept his vigil in the tomb until Dara came to him, victorious, Shahshuja had been defeated and now fled back to Bengal. Dara laughed with delight and his mirth echoed around the tomb.

The emperor remained kneeling: 'And Aurangzeb?' Dara fell silent. 'He marches now with Murad. Aurangzeb has proclaimed Murad emperor,' He chuckled, 'I will defeat Murad as easily as Shuja.'

'But he has Aurangzeb,' Shah Jahan spoke gently. He turned to Isa: 'Do you believe Aurangzeb would allow Murad to become emperor?'

'Who can truly read the mind of Aurangzeb, your majesty?'

'Then I must lead the army against them. Only my experience and my presence can defeat Aurangzeb.'

'No,' Dara shouted. 'If I am to rule one day, I must fight Aurangzeb.' He turned and stalked angrily out of the tomb, like a child deprived of his toys.

Shah Jahan, wounded, looked at Isa: 'Am I wrong?'

'No, your majesty. Only you can defeat Aurangzeb. Dara has not the experience.'

'But I have made him unhappy.'

'It will pass,' but even as Isa spoke he sensed the emperor sway from his decision and he felt dread.

It was as he had spoken. On the banks of the Chambal, while Shah Jahan and Isa waited in the tomb, Aurangzeb defeated Dara. Thousands died in the day-long battle, and when Dara retreated, his army fled. Dishevelled and dispirited he returned to Agra. His father, forgiving and loving, comforted him even as Aurangzeb now turned on the foolish Murad. Aurangzeb bound Murad and placed him on an elephant which took him to an unknown prison. At the same moment, three other similar elephants were sent to the other points, of the compass.

'The monster!' Shah Jahan raged. The deceiver. He has always intended to become emperor.'

'He has vowed to imprison me too,' Dara said hopelessly. 'He hates me.'

'We will defeat the bi-daulat. We will raise another army.' Then, as if to defy the very forces of destiny that moved against him, he proclaimed: 'Dara is now Emperor of Hindustan.'

Isa watched the new army stretch out across the dusty plain outside Agra. The sun glittered on helmets and lances, cannons and jezails. The men and beasts appeared countless, but he knew it was a hollow force. Agra had been emptied of butchers and cooks and carpenters. They would be no match for Aurangzeb.

And Aurangzeb, chaining the foot of his war elephant to a stake in

276

the earth, vowing victory, only defeated Dara by the betrayal of Dara's commander, Khallihillah Khan. Dara fled west, while Aurangzeb marched on to Agra.

1068/AD 1658

Shah Jahan peered down from the battlements. The soldiers stared up. No one moved. From the roof of the mosque the cannon boomed. He did not flinch as the shot struck the walls of the fort and splashed into the moat.

'Bi-daulat,' he shouted, and shook his fist at the army that surrounded the Padishah, the Great Mughal, the emperor of Hindustan, Shah Jahan, Sovereign of the World. 'Bi-daulat.'

His cry did not carry; the army did not vanish. 'What have I done?'

'You fell ill,' Isa said. 'And Aurangzeb wants to be emperor.'

'Well, he cannot, until I die,' Shah Jahan said petulantly. 'I fall ill for three days, and great armies march. What did he expect would happen to me in those three days? That I would die? The badmash.'

'He claims he came only to aid you,' Isa said. To give you protection against your other sons.'

'He is a liar. Dara, where is Dara? If only he'd listened to me, my dear beloved son could have saved me. Aurangzeb knew Dara would never harm me.'

'I know,' Isa said softly. 'Dara fought to protect you, but he did not have Aurangzeb's experience in warfare. Who knows where he is now? You loved Dara too much, your majesty, and Aurangzeb not enough. You gave Dara the dream that he would become emperor, but by keeping him at your side, you weakened him. Each caress, each kiss of affection lessened his strength to survive against Aurangzeb. And each kiss, each caress only strengthened Aurangzeb's hatred. Now he hates Dara.'

'I curse you, Isa, for warning me too late. Warning? You read the rites over our graves. Oh God, where is Dara?'

'He flees.'

'We must give him time—time to escape, time to raise another army and defeat Aurangzeb.'

The emperor's pearl prayer beads clicked, counting away the time. They could be heard across the river. His only solace now was God, and he went to Him in the Mina Masjid—only there was there peace for an emperor.

Taktya Takhta.

It was carved on his heart. He could not erase it. His own whisper echoed across the years, it could not be retracted. In the brevity of words lay the swiftness of events. The emperor's authority had seeped away. He was a ghost who whispered from behind the throne, but none heard him.

Shah Jahan descended from the Mina Masjid. Prayer had been no balm; age scythed at him, cutting furrows in his face.

'I will invite Aurangzeb to come to me and discuss the matter. Then he must return to his post.' For a moment Shah Jahan raged, fierce and dangerous, then as quickly calmed. 'I will beg him to return to the Deccan, to go in peace. I will forgive him.'

Isa went. He carried Alamgir, the sword fashioned from a star. The hilt was of gold, studded with emeralds. On the pommel was a stone the size of a clenched fist. The scabbard was also made of gold, encrusted with pearls, diamonds and emeralds. The wicked, curving blade never lost its brilliance or sharpness. Alamgir: Seizer of the Universe.

Aurangzeb awaited Isa in Dara's palace by the Jumna, the residence of the prince Shah Jahan and his wife Arjumand. Isa was suffocated by memory. He had not entered here for years. Aurangzeb stood where Arjumand had spread her silver trinkets and won back the heart of her prince. He trampled the grass, uncaring. He took the sword from Isa and drew it from the scabbard. The sun sang on the blade.

'Alamgir. It is well balanced. What else does my father send, Isa?'

'He invites you to discuss the matter.'

Isa amused Aurangzeb. He smiled and looked back at the fort.

'No doubt he would like me to return to my post. He orders me to run here, run there. All these years I have run for him, to attack Kandahar, to attack Samarkand. I have marched through cold mountains and burning deserts on his bidding. I have been a dutiful son, haven't I, Isa?'

'You speak as if your duty were over.'

'It isn't,' there was fervour in his voice; his eyes never left the fort, but brooded with longing. 'Whose fault is it? Mine? I would have loved him, but all his love flowed to that usurper, Dara.'

'Dara did not usurp the throne, your Highness. The emperor . . .'

'You too will only speak well of Dara. You loved him as if he were your own son. Why? Because my mother loved him. The firstborn—I watched her smother him with her affection. He received all her kisses; we others were forgotten.'

'You are fortunate to find so many to blame, your Highness.'

'You have a wicked tongue, Isa. One day you might lose it.'

'Do you expect me to fear the child I once carried in my arms?'

'You put too much faith in my affection.'

'I will not make that mistake again, your Highness.'

'Ah, Isa.' Aurangzeb smiled forgiveness in a comradely manner, slapped his arm. It was a stiff and formal gesture. To Isa, Aurangzeb the man was no different from Aurangzeb the child. 'I would not harm you, but Dara has harmed me. He hates me. He has poisoned my father's mind against me, as Mehrunissa poisoned Jahangir's against him. If I retreat from here, he will return. And once more we will battle, and once more I will win. The fool knows nothing of warfare; he only knows his foolish tolerance of all men. He would love the Hindu more than the Muslim; he would give him freedom to worship, freedom to propagate that evil religion and suppress the true faith. I cannot permit that to happen. We must crush the Hindu so he will never rise again.'

Aurangzeb's fervour chilled Isa. He believed himself the true defender of the faith, the true Scourge of God. Babur, Akbar, Jahangir, and Shah Jahan had believed too, but not like this, not like this.

'Then there will be no peace in your lifetime,' Isa said. 'If you declare war on your subjects, they will declare war on you. The throne will shake and fall, for it stands only on the foundation laid by Akbar and built upon by your father and grandfather. They decreed that all people should be treated justly. If you unleash hatred, you will receive hatred in return. What you do will echo through time, just as what has occurred in the past echoes today. There will be no escape from the consequences of your actions. Aurangzeb will be a name to be hated by generations to come.'

'You talk like Dara the fool.'

'Maybe I am a fool too, your Highness.'

'Then I am wasting my time. You may return to my father and give him my message—he will hand the fort over to me.'

'He will refuse.'

'Don't speak for the emperor, you fool.'

'And don't speak as if you already were one, your Highness.'

'Your familiarity angers me. I will not always remember that you carried me as a child.'

Isa returned to the fort and reported to Shah Jahan. He knew his ruler well; Shah Jahan refused.

'We must give Dara more time. Even now he is raising an army. I know he will rescue me.'

'But he cannot defeat Aurangzeb, your majesty. Only your skill can do that, and it is trapped within these walls. Dara has not had enough experience.'

'Ah, but God is on his side. You always were a nuisance, Isa. Did Aurangzeb tell you what would happen to me?'

'No, your majesty.'

'He intends to murder me, I know that.'

Takhta, he whispered to himself, and for a moment he thought his voice sounded like Khusrav's. Too late. He should have heeded Arjumand.

Gopi, Ramesh and Savitri huddled together in their hut. The street was quiet, the silence hung with dust. They had seen the soldiers surround the fort. They did not know what was happening; a thunderstorm seemed about to rage over their heads. For two days they remained hidden, as everyone did in the city. Then on the third day, driven by hunger, Gopi ventured out to the bazaar to buy food. He went quickly, furtively, but the soldiers paid no attention to him. Some stalls were open, and hurriedly he purchased what they needed.

A tall, plainly dressed man, surrounded by soldiers, entered the bazaar. He might have been a commoner, except for the authority in his manner. He stopped, and looked around haughtily and possessively.

'Who is that?' Gopi asked a soldier.

'Prince Aurangzeb, the emperor's son.'

Two Muslim priests approached the prince and bowed deferentially. Their faces were lit with a fierce piety. A third man followed, carrying a gunny bag. Gopi watched them take the gunny bag and throw out the contents at Aurangzeb's feet. Gopi felt ill with shock. There, still garlanded with diamonds, still smeared with kum-kum, still clothed in silk, lay his father's Durga.

The diamond chain was removed and handed to a slave and the priests fetched a large iron-headed mallet. Aurangzeb took it in both hands and swung it above his head. With demonic force he brought it down on the marble of Durga, shattering it.

Seeing the splinters fall in the dust, for the first time in his life Gopi experienced a deep, unreasoning fear. It was followed, like the surge of a wave, by hatred for Aurangzeb.

the love story 1032/AD 1622

Arjumand

My beloved had to bid Bairam farewell, and it almost broke his heart.
The old scarred beast was the most loved and trusted companion he
had, as gentle as Isa, as faithful as Allami Sa'du-lla Khan and in battle as
sagacious as Mahabat Khan. But his stubborn loyalty and unshakeable
refusal ever to be upset or hurried were the very reasons why we had
to leave him now. He seemed to understand that it had to be so; he
curled his trunk round Shah Jahan's body in a loving embrace and tears
gathered in his wise, wrinkled eyes. He had borne my love back and
forth across the empire without complaint, had carried him into
countless battles, great-hearted as any true warrior. Shah Jahan clasped
his trunk and wept like a child; he begged the mahout, every second of
whose life was his prince's to command, to look after his old friend
and keep him safe and well.

The unearthly quiet of the land magnified every sound so that the
din of our escape was deafening. Though the men only whispered, it
sounded as if they shouted. Weary beyond fatigue after the long battle,
they staggered and scrambled to saddle horses, awaken surly camels,
fold the shamiyanas, load the carts, abandon the wounded, the cannon,
the elephants.

283

As we left the camp, Shah Jahan turned in the saddle once more; Bairam raised his trunk black against the stars and let forth one great cry of grief, rage and loss, so shrill that it must surely reach out to every corner of the empire to tell the people that their prince was fleeing in defeat.

The land was silvery grey, empty. Moonlight stole the harsh purple reality of the hills and trees, boulders and ravines, reduced their substance to an illusion. We drifted through mist, and rode through shadows. We could not see where we were going nor from where we had come.

Only the children revelled in our plight. They were woken by Isa and dressed and, though somewhat querulous, enjoyed the excitement and secrecy. The little girls clung to me in fear. Dara, being the eldest son, philosophically accepted our defeat, although he did not understand what it meant. His little arms around my neck gave us both comfort, assured me of his love. Shahshuja was stolid and unemotional; Aurangzeb remained awake as we moved out of Balockpur, his face grave. He took the defeat as a personal affront. His eyes glistened, but he did not allow any tears to fall. He neither sought comfort nor gave it.

Only five thousand horsemen, loyal soldiers, fled with us. The remainder of the army, like smoke blown by a breeze, dispersed into the night. Some would return to the Deccan, others to their villages in the north. My beloved was no longer able to hold them. He could no longer afford to pay them, and they abandoned his cause. I had little doubt many would join Mahabat Khan; the Great Mughal would pay them well to hunt down his son.

By dawn many miles lay behind us. With the daylight came the immense heat, striking down horses and men, littering our path with armour, swords, shields, muskets, bedding. We could not rest, could not, like the men and beasts we passed, lie in the shade. News of defeat preceded us swiftly. All knew of it. Villages were closed, silent; we

284

caught glimpses of fearful people watching our progress from within and praying that we would not seek their poor shelter. The land looked deserted, cloaked in a deceptive peace, but I knew that peace was an eternity away from us. A limitless empire had shrunk to a handful of earth. Where could we scurry, where could we hide? The earth was laid bare; Jahangir's eyes pierced every nook and corner. There were no secret places; eyes watched, ears heard, tongues betrayed. The defeated were met by hostility. We moved south. For two days and two nights our column travelled slowly, painfully, each step wearier than the last. Horses stumbled and fell, heaving great sighs as they died. Men took to foot, looking behind fearfully to see whether they could descry the dust of the Mughal army. The horizon remained clear.

My beloved rode ahead, harrying the earth for shelter. None was to be found; palaces were closed, forts barred. Ranas, nawabs, amirs, nobles, all ignored our existence as though Jahangir had stretched out his hand and shut their eyes. I could not blame them. An emperor's wrath or a weary prince's gratitude—there was no choice. Each day he returned with exhaustion and despair cut deep into his face. Dust embraced him from turban to toe, changed his colour, reduced his proud authority to haunted stiffness. I knew I was a burden to him, a boulder that dragged at his feet.

'Go. You can ride faster without us.'

'No.' He lay beside me, resting briefly in the stuffy shade of my ruth; we jolted against one another. His eyes were bloodshot with dust and exhaustion, and I bathed them gently, wiping his face.

'We will be safe. No harm will befall us. Neither the emperor nor Mehrunissa will touch so much as a hair on our heads.'

'I know.' A smile rose to his weary face, sad, unbearably sad. They will not break the Timurid law. I have.'

'That is past. We cannot undo what has happened.'

'You would take the blame for me, then?'

'We are one and the same. Let us not think about that any more.

285

Khusrav is dead. You live. You must be safe.'

'I cannot leave you. Or do you wish to be left?'

'No. But we slow you down.'

'Mahabat Khan is only two days behind.' He smiled affectionately. The old tiger gave me time. He must have known of our escape even as we crept away. Jahangir has sent Parwez to join him.'

'Not Shahriya? That would have given him some experience,' I said with bitterness.

'Mehrunissa doesn't want to risk his life. The future emperor must remain safe, hidden in the haram.' He kissed me. 'You are well?'

'Yes, always when I am with you,' I spoke dishonestly, but it pleased him and he closed his eyes, resting against me in the cart.

He slept, and I watched. The lines were still there, the brief respite from exhaustion was not enough to erase them. I tried to smooth them with my fingers, but they returned immediately and he stirred. I knew my own features were likewise furrowed. Though I had not battled, I felt I was crumbling inside. My body ached; it shivered. I had not yet recovered from the recent birth; it had been difficult. Each child took its toll of my body and the journey to recovery was longer each time. With Dara I had been vigorous and joyful in my return to health. I grew melancholy now. I only wished to sleep and rest, to fall into the warm soothing comfort of a hamam, to lie without moving as a breeze cooled the fever in my body. How long? How long? I could not lift the screen of eternity that lay before us.

Shah Jahan awoke at dusk. He did not look refreshed, but weary; his sleep had been filled with the ghostly figures of Jahangir, Mehrunissa, Mahabat Khan, Parwez, and a host of horsemen.

'Where shall we go?'

'I don't know. No one will hide us. Perhaps we can return to Burhanpur. I still have authority there.'

'But for how long? Your soldiers will have told them that we were defeated. The Deccan princes would readily betray us to Jahangir so as

286

to remain in his favour.'

'All princes would, not only those of the Deccan.' He sighed. 'Mahabat Khan will assume that we're returning to Burhanpur. If we travel to the west, perhaps we can find shelter with one of the Rajput princes.'

'Which one? Jaipur rides with Mahabat Khan. Malwar too.'

'We will go to Mewar.'

'Karan Singh will always remember his father's defeat at your hands.'

'He might also remember our kindness towards him. I will send a messenger ahead asking him to give us refuge from my father. He might take delight in defying the emperor.'

'Or in killing us.'

'Anyone would do that, my love. Betrayal is the natural trade of all men. I would distrust anyone who said it was not so. Our survival depends on the desirability or otherwise of our presence, and both are beyond our control. They can change from minute to minute, day to day. We may be welcome one day, unwelcome the next, depending on the storms that rage in men's hearts and minds. They will look at us and think: what can we gain? The thought will beat in their heads night and day, and as they watch us, we must watch them. Am I worth supporting? Am I worthless? I can promise great wealth, great honour, but they know the more desperate a prince becomes, the greater grows his generosity.'

His face conveyed the despair of his words. The smallest plot of earth would have seemed to us a limitless space in which to hide. We would have only so much as was contained in the heart of a man. If it were a strong heart we could remain hidden forever; if it were weak we might be delivered up in chains.

'Send a messenger then to Karan Singh. He may lie to entice us there. But what else can we do?'

'Nothing. I will also send Miami Sa'du-lla Khan and what men we can spare to continue south towards Burhanpur. Mahabat Khan will follow them while we return west to Mewar.'

Only one hundred horsemen accompanied us on this journey. The remainder rode south under Allami Sa'du-lla Khan's command. For one month, longer if possible, they were to lead Mahabat Khan, Parwez and the Mughal army as far from Mewar as they could. Then they would disband, re-group after having shaken off the pursuit, and join their prince in Udaipur.

We no longer bore the outward appearance of a prince of the empire, his princess and a royal family. Instead, having cast off his rich clothing and jewellery, my Shah Jahan looked like a very minor noble travelling to visit rich and powerful relatives. He could not be other than minor, for did he not have only one wife? The soldiers too no longer wore the prince's colours, but looked like dacoits. We travelled with less haste, since we knew the Mughal army moved south, but with no less caution. The subas we passed through were the Mughal's and all the Rajput kingdoms were under his suzerainty. We began our journey at dusk and halted at dawn, slipping quietly through villages, avoiding towns and forts, clinging to the shadows of hills and jungles. We made camp in ravines or in deep forests, hidden from the sun and the eyes of men.

The children suffered. They slept fitfully, and our lack of comfort dispirited them. They were trapped with each other, and quarrelled, fought and reconciled, choosing enemies and allies like little kings. Dara and Jahanara would join forces against Aurangzeb and Raushanara, and sometimes Shahshuja and' Aurangzeb would fight side by side. Never did Dara and Aurangzeb join together. They chose only those who would move against the other. Shah Jahan allowed the boys to ride with the soldiers; it was a makeshift school in which they would learn the craft of warfare, Aurangzeb was the most eager; Dara preferred the company of Isa, and the few books that we still had with us. All the children read the Quran, and the *Babur-nama* and *Jahangir-nama*. It was a bitter amusement that we carried this testament of love

288

for Shah Jahan, while being pursued by the armies of him who wrote it.

At the border of Mewar we were met by the Sisodia Karan Singh himself, and his horsemen. Karan Singh dismounted and touched Shah Jahan's knee; they embraced with great affection. My beloved could not hide his relief at finding an ally in this desolate world.

'You can stay as long as you wish,' Karan Singh announced.

'I will stay only as long as it is safe for us all. We need rest. Arjumand is very tired and weak, and I must give her time to recover her strength.'

'She will rest in my lake palace at Jag Mandir. Her courage is no less than that of my ancestor, Queen Padmini, who led the women into jauhar rather than be taken prisoner. I will honour Arjumand as I honour her.'

I, of course, knew the legend of Queen Padmini. Over three centuries ago, the Pathan king Ala-ud-din Khilji heard of Padmini's great beauty. She was the wife of the ruling rana's uncle, Bhim Singh. Ala-ud-din Khilji attacked Chitor and said that he would only withdraw his forces if he could see Padmini. For a Muslim to look upon a Hindu princess directly was impossible, but in order to accommodate Khilji and to have the siege lifted, the Rana permitted the Pathan king to look upon Padmini's reflection in a mirror. Khilji became so infatuated by this sight of Padmini that he broke his promise and redoubled his efforts to capture Chitor. But just as he neared victory, the princess led all the Rajput women into an underground cave and they committed jauhar. The Rajput men then donned their saffron robes and died in battle.

We left the dust and dirt and the hard road behind and were borne to the palace which was like a marble cloud afloat on the water. It lay low and serene on the surface of the lake, and as the barges transported us towards it, I could not imagine a more peaceful refuge. I yearned for its silence, for the blessing of the lapping water, the cool breeze on my burning skin, the cold marble underfoot and the air clean of choking dust.

Jag Mandir was not Hindu in architecture, but Muslim. My beloved looked on it with great interest, and once we were within its walls he spent many days in the company of Karan Singh exploring every corner of the palace. The Sisodia had observed the red sandstone palace in the Lal Quila, and the equally magnificent but abandoned palace of Akbar at Fatehpur Sikri. Red sandstone was not available here, so he used marble. The light playing on the stone and the reflection of the building in the water without any imperfection delighted my beloved. In the moonlight, as we lay on the balcony looking out towards the distant shore, the image turned to silver. He would look down at it for hour upon hour, and fell in love with the beauty of it.

For days and weeks we lived suspended in tranquillity. Battle, defeat, the harshness of our journeys, all were now distant and unreal. This was our reality: we could foresee no other. Awakening to gentle light glowing in our bedchamber, bathing at leisure in the hamam, lying perfumed and resting with the breeze cooling me until twilight, and then listening to the singers who sang of great Rajput princes and their bravery and how they fought the Mughal Akbar—thus were our days passed. When the palace fell quiet, we would lie together and love each other until we were exhausted and sated. In all the confusion of our circumstances, our love never changed. His tenderness and passion never faltered, never waned. We did not speak of our future; for all we knew, we had none. We did not talk wistfully of the time when he had been crown prince of Hindustan We lived only for the present, taking pleasure in the moon, the stars, the beauty of the night sky, the colours of dawn and dusk. Yet, we knew it was all but a dream. Over the distant horizon Mehrunissa brooded. Though Karan Singh hid us, others had eyes and knew of our presence in Jag Mandir. We heard the whispers against her, and my father wrote to tell us that the

290

nobles stirred in unease, unhappy about her relentless pursuit of my beloved.

I knew that Shah Jahan strove to hide his worries from me. Unaware of my gaze, he would frown and look out longingly towards the empire that surrounded us. Towards the hundredth day of our stay, Allami Sa'du-lla Khan came. He looked thinner and tired. He had led Mahabat Khan as far south as Mandu, then the Mughal army, sensing trickery, had turned back and begun to search for us. It would not be long before they discovered our retreat. I spent each day in breathless fear, dreading the warning that we would have to run from our island seclusion. Every evening, I would pray for us to be given another day. I had regained my strength, but my mood darkened when I discovered that I was with child once more. Ah, if only we could separate pleasure from its consequences, how much sweeter would be the enjoyment and pleasure of it. I did not tell my beloved; his face had grown taut and thin as he waited for danger to strike.

It came at night, while we slept, Isa called to us, and even through our drowsiness we heard the urgency in his voice. He held a lantern and in the pale yellow gleam I saw the children gathered together, rubbing sleep from their eyes. He had prepared them before waking me to give me a longer rest.

The wily Mahabat Khan had doubled back up to Ajmer, and now moved swiftly towards Udaipur.

'He is but a day's ride from here,' Karan Singh said as we hurried down the corridors; our shadows lagged far behind, reluctant to leave such a haven. 'His men gallop and won't stop to rest until they reach that shore. I will send my army to meet him.'

'No. You have done enough for us. A day is more than we need. We will escape him again.'

There was no moon on the night we left. The sky was dark with swollen clouds that threatened rain, and Jag Mandir was only a flat, shadowless mass rising out of the waters. There was no reflection, no beauty, and we lost sight of it long before we reached the shore. Already it was only a memory. It had all been a dream. Despair settled swiftly.

We rode through the monsoon. The rain fell in shafts, obscuring the world around us. We moved in a huddled, dispirited group, isolated from all other living things. As they sought dry shelter and relief, we moved on. The dust turned to mud, the mud to puddles, the puddles to streams, the streams grew into rivers, and the rivers became raging torrents. They boomed, carelessly smashing through their banks, shattering them and consuming all life on either side, flattening out across the land to become a vast lake drowning villages and fields. The waters were littered with the dead; cattle, men, women, children, pi-dogs; their stench filled the air. The foulness, not only of corpses, but of rotting trees, sodden earth and clothing, choked us. Mould and mildew grew on the soaked divans, the shamiyanas tore, our clothes rent easily.

All the world was sweat and heat and rain. Even my hair felt as if it rotted in my head; it stuck to my face and back and neck, like roots desperately clinging to the earth.

Shah Jahan

I could not move north; my father waited there, I could not move east; Mahabat Khan raced towards us. I could not move west; Persia was at war with us. Perhaps, to spite Jahangir, the Shahinshah would have offered us shelter, as he had my great-grandfather Humayun, but to move so far from my father would have been foolish. It would take too long to return to claim the throne on his death. I would have to remain within the boundaries of the empire.

So we moved south. In the Deccan we would find refuge, however temporary, for Arjumand to rest. She could have remained in Jag Mandir in the care of Karan Singh, but the desolation of being without her on this long, endless pursuit was unimaginable. I needed her comfort, her courage, her love: I could not expect these from anyone else in the world. Except for her I was truly alone; without her I would despair. When I looked on her enchanting face, heard her soft silky voice which still reminded me of the rising of incense smoke, felt the caress of her fingers on my face and on my lips, I would briefly forget our wretchedness, and for a minute, an hour, my troubles ceased. She neither complained nor protested, while my men ceased to do neither. I could not blame them. They were following Jahangir's bi-daulat and their reward would be scant. Betrayal lurked in every heart except Arjumand's.

Our path was not straight. We could not ford the swollen rivers, so we meandered south and north searching for crossings. Our shelters were a village hut, an abandoned fort, a cave. Such small comforts were all that the Sovereign of the World could command.

The rain ceased, and the sun steamed the earth. For a few days we travelled through a tender green landscape filled with flowers and shrubs and new-born animals. This blessed time was too brief. We had escaped the welter of rain only to be crushed by the heat. We discarded our rusting armour and kept only our swords and shields, scant protection in case of battle. The passing of the days ceased to have any meaning; they came and went, and we moved further south. On the ninetieth day, we reached the outskirts of Mandu.

We could not move further. Arjumand bled. The hakim staunched the flow as best he could, and refused to allow her to move. I prayed. The bleeding ceased, but the child was lost. I wept, not for it but for Arjumand, so pale and tired. If I could have given her my life, my blood, I would have. I remained by her side for many days, uncaring of the danger. Ten days passed before she could sit up; Isa and I held her and fed her. Slowly, her colour and her strength returned. We could not move until she was well again.

I was not granted such a luxury. Allami Sa'du-lla Khan came to me, accompanied by a soldier who had been despatched to report on

293

Mahabat Khan's movements.

'Your Highness, Mahabat Khan is a few days behind us. He is nearing Indore.'

'Arjumand must not travel.'

'She must.'

'"Must?" You tell me "must", when I tell you she can't? Forgive me, my friend, for giving orders as though I were a prince.'

'You are, your Highness,' Allami Sa'du-lla Khan smiled wryly. His teeth were red with paan. He had grown lean, like all of us; fat only gathered at court. How long had I known him? For a century it seemed, and he had never wavered in his loyalty. I knew he had little wealth, and it surprised me continually that he remained loyal to one as impoverished as I. Mehrunissa would have rewarded him greatly for his betrayal.

'One day you will be Padishah. Until then, we must run. We cannot move south. Mahabat Khan has sent a detachment ahead under your brother Parwez. We cannot return. We can go only east or west, and there are only narrow passages through Mahabat Khan's buffalo horns.'

'You suggest surrender?'

'No. Who knows what Mehrunissa will do? Your father won't harm you, but she isn't of the Timurid line. She might persuade him to take your life.' He shrugged. 'West, I would suggest.'

We brooded. The choice was pitiful. I felt the weight of defeat heavy on my heart.

A soldier approached as we held our council, and a step behind the soldier came a thin, small man. He stopped some paces away.

'Your Highness, this man says he wishes to help you.'

I looked at the bearded face. It stared back at me boldly, awaiting recognition. His clothes were threadbare, his turban dusty. He stood in the manner of a man accustomed to carrying a weapon, alert, wary, hunted.

'Who are you? Why do you want to help me?'

'The prince Shah Jahan doesn't remember me? No matter. It was an insignificant incident in the great prince's life.'

'You mock me with your flattery?'

'No, your Highness. I would not insult the man who saved my life.' He saw that I was still puzzled. 'My name is Arjun Lal. Many years ago, while you were travelling to Burhanpur, you came across a man, his brother and his cousin. They were to be executed for planning to murder a thakur. You heard my plea for justice, and instead ordered the thakur's execution.'

'Shabash. I remember. Was he executed?'

The man smiled without humour, 'Not by the officials. I was thrashed, and set free, The thakur was allowed to live . . . for a while.'

'I don't wish to hear further. Let it be your secret. How can I help you now?

'It is I who can help you. I can lead you to safety. I know these hills and ravines well; they are my home. I know a place where you can rest until it is safe for you and your princess to travel.'

I had no choice. At nightfall, we carefully and slowly moved Arjumand east in her rath. The dacoit took us on a winding path through ravines, down dried river-beds, and into a deep cave that appeared unending. Finally we emerged on the other side, far away from Mahabat Khan and my brother. They could have searched for our path for months and not found it. We rested in a tiny hidden valley until Arjumand regained her strength.

'When I am emperor, come and ask what you will. It shall be granted.'

'If I live that long, your Highness, I shall approach you to ask only for justice. I am a farmer and I want to return to my land.'

'I will remember what you have done for us.'

How could I mark and count the days, the months, the years? We snatched shelter and comfort as others snatch at sleep. We lived on what we could plunder from towns and villages. Princes whom I had once fought and conquered now, from convenience, gave me support until, out of inconvenience, they withdrew it. The ranks of my men dwindled and swelled, depending on the alliances I could create. I, Shah Jahan, begged favours of mean and petty men, unjust men. I was profligate with my love, extravagant in my gratitude for the roof over our heads, the food for our bellies, but silent in my vow to avenge betrayal.

We moved eastwards, resting little and hoarding our meagre resources, until we heard that Mahabat Khan and my brother drew near. The numbers that rode with them never lessened—over thirty thousand horsemen, fifty war elephants, thirteen cannon and countless camels carrying provisions. They moved with the slow and steady dignity of a tide which knew that eventually it would prevail, would conquer and drown.

It was at Surguja, deep in the hills, that I fought Mahabat Khan again, not from choice, but because of betrayal. It happened during the second winter. We enjoyed the hospitality of the Nawab, a generous, kind host. He was a patron of music, and for many evenings we listened to the men and women who gathered at his palace to entertain him. And what did he not give us? Gifts, food, gardens in which to wander, horses, elephants. He was not effusive, but gently solicitous, as though for an errant son; he was old and had only female children. He had no lack of wives, whom he used as frequently as his ailing strength would permit, but it was his misfortune to have no male heir. I believed myself loved, and would have remained throughout the winter in this isolated kingdom if Malik Ambar had not sent warning. Ambar was the Abyssinian general who commanded the combined forces of the Deccan princes when I defeated them years ago, and my former enemy had intercepted a messenger riding back towards Surguja. The messenger had informed Mahabat Khan of our hiding-place. Ambar sent me word that already Mahabat Khan rode towards us.

It was too late. Even as we hastily fled the Nawab's hospitality, the Mughal army was within five or six kos of Surguja. They had abandoned their elephants and cannon in order to make speed. I could not meet so many horsemen with the hope of anything other than defeat. I sent Arjumand, the children and Isa on ahead. They were to ride fast and not halt until I and my men caught up with them. Where that would be, I could not tell.

'They are too many, your Highness,' Allami Sa'du-lla Khan warned. 'We should run too.'

'We will be caught. The best we can do is give them little stings, like flies worrying an elephant. The terrain is our only advantage. It is impossible for such a large army to fight a battle in hills and ravines.'

'What difference does that make? We only command two and a half thousand men. And how many of them will desert when they see the force they have to meet?'

'But we will be swift. I learnt from Malik Ambar how a smaller force can harry a huge one. We will hide in the hills—yes, like dacoits hit them quickly and withdraw. It will confuse them, slow them down.'

We divided our meagre forces into five commands, five hundred horsemen in each, pitifully small numbers against the flowing mass. But a whole river can be shifted by a small log felled across its course. We would not fight, but make raids, riding swiftly to strike the enemy's flanks and, before the army turned, fade back into the ravines where they could not pursue.

The Mughal army came, and I could not help feeling a rush of pride. It was an impressive force of men, disciplined and guided by Mahabat's cunning. However, like all huge forces, it was arrogant in its invincibility.

I attacked the right flank, cutting and chewing into men and horses, and by the time the command was given to confront me, I had turned and fled back into the shadowed valleys. Then the other commanders, one by one, attacked a different limb of the unwieldy monster that could only snap, but not turn fully to destroy the insects that buzzed at it. For three days and nights, in spite of our weariness and heavy losses of horses and men, we harried Mahabat Khan. On the fourth day he halted and, with the same dignity with which he had marched forward, now retreated to the flat plain, hoping I could be drawn to do battle in the open.

I caught up with Arjumand and the children ten days later in Jaspur, They were as weary as I. The children, with all the resilience of youth, had grown accustomed to the hardships, the race over the harsh countryside, the nocturnal passage through sleeping villages and brooding hills. We had to stop for many days, as we waited for the birth of another child. It was a boy, Murad, and to our surprise he lived. But there was no more time to squander, Arjumand herself still made no complaint. We had lost over three hundred and fifty men in the battle; it was a grievous loss. Those that were wounded we left in Jaspur, then we moved further east. Mahabat Khan would return, possibly with fewer men, for he was a man quick to learn the lessons of warfare.

The terrain had aided me then but it slowed us now. The steep hills and low valleys made progress difficult. We moved only a few kos every day, winding and unwinding like a blinded serpent seeking to escape.

1035/AD 1625

By the third winter, we reached Bengal. It was not winter in this land. It steamed with moisture, and the ground was broken by countless little rivers, all of them impassable except at great cost in boatmen. Arjumand could not take to this climate. She fell ill with a fever that came and went, and shivered as if she lay in the northern snows. Her sweat soaked the divan, and with the sweat her strength seeped too.

I was told of a fort on the banks of one of these rivers. It had some comforts, medicines, and because it was at the farthest reach of Jahangir, I sought its shelter for Arjumand. It was a small place, built with thick brick walls pierced by openings for cannon, and it faced towards the sea. The sea itself was beyond our vision, but large ships with tall masts lay on the water by the walls. I had not seen such vessels before. The fort too was unlike ours; it was mean and bare of any decoration. Those who built it had no eye for beauty, only bare utility. But it would provide shelter and rest for my Arjumand.

Isa

The prince Shah Jahan, Allami Sa'du-lla Khan and I rode in with fifty horsemen. The fort contained a few low buildings and, in the very centre, their church. There were few of our people to be seen, but many feringhis. They dressed in thick clothes which held the stink of their flesh, for they were not a people who believed in the cleansing powers of water. To my eye they looked no different from those who had insulted my Agachi many years ago in Agra. They all had beards, and carried jezails.

They did not look on Shah Jahan with any friendliness. He rode erect, ignoring their hostility. In spite of the years of hardship, one could not mistake the authority of a prince, it was as much a part of him as his bones. It clung about his person, visible even to the most ignorant. Yet these men barely gave him any recognition; their faces were surly and as cold as the air was hot. The commander of the fort was a tall, thickset man, bareheaded, with hair which flowed down to his shoulders. He was accompanied by his priests, small, furtive, watchful men who wore black from neck to ankles. They reminded me of the mullahs; the same glare of fervour flamed in their eyes. Around their necks were wooden crosses which they toyed with ceaselessly. They seemed to hold more authority than the commander, and in their arrogance appeared to stare down at the prince Shah Jahan on his horse. The commander made a brusque obeisance, for he knew who approached him. The priests made no attempt to show respect.

'I wish to spend some time in the shelter of your fort,' Shah Jahan addressed the commander. 'My wife is sick, and I have been informed that you have medicines here which will cure her.'

The commander would have replied, but without permission one of his priests stepped forward and directly addressed the prince. 'I do not see her. I only see soldiers.'

'I am speaking the truth,' Shah Jahan said with patience. 'She is in her conveyance. We will fetch her, but you cannot look upon her face. We have been travelling many, many days, and the children too need rest here.'

Slowly, more of the feringhis crowded around, looking on the prince with curiosity mixed with dislike. They made no attempt to disguise their arrogance. I had not known that so many of them lived in this fort along the riverbank. They worshipped a woman, and forced all who came near them to do the same. I have never been able to understand why men should force others to worship as they do. Does it arise from—not belief—but fear? A fear of solitude, a suspicion that God may not exist as they imagine him, and a belief that by increasing their numbers it will reassure them that they are not fools?

'It would be possible,' the priest said quietly, squinting up. 'But that depends on the prince.'

'I will do what you wish.'

'You will visit our place of worship and give thanks for your safety, then. The blessed mother will show you great mercy.'

'The prince cannot do this,' Shah Jahan said. 'I do not ask you to pray in the mosque. Why should you demand that I pray in your place of worship?'

'That is our condition. If you do not wish to fulfil it, you must leave.' He spoke swiftly as if he had triumphed in a skirmish, and he

300

waited to see what Shah Jahan would do. 'The medicine too will be available for your wife, should you reconsider your decision.'

Shah Jahan glanced towards the commander in disbelief; the man merely lifted one shoulder and let it fall. He was commanded by the priest. The prince returned his gaze to the priest. His eyes had grown darker and his exhaustion evaporated. He studied the priest: a plump man with a reddish beard, his face was the colour of tomatoes that have turned bad, and his eyes had a habit of winking. But around his mouth lay evidence of his strength. His lips were pressed and firm, and revealed no weakness. The prince looked hard, but only to remember the man.

'What would conversion to your religion offer me?' Shah Jahan enquired. I knew his mildness to be deceptive; within he raged. 'Other than the medicine I wish?'

'Salvation,' the priest said eagerly.

'Ah . . . salvation.' He considered the word with curiosity. 'Salvation from what? Can your god make all my hardships vanish? Is that salvation?'

'From your sins. When you confess you will be forgiven and you will enter a state of bliss.'

'But what if I … sin again?'

'With confession you will be forgiven. But you will come to understand the nature of sin and will desist.'

'It is not easy for men such as I to cease from sinning. But it sounds a fair bargain. Each sin is forgiven. And the idol you worship is the one who forgives?'

'It is not an idol,' the priest spoke sharply. 'The Virgin Mary is the symbol of all-powerful God.'

'She is very much like the Hindu idols. You drape her in silks too. What is the difference? I see none. I can enter a temple and worship and be forgiven of all my sins. This forgiveness is authorized by you. Or does your virgin utter the words of forgiveness?'

301

'You mock me.'

'And you treat me, the prince Shah Jahan, like a fool. I ask for shelter and you make bargains. The health of my wife is not a saman in the bazaar. Because I need your help, you think that you can convert me to your religion. My father and my grandfather allowed your people the freedom to practise what they wished—in fact you tried your tricks in the court of the Great Mughal Akbar too, and he lost patience—and you do not even have the courtesy to treat me with the compassion your religion professes to offer its people, I do not see even a cup of water offered according to the custom of all people in this land to the meanest of beggars.'

'And what will you do, prince Shah Jahan?' The priest was amused by Shah Jahan's cold anger. 'Send soldiers? You have too few. Your father will be pleased to know where you hide. Now go, before we send a messenger to the Great Mughal to tell him his son hides in this suba.'

'And my wife?'

'We cannot help her.'

The priest turned and strode away. The others stood about staring at us in silent defiance, expecting some reaction from Shah Jahan. He said nothing, but slowly looked round at the fort and the gazing faces. He reined his horse, and we followed him out to join the main party. On the short ride, he did not utter a single word, did not glance back at the closing gates of the fort or the men peering down at us. I could not tell what his thoughts were, his face was set in stone. The children came to greet us; the boys were eager to explore the strange fort. He ignored them all, except Dara. When he dismounted he took Dara by the hand, and they went to sit with Arjumand in her rath. My attention and affection were a poor substitute for his, but I took the others as close to the fort as was wise without endangering them. It was not possible to judge the temper of these feringhis. Aurangzeb held up his arms to be lifted so that he could see better. He turned round once to gaze at the closed rath.

'Your father has many worries, your Highness. They preoccupy him and don't leave him much time to spend with you, as he would wish.'

'Dara, then?'

I could not reply immediately. Aurangzeb stared at me. The pain sparked, then the soft gauze of introspection veiled it. No explanation would satisfy the child, only his father's love.

'He is the eldest and needs to be consulted. When you grow older your father will discuss such matters with you. You must remember, your Highness, that your father could have left you all behind In Agra with your grandfather. But he wished to have you with him.'

'My mother wanted it.'

'Your father also. He could not abandon you.'

'Why not? Allah would have watched over us.'

It was a strange answer. He had been taught the Quran, as had the others, but his belief was stronger. His solace was Allah, a cold substitute for love.

We moved north to escape the cloying, heavy climate. It clung to my Agachi like a sweaty shroud, making her listless.

We crossed the Damador and turned east until we reached the banks of the Jumna. Even though we were far from Agra, the sight of the river filled us with longing. We could imagine these same clear waters rushing past the fort, winding through the familiar city. We remembered the sights and smells and the companions we all had there. It had been so many years since we'd seen them, and we fell into a sad and musing silence that lasted a long time. Shah Jahan dipped his hands in the river, and let the waters of his city, his home, run through his fingers.

Arjumand bathed in the waters; she rose fom the immersion as one would from the Ganga, refreshed and stronger. Her gaiety returned, and her laughter. She talked about all the things she'd done as a child in Agra, chattered about her parents and grandparents as if

303

she might see them at any minute. We had never been so close to home before, and we felt ourselves pulled towards it. The urge to return was powerful; the urge to rest in the cool palace by the side of the Jumna, to ride and play *chaugar* on the maidan beyond the fort, to sit in the twilight sipping wine—a luxury Shah Jahan greatly missed—and talk until the moon rose and gave light to the world. How clearly we recalled the tiniest details of our old life; our youth was a dream remembered and we regaled each other with the telling and re-telling of it.

Shah Jahan stared north towards Agra and spent many hours alone with Arjumand. They would sit by the river together and we had little doubt that he had grown too weary to continue. He longed to travel north, to reach the familiar walls of the red fort, prostrate himself at the great gates and go in.

But it was not to be. Mahabat Khan still rode. The Mughal army, fearing that Shah Jahan might attack the fort, blocked our way and began to march south towards us. Once more the rest was too brief; we turned round and moved swiftly south. We returned by the route we had already travelled, this time avoiding the feringhi fort, until we reached the boundary of the empire, the edge of our world. There, we turned west. We travelled along a line narrow as rope; on one side lay Hindustan, on the other the land where I was born. I looked south often; the village was no more than a blur in my memory, only its vivid greenness, the soft tranquillity of the life there, came to mind. I did not speak of these things to my lady; my old life was too remote in distance and time. I knew I could not go back. What of my brother Murthi? What of Sita? They would have forgotten me. My parents were probably dead. How different and dull life would be there now. Karma had snatched me from that security and driven me into this wandering life.

Once more, near Kawardha, Shah Jahan fought with Mahabat Khan. It was not a battle, merely a brief skirmish, a touching of swords, for both men were exhausted. We withdrew, and Mahabat Khan remained in position, though he could have overwhelmed us with his superior forces. Tigers too, after a display of ferocity, retreat from battle.

Shah Jahan was serene. He sat in his shamiyana, bent over the document he wrote in his own fine hand. He sent me to fetch Allami Sa'du-lla Khan and when we returned we stood waiting until he had completed his letter. It was addressed to the Conqueror, Seizer of the World, Lord of the Rivers, Lord of the Seas, the Dweller in Paradise, the Padishah, Emperor of Hindustan, the Great Mughal Jahangir.

'Father,' Shah Jahan read, not looking up. 'I, the most wretched of your sons, beg your forgiveness. For my past misdeeds I have been treated as I justly deserved. You could not but have thought me a most ungrateful son who showed your love and honour no respect. In these past years, as I have wandered through your great empire, I have thought deeply of my ill behaviour towards your kindness and feel myself unable to pursue this course any longer. I am weary of our enmity, as are my wife and children, and we wish only to live in peace and harmony with my beloved father. I lay before you my life, with which you may do as you wish.'

He sealed it and handed it to Allami Sa'du-lla Khan.

'You must deliver it to him personally,' Shah Jahan ordered.

'She will not permit it. I will have to give it to her wazir, the eunuch Muneer. Whether you receive pardon or not will depend on Mehrunissa.'

'She will be ready to listen. Mahabat Khan has grown too powerful. Each year of the pursuit has increased his strength.'

Allami Sa'du-lla Khan shrugged. 'Mehrunissa isn't your father. Who knows what she thinks about you or Mahabat Khan? But I will do my best, your Highness. I shall whisper your surrender to every ear at court, so that all shall know you are no longer at fault.'

We waited tensely near Burhanpur. It was not possible to judge the whereabouts of Jahangir. If he were in Agra, we would have

Mehrunissa's reply soon, if he were in Lahore, later, and if he were in Kashmir, much later. From the great time it took to reach us—one hundred and eighteen days—we judged him to be between Lahore and Kashmir. The reply was not written in his hand, but in Mehrunissa's, so open was her power. She forgave. Her terms for peace were lenient. Shah Jahan would surrender his forts and accept the governorship of Balaghat, a remote and useless suba.

He would also send Dara and Aurangzeb to her as hostages.

Shah Jahan accepted her terms immediately waited for the Imperial messenger to bring the *firman*, confirming the terms of our peace. When it came Shah Jahan placed his forehead on it, signifying his humility and obedience to the emperor. But he was still wary of Mehrunissa's stratagems where his own life was concerned, so he and Arjumand decided to remain where they were in the Deccan.

Mahabat Khan sent an escort of ten thousand horsemen for the two young princes. Arjumand ordered me to accompany them back to court. She embraced them both with equal passion, kissing their faces and hands. Shah Jahan kissed them too, but I noted the averted face of Aurangzeb.

'You will look after them, Isa. Protect them from all harm.'

As we rode away Dara looked back often at his parents, Aurangzeb not once.

twenty-two

the taj mahal 1068/AD 1658

Betrayal, betrayal, betrayal. The word had a stench of its own, vile as
the rot of a human soul. It darkened the air and filled each breath with
despair. It could not be washed away; the weight of it was insupportable.
It could misshape destiny and torture it along new paths. Though the
word was small, the consequences of it could be monstrous. If the
man betrayed was unimportant, the ripple would touch but one man,
one family, one village, then disperse and be forgotten. If the man
betrayed was a prince, then the act, like the pulse of the very earth,
would beat on into eternity.

Or is betrayal the natural impulse of all men? Isa recalled Shah
Jahan's belief: according to convenience or inconvenience, *taktya takhta*.
Were even the lives of kings, with such bounty surrounding them,
reduced to so stark a choice?

'Dara. Save Dara. Save your brother,' the Great Mughal Shah Jahan
had commanded his daughter Jahanara. 'You are loved by Aurangzeb.
He will listen to your prayer, not mine. What I love, God destroys.
That is the curse on my life. My loved and cherished son I had hoped
to see him become king peacefully, but none can fathom the secrets of
the Lord Most High. I am now powerless to do more, but I pray that

307

his life will be spared and that he will survive to become emperor of all Hindustan. Whose fault is it that destiny has defied an emperor's command? The emperor's? In his love, he was foolish. Is that a crime? Would he be made to suffer all his days for having loved too much? I loved Dara too dearly, Aurangzeb not enough. In such careless apportioning lies the downfall of a king, not in the vast armies he can command or the power he wields, but in the careful measurement of love. For that I will be held guilty by Aurangzeb; for that I will be punished, and for that alone will Dara pay the highest price. Ah, if only he had escaped, if only he had not been betrayed by those he trusted. Trusted? Did he not save the very life of the man who betrayed him from my wrath? I would have executed Malik Jiwan for his misdeed. I had even ordered him to be trampled by elephants, but my cherished Dara placed himself between me and that wretch. He begged me to be lenient and, listening to his soft and gentle voice. I forgave Malik Jiwan. Oh God, how I regret now that I listened. If Jiwan had died then, Dara would now be secure under the protection of the Shahinshah instead of lying in Aurangzeb's dungeon. By such tiny acts, like the sands which can consume a river, grain by grain, does destiny change the lives of men. Hurry, Jahanara, hurry. Aurangzeb will listen to you. Use his love for you to save Dara. Use his love, as Aurangzeb used my lack of it. I have already lost Shahshuja, murdered by dacoits in Bengal, and Aurangzeb has by treachery captured Murad. God alone knows where he imprisons him. Four elephants with matching howdahs left Aurangzeb's camp at dawn. In which was Murad? Only Aurangzeb knows. And so my beloved Arjumand's child has consumed his brothers. How, out of so much beauty and love, can such vileness be born?'

Shah Jahan was distraught, fretful, weeping; he sat staring across the Jumna to the Taj Mahal. They were separated by water: both were imprisoned in marble. The emperor's bars were the jewelled walls of his palace. Shah Jahan had capitulated to his son in three days, but they could not be reconciled. Aurangzeb remained without, Shah Jahan stubbornly within. Isa and Jahanara wished them to meet, to embrace. The emperor finally consented, but he ordered his Tartar slave women to wait in ambush for the bi-daulat Aurangzeb. As father and son held each other in their arms, the women would strike. But how, without love, could trust exist? Aurangzeb stayed without. He managed to intercept a message from his father to Dara: 'My cherished son, my beloved son.' It filled him with bitter melancholy. Power changed, love did not. He turned his back on the fort and pursued Dara.

'Hurry, hurry,' Jahanara ordered.

The horses felt the whip and surged forward; their eyes bulged with exhaustion, their mouths foamed and their flanks were streaked with welts and sweat. The moonlit road from Agra to Delhi led straight to the horizon. Eight horsemen rode ahead as escort, Isa beside the rath. Men, women and sleeping beasts stirred from rest by the roadside to watch the speeding horses, returning to slumber when they had passed.

The Great Mughal Aurangzeb awaited Jahanara and Isa on the battlements of the Delhi fort. It had been built by his father and the work was not yet completed. The scaffolding still stood around the emperor as he gazed down from the Delhi darwaza. 'Come and see,' he commanded.

Below, a huge crowd gathered. Imperial soldiers formed a narrow path through the mass which stretched into the city, clinging to trees, perched on roofs, ominously silent, waiting. Kites wheeled overhead, vultures crouched in grave dignity on the river banks. The sky was a faded, worn blue. Within, a procession was being prepared. A sick, bony elephant, his sides sticky with running sores, swayed weakly. The howdah was open. Behind it sat a slave with an executioner's sword;

the cruelty of the sword lay not in its sharpness, but in the crust of rusted blood. The second elephant was a strong, healthy beast, richly decorated. Its howdah was of jewelled gold, and on its forehead was a gold and emerald covering. Its tusks were tipped with gold.

'Fetch him,' Aurangzeb commanded.

Dara emerged from the dungeon, blinking in the sunlight. He was bound cruelly in chains, his clothes were torn and filthy, dirt caked his face and body. He stumbled and the soldiers dragged him towards the diseased elephant. In spite of the indignity, he remained calm.

Isa groaned.

Jahanara wept. 'My brother, forgive my brother. His only crime has been to obey the commands of his father whom he loved so dearly. He has been a good and obedient son, and a kind brother to us all. I am not asking you, I am begging, like the poorest person in the land—look, I kneel and kiss your feet—not for his freedom but for his life. Imprison him in the most remote part of this vast empire. Enclose him among the rocks of the mountains or in the deepest forests. Build a fort and guard it so he may never escape, never look on your face again, as you have done with our brother Murad. You have defeated Dara, bound him in chains, treated him vilely. Now, like Allah, show him mercy. You claim you have always had great love for me. Look at him through the eyes of my love. Let it temper your hatred. I will serve you all my life with love and devotion. If you love me, forgive him.'

'Should love be subject to such conditions?' Aurangzeb enquired quietly.

'At times they are necessary to preserve it. Love is a most fragile thing and if we did not command others to respect it, it would crumble to dust. It cannot be abused.'

'So you will use our love to save your brother?'

'What else do I have? I have no armies, I can use no weapons. I am your sister. I am a single woman. Our blood is the same. Aurangzeb, when I lay ill and near to death you rode a thousand kos to kneel by my side. It was an act of love. Perform another for me now, forgive Dara.'

'And when I came to your side, my father ordered me out like a pariah dog who'd slunk in to sniff for a scrap of affection. I have not even received that from him. Have I not been obedient too? Have I not obeyed his every whim? I have served my father more faithfully than Dara ever did, but because of Dara he couldn't see me. Dara loomed between us like a dark cloud that hides the sun from worshippers' eyes. Tell me, my beloved sister, who pleaded for Khusrav?'

'Our mother.'

'Did it save him?' Aurangzeb stared into Jahanara's eyes. His own were unblinking, set in the hard face like glowing coals. Jahanara's were grey and filled with tears. Her stare wavered and fell.

'Did it save him? My mother cried too, as you do now. Did it save Khusrav?'

'No.'

Then why should I heed you now? Taktya takhta. Those were my father's words to Khusrav—a cruel choice for a blind prince. He had no choice. Now I give Dara no such choice: the coffin is his destiny. When you see him remind my father that I only imitate him.' His thin smile mocked her. 'What more can a son do than flatter his father by copying him?'

Aurangzeb looked down to the courtyard again. The soldiers faltered back a step, releasing their hold on Dara, He swayed but remained upright, looked around, aware now of those who surrounded him: soldiers, nobles, servants, slaves, executioners and, beyond in the palace, the invisible presence of the women. Even over such a multitude within and without, the buzz of flies around his head could be heard distinctly. They settled, he shook, they flew and realighted, tormenting his helplessness. Finally he lifted his head to look up at his brother on top of the battlements of the Lahore darwaza. To the right stood his sister Jahanara, anguished, weeping, dishevelled; to the left, faithful Isa stood with the sunlight glinting on the rivulets that stained his cheeks. Aurangzeb himself was just a black shape shutting out the sun. Dara sighed; the crowd stirred in discomfort, in mute compassion.

It was a portent. Aurangzeb ignored it. He wanted to savour, to gloat; hatred could not be allowed to die too swiftly, yet nothing stirred in his heart. It remained still and sullen, unable to pound with pleasure at his brother's wretchedness. He could not recognize Dara, but looked down on a stranger who had only just entered his life. Aurangzeb's fist clenched and unclenched to the slow beat of his pulse. He realized with sudden clarity that he held his brother in chains, in hatred, only as hostage for Shah Jahan's love. This hatred could cleanse him of a need to be loved, though envy remained, sour and bitter. But it was a small emotion compared to the immensity of his hatred. He felt undermined by this knowledge. He could forgive Dara, even free him. It was in his power. He was the Great Mughal—not his father. It could all have been resolved, if only his father had come. If Shah Jahan had ridden swiftly to his side, begged him as Jahanara had, just once embraced him with the same love as he had often embraced Dara, he would have granted Dara his life. The gift of life was mercy enough; Dara would never have his freedom, but would live imprisoned behind stone walls as did his other brother, Murad.

Aurangzeb lifted his hand.

Dara was taken to the mounting platform. The emaciated elephant came alongside and Dara was lifted into the open howdah, chained into position. Behind him sat the executioner, sword raised. The elephant swayed uncertainly.

The nobles made way silently. The traitor Malik Jiwan strode into the open space. He was tall, glittering and arrogant with the precious gifts Aurangzeb had bestowed on him. He expected applause, faltered at the ominous quiet. He would have mounted the steps of the Lahore darwaza, sought comfort at Aurangzeb's side. Alamgir, Seizer of the Universe—Aurangzeb had taken for himself the name of the holy

312

sword—stopped him with one finger. Malik Jiwan approached the richly decorated elephant and mounted it. Once he was settled within the howdah, the gates were opened.

Slowly the two beasts passed under the gate and down the slope between the high walls. The soldiers looked once, then turned their heads away. Aurangzeb was irked by their compassion. Would Dara, the beloved gentle Dara, have treated him any differently if he had been the victor? He looked at his sister. Jahanara's face was averted, now as emotionless as his own. The elephants passed under the second gate. The crowds on either side stirred, their sighs gathering like a storm. Aurangzeb heard the first cry, a sad, keening wail. It began to echo in every throat as Dara passed on his way through the narrow streets of the walled city. The bazaars were shuttered; commerce had ceased. People wept openly at the sight of their prince.

'Why did our father not come?' Aurangzeb turned to Jahanara.

'Would you have forgiven Dara at the sight of your father?'

'Possibly. If he'd begged me.' He watched Dara fade into the mass. 'Why could he not have loved me as he loved Dara? What had I done to choke his affection for me? Or was it the wish of our mother? Yes. She hated me.'

'You cannot believe her capable of such a thing.' Jahanara was listless, indifferent, distracted by the swelling cries of the crowd. Her childhood had been soiled and spoilt, burned and bloodstained. 'Our mother would have wept as I do to see one son destroy another. She loved us all so much.'

The crowd wept for Dara and cursed Malik Jiwan. Animal cries of pain and rage swept the city, full-throated, baleful. The tamasha grew louder, they heard the clash of soldiers, swords beating shields, beating back the people. Aurangzeb stirred uneasily.

'They wish to kill your traitor. They defy you.'

'It will not last. They will learn who rules, not their soft Dara, but I!'

313

He signalled.

A soldier ran out to bring the procession back before it went further. Aurangzeb was not afraid of the people, he was afraid of their love for Dara. They would not be allowed to weep for long.

'Come, we must receive our brother after his triumphant tour of Delhi.'

Jahanara and Isa followed the emperor across the lawns to the diwan-i-am. Aurangzeb climbed to the alcove above the audience and Jahanara retreated to the women's enclosure. Isa remained at a distance. The nobles gathered under the pillared sandstone ceiling. Aurangzeb settled on the gold awrang, leaning back on the cushions.

The flies massed on the sores on the elephant's sides. Nothing unsettled them, its shambling, stumbling walk, the weeping of the crowds. As the elephant's shadow fell on Gopi, he smelled the odour of decay, of death; it was a flat, evil smell that pinched his nostrils. He held his breath and looked up into the eyes of prince Dara. He was startled, the prince *saw* him. The regard was not glazed with outrage or fear, it was grave and observant. It set a value on Gopi's features, he felt they had been given the worth of a prince's study; then he was gone, searching for another face. What did he search for? A saviour? There was nothing to hope for from the crowds, only compassion and tears, and they were worthless against the steel of the Imperial soldiers, the iron of Aurangzeb. Gopi's eyes blurred and he too began to weep. How confused was the destiny of princes and their people! Like all who watched, he wept for Dara and for himself. Dara's rule would not have been a yoke, but gentle, caring and, above all else, tolerant of the many religions in the land. Aurangzeb had already declared his intent. Like Timur-i-leng, he would be the Scourge of God. He would crush the people with his fervour, razing temples and churches, as if with these acts of violence he would bring them all to Allah. The crowds

314

wept for the future, knowing that the events of this day would echo for countless years.

The soldiers returned and the elephants wheeled slowly to begin their return to the fort. As Malik Jiwan passed, Gopi picked up a handful of dung and hurled it at the golden howdah. It splattered the traitor, who cringed from the touch of the filth and the anger of the crowd. An Imperial guard struck Gopi with the haft of his spear, not hard, but enough to stop any more disobedience. He was a grey-bearded, portly man, sweating in the heat. His helmet was tarnished, and the chain-mail hung like locks, rusty.

'What will happen to the prince?'

The soldier gestured with one finger across his throat. Gopi flinched. He was an Acharya, a carver of gods, and violence frightened him.

The soldier softened. 'It is their karma. Brother kills brother. How could it be otherwise, when Shah Jahan killed his brother Khusrav? I was Khusrav's keeper and served him loyally, but when the time came in Burhanpur to protect him from his brother, I failed him. The memory of it haunts me. Shah Jahan was a brave prince then, glory shone in his face . . . until that day. His beautiful wife Arjumand pleaded and wept to save my prince Khusrav, but Shah Jahan would not be moved.'

'You saw her?' Gopi did not believe a common soldier had looked upon the face of Mumtaz-i-Mahal.

'Yes. Briefly. She had luxuriantly beautiful eyes, my friend, and when they looked on you, you caught fire. They set you dreaming to possess her. I dared to lust for her, and that frightened me.'

The soldier remembered her sensuality and anguish. Gopi only saw her as the marble which he had shaped.

'What happened then?'

'I did not stay to witness his death. Shah Jahan let me go free. I returned to my village, Sawai Madhapur, but could not remain idle for long. There was no rain, and my land was worthless dust. I returned to serve Shah Jahan, and now I serve Aurangzeb. But I am getting too old and the times will be bad.'

The crowd dispersed and the soldier followed his comrades back to the fort. Gopi made his way through the deserted bazaar. An ominous quiet hung over the city; suddenly it felt abandoned.

Gopi began trudging along the banks of the Jumna towards Agra. He had been summoned to Delhi by the old man, Chiranji Lal. It was he who had built the Hindu temple outside Agra, who had commissioned his father to carve the deity, Durga. Now he wanted Gopi to carve another Durga. They had discussed the matter at length, but because of the uncertainty of the times, no decision had been reached. These were dangerous days for Hindus and if they should be caught building another temple, Aurangzeb's retribution would be swift. His mullahs eagerly spied on all unbelievers, scurried to report even the palms pressed together in prayer. Gopi was relieved that he had been released from his obligation.

It was a long journey to Agra. He followed the river, sometimes on foot, and, when he could, rode a passing cart. The journey gave him time to think. He felt uneasy and unsure. He carried the responsibility for his sister and brother; their lives, their futures, were in his hands. They could remain in Agra, he had employment. The tomb constantly required work, repairs, additional touches, the gates to be inlaid with marble. A man of his skill would always be assured of work. The Princess Jahanara was planning to build a huge marble mosque opposite the Lal Quila. But despite that, he remembered Aurangzeb smashing the Durga his father had carved so painstakingly. He felt his own life lay under a hammer. He thought of the home he'd left as a small boy so many years ago, though the memory was dim. He could recall fields, serenity, the security of a forgotten family. There would be work there too, not so well paid, of course, but at least he would have some status there. In the court of a Raja, he could carve Lakshmi or Ganesh or Siva. Then Gopi felt an immense loneliness. He was of the age for marriage, but

316

now that his mother was dead, he had no one to search for a bride. She would, naturally, have to be from his own caste. What chance was there of finding an Acharya family in Agra? And then there was the burden of his sister. She was of marriageable age too, and the sooner she went to her husband's household the better.

'We will return to our village,' he announced abruptly to his brother and sister as he entered their hut. 'I will ask our uncle Isa to come with us. He is an old man and someone must care for him now.'

With the decision made, Gopi felt some relief. After the midday meal, he and his brother trudged up the dusty footpath towards the Taj. As they drew near, it swelled in size and height, and by the time they reached the walls it dwarfed them with its icy magnificence. It gleamed in the harsh sunlight, forcing them to shield their eyes from the glare. It wavered in the air, as if made of hanging silk. He stopped in surprise. Over the years he had grown accustomed to the soldiers guarding the monument. Today it was deserted. By removing the soldiers, Aurangzeb had diminished its importance.

twenty-three

the love story 1036/AD 1626

Isa

Jahangir watched us approach. He was reclining on the awrang, his face shadowed by the alcove. I caught the glitter of his eyes as he leant forward to study the two boys. It had been four years since he had seen his grandsons, and he seemed curious and expectant, perhaps seeking in them the features of Shah Jahan.

The banners of silk hanging in the diwan-i-am wafted in the soft breeze. The nobles were packed behind the vermilion-painted barrier, the plumes on their jewelled turbans nodded and rippled as they turned to watch our progress. I heard the indistinct whispers. How will Jahangir greet his bi-daulat's sons? With kindness or with cruelty? To the right of the alcove, behind the jali, I felt the presence of Mehrunissa. Jahangir would act only in accordance with her wishes. If she spoke: *Kindness,* then that would be our lot. And if not. . . .

I had tried to discover her mood before entering the court with Dara and Aurangzeb, but none would answer my questions. Possibly she brooded angrily on the disobedience of Shah Jahan and her niece Arjumand—Arjumand, of her own blood who had fled with her husband into rebellion. She had expected an ally in Arjumand, not an enemy.

The solemn gurz-bardar approached the wooden barrier and opened the gate. We walked through, escorted by him past the silver barrier that held the captains and high officials and halted within the enclosure of the gold railings. There we performed kornish to the Great Mughal Jahangir.

After four years of flight—discomfort, bare shelter, suspicion, strange fortresses and hardship—his magnificence affected me like a blow. I could smell the cool odour of diamonds and pearls and emeralds, sweetish and light. Dust and dirt, our constant companions, were hidden under silken Persian carpets, and the bones of the people around us were clothed in soft flesh. I felt as if the dust still parched our throats and the dirt lay on us in drifts. Such unease only stiffened our movements, as though we had just dismounted after a long ride. We found ourselves gazing around with awe at the court of the Great Mughal. From the rim of the empire to the hub, to gaze at the sun itself and feel the warmth of his nearness, was a mental journey we had yet to complete. Surely we were in a dream and on wakening would find ourselves back in Burhanpur with Shah Jahan and Arjumand.

The boys stood apart. Dara, at ten, was a head taller, prouder and straighter than the seven-year-old Aurangzeb. He looked the braver too, for his face trembled on the brink of tears, but by his will none was spilt. They wore princely dress, pale blue and pale green turbans of silk, each with an emerald of great size, voluminous silk *takauchiyas* of stiffly woven silk and gold thread around their waists. Their slippers were embroidered with pearls.

Our journey from Burhanpur had taken forty days, travelling slowly in the company of Mahabat Khan. In spite of their proximity, the sons of Shah Jahan had remained mute towards each other. There was a flaw in both their visions: they noted all things except the physical presence of the other. I tried to coax them into friendship, for they were too young for such antagonism, but nature herself conspired to make them enemies. As Shah Jahan and Arjumand had instantly loved, so Dara and

Aurangzeb instantly and instinctively—for that is a secret part of our natures—disliked. Of the two, Dara was the more companionable, the more amenable. He made an effort to befriend his younger brother, but the aloof coldness of Aurangzeb immediately discouraged him, and despite my efforts I could not reconcile them. I thought they might be the reincarnation of ancient enemies, for the soul must carry its memories into each new life.

Dara was a joyous prince; he laughed easily and took delight in the progress of events. In his nature, he was closer to Arjumand. His character had the same softness and warmth, and he missed her presence more than did Aurangzeb. I saw in him too a part of Shah Jahan, and even a part of his grandfather, Jahangir. His curiosity was limitless: the flowers, the animals, the temples, the people, the mysteries of God and His works, all these things fascinated him. He sought my company frequently, for I had a greater knowledge of the places we passed through than did the old general Mahabat Khan. To him the land was a blank page on which to write a history of strategy, conquest, rule. Dara shunned his company.

Aurangzeb's vision of the world was a narrow one. He was a grave boy, keeping his own company in the main and riding in silence beside the general. Occasionally he would reveal some curiosity, but this curiosity only extended as far as the movements of the soldiers who rode with us. He would listen to the stirring tales of battle and valour, of charges and retreats, of the conquest of other lands. When the general paused, Aurangzeb would command: more. Over these stories alone he showed all a boy's greed for excitement. But then, abruptly, he would withdraw and return to his dark brooding. Sometimes I would catch him glancing with disapproval at the magnificence of Mahabat Khan and the splendour of his escort. If those glances were furtive, his outward display, even at that age, was disturbing. Every devout Muslim prays five times daily, and where Mahabat Khan was dutiful in this ritual, Aurangzeb was punctilious. No one could move until the prince had completed his prayers. This intense show of zeal caused me to remark: 'In battle there will be no time for prayer, your Highness.' Aurangzeb gravely replied: 'In battle there is always time.'

Even at court he revealed his indifference. While they awaited their grandfather's signal, Dara looked around with pleasurable anticipation—he was returning to a familiar world after a long exile—but Aurangzeb only stared unblinkingly at his grandfather.

Jahangir rose stiffly, an old lion staggering to his feet. None could help, for the monarch sat alone in the alcove and only when he reached the bottom of the steps did a slave step forward. He had aged swiftly in these four years. Time had swollen his face and body, slashed weary furrows on his cheeks and forehead. His skin had become wafery, reddish, and bloodshot eyes burned more sombrely. He moved slowly, dragging his right foot, and the air now seemed even more reluctant to enter his body. Even though we stood only a few paces from him, he paused twice to gasp for air, greedily sucking it in, wheezing like a mechanical device grown rusty. But the Great Mughal had lost none of his splendour. The Imperial emblem in his turban—a large emerald set in a gold brooch with diamonds—the pearls about his neck, the gold bands on his arms, and the gold belt round his waist, all spoke of his magnificence. The perfume of sandalwood preceded him.

He halted in front of his grandsons. His face revealed little as he examined them as carefully as the cranes he'd once studied so carefully, noting their habits. His hands were stiff, the ringed fingers set into claws; they shook as if in a fever.

'Which are you?' he asked Dara.

'Dara, your majesty. Son of the Prince Shah . . .'

'I know whose son you are. The bi-daulat.' He sighed heavily. 'A father has to bear the burden of betrayal by his son. In my old age, I wished only for peace. Instead I have squandered my strength for the past four years waging war against my own son. Your father.' He glanced at Aurangzeb, ignoring the boy's stiff body. The punkah of peacock feathers stirred the warm air into our faces. 'But I am pleased that he has come to his senses while I still live. We have peace in the empire, but because of him and his disobedience we have lost Kandahar to that Persian bandit.' He would have railed on but, aware of the occasion, he stopped himself. 'That is past and we must reconcile ourselves to its loss, until we can retake it.' He opened his arms slowly, an eagle spreading its powerful wings. 'Come.'

First Dara entered the emperor's embrace. He was kissed on both cheeks. Aurangzeb followed and also received his grandfather's kisses. The nobles behind us shouted, 'Shabash, shabash.' In their cries I detected relief. Jahangir, with his kind treatment of his own flesh and blood, had prevailed over whatever counsel Mehrunissa may have given. She was not of the line of Timur.

The boys were seated on the carpet, and slaves brought forward basins of diamonds, emeralds and rubies. Jahangir dipped his cupped hands into the priceless stones and poured them over the two boys. Another slave brought two golden scabbards and metal *pulquars* with jewelled handles; each boy received one as a gift. *Khandas* of equal beauty were tucked into their *patkas*. Aurangzeb could not control his eagerness to examine the weapons and, unthinkingly, began to draw the blades from their scabbards. A growl from the soldiers guarding the emperor made me seize the boy's arm hastily. He looked around in surprise, slowly grasping the fact that he was within a sword's length of the heart of the empire. The captain of the Ahadi gently removed the weapons and laid them out of Aurangzeb's reach.

'How is my son?' Jahangir addressed me above the heads of the boys.

'He sends his love and respect to the Padishah, your majesty.'

'Why did he not come himself, then?' Jahangir asked petulantly. He was tiring of the ceremony and his irritability was beginning to show.

'Your majesty, the prince Shah Jahan wishes only to serve you to

322

the best of his capacity and as an obedient son did not feel he should leave his post.'

'Burhanpur isn't his province. It's mine. He should have gone to Balaghat.' He chuckled. 'It is a miserable place for a most miserable son.' He began to choke for breath and the hakim hurried forward to administer a potion. Jahangir waved us all away. 'Take them to see the Empress now. I will rest; though my body must remain in this place, my spirit roams the cool valleys of Kashmir.' Then sharply: 'I only dragged myself here to receive them.'

We bowed and he withdrew, not to the alcove, but to the gulabar pitched in the gardens.

Mehrunissa received us in Jahangir's palace. We passed through the splendid red sandstone courtyards to her quarters overlooking the Jumna. She reclined on a divan, her back to the jali filtering the sunlight and the cool breeze into the room. State papers lay neatly stacked by her side and, on the table in front of her, was the Muhr Uzak. Muneer, fatter, slyer, the riches of his position apparent in the rolls of fat that cushioned his body, stood servile and suspicious to one side. His dislike of me had in no way abated and I could feel his triumph at the capitulation of my master to his mistress.

Though Jahangir had grown old, Mehrunissa remained ageless. True, her eyes had shadowed, but her beauty was still remarkable. The long black hair that fell to her waist was unstained by grey, and her waist could still be spanned by the two hands of a man. Her authority was stamped in her upright posture, and in that silence which those in power use to humble others. Power is silence, for the powerful do not have to negotiate; they only command. That weapon gave her a secretive serenity.

The boys bowed and, like Jahangir, she studied them closely. They were future emperors, should Shah Jahan mount the throne after his

323

father's death. Or did she look upon Jahangir's son and grandsons as fallen runners, to be kicked aside. She still supported Shahriya's claim and had ambitions to rule Hindustan for yet another generation through Ladilli. She gestured; the boys sat. Muneer fetched jalebis, mithai and lassi. Dara chose from the gold platter delicately; Aurangzeb ignored the sweetmeats and only sipped the lassi. They were dimly aware of her position, and seemed more awed by her beauty than by her power.

'How is Arjumand?' Mehrunissa asked.

'It was a difficult time for her, your majesty. The constant travelling has not improved her health. But, otherwise, she is well and sends her affection to her aunt.'

'Affection?' An eyebrow was raised. 'Shah Jahan sends love to his father; Arjumand has only affection for the empress. Is she angry with me, Isa?'

'I cannot tell, your majesty.'

'Even though you know every corner of her soul better, even, than her husband? You always were discreet and too moral, unlike Muneer who will do anything for baksheesh. It was all Shah Jahan's fault; he brought it down on his own head.'

'But did not the Padishah . . .' I paused, knowing I really spoke of her, '. . . take back the jagir of Hissan Feroz and give it to Shahriya? Shah Jahan felt himself betrayed then.'

'A title, a piece of land—he attached too much importance to it.'

'An empire, your majesty, is also nothing more than a title, a piece of land. But the prince now wishes only to be at peace with you.'

'He still harbours his ambition?'

'What else would the true son of the Mughal dream of, your majesty?'

She flushed: 'Your sly tongue will lose you your head. Shahriya is also the true son of the Padishah, and a more obedient one than Shah Jahan.' She softened the barb with a sweet smile. 'The misunderstanding is in the past, and we bear no malice against Shah Jahan. You will tell him that.'

'I will convey your affection . . . and your forgiveness, your majesty.'

'I hope he will keep them in his heart for many years.'

Her stare did not waver, but she could not disguise her annoyance. Already she sensed a change in the old order, the leash of power gently slipping from her grasp. It was time to compromise, to concede a little in exchange for a promise of safety when she no longer commanded great armies. We looked at the two boys. They had fallen asleep, sprawled and vulnerable, no different from other children exhausted by the excitement.

'They will be safe.' The unspoken question hovered between us. She paused, and then went on.

'I too will obey the Timurid law. Will Shah Jahan?' I made no reply. 'Why do you hesitate to answer, Isa? Is he not also the descendant of Timur-i-leng, the son of his father? Or do the Timurid laws not apply to the Sovereign of the World?'

'He will obey them.'

'On the word of a slave?' She mocked. 'Arjumand could not save Khusrav. Why should I believe that you will save my son-in-law?' She leaned back against the cushions. Taktya takhta. There is precision in those words, such a stark choice. If only between them there were a third, an escape.'

'There is exile. The Shahinshah will always give shelter to a Mughal's son.'

'Exile. For how long? For ever? No, exiles always return at the head of invading armies. Taktya takhta. Shahriya had no ambitions for the throne, but I forced them on him because of my own. And now I have presented him with the coffin. He is a weak fool, too easily pleased, too childish. He would not have had the strength to rule this empire. I would.'

'Of course.'

'Your tongue, Isa—guard it. I am still empress, and you are a slave far from the protection of your master.'

325

'A servant.'

'The same thing.' She returned to her musings, ambitions and confessions. They were not idle words; I was to convey them to Shah Jahan. She was bargaining for Shahriya's life.

'If Shah Jahan should become emperor, Shahriya will be quite content with a governorship: Lahore, the Punjab, as far away as Shah Jahan wishes. Ladilli will ensure that he does not continue to harbour any ambition to mount the throne.' The light from the jali set a softening pattern on her face. The sun was mellow, turning hazily golden, and it transformed her from an empress to an ageing woman. 'Ladilli sends her love to Arjumand. She always loved her as if she were a sister. She talks about her constantly: "Arjumand is so strong, Arjumand is so brave."'

'I will convey her wishes to her Highness.'

'Love. You always muddle your messages, Isa. Love.' She stopped abruptly. 'What a price Arjumand paid for her love! Endless children, years of hardship. She could so easily have stayed here, by my side, instead of running all over the empire with that . . . Shah Jahan.' She laughed drily, 'At least she would have had some rest from his unending demands. I told her years ago . . . but never mind that. She will remember my advice. Because of her love, she didn't follow it. Babies, deaths, babies, deaths. The pain! One was more than enough for me. I cannot bear pain, I hate it. Lying there screaming and bellowing like a beast. What for? A child.' She looked down at her body, through the silken choli her breasts were still round and firm, the nipples painted red, her belly above her churidar was flat with barely a wrinkle, her legs remained slim and strong.

'She must have grown fat and heavy.'

'Her Highness's beauty is unchanged.'

'Your loyalty is transparent, Isa. Nature has never served one woman differently from another. She treats us all unkindly in the end.' She waved me away. 'Try to remember what we have spoken of, Isa, and in the telling be accurate.'

'As always, your majesty.' I moved to the boys.

'Leave them. When they wake I will send them to their rooms.'

Arjumand

I missed Dara, and Aurangzeb; I had a longing to clasp them in my arms. Many months had passed and, like a breached fortress, I felt as if I had two ragged gaps in my heart. I was comforted by my beloved and by the other children, but each time I looked on their faces, I missed my two first sons.

The serene flow of the Tapti past the palace soothed me. For hour upon hour I watched the clear, blue waters from the balcony. Below, the people worked slowly; the farmers washed the buffaloes until their black hides glistened like rocks; the women beat their washing on the stones, thuck, thuck; boys splashed and swam naked, their bodies gold in the sunlight. To the north, where the river curved away, small white temples dotted the sandy river banks. They could have been there since the dawn of time, I mused, and this gave me a sense of peace after all our years of flight. Across the river, the fields gently sloped away to the distant, hazy hills.

While I was tranquil, Shah Jahan was not. He sensed that the time was approaching for him to march north to take the throne, and daily he looked in that direction. He had men posted on the battlements of Asigarh fort. From that vantage point it was possible to see beyond the valley almost to Agra. There was now a purpose to our waiting. Peace had strengthened his hand: he was no longer the bi-daulat. My father sent us word that at court the nobles were openly supporting my beloved's claim. Because of Mehrunissa's support, Shahriya was unpopular. Only Parwez remained, but he did not wish to usurp his brother. It was only Shahriya who, like Khusrav, had been touched by the dream of unlimited power. It infected all who came within its reach, like a disease that could not be cured, for to be the Great Mughal was to command the world. Homage was a heady intoxicant; it swelled the importance of men, making them think they were gods.

I could not contain my misgivings. Empress! How burdensome the title felt, how constricting the position. I had neither wish nor ability to play the role as Mehrunissa did. I would be content to remain here by the Tapti—or some cooler river, for I found the summer heat here unbearable—and watch time slide by with effortless ease. My spirit no longer had any will to do battle, to enter into the continual intrigues of court. Our flight had given me a taste of freedom from petty jealousies, quarrelling women, protocol; if only we could stay here—but I knew it could never be.

1037/AD 1627

The messenger came in the winter. He was escorted by a thousand horsemen and Shah Jahan received him in the palace. His message was a simple one: Jahangir had died in Kashmir. At least his wish had been granted. His spirit would be content to roam the mountains and, if it breathed, to taste the clear cold air. My beloved ordered one hundred days of mourning throughout the empire. I prayed that Jahangir had found the peace he yearned for. Though he mourned his father's passing, my beloved knew he had to move swiftly. We went to the great Masjid in Asigarh where, reading the Quran, he declared himself emperor. He prayed: 'Lord! Confer Thy great honour upon the faith of Islam and to the professors of that faith, through the perpetual power and majesty of the slave of the sultan, the son of the sultan, the emperor, the son of the emperor, the ruler of the two continents and the master of two seas, warrior in the cause of God, the Emperor Abdul Muzaffar Shahabuddin Mohammed Shah Jahan Ghazi.'

It was but a gesture and he wasted little time. His men were prepared, and we began the march north to Agra. Our passage was no longer furtive, we rode through the glowering land in triumph. Rajas and nawabs and umaras, the governors of the subas, all came to pay homage to the Great Mughal Shah Jahan. No longer was the small red pennant of the prince of the empire flying ahead of us atop elephants, but the banner of the emperor.

I felt myself little changed. The land did not blossom for us, the people were still timid and poor. The Adhivasi families still sheltered under the spare shade of scrawny trees, watching us with an age-old mistrust. The heat of the sun did not abate because the Mughal passed by; the rivers did not cease to flow. I was empress, I spoke it aloud to myself in the privacy of the rath, as if to awaken myself from a dream. But Arjumand slumbered on, unchanged.

In spite of Shah Jahan's boldness, the threat of a challenge from Shahriya lingered. Mehrunissa lurked unseen, manipulating her son-in-law, building armies, beating the drums for war.

Shah Jahan

To grasp the sceptre, to ride behind the Imperial banner rather than behind my father, was to feel the very vibration of the earth. The homage I disliked, distrusted. That men should place their heads in their hands as if they worshipped a god was repugnant to me. I put a stop to the practice immediately. A bow would be sufficient. That was my first law, and my uttering it caused all men in the empire to cease to perform kornish. Even as prince and governor I had not possessed such might. My word then was not law; my father eclipsed me. Now, no one did. My breath, my thoughts, my heartbeats were now beyond price. But with this immense power came its companion, desolate loneliness. I moved in a separate world from other mortals; they were by my side, surrounding me, yet the distance between us was immeasurable. My old companions looked on me anew. What was it I saw in their faces? Awe, fear, wariness, servility? Once, they had approached me as friends, now they cringed, not from me, Shah Jahan, but from the Great Mughal. Even Allami Sa'du-lla Khan changed. My second enactment was to make him my Vakil. He had been loyal for all these years, and I believed him to have the qualities Akbar deemed important in a prime minister: 'Wisdom, a nobility of mind, affability, firmness, magnanimity, a man able to be at peace with anyone, who is frank and singleminded towards relations and strangers, impartial to friends and enemies, trustworthy, sharp, far-sighted, skilful in business, knowledgeable in state secrets, prompt in transacting business, and unaffected by the multiplicity of his duties.' Yet even he, in spite of his importance, now showed great deference to my person.

The only true companion I had, who showed no change towards me, remaining as transparent and serene as water, was my beloved Arjumand. To her I had never been a prince, nor was I an emperor now. I was her husband, her lover, my heart was still entwined with hers. Our love was trust; they were fused as if wrought of finest metal. I could not breathe beyond her presence; in it, the loneliness was dispelled. It never went far, but awaited just beyond the light of her companionship, sombre and heavy like a night without wind. On our march north, she was my solace once more. Already the duties of the monarch consumed my time. Before daybreak I had to reveal my presence at the jharoka for nobles and commoners alike. The sight of my face meant a continuity of rule and this comforted them. The morning was taken up with audiences for nobles and ministers and the servants of government. Though I was not to be crowned until we arrived in Agra, I was heartened by the evidence of support.

But Shahriya continued to press his claim, goaded on by Mehrunissa. How could she relinquish the sceptre? Only those who lose power ever truly savour the exhilaration of it. I could not banish my unease. First Khusrav had threatened, now Shahriya. I must act swiftly, otherwise the empire would be unsettled by war and there would be no peace until one of us was victor.

'Exile him,' Arjumand counselled, caressing my arm. We sat alone in her khargah after the evening meal. The servants had been dismissed and she poured the wine. It was the time I enjoyed the most, reclining beside her on the divan, listening to the cicadas. 'Order his imprisonment and then send him away.' She was mercy to my implacability and I acknowledged her compassion.

'But he will return. If I were him, I would, too. I would gather an army and come to battle. How can a man turn his face and heart away from the chance to be Great Mughal? It is the richest throne on earth.'

'Then keep him imprisoned.' She searched my face for an answer and read it too easily. 'But you will not, will you? He is an idiot and his followers will leave him. A little time and his ambition will die.'

'It is not his ambition I fear, but Mehrunissa's. There will be no end to hers. I can only break her power by . . . .'

'No, my love. Spare him. It is not his fault. His blood is your blood and Khusrav's blood, and if you spill it, it will stain our lives once again.'

'If Khusrav had lived, what would be the state of affairs today? Another claimant, more war? The empire must not be weakened by these battles for the throne.'

'He is our kin.'

'Kingship has no kinship.'

Though harsh, I was right, and my Arjumand found it repugnant. She cringed as if I had struck her. 'If I show compassion towards Shahriya, every upstart prince will rebel against my authority. They will think Shah Jahan lacks courage.'

'Let them think so. Then crush them. But the duty of a king is to be a father to all his people.'

'I too have read my grandfather's advice,' I said sharply. A king must also have a great heart so that the sight of anything disagreeable does not unsettle him, Akbar wrote. 'Shahriya commits treason against me, the Padishah, and must die.'

331

I had spoken. It was law. I watched and waited, but she made no further effort to dissuade me, My power cowed her, although I did not want it to. I wished to follow the dictates of Akbar: compassion and justice in all matters. But the throne and my person had to be protected. Royalty is a light emanating from God, a ray from the sun which illuminates all the universe. I wore the *kiyan khura* which is bestowed by God on kings. It cannot be threatened.

Arjumand could not understand. She had, through loving me, excluded all her own ambitions. Some women in the haram practised commerce, accumulated riches; others whined for vast jagirs or lavish gifts. Nothing satisfied their greed. Arjumand loved me; her existence began and ended there. Like a sanyasi, she had few needs. The bare necessities—food, drink, her love—were enough to sustain her. A king cannot but admire such spiritual richness, but his duty does not permit him to embrace it. He may envy the simplicity of the holy man, for the burden of a king is great, but he cannot leave his subjects to wander like sheep. I have never been able to condone the actions of the Gautama. Siddhartha was the prince of the realm, the husband of his wife, the father of his child, and he deserted his duty to become an ascetic. He betrayed his wife, his child, his duty, his subjects. Surely it was his duty to shoulder the burden of kingship? Doubtless a Buddhist will excuse him, saying: 'he became The Enlightened One', but I cannot excuse him. Which does the world need: more gods or better kings?

Arjumand watched the thoughts in my face. Intuition, the magic of women, the power greater than a king's, told her that I would not be moved. She had shed tears for Khusrav, but there were none now for Shahriya.

'Already you have changed.'

Her face remained in the shadows, turned away; I heard her sadness. I moved out of the light, the yellow flames illuminated her alone, turned her golden and mysterious. My heart was moved by her sombre face. I wanted to touch her mouth and eyes and cheeks, feel their silken smoothness, but when I moved my hand, she drew away.

'How could I still be the boy who first saw you in the Royal Meena Bazaar so many years ago? The world doesn't stand still. A moment cannot be held, we cannot transform it into eternity. I am not the boy, as you are not the girl, of that distant minute. I am Emperor, I must change. I hold the office, I hold the power. That child would not have been able to rule; this man can. Life hardens the heart and the mind. We would remain untouched and unchanged if it were not for the acts of other men; their betrayals, their ambitions, their love, their cruelty. And by our own acts, we in turn change their lives and destinies. If we were two villagers we would lead simple and untroubled lives. But that was not to be our destiny.' Her head was bowed, bent by the burden of my words, her long gleaming hair touched the divan. 'What would you wish for?'

'Nothing now; it is too late. We are no longer a boy and a girl. You are Emperor, I am Empress. What chance is there for escape? Maybe I too will change in the coming years. It is not my wish, but you say we cannot live our lives untouched and unmoved by the actions of others. But my love for you will never change. It cannot be stolen, it cannot be soiled, and perhaps, by its power alone, I will remain the girl you first saw.' She took my hand and kissed it, as if in farewell. 'Stay here this night.'

I rose. 'I will return.'

'No. Not this night, then. Another. I do not want the dream of the distant night to return. It reveals itself piece by piece—blood first, and a face I do not know coming out of the mist.'

I did not return to her that night. I sent a message to her father in Lahore. It was the third of my reign: Execute Shahriya and his sons. I did not wish to be hounded by the vengeance of his children for, under Muslim law, they could demand justice from the courts for their father's death. I remained awake. Taktya takhta. Can any king reach the throne without leaving footprints in blood? Only if he is fortunate, and an

333

only son. I vowed to ensure that when the time came, I would control the destinies of my own sons. They would not spill each other's blood.

On the day we reached Agra, Shahriya died, together with his two sons. I did not enquire how it had been done; the emperor's command had been obeyed. The land had but one king.

The city welcomed me. Men, women and children, nobles and beggars, soldiers lined the streets. I rode through them, drunk with the tumult of their cries—Zindabad, Padishah, Zindabad—the beat of drums and joyful music. Rose petals showered down on me and I scattered gold coins for the people to spend in celebration and rejoicing. I passed through the Hathi Pol darwaza of the Lal Quila, dismounted and kissed the earth. More than four years had passed since I last set foot within the walls of the fort. I looked around for changes, but could see little. The sombre red sandstone of the palace still loomed against the clear blue sky above the walls. The garden was, however, even more beautiful. It had been my father's passion and he had greatly improved it with extensions and more flowers, devoting much time to their care.

In the diwan-i-am the nobles and captains of the empire waited. I noted the presence of Karan Singh among them, adorned with jewels and gold finery standing behind the vermilion barrier. The Sisodia of Mewar looked delighted at my position. With my power, his power had increased as well. He would have bowed, but I embraced him. Hidden by a distant pillar lurked Mahabat Khan. He did not lack courage, his position was chosen out of discretion. He had aged; his beard had turned grey and the pouches beneath his eyes had deepened, but the face still bore the dignity of a commander.

There had been a curious episode concerning him and my father a few months previously. Inaction turns the mind to mischief, and Mahabat Khan, having ceased his pursuit of me, fell prey to it. In a fit of madness or boredom, he had entered my father's camp, taking the emperor prisoner. He then seized Mehrunissa, and took them both to his camp, holding them as hostages. What he hoped to gain, none knew. He had the empire in the palm of his hand for one day, but then Mehrunissa managed to escape. She rallied the Mughal army and personally led it into battle against Mahabat Khan. Even as a general, Mehrunissa was victorious; she killed a few men in the skirmish, but I suspect that Mahabat Khan, having come to his senses, fled the battlefield. I vowed I would discover more of this affair.

He did not tremble or cringe as I walked purposefully towards him. I stopped a pace away; his eyes did not falter, though I saw their sadness. I recalled his strong hand on mine guiding my boyhood arm in swordplay, lifting my heavy shield higher, hoarsely instructing me in warfare. He still smelled the same: of sweat, dust, gunpowder, metal, blood. I knew he silently spoke: Inshallah. If I commanded his death, he would die. He bowed; I acknowledged it.

'Your majesty looks well,' he said, and could not resist adding: 'Doubtless, it was I who kept him in this fine condition.'

'You did.' I patted my stomach. 'Hard riding has not made me soft and round like a woman. What do you want?'

He stared, trying to read my mind, delicately assessing the weight of his past deeds. He could not judge which way the balance would tip.

'I am an old general. As a youth I served your grandfather and your father as a man. I am only what I am commanded to be. I await your word.'

'Lead my armies then, old friend. I do not hold it against you that for four years you gave me no rest or peace. If you had disobeyed my father's command, I would not respect you. You might as well serve a third emperor with the same loyalty as you served the other two.' I began to turn: 'And you will explain your mischief-making later.'

He flushed. I had never seen a man so embarrassed. I suspected that he had no explanation, and still continued to puzzle over his erratic behaviour. Men find the greatest mysteries in their own actions.

For the first time in my life I crossed the gold barrier and mounted the steps into the alcove. It was narrow and as dark as a coffin. The enclosure and pillars were meant to shield the might of the emperor from probing eyes. I laid aside my sword and lowered myself on to the awrang. It had been the seat of my grandfather, a simple piece of furniture covered with beaten gold and inlaid with precious stones. It was a half-circle built low, not truly reflecting the power and splendour of the Great Mughal. Like the sun, it should have emanated rays of glory; instead it crouched like a flattened toad. The *chatr* above my head was of solid gold, studded with diamonds. The ceiling of beaten silver dully reflected the assembled nobles, and the wooden roof showed rot. It would be changed.

I looked down: row upon row of faces looked up. From such an elevation, vision changes. The world had shrunk in size; I had increased in glory and I looked into the souls of men. The awrang felt comfortable; I settled into its cushions and felt my whole being take on the nature of the monarch. But there also settled on me, unbidden, a leaden isolation. Neither to the left nor right would I find companions; laughter had ceased and silence held sway. I looked over the massed nobles, silently reached for Arjumand beyond the jali; I thought I saw her face in the shadows and her barely visible presence gave me comfort. Below me stood my sons: Dara, Shahshuja, Aurangzeb, Murad. They stared in awe, then hastily bowed. Even them I could not embrace: they were not permitted to step into the alcove. Dara and Aurangzeb had grown— they had left boyhood and entered youth. Dara looked up at me with suppressed affection—our separation had distressed him—Aurangzeb's face was of stone.

I was truly Ruler of All.

The formalities remained: the reading of the Quran in the Masjid, the Durbar and the swearing of allegiance to my person. A week was spent in these ceremonies. The princes and nobles attended me, bearing priceless gifts with which to fill the treasury. Already it overflowed; none could calculate the wealth that glowed in the rooms below the haram. Every day I gazed upon it, the blood and muscle of the empire, my blood and muscle. How could such wealth not arouse the avarice of men?

An emperor cannot forget friends, favours or enemies, and I had many to remember. Each had to be dealt with justly. I appointed Arjumand's father Mir Saman, and summoned Mehrunissa to attend on me in Agra. She came with reluctance. Arjumand and I received her in the privacy of the haram, sitting alone on the balcony.

That night, before she came, I presented Arjumand with the most powerful gift an emperor can bestow on a trusted companion. She took the gold box hesitantly, allowing it to rest on her lap as she searched my face.

'Open it.'

'What is it?'

'You will see.' She remained still. 'It is my heart, of course. What less can I give to my empress?'

She peeped inside, expecting perhaps a precious stone, then frowned and slowly removed the heavy object.

'I saw this on Mehrunissa's table many years ago. When I touched it, she became angry.'

'You will keep the Muhr Uzak. It is the symbol of my power, and of my trust. You will temper my judgement with your kindness and love; you will be the rein on my injustice, if Allah should so blind me.'

She held it for a moment, then passed it to me. The metal had been warmed by her touch.

'You are the king, my beloved, not I. I have no wish to rule like Mehrunissa. I know you will be gentle and kind to your people as you have all these years been towards me.'

I opened her palms and returned the seal to its keeper. 'An emperor needs a curb. You must be my guide in what is good and what is bad.'

'If you wish it. And . . .' she added gravely, '. . . if you will listen.'

'What you are holding and your sweet voice will make me listen.'

She placed the Muhr Uzak on the gold table by the divan. It was there for all to see, within her reach, not mine. Mehrunissa noticed the Imperial Seal immediately—more precious and powerful than gold or armies—she displayed no humility, merely resignation. She accepted defeat and awaited my command.

I was frozen. All the years of hardship and, even worse, the loss of my father's love and trust, had stemmed from her. True, my father was at fault; to gain her love, he had turned his face from me, yet I could not hold him to blame. She had used his weakness to further her own ambitions, and I had suffered. It was she, too, who had brought down the weight of my power on Shahriya's life. How often, during these past four years, had I cursed the name of Mehrunissa? With my daily prayers I had called down upon her the venom of my heart, and I could not look upon her now without bitterness in my eyes.

Arjumand rose immediately and embraced her aunt. In her, there was forgiveness. My Arjumand looked the older, her body thickened by the years of illness and childbearing, her face worn with exhaustion. And yet to me she was infinitely the more beautiful.

'Your majesty,' Mehrunissa bowed. She was swift to realize that she would be sheltered from the storm by her niece. 'I come humbly to pay my respects to the Great Mughal. I wished, of course, to remain in Lahore to mourn the death of my husband, your father, but I could not disobey your summons.'

She settled down beside Arjumand, sighing in mourning, although her sadness had in no way lessened the glitter of her finery.

'I only wish I had been able to look upon my father's face before his death. For four years I had not seen him.'

'Inshallah,' she spoke blandly. 'He is at peace. My only wish is to return to Lahore to build a monument to his greatness.'

'Nothing more?'

'We can discuss these things later,' Arjumand guided me away from anger. 'How is Ladilli? Is she well?'

'She mourns.' Mehrunissa drew from that word every nuance of reproach. 'She loved Shahriya devotedly, and his death has deeply affected her.'

'You married her to him only to gain power.'

'Do you blame me?' Her flash of spirit returned. 'I was not meant to remain a weak, silly woman whiling away her years and her energy in the haram. Counting jewellery, perfuming my body, waiting eternally for my husband to visit me—that was not a life I relished. Your father only too gladly gave me that . . . .' She pointed to the Muhr Uzak. 'He said: "Do with it what you wish." He wanted only to enjoy himself. The burdens of state tired him and distracted him from his enjoyment of painting and, of course, drinking. His mind had been weakened. I could not allow the empire to disintegrate through his neglect. I ruled as best I could. You understand power as well as I. I could not relinquish it easily. What will there be for me to do now? I will be like a candle guttering through the long and lonely night with no one to notice my flame.'

Mehrunissa waited for my judgement. The silence pinched the muscles in her face. I glanced at Arjumand. Her wish was to be my command. She placed her arm affectionately around Mehrunissa's shoulders.

'You will build a great tomb for Jahangir. It will be as beautiful as the one you built for my grandfather.'

So I forgave.

There were others I could not forget. I summoned Mahabat Khan to the diwan-i-khas on the following morning.

'You will go to the jungle surrounding Mandu and search for a dacoit by the name of Arjun Lal, if he still lives. When you have found him, deliver the greetings of the Emperor Shah Jahan, and tell him this: "Shah Jahan has not forgotten his loyalty and in gratitude returns to him all his lands, and twice more besides. From this day he will live at peace with the emperor."'

The wazir wrote down this command, and another: 'You will take twenty thousand men into Bengal. On the banks of the Hoogli, you will find a feringhi fort. You will raze it to the ground, and those who do not die in the battle you will bring in chains to the palace. One, only one, I wish to look upon. A priest with a red beard, the colour of carrots. He will live only until he has seen my face.'

The wazir wrote these commands. Arjumand set the seal upon both.

the taj mahal 1069/AD 1659

Isa wept. Tears glazed the sunlight, dissolved the faces of the people, and reduced the marble and sandstone palace into a grotesque shape. The silence was crushing. A frozen frieze of men surrounded him— soldiers, nobles, princes, an emperor. And a prince, separate, cut from a different stone. He looked around him with an air of regret. He knew his own mortality, knew that everything he could see would vanish. Did men die, or was it the world that died? Our grasp of mortal things, Isa thought, is tenuous. When Dara died, he passed from our sight. Or is that an arrogant thought? Did we pass from Dara's sight? The puzzle eased the ache in his chest. It was a subtraction, but of what, from what? If the soul returned to Brahma, that was then permanence, the world impermanence. We are subtracted then, not the dead. The conclusion failed to comfort him. All men of all faiths yearned for comfort; all belief depended upon it. We are promised comfort, but with no proof, and we believe because we must.

The silence unsettled the emperor, Aurangzeb looked at the sullen faces. He saw the grief, but could not understand that he was the source. He was the victor; there stood the villain. But the silence reversed their positions, and somehow the very air played tricks. He stifled an

341

unwelcome thought—if he were in chains, the faces would be joyful. He had judged Dara fairly. The emperor was the shadow of Allah, the Scourge of God. Dara had failed. He had displayed open affection for the Hindu. He was flawed. Death awaited.

Instinctively, Aurangzeb knew that blood could not be spilt in the open. The mood of the crowd was unstable, the rage around him barely stifled; one drop would release the flood. He did not look at Dara. Instead he gestured, dismissively. The guards pushed Dara towards the dungeons below the palace. The executioner looked up; the emperor nodded.

It was cool below the palace. A breeze came off the Jumna. Dara smelled the dust and water. He felt a natural relief from the heat that had beaten on his back all morning. The steps down and down were endless. Candles guttered in niches, shadows leapt and waned with his passing. As they went deeper, the darkness increased, the flames burned more bravely. So far from sunlight, time itself ceased to move. A stone room, a dirt floor, a block of wood. Dara experienced a sad and desolate loneliness. He wished for comfort at this moment, but none he loved was near him. He saw his mother's face with startling clarity, as a child might, from below, as if he lay on her lap. Her perfume surrounded him, musky, of roses. They laid him face down in the dirt, his head on the block. He dozed against the velvet comfort of her shoulder, covered by her long black hair.

Thuck.

Thuck, thuck, thuck. Shah Jahan listened to the washer women beating on the stones. Buffaloes lay supine in the lap of the river. His heart twanged, plucked like a bowstring by an unseen hand. In the haze of sunlight and dust, the Taj Mahal wavered; only the dome remained in

342

reality, supported by air. He groaned: Arjumand, Arjumand, summoning her to escape the weight of marble and come to his side. She came often, at night. He dreamed she lay by him, healed his loneliness. He woke at times, head bent as if he nuzzled the crook of her shoulder. Flesh, he would demand then, wanting comfort in his solitary bed. The women waited for his call, knowing his needs, and lay beneath him, and when he called out, it was not for them.

Isa turned. A soldier called. Another stood by holding a golden bowl that shone in his hands like a ball of flame.

'What is it?'

'We wish to approach Shah Jahan.'

'His majesty.' Isa corrected, but the soldiers paid no attention. The land had only one majesty—Aurangzeb. Isa did not grant permission, but they walked boldly into the Saman Burj. Shah Jahan reclined on the divan by the marble rail, staring out, his back against a pillar, his reflection trapped in the angles of myriad diamonds set into the walls of the room. He did not look at the soldiers, but at the bowl. Fear hollowed his face, his eyes started. He averted his head, and Isa knew then what the great dish held.

'Go away.' He moved swiftly and pushed the soldiers. A dagger touched his throat, a sword-point rested on his chest.

'Who are you to command us? The Padishah Aurangzeb has sent a gift for his father. "Here lies his love and comfort", the Padishah said.'

The soldier removed the cover.

Sightless, Dara stared.

Gopi stepped cautiously through the portals into the harsh sunlight. The garden was deserted, no one guarded the tomb. He looked down the long narrow canal; the fountains were still. The blazing white image was reflected in the dark water. He listened to the drowsy hum of insects. He could hear no sound of men; they were distant, across the river, beyond the high walls. The world had shut its eyes; the tomb was his. He hesitated in the shadow of the gate. He stepped down, still expecting a challenge, the brutal authority of an Imperial soldier driving him back. He could not believe he was in the garden, looking on such beauty—the green and watered lawns, the rose beds, the canna lilies, the marigolds. For Muslims, the marigold was the flower of death and these were abundant in their colours and mass. Fringing the garden were all kinds of trees: mangoes, lime, cypress. The cypress too appeared in the carving on the tomb; the tree of Timur.

Gopi walked along the footpath beside the fountain, catching glimpses of his reflection moving over that serene image. The building loomed as he approached. From a distance—he had only ever seen it from beyond the wall—it had not possessed such grandeur. As he entered its shadow, he felt the magic. Its delicacy was illusion, created to give an effect of fragility. It towered over him, and he craned his neck to look up at the dome. He lost sight of it as he neared the plinth and hurried up the steps to the door. The fragile marble fretwork stretched high above him. In a corner of the arch, bees had built a black and swollen nest. He pushed open the silver door, and saw the jali.

From the threshold, Gopi stared. The light broke through the marble tracery of the western window, mellowed, muted. It struck the jali and changed the very texture of the stone into something fragile, translucent, luminous, until the stone itself became a source of light. In the dark, he thought, it would glow with its own life. The inlaid patterns: leaves and flowers, reds, greens, blues, shimmered like the glow-worms that lit the gardens at night. He knew instinctively which panel his father had exhausted a lifetime in carving. He was drawn to it, his fingers caressed the polished marble, touching every part like the body of a woman, striving to reach his father through the cold

344

stone. Sadness overcame him: to have created such beauty, but never to gaze and kiss.

At last, he saw the sarcophagus within. Cautiously, he entered the enclosure and walked round, but did not touch, the marble block. He could not comprehend the strange behaviour of the Muslims: they built monuments to their dead, but the body was transient, worthless after death. He looked up at the golden lamp, unlit, and to the great dome. He sighed at the splendour, and the echo replied softly, mocking him. He felt at peace now, knowing he had the luxury of time to spend examining the building. Respecting the spirit of the tomb, he drifted quietly through the chambers, studying the pattern of light, marvelling at the enormous labour that had been expended. And from each chamber he would gaze through windows to his father's jali. He possessed it now, finally after so many years. It was his father's, and his. His childhood had been invested in the carving, along with those other childhoods, lives and deaths—his brother, his father, his mother. Their spirits too were in the tomb, along with those of countless others who had laboured all those years to lift such loveliness from the earth.

Gopi touched the walls, his fingertips caressed the diamonds and rubies, emeralds and pearls set into the flowers, each one of fabulous value.

He realized, suddenly, that he had come here to say his farewell. The courage to enter the tomb, stifling his fear of punishment, had risen from this desire. He had not known what to expect, and he wished now it had remained a mystery. For all these years he had imagined it to be hollow as a shell, not filled with such splendour. How could he leave? How could he return to a village he barely remembered, two thousand kos to the south? He could not desert the spirits of his father and mother. No, he deceived himself. It was the tomb he could not desert. He sensed its need for his skill, and his own need for its beauty.

Gopi walked out into the sunlight, trudged down the steps and up

345

the path to the gateway. He did not look back. He was absorbed in his thoughts; his life would have to be changed to make room for his new love. He could not return to strangers, he would be a stranger now in that tiny village nestling in the green fields. He had a family here, a brother, a sister, an uncle—distant but benign. They would stay. He would not forget that he was an Acharya. It was his identity, his profession and, if the gods willed it, he would find a woman of his own kind to marry, a wife for Ramesh, and a husband for Savitri.

He returned to his position beyond the wall, beneath the shade of the peepul tree. Then, as his father and his father's father had done, he contemplated the block of marble. It was a foot high, a foot across and a foot deep. He shut his eyes, saw the god in the stone, not Durga, but Ganesh, the god of luck and learning and wealth.

1076/AD 1666

The years passed; dust and age weighed upon them. The palace hung like an enchanted ruin on the massive walls of the Lal Quila. It looked abandoned, except for pinpoints of light fluttering in marble niches at night; except too, for the soldiers who surrounded it, permitting none to enter. Theirs was a lazy duty; the empire had ebbed away, the tumult had died, and only silence and those few figures remained to haunt the palace.

Shah Jahan was entombed in marble and sunlight. He had ached for his own passing; life was drained of all purpose, reduced to mere existence. Isa read to him daily from the *Ain Akbari* or the *Babur-nama*, and occasionally the emperor would listen to letters from the emperor, his son. "'I wish to avoid your censure,'" Isa read, "'and cannot endure that you should form a wrong estimate of my character. My elevation to the throne has not, as you imagine, filled me with insolence and pride. You know, from more than forty years' experience, how burdensome an ornament is a crown, and how with a sad and aching

346

heart, a monarch retires from the public gaze. You seem to think I should devote less time and attention to the consolidation and security of the kingdom, and that it would better become me to devise and execute plans of aggrandizement. I am indeed far from denying that conquests ought to distinguish the reign of a great monarch, and I agree that I should disgrace the blood of the great Timur, our honoured progenitor, if I did not seek to extend the boundaries of my present territories. At the same time, I cannot be reproached for inglorious inaction. I wish you to recollect that the greatest conquerors are not always the greatest kings. The nations of the earth have often been subjugated by mere uncivilized barbarians, and the most extensive conquests have in a few short years crumbled to pieces. The great king is he who makes it the chief business of his life to govern his subjects with equity."'

'I do not want to be subjected to his letters!' Shah Jahan said querulously. They only dredge up forgotten grief. I am an old man. He should banish me from his thoughts, as he has banished me from his life.'

'He seeks forgiveness, your majesty,' Isa spoke gently.

'From me? Eight years have passed and he still asks an old man to forgive an emperor? Of what use is my forgiveness?'

'You have not granted it.'

'How can I? He murdered two of my sons, imprisoned a third. How can a father forgive? You tell me, Isa. The sons of Arjumand lie in their graves; her husband lies in this prison. There will be no forgiveness.'

Isa did not pursue the argument. Every time it ended the same way. He would not be heard. Jahanara, who cared lovingly for her father, also would not forgive.

Immediately after receiving a letter, Shah Jahan would retire to the Mina Masjid. If he prayed for Aurangzeb's death, he was not answered. If he prayed for his own, he was not answered. Time was squandered in listening to music, eating, drinking, consuming the slave girls nightly. His passions had not ebbed—their bodies and perfume and softness sustained him. Pleasure eased his restless spirit.

And then, one day, when Isa came to wake him, the prayers had been answered. Shah Jahan lay on his divan, staring out at the pale, pink dawn alighting gently on the dome of the Taj Mahal. Isa closed his eyes, gently kissed the sunken cheeks and embraced the corpse of his emperor. Once his private farewell was done, he called Jahanara.

He went at night, when the funeral was over. Shah Jahan lay beside Arjumand, encased in a simple block of marble. It was dark in the heart of the tomb. Isa savoured the incense and crushed rose petals that still lay on the floor. He knelt and kissed the cold stone that was Arjumand. His lips lingered, turning cold too, and his tears streaked and slipped down the marble. How long he remained there in a last caress, he could not tell. He was aware of a lantern light, and the footsteps of a solitary figure. Quickly, he withdrew to a corner.

Isa recognized the emperor in the pool of yellow light. Aurangzeb stood passively, staring at the two tombs. He set the lantern down, and crouched at the tomb of his mother. He placed his forehead first on the cold stone, and then his lips. He performed the same ceremony at the tomb of his father. As he stood and turned, he saw Isa.

'Do I surprise you, Isa?'

'No, your majesty. You are their son.'

The flame leapt, illuminating Aurangzeb's face. Isa had not seen him for many years. The eyes shone too brightly, glazed with sorrow. Before the light faded, Isa noticed too the look of withdrawn loneliness which crept into the face of every monarch.

'I looked on his face a last time—he had not appeared to age.'

'You were fortunate. He did not look upon yours.'

'Was that my fault? His life was an echo of things past. He did not

348

look upon his father's face.'

'The blame then lies buried in the tomb.'

'Blame! I could not have chosen a different path. I destroyed my brothers for the same reasons he destroyed his brothers. But he blamed and cursed me for my actions. That was not just.'

Then, in a lower voice: 'But I spared him; and I spared Murad. I wonder, at times, might it have been different if she had lived?'

'Might? Would you have listened to your mother's voice pleading for Dara?'

'Perhaps, but we were set in conflict all our lives. The balance of loving—Inshallah.' He took up the lantern. 'And you, Isa?'

'I loved you all, your majesty; one no less than the other.'

'You took nothing from us, unlike so many others. I will care for you until your last day.'

When the emperor had left, Isa returned to his vigil.

the love story

Arjumand

The sickness began again within the first month of my beloved's reign. It struck, as always, without warning, in the pale soft light of dawn, having lain coiled and waiting in my belly throughout the dark night. I could not bear the thought of another child. This one lay heavy in me like a dull sullen stone, dragging at my spirit. For days I plunged into a mood of such blackness that I seemed to live in a nightmare. I lay entombed in the lightless room unable even to see my own body. I heard hushed voices, whispers indistinguishable beyond the walls of my chamber.

It was the hand of my beloved, his kiss on my lips, that awoke me from the darkness. I saw his face, drawn with worry, his eyes red and sleepless. I smiled, lifting his burden of guilt. He had taken my willing body on the day he became emperor in Agra. He could not be blamed for my own lust. Still I weakened at his glance, and my blood raced to his touch. We had resisted for many months, but on that night our lovemaking had been part of the frenzied celebrations.

'The hakim has advised rest and quiet,' my beloved whispered. 'No one is to disturb you.'

I could not contain my disappointment, 'How long we've waited for your rule, and now I cannot enjoy it, but must remain in my sickroom night and day.'

'You will recover soon.'

'Nine months isn't soon. It's a lifetime. I feel as if. . .' I could not speak my foreboding. It hung on my heart like an impenetrable veil.

'What?'

'Nothing. I feel nothing has changed. I remain a princess, I remain confined.'

'But you are no longer the princess Arjumand Banu. You are now the empress of my heart and soul and empire. You are the Chosen One of the Palace.'

'It is a pretty name. Mumtaz-i-Mahal. But it lies strangely on my tongue. Let others call me that, my beloved. I want only to be what I have always been to you—Arjumand. I am still the same woman.'

'It will be as you wish, my love.' He kissed me and rose. I felt him fading from my sight and I was afraid, but held my tongue. 'But from now on the world will know you as my Empress, Mumtaz-i-Mahal.'

Such grandeur was undeserved. The name slipped from my memory as I lay in the still, heavy heat. Bathed by my maid, fed and cared for by Isa, I cursed this unborn child that so incapacitated me. It fretted within me, gave me no peace or rest, and I lay for hour upon hour only dimly hearing and seeing those who attended me.

Possibly, it heard my curses. God forgive me. I felt one dawn that it had begun to slip from my body, a spirit fleeing its earthly shell. I did not call out; the blood could not be dammed, and with the passing minutes I felt a lightness take my body, setting me afloat, as though I too were escaping from my flesh. Only then, clinging stubbornly to my body, I called. Isa came, saw the blood on the divan and fled to call the hakim. He gave me a potion to make me sleep and staunched the flow with his herbs, I slept for many days, and when I woke I felt refreshed.

351

I could not yet quite suspend my disbelief. I awoke expecting a different roof over me, a different sound outside, a different land, different faces, different smells. I was sensitive to the odours of this land and could tell where I was from the softest breeze bearing the dust of rice, wheat, pepper, mustard, the fragrance of humid jungle or bleached desert. Jaspur, Mandu, Burhanpur, the Jumna, the Tapti, the Ganga; each place had its own scent. Here it was a mixture of the river, men, armour, elephants, horses and the sweet musk of power.

I relished the peace and the permanence; the dread of having to live on the march, rudely shaken in a rath, from dawn to dusk, still haunted me. But the Empress of the Great Mughal, once woken, looked out upon a day of pleasure. I was bathed and dressed and perfumed, which took an inordinate amount of time because such had been the custom of the empress before me. Countless women and eunuchs waited upon me, making me feel trapped and smothered after a few days. I had grown accustomed to the attendance of only one maid for my toilet and, for all my other needs, Isa. We were drowning in people, formality, ritual. It was, I thought, truly more arduous than our spare existence during our time of flight. I had never lived in the palace before and found it difficult to accustom myself to the life here. My comings and goings were noted, each word I spoke repeated, every gesture interpreted. I was supposed to behave with the grandeur of an empress among the other women in the haram, but could not summon up enough interest to play this role.

Jahangir's concubines still remained in residence with their countless attendants, all vying for importance. The haram continued to be guarded by those sullen, Tartar women who now showed me grudging deference. To the puzzlement of all, but to my own relief, I did not have to contend with other wives. No doubt I would still have been empress, but the jealousies would have shrivelled my soul. Whom my husband chose for his evening's pleasure, whom he rejected would, as it did for both Akbar and Jahangir, have caused sulks, fights and bitterness.

Out of habit I slept in the gulabar pitched on the lawn. As if I were of the blood of Timur, I could not bear a fixed roof overhead. This was fortunate for, within the first month of his reign, my beloved began to tear the palace apart. The treasury overflowed. He could not curb his impatience to build and enhance the glory of the Great Mughal. If his father had loved paintings and gardens, my Shah Jahan expressed himself in the splendour of buildings. The wooden roof of the diwan-i-am was pulled down and workers began to replace it with the red sandstone of the pillars and the fort. Work also began on other parts of the palace, using the stone which he loved so much, white marble. He always remembered the audiences with his father in the dim and gloomy diwan-i-khas, and had contained his yearning all these years to transform it into a light and beautiful chamber fit for an emperor.

The exercise of power rejuvenated my beloved. His energy was inexhaustible. He rose before dawn to show himself at the jharoka-i-darshan, patiently attending to the petitions that were attached to the chain of justice. He would return to my side to doze for an hour or two, and would then spend the remainder of the morning in the diwan-i-am hearing other petitioners and settling the disputes that arose between his nobles. Then after a light meal, he would meet his ministers to discuss the management of the empire, receiving them in the diwan-i-khas or the ghusl khana. Once official matters had been dealt with, he turned his mind to his building; his passion for detail demanded the attention of countless craftsmen. He summoned them from all parts of the empire, Muslim and Hindu alike, for ability and an eye for beauty are not limited to one creed. They came from Multan, Lahore, Delhi, Mewar, Jaipur, and some even from Turki, Isfahan and Samarkand. Towards evening my beloved would seek my company. We would spend an hour or two watching elephant fights on the maidan, then we would retire to the gulabar, attended only by a few servants and Isa, while the court musicians and singers entertained us. At the evening meal, the children and other relations and friends would join us in the palace.

If an emperor must love his subjects, so must an empress. I now had unlimited wealth. It had always been a tradition of the Mughal emperors to keep a large leather sack of money, one lakh of dams, to distribute to the needy. One stood at the entrance to the palace. I made sure it was emptied, and daily it would be refilled. I no longer needed to beg for contributions. I was empress, and as my beloved built palaces, I built humbler places: schools, hospitals for the treatment of the sick, homes for the homeless. Each week, still in the company of Isa, but now escorted by soldiers, I fed the poor. I could not in truth claim, as I became more used to it, that I disliked my position.

In the eighth month of Shah Jahan's reign, Mahabat Khan returned from Bengal. We watched the rising dust of his approaching army. Behind, in chains, walked the survivors from the feringhi fort. It was summer, and the heat was immense. I felt no pity for those who had shown neither me nor my beloved any compassion in our need. I could not forgive them for their insulting treatment of me all those years ago when I was still a child. They had walked two thousand kos, chained together, suffering the consequences of their harsh behaviour.

Those who rejoiced most were the Sadr and the mullahs. They believed that at last my beloved was going to begin a campaign to crush the unbeliever. The Christians were but a tiny irritation to them, and punishment satisfied them. The Hindus were their chief enemy, and they expected Shah Jahan to move the army against them. He did not correct their belief. If his revenge was misread, but placated them, then two purposes were served.

Mahabat Khan entered the diwan-i-khas to report to his emperor.

'Your majesty, I found the dacoit Arjun Lal—a bold rascal and difficult to catch. He evaded my forces for many days in spite of

assurances sent to him. I finally trapped him in a gully, and he would
still have fought the whole army.' He stopped to drain a cup of chilled
wine. He could not hide his appreciation; a pleasure of the court was
the daily supply of ice that was carried down the Jumna from the
Himalayas.

'I shouted out the greetings of the Emperor Shah Jahan. That quieted
him. Of course, in such wild country, they had not heard of your ascent
to the throne, your majesty. He accepted your peace, and I returned
to him his lands and twice as much again.'

He went to stand on the balcony, and looked down on the maidan
between the Jumna and the fort.

'I have your priest—alive. The commander of the fort died in battle.
He was a good man.' He would not deny him respect. 'He died in his
duty.'

'How many others were killed?'

'A few hundred. The remainder I brought. There were many
converts to this Christianity, and I did not wish to leave them behind
to carry on their religion.'

The prisoners lay exhausted on the ground, strangely still. They
did not raise up their heads towards the palace; hope had fled, and
with it all curiosity. They waited for death. 'Give them a choice. They
must forsake their religion or die,'

The wazir was despatched to read the emperor's command. How
swiftly men and women forsake their god. If another will allow them
life, is that not proof of his miraculous powers? The Christian god had
not protected them during the long march; many had died on the way,
and he had remained indifferent to their pain and hunger and thirst.
Now, another succoured them, the god of the Great Mughal and all
Islam, and they fell in worship. Only the feringhi priests refused. They
stood apart and shook their heads in defiance.

'Fetch them.'

The one who led them had hair on his face coloured like carrots, a watery red with some greying hairs. He did not bow, and the others, taking their instructions from him, also remained upright. Their hands were bound. The leader, his face gaunt and savage, had angry eyes which burned in his head like fierce, anguished flames.

'You recall me.'

'Yes.' The priest had a brutal, hard voice. He was used to command and humble speech came reluctantly. 'You have committed sacrilege . . . .'

'Doubtless. And you, of course, have not. Since our first meeting, I have read your holy book. It says that men should show compassion to one another, as well as many other interesting things. Like us we believe in a hereafter, a paradise you call heaven. But that reward depends on one's actions in this present life. Will you go to heaven, priest, when you die?'

'Yes, I will. I have led a God-fearing life and sung His praises. God will reward me for my love.'

'You are selective in your love. You love god, yet not man. Does that not strike you as strange since god, your god, claims to love all men?'

'Only those who follow His teachings.'

'He is selective then, in his love. He places conditions on his compassion.'

'And does not your god do likewise?'

'He does. And that has always puzzled me. But I am not . . .'

Shah Jahan hesitated, A thoughtless word and our own priests would hear, and he would have to placate their sulking anger. 'I am a true believer, but the duty of an emperor is to love his subjects equally. I cannot indulge in the luxury of following only God's dictates. I listen to my conscience too. Do you?'

'God is my conscience.'

I could not stifle my loathing. This man and our own priests were of the same stuff: stubborn, pedantic, narrow. The rich juices of life and love had drained from their hearts; stringy souls dangled within their bodies.

'And he spoke nothing of charity towards those who seek it? My God dictates charity.'

'Does a prince have need of charity? It is meant only for the poor.'

'A fine distinction, since princes can be poor, too. Are you not afraid of me now?'

'I do not expect God's punishment for my act.' He stared boldly. 'And I am not afraid of yours.'

'I ought not to keep you then from your appointment with God.'

Shah Jahan's words gave the priest pride. He was to be martyred, and the emperor was the instrument of his salvation.

'You believe in the power of your god to save you?'

'He will save my soul from eternal damnation. He is all-powerful.'

'You are as foolish as the other men, priest. You believe you have power that will place you above your destiny. The difference between you and me is a subtle one. As a monarch, I understand the mortality of power; as a priest you deceive yourself by believing in the immortality of power. When the blade falls and God is not waiting to receive your soul, where will you wander?'

'He will be there.'

'But not yet. You will be imprisoned for two years, and flogged daily. At the end of your imprisonment, you will leave the empire of the Great Mughal.' The emperor wearily straightened his back. Apart from being a priest this man was a feringhi and a constant irritant to the throne. 'Otherwise, the Mughal army will raze Surat and expel all your people.'

I too was disappointed; for the first time I did not wish my beloved to show leniency. I sent Isa to fetch the emperor, who left the alcove and came to me. I did not speak until he sat beside me.

'Should you not have been more harsh?'

357

'I cannot execute a man of God—even though he behaves as if he were a man of the devil. His only crime is lack of compassion, and that can afflict us all. I have punished him and his people enough.'

'But will they learn? They grow too bold.'

'You would like an example made of him?' He waited, gently stroking his beard. His face was unreadable, even to me. It showed the features of an emperor, immobile, waiting behind the mask. His silence permitted consideration.

'No. I am sorry. I was swept away by my anger at the man himself. He disgusts me.'

'But that is not enough. Examples only distort justice. And his death would bring certain difficulties on our heads. We need the feringhi ships to take the true believers to Mecca. The route by land is hard and dangerous.'

'You are right, but I could not hide my feelings for that man and his people from you.'

He rose and returned to the awrang. I knew that if I had persisted he would have bowed to my wishes. The guards took the priest and the others from the diwan-i-am. The unclean smell of their bodies and the reek of smug sanctity went with them. I was not the only one to be disappointed; so were the mullahs. All priests thirst for blood.

1039/AD 1629

Sweetly and quietly the time passed. We did not leave Agra, even in the summer. I had no wish to journey north to Kashmir to escape the heat. I felt a great serenity in remaining where we were.

In the spring we held the Royal Meena Bazaar—an echo from our past—in the gardens of the palace. I could not suppress my childish pleasure in abandoning my beatilha once more, if only because it reminded me of our first meeting. If I had kept my veil on that day, my life would have been far different. I could have loved him, but not him

358

me. How can one fall in love with a piece of cloth?

The wives of the *omrahs* gathered in the palace before dawn. This time, I was not a lost and lonely girl trailing in the wake of Mehrunissa; now they gathered around me, countless faces, giggling, laughing. The air boiled with anticipation of the evening. I did not wish to dazzle all eyes; what had I to sell to an emperor of Hindustan? Silver, not gold and diamonds, was the magic that had changed my life. Isa thought it did not befit an empress to sell such a lowly metal.

'It will enchant him once more, Isa. We will return to that moment twenty-two years ago.'

The past returned as if in a dream, and I thought it would be pleasurable to be again the girl innocently awaiting the impact of destiny. But, inexplicably, I felt a darkening, a greyness that pervaded my being, imprisoning me in a cold and clammy mist.

'What is it?' Isa startled me from my thoughts.

'I don't know. For a moment I felt cold.'

'In this heat you are fortunate if you feel cold, Agachi.' He looked at me with concern. I was severe and unsmiling, frightened too. 'You're not well?'

I was grateful for his familiar presence. He was the shadow of my life. Only once, from deference, had he addressed me as 'your majesty'; I was swift to correct him. His familiarity was a reminder that I had not always been in such an elevated position.

As empress, I had a stall in the most advantageous position: by the entrance, within the circle of lanterns and candles. I could not help but glance towards the shadows where I'd once stood, beyond the light. There was a woman there, the wife of a minor omrah. I was disappointed. Somehow, I'd hoped to see a young girl, another Arjumand.

The dundhubi beat his approach; my heart too made just such a thunderous sound. The Emperor Shah Jahan, more resplendent than his father Jahangir, handsome, assured, entered the Royal Bazaar. His

turban was of scarlet silk and gold, and the diamond set in the brooch
that held the long heron plume was as large as a mouth agape with
awe. He wore a long necklace of pearls, each the size of a pigeon's egg;
his gold belt was fashioned like chain-mail and encrusted with emeralds,
and the *jam khak* had a gold handle also decorated with emeralds, as
were the handle and scabbard of his *shamsher*. His sarapa, brought from
Varanasi, was heavy with gold thread woven into flowers and leaves,
all encrusted with precious stones in harmony with the design. He
was accompanied by Allami Sa'du-lla Khan, Mahabat Khan and my
father. Without hesitation, he came to my stall, and in mock gravity
examined my offering, a paltry heap of silver. The pieces were the
same ones he had purchased twenty-two years ago.

'What is your name?'

I am Arjumand, your majesty.'

'Who is your father?'

'He is the son of Ghiyas Beg, the Itiam-ud-daulah. You stare. Have
you not looked upon a woman before?'

'Before such beauty I cannot help myself. Do you order me to
turn away?'

'No. This is the Royal Bazaar and it is your privilege. Will you not
buy a trinket from my stall?'

'Of what use will the money be to someone like you?'

'The poor always need it more than I do. I will give it to them.'

'Which poor?'

'Has not his majesty noticed them outside the fort? They huddle
against its walls.'

'Yes, I have. I shall buy all that you are selling . . . that is, if you will
sell it all to me?'

'Everything is for sale. A poor bazaar girl keeps nothing for herself.
But it must please you.'

'It pleases me to buy everything. How much?'

'A lakh.'

The emperor laughed aloud: 'The price has risen, but I have a bargain. I will see you again.'

'If it is your wish.'

It was.

He came to me an hour past midnight. I was sleeping but woke immediately at his kiss. The soft glow of the lamp faintly illuminated him. He had disrobed, and his silken wrap fell away as he knelt and then lay beside me. His body had changed little, it was still firm and muscled. I felt his hardness at my thigh.

It had been—how long?—months, nearly a year now. We resisted each other, although for him the abstention had been easier. I had chosen the concubines he lay with; they were pretty, but not of noble families. There were Turks and Kashmiris and Bengalis and Panjabis, Muslim and Hindu. They remained in the haram, leading leisurely lives, and I ensured that no single one was summoned to his bed more than once. I could not always contain my jealousy, as his need was constant. I myself could not satisfy him because of my fear of another child. The hakim, with acerbic pleasure, was the constant sentinel of my celibacy.

This night was different. I could not resist my need for him any longer. My body ached and yearned to have him once more inside me. His kisses tasted of wine and his hands, strangers for so long, stroked my breasts and caressed the nipples. He explored me as though I were a fresh young girl brought to his bed. He too could not hide his eagerness, even after all these years. I held his organ in my hand: how amazing and hard it felt! I had forgotten its strength.

'I have missed you,' he whispered. 'Every woman is you in my heart and my mind. I call only your name—Arjumand.'

'My beloved, I have heard you in my heart. I still cannot breathe in your presence. My whole being has become a part of you, and my longing for you has been an unbearable pain. Hurry. Enter me, my beloved, and thrust hard.'

I cried out, not from virginal pain, but with pleasure to feel him

361

entering me, slowly, gently, gradually, until he was fully inside. I wished him to never cease the delicious movement; I wanted to hold him and feel every part of his body descending and rising above me. My greed was insatiable, but all too soon I felt it begin to fade as my body burst with the pleasure of our lovemaking. I was awash and languorous, dimly hearing him whisper: Arjumand, Arjumand. Then he rested by my side. We lay in each other's arms and slept. When I awoke he was gone. It was nearly dawn and I heard the dundhubi beat his presence at the jharoka-i-darshan.

1040/AD 1630

Every act has its consequence. Long after we have forgotten, there follows an echo; strident or soft, it awakens our destiny. Our flesh is our weakness; we cannot but succumb to its greed. Through it, God has inflicted unjust punishment on us. I wept, I raged; even an empress was not more powerful than her husband's seed. I was no more than a beast of the earth in which all things became fruitful. Prayer and tears and potions, nothing could prevent the growth of the child within. Other women lie with men night upon night and satiate that lust, but nothing stirs within them. Yet after one night with my beloved husband, I was once more brought low by a pregnancy. It was my fourteenth.

Once the flare of rage mingled with despair had passed, I became calm. This surprised my beloved, the hakim, Isa. They expected my dark fear to continue until the birth. I could not myself explain this spirit of acceptance. It entered me quietly, soothing my turbulent spirit. The winter days passed like a murmur. At dawn I was carried from the gulabar to the palace balcony. There I would lie on a divan while Isa read to me or, if I was tired, I would look out upon the ever-changing scene below me. At dawn the people bathed and worshipped, in the morning they washed clothes and worked, the buffaloes and elephants lazed in the afternoon after labour, and at twilight the people bathed again before prayer.

But while I was in a tranquil frame of mind, the peace of the empire was threatened and disturbed. The princes at the fringes of the empire had been deceptively quiet, calculating the temper of their new emperor. They thought him too occupied with his duties, and the troublesome spirit of the Deccan once more began to assert itself. The thousands of men and the immeasurable wealth that were expended on that harsh and barren land could have made of it a green and luscious garden. But its forts and deserts and the Vindhya mountains were barriers that protected the rich south from conquest. We knew wealth lay beyond, wealth as great as that of the Mughal.

Shah Jahan could not send Dara, The eldest son of every king had gained his military experience in the Deccan, but Dara was still only a child. Nor could we despatch Mahabat Khan. Once already, the general had shown a tendency to work mischief if he commanded too much power, and my beloved would not entrust the whole Mughal force to him.

Shah Jahan came to me on the balcony and sat by my side, staring out with intense force at the river curving and winding into the hazy heat, its sandbanks white and bleached. He looked despondent.

'I had hoped the trouble would die down. Our strength is being drained by these useless wars,' he sighed. 'But the rats continue to nibble at my borders, threatening my peace, and Shah Jahan will not be remembered as the king who released them from the empire. Let another do that. I will have to march south myself to subdue them.' He took my hand and placed the palm against his lips.

'You wish me to come with you?'

'Yes. It will be a year or more before we can return. I could not bear to be parted from you for so long.'

'The hakim does not wish me to travel. And the journey will be arduous.'

'I am no longer the bi-daulat fleeing my father's forces. We will travel slowly and if you should need rest, we will remain in one place as long as necessary.' He stroked the swell of my belly gently. His face was mute with loving, and sadness. 'I am sorry.'

'For what? For my child? I wanted you that night. I had wanted and waited too long, I am content that we made love so pleasurably.' I kissed his hand. 'Order the Mir Manzil to construct the most luxurious rath for my comfort.'

'It will be done.'

The Mir Manzil fulfilled the command literally; he built a rath that reflected the splendour of an empress. It was the size of a room, with Persian carpets and many divans filled with the softest feathers. The roof and pillars were covered with beaten gold and decorated with precious stones. But even the many divans could not completely soften the uneven road; the emperor himself could not command the earth to be flat and smooth.

Although I did not ride, my rath was followed by the customary seven elephants. On each was mounted a gold and azure *meghdambar*, lined with velvet and silken cushions, but they remained empty throughout the journey. This time I was not placed midway in the huge column, but travelled close behind my beloved.

Each day, two hours before the dawn broke the blackness of night, the column began its march south. The first to leave the camp were the heavy cannon drawn by one hundred elephants, accompanied by 30,000 siphais. With them, roped onto a large bullock-drawn cart, went the royal barge. At river crossings, it would take us in comfort to the opposite bank.

Then, one hour before dawn, my beloved would rise. To the accompaniment of the dundhubi and *sanjs* and *karanas*, he would show himself in the jharoka before mounting his elephant. Small signal guns were discharged to announce his position and his captains and nobles and their ladies would shout: 'Manzil Mubarak!'

Little had changed in the order of march since the days of Jahangir, except, of course, for my own more prominent position. A hundred thousand horsemen and their syces, and all their baggage and feed, followed us, and the column took a whole day to pass any given point.

The journey to the south was leisurely. My hakim, Wazir Khan, rode by my rath and, when he felt that I had grown tired, would command the column to halt. He had as much power as the emperor in these matters, but fortunately I found I did not tire as easily as he expected. But my belly grew larger and larger as we neared Burhanpur and I found that in the dry, dusty heat, my breathing grew difficult under the weight of the child. I did not wish to delay any longer, only to hurry onward, to cross this savage broken land, escape the desert, and reach the comfort of Burhanpur. I calmed myself by thinking of the cool waters of the Tapti flowing past the palace, and the gentle sounds of the people working on the river banks. I wanted the child to be born there, in tranquillity, not here on the road, even though the gulabar offered every luxury and comfort.

We reached Burhanpur in the middle of summer, a haven after the turmoil of travel. Wazir Khan no longer frowned so often, but, calmed by the placidity of my condition, smiled and joked with me. I had kept him well employed all these years.

Our arrival was timely. I had only rested for a few days when I began to feel the first pains of birth. They were sharp and brutal, stronger than for any of the other children, and I could not control my screams. For the first time these natural pains frightened me. They took hold of my body and wrung from it all my strength. I sweated as if I bled from every pore, and each drop weakened me further.

'Where is my beloved?' I asked Isa in between the pains. They came too swiftly, and my whisper was hoarse from my screams.

'He is in Asigarh.'

'Send someone to fetch him. Hurry.' My urgency frightened him. I could not explain it. There would be many days and years for me to look upon my beloved, yet something in me gave the command.

'It will be done at once, Agachi.'

How lonely we are with pain. Our love, joy, even sorrow, can be shared and experienced with others, but pain is a demon to be fought alone. It will not be coaxed away; it clings to us with a strength of its own. All afternoon and through the night, it attacked ceaselessly, swifter and swifter each time, lingering long like the twitch of a dying serpent. I could not see, or hear, could not feel anything else. All my senses turned inward, becoming mute under the assault.

'It must be a big child. A boy!'

I faintly heard the hakim's words. Isa and the maid held me. The other women hovered beyond my vision. Shadows jerking in the lamplight, they loomed over me, watching and waiting like birds of prey crouched in trees.

I felt the child then, beating, pushing against the walls within my body. The hands of the hakim blindly groped through the fine netting, reached inside and took hold. I only prayed he would pull it free from me, release me to surface in cold, clean air, instead of this dark swamp in which I drowned. It was not to be. We battled with the child. I pushed, Wazir Khan pulled. And then, when all strength ebbed and I abandoned hope, so weary I did not care, the child slipped free. I felt relief, a release, and the drowning ceased.

I must have slept then. I awoke to find Isa holding my hand rightly.

'What is it?'

'A female child, Agachi. Do you feel well?'

'A girl. I prayed for her. We have enough sons.' My body felt distant, beyond reach. I could not think what to reply to his query, except that I experienced a great and heavy fatigue.

'I am so tired, Isa. Where is my beloved?'

'He is coming. Sleep now. When he arrives, I will wake you.'

'No. I don't wish to sleep,' I dimly perceived his face beyond the netting. 'My friend Isa.' I could not explain why I wished him to know of my affection.

366

'Your slave.'

'Servant,' I corrected. 'And my friend. I will miss you.'

'But I am not leaving.' He sounded worried.

He held my hand still, 'You are very cool.'

'I feel cool. Do they bathe me?'

'No, the hakim thought it should be left until the morning.'

'Yes, that will be good.' I struggled to remain awake, to talk away the lassitude that had begun to creep into me, dragging a heavy weight behind it, 'You will promise me one thing, Isa. You will remain always by my beloved.'

'I promise. And by you too, Agachi.'

'Yes, of course; by me too. But always by him, Isa.'

I felt him turn as if to leave, and tightened my grip on his hand. It held me to the world, I thought.

'Don't go.'

'I will not. His majesty is here.' Gently he released his hand and stepped aside.

My beloved bent down. The dust and sweat of the ride from Asigarh clung to his face. I felt calmed by the familiarity of his beard and nose and mouth and eyes. His touch comforted me.

'I cannot see you.'

'Bring light.'

I saw the glare of the lamp, but still he remained just beyond my vision. I drew him nearer, and dimly saw the contours of his face. He looked bewildered; his face was hollow with despair. I felt him holding me, pulling me closer to him. What could not the Great Mughal command? He could bring light, but not chase away the darkness. It crept closer. Even though his face was next to mine, he seemed to recede from me.

'Stay.'

'I am here, by my beloved Arjumand. What is it?'

'Sleep,' I whispered. 'I must sleep soon. Stay by me.' He kissed my eyes and cheeks, brushed my lips. 'I dreamed the same dream. Why does it not let go of me? It comes again and again. I saw . . . I saw a face. It was dear, with strange eyes, but I did not know whose it was. A man. Handsome and princely. But it was only a face. The head had no body. It lay in a desert, like a stone. What does it mean?'

'Calm yourself, my love. It is only a dream.' His hold tightened, gripping me so that I could not float out of reach. I heard him call the hakim. They talked, I could not distinguish the words. Sleep crept closer and still I fought it.

'My beloved, I will sleep soon. I cannot resist it for long, it is too strong for me.' His breath on mine, wishing to fill my body, was sweet and cool. 'You must make me a promise.'

'Whatever you command.'

Shah Jahan

I felt tears roll down my cheeks into the hollow of her neck. They tickled; she smiled a little. She tried to wipe my face, but could not move her hands.

'Do not marry again, my beloved prince. Promise me. Otherwise my sons will battle with hers and there will be great bloodshed. Make them love each other . . . treat them equally . . . like your subjects.'

'I promise.'

'And promise . . .' She needed comfort, promises to cling to in her endless sleep, words spoken by the Great Mughal Shah Jahan—her beloved. 'You will not . . . forget your Arjumand?'

'Never. Ever, ever, ever, ever.'

'Kiss me.'

Through the tears she felt my mouth on hers. It was not gentle, but harsh with all the passion and frenzy of our youth.

With my love I stole her last breath away.

Epilogue 1148/AD 1738

The air, metallic with death, hung dusty and malodorous over the land, extinguishing hope. The vibrant sky burned the eyes of men and the sun had ceased to move. Vultures squatted on the earth like carved idols awaiting worship, the burnished silver langour sat in his tree whispering melancholy secrets to the leaves, and parrots, luscious as emeralds, peered down with malice. The river was sluggish with corpses, floating slowly into eternity.

The Mughal Empire had fallen.

The Persian soldiers hacked through the undergrowth that seemed to close in behind them, smelled the rot of flesh and the sour odour of their own bodies. They rested on their swords for a moment, their armour dark with rust and blood, then continued their determined progress. They entered through a gate and found themselves in a huge courtyard, its walls lined with red sandstone chambers. There were three other gates, the one in the north wall a massive arch inlaid with marble and Persian lettering. At the great gate, strangled with vines, and speckled with bird droppings, sadly powerless to bar their entry to what lay beyond, they paused to gaze up at the inscription. The dust and dirt of the years obscured it and impatiently they marched under the arch into the great overgrown garden.

What is that? they asked.

A tomb. The Taj Mahal, one replied.

Shadowless, it floated above the earth, moored only by the slender thread of their imaginations. It was as white as the noonday sun, and they shielded their eyes from its brilliance. It seemed alive, wavering in the luminous air, unafraid of these puny conquerors. It had stood from the beginning of time, and would remain there to the end of time, while all who looked upon it would return to the dust from which they came. It soared sublime beyond reason; there was no man courageous enough to destroy it. Its invincibility lay in the knowledge that what it guarded was worthless to all. This knowledge gave it a melancholy serenity; its immortality was the dust within, the dust of dreams and the passions which all men must feel if they are to exist beyond the limits of their mortal bodies.

The soldiers listened. All movement and noise had ceased and they were alone; they had stepped out of their world into another. The sky was empty of birds, the monkeys cowered beyond the gate, no small animals scurried through the overgrown garden. The sun was veiled and it was sweet and cool. The perfume of lime trees hung in the air, though they saw none, and they thought they could hear voices and weeping. There were fountains leading to the building, black and empty now, like pits of dead fire, and the paved pathways on either side were cracked and sprouted weeds. The soldiers halted finally at the plinth of the tomb and lifted their heads, stared into the eye of the sky, and saw the dome as a part of it, for the whiteness was the same as that which edged the sun.

They mounted the narrow steps, their feet leaving a jumbled trail in the dust, and approached the black doors that stood like rotting teeth in the ornate marble facade. They looked up at the inscription.

What does it say?

The pure of heart shall enter the gardens of God.

A soldier struck the door with his sword, and they heard the hollow echo, like a reply. The sword had scratched the great door and they peered at the mark and whispered to each other: silver. The door opened easily. The gloom reeked of dust and the droppings of bats, but beneath, like a tendril of smoke, lay the sweet delicacy of incense. They looked to see where it burned, but it was as if the spirits held the tender perfume. They touched the walls. Jewels, they whispered; then their laughter rose up and up and the high dome resounded with it.

One soldier struck an inlaid rose with the pommel of his sword, shattering the marble, and removed a ruby. The echo sounded like a sigh of pain. They looked up and saw the huge gold lamp that hung from the centre of the dome. Their hearts swelled with avarice. They had been promised plunder and here it waited to be plucked.

Beyond the marble screen, delicate as a veil, so fine that the muted light flowed through like water, they saw the sarcophagus. It lay in the centre, directly beneath the dome, it was of snow-white marble, inlaid with brilliantly coloured flowers and leaves and lavish with jewels. Beside, although higher, was another, humble in the shadow.

What does it say?

Here lies Arjumand Banu called Mumtaz-i-Mahal, exalted one of the palace, Allah alone is powerful.

Who was she?

An empress.